SUMMER DEATH

SUMMER DEATH

A Thriller

MONS KALLENTOFT

EMILY BESTLER BOOKS
—
ATRIA

New York   London   Toronto   Sydney   New Delhi

ATRIA BOOKS
A Division of Simon & Schuster, Inc.
1230 Avenue of the Americas
New York, NY 10020

Copyright © 2008 by Mons Kallentoft
English language translation © 2012 by Neil Smith.
Originally published by Natur & Kultur in Swedish as *Sommardöden* in 2008.
Published by agreement with Nordin Agency.

First Emily Bestler Books/Atria Books hardcover edition June 2013

EMILY BESTLER BOOKS / ATRIA BOOKS and colophons are trademarks of Simon & Schuster, Inc.

For information about special discounts for bulk purchases, please contact Simon & Schuster Special Sales at 1-866-506-1949 or business@simonandschuster.com.

The Simon & Schuster Speakers Bureau can bring authors to your live event. For more information or to book an event contact the Simon & Schuster Speakers Bureau at 1-866-248-3049 or visit our website at www.simonspeakers.com.

Manufactured in the United States of America

10 9 8 7 6 5 4 3 2 1

The Library of Congress Cataloging-in-Publication Data has been applied for.

ISBN 978-1-4516-4254-4
ISBN 978-1-4516-4256-8 (ebook)

For my mother
And for Karolina, Karla, and Nick

Prologue

Östergötland, Sunday, July 25

IN THE FINAL ROOM

I'm not going to kill you, my summer angel.

I'm only going to let you be reborn.

You'll become innocent again. All the dirt of history will vanish, time will deceive itself, and everything that was good will reign in isolation.

Or else I really will kill you, have killed you, so that love can arise again.

I tried not to kill, but that made rebirth impossible: The substance remained, clinging obstinately to material, and everything shameful vibrated within you and me like a hot black worm.

Pupated evil. Shredded time.

I tried in various ways, feeling my way, but I couldn't get there.

I scrubbed, washed, and cleaned.

You, my summer angels. You saw snow-colored tentacles, tearing spiders' legs, and the rabbits' claws.

I watched over you, gathered you in, and took you.

I'm there now.

He's sitting on the sofa.

His gut is open and rippling black snakes are sliding out onto the floor.

Can you see him?

Now he can't hurt anyone anymore, so say that you want to, say that you dare to come back. No oak floorboards will ever creak again, no alcohol fumes will ever make the air glow with anxiety.

The world is burning this summer.

The trees are transformed into withered black sculptures, monuments to our failures and our inability to love one another, to understand that we are one another.

We are the same, fire and me. Destroying so that life can arise again.

Someone has captured vipers, thrown them into an open oil drum, poured on some petrol, and set them alight.

The mute creatures crawl as they burn, making vain attempts to escape the pain.

Stop crawling, little girl.

I drove past the burning forest just an hour or so ago. I heard you beating against the inside of the car, ready to come out, come back, pure and free from anyone else's guilt.

She thought she knew something about me.

So foolish.

But don't be scared. The person you still are.

This is how it is: No one can live in fear, only in trust. Death is the penalty for anyone who deprives another person of the ability to trust.

That sort of trust is a close neighbor of love, which means that it's a close neighbor of death and the white spiders' legs. We needed you in spite of what you did, in spite of that. You owned our world. We couldn't escape even though it was the only thing we wanted, and we went to you sometimes because we had no choice. It has haunted me, this enforced seeking after darkness. I know now that I will never be able to choose anything except wishing myself harm.

But when you are reborn, that curse will be lifted.

So it will all be over soon.

Everything will be clear, pure.

White and light.

You will feel nothing within you, just as we once did.

You are shaking and twisting on the floor.

But don't be scared.

Only love will be reborn. Innocence.

And then we will cycle together along the bank of the canal, in a summer that lasts forever.

{PART I}

Love Reborn

1

What's that rumbling, rolling sound?

Trying to get out?

It's the sound of rain coming. Thunder. Finally, a drop of water upon the earth.

But Malin Fors knows better. The heat of this summer is devoid of mercy, has made up its mind to dry all the life out of the ground, and rain will be a long time coming.

Through the noise of the lingering customers, Malin can hear the pub's air-conditioning unit rumble like thunder, shuddering, protesting at having to work such long, demanding shifts, that there doesn't seem to be any end to the overtime this summer. The entire contraption seems on the point of collapse, its joints clattering, saying, "Enough, enough, enough. You'll just have to put up with the heat or slake your thirst with beer. Not even a machine can go on indefinitely."

Is it time to go home?

She is sitting alone at the bar. Wednesday has turned into Thursday and it is just after half past one. The Bull & Bear stays open all summer, and the dozen or so customers occupying the tables have fled the draining heat of the tables outside and taken refuge in the blissful cool indoors.

Bottles on shelves in front of mirrors.

Tequila. Cask-matured. Should she order a single? A double?

Condensation on glasses of freshly poured beer. The smell of sweat and rancid old spilled alcohol is clearly noticeable in the smoke-free air.

She sees her face in the mirrors in the bar, from countless angles as it is reflected and then reflected again in the mirror in front of her and the one behind her, above the green leather sofa.

A thousand reflections, but still one and the same face. Skin slightly tanned, her prominent cheekbones framed by a shorter blond page-boy cut than usual because of the summer heat.

Malin had gone down to the pub when the movie on television ended. It was something French about a dysfunctional family where one of the sisters ended up killing everyone. Psychological realism, the announcer had said, and that could well be right, even if people's actions seldom have such clear-cut and obvious explanations in reality as they did in the film.

The flat had felt too empty, and she hadn't been tired enough to sleep, but awake enough to feel loneliness dripping down the walls in almost the same way as the sweat now running down her back under her blouse. The increasingly tired wallpaper in the living room, the IKEA clock in the kitchen, whose second hand had suddenly fallen off one day in May, the blunt knives that could do with being honed back to finger-slicing sharpness, all of Tove's books in the bookcase, her latest purchases lined up on the third shelf. Titles that would be advanced for anyone, but improbably difficult for a fourteen-year-old.

The Man Without Qualities. Buddenbrooks. The Prince of Tides.

Hello, Tove? Can't you hear Marian Keyes calling you?

Reading.

Infinitely better than a lot of things a fourteen-year-old could come up with.

Malin takes a gulp of her beer.

Still doesn't feel tired.

But lonely? Or something else?

Summer lethargy at the police station, no work to tire her out,

or that she could be swallowed up by. She had spent all day wishing
something would happen.

But nothing had.

No bodies had been discovered. No one had been reported missing. No summer rapes. Nothing remarkable at all, apart from the heat
and the forest fires that were raging up in the Tjällmo forests, resisting
all attempts to put them out, and devouring more and more hectares
of prime trees with every passing day.

She thinks about the fire brigade, working flat-out. About all the
volunteers. A few police cars there to direct the traffic, but nothing
for her or her partner, Zeke Martinsson, to do. When the wind is
in the right direction she can smell the smoke from the fires, which
seems only fitting seeing as the whole of Linköping is enveloped in a
hellish heat, day and night alike, in the hot winds from the south that
have parked themselves on top of the southern half of the country, as
if they had been screwed down onto the landscape by the prevailing
area of high pressure.

The hottest summer in living memory.

Malin takes another mouthful of beer. Its bitterness and coolness
ease the residual heat in her body.

Outside the city is sweaty, tinted dull sepia, pale-green, and gray.
Linköping is empty of people, and only those who have to work or
have no money or no place to escape to are left in the city. Most of the
university students have gone back to their hometowns. The streets
are eerily empty even in the middle of the day, businesses stay open
only because they have to, seeing as the summer temps have already
been taken on. Only one business is booming: Bosse's Ice Cream,
homemade ice cream sold from a hole in the wall on Hospitalsgatan.
Day after day there are queues outside Bosse's; it's a mystery how everyone gets there without being visible anywhere along the way.

It's so hot that you can't move.

A hundred, a hundred and one, a hundred and two degrees, and
the day before yesterday a new local record was reached: a hundred
and nine degrees at the weather station out on the plain at Malmslätt.

"Record-breaking heat wave!"

"Old record smashed."

"This summer unlike any other."

There's a cheerfulness in the tone, an energy in the headlines of the *Östgöta Correspondent* that isn't matched by the pace of life in this heat-stricken city.

Muscles protesting, sweat dripping, thoughts muddied, people searching for shade, coolness, the city drowsy, in sympathy with its inhabitants. A dusty, smoky smell in the air, not from the forest fires but from grass that's slowly burning up without flames.

Not a single drop of rain since Midsummer. The farmers are screaming disaster, and today the *Correspondent* published an article by its star reporter, Daniel Högfeldt, in which he interviewed a professor at University Hospital. The professor said that a manual laborer in this sort of heat needs to drink between fifteen and twenty quarts of water a day.

Manual laborers?

Are there any of those left in Linköping these days?

There are only academics. Engineers, computer experts, and doctors. At least that's what it feels like sometimes. But they aren't in the city at the moment.

A gulp of her third beer gets her to relax, even though she is really in need of an energy boost.

The pub's customers disappear one by one. And she can feel loneliness demanding more space.

Tove with her bag in the hallway eight days ago, full of clothes and books, some of the new ones she's bought. Janne behind her in the stairwell, Janne's friend Pecka down in the street in his Volvo, ready to take them to Skavsta Airport.

She had lied several days before they left when Janne asked if she could drive them, saying that she had to work. She wanted to be short with Janne, to show her disapproval that he was insisting on taking Tove with him all the way to Bali, on the other side of the fucking planet.

Bali.

Janne had won the trip in the public employees' holiday lottery. First prize for the heroic fireman.

A summer dream for Tove. For Janne. Just father and daughter. Their first real trip together, Tove's first trip outside Europe.

Malin had been worried that Tove wouldn't want to go, that she wouldn't want to be away from Markus, her boyfriend, or because Markus's parents, Biggan and Hasse, might have plans that involved her.

But Tove had been pleased.

"Markus will manage," she had said.

"And what about me, how am I going to manage without you?"

"You, Mum? It'll be perfect for you. You'll be able to work as much as you like, without feeling guilty about me."

Malin had wanted to protest. But all the words she could have said felt lame, or, worse still, untrue. How many times did Tove have to make her own meals, or go and put herself to bed in an empty flat simply because something at the station demanded Malin's full attention?

Hugging in the hall a week or so ago, bodies embracing.

Then Janne's firm grip on the handle of the bag.

"Take care."

"You too, Mum."

"You know I will."

"Bye."

Three voices saying the same word.

Hesitation.

Then it had started up again, Janne had said silly things and she was upset when the door finally closed on them. The feelings from the divorce twelve years ago were back, the lack of words, the anger, the feeling that no words were good enough and that everything that was said was just wrong.

Not with each other. Not without each other. This single stinking love. An impossible love.

And she had refused to admit to herself how insulted she felt by their holiday, like a very young girl being abandoned by the people who ought to love her most.

"See you when I pick you up from the airport. But we'll speak before that," she had said to the closed gray door.

She had been left standing alone in the hall. They had been gone five seconds and already she felt an infinite sense of loss, and the thought of the distance between them had been unbearable and she had gone straight down to the pub.

Drinking to get drunk, just like I'm doing now, Malin thinks.

Downing a shot of tequila, just like I'm doing now.

Making a call on my mobile, just like I'm doing now.

Daniel Högfeldt's clear voice over the phone.

"So you're at the Bull?"

"Are you coming or not?"

"Calm down, Fors. I'm coming."

Their two bodies facing each other, Daniel Högfeldt's hairless chest beneath her hands, slipping moistly under her fingertips. I am marking you, Malin thinks, marking you with my fingerprints, and why have you got your eyes closed, look at me, you're inside me now, so open your eyes, your green eyes, cold as the Atlantic.

Their conversation in the pub just ten minutes before.

"Do you want a drink?"

"No, do you?"

"No."

"So what are we waiting for?"

They took their clothes off in the hall. The church tower a black, immovable shape in the kitchen window.

And the sounds.

The ringing of the church bell as it struck two, as Malin helped him out of his worn white T-shirt, the cotton stiff and clean, his skin warm against her breasts, his words: "Take it slow, Malin, slow," and her whole body was in a hurry, starting to itch and ache and hurt and she whispered: "Daniel, it's never been more urgent than it is now," thinking, you think I've got you for slow? I've got myself, other people for that. You, Daniel, you're a body, don't try to smooth talk me, I don't fall for that sort of thing. He pushed her into the kitchen, the crippled IKEA clock ticking *ticktock* and the church gray-black behind them, the tree branches brittle with drought.

"That's it," he said, and she was quiet, spreading her legs and letting him get closer, and he was hard and rough and warm, and she fell back on the table, her arms flailing, that morning's half-full mug of coffee sliding off onto the floor and shattering into a dozen pieces on the linoleum.

She pushed him away.

Went into the bedroom without a word.

He followed her.

She stood at the window and looked out at the courtyard, at the street beyond, at the few hesitant lights in the windows of the buildings.

"Lie down."

He obeyed.

Daniel's body naked on the bed, his cock sticking up at a slight angle toward his navel. The gun cabinet with her service revolver on the wall next to the window, Daniel closing his eyes, reaching his arms up toward the pine headboard, and she waited a moment, allowing the ache of longing to become real pain before moving toward him, before she let him in again.

I dream that the snakes are moving again, somewhere. How a girl the same age as you, Tove, is moving through the green-black trees of something that seems to be a park at night, or a forest beside a distant, black-watered lake, or shimmering blue water that smells of chlorine. I imagine her drifting across yellowed grass, as far, far away a water sprinkler wisps corrosive drops above a freshly cut lilac hedge.

I dream that this is happening, Tove.

It is happening now, and I get scared and stiffen as someone, something creeps out of its hiding place in the darkness, rushing up behind her, knocking her to the ground, and the roots of the surrounding trees wrap around her body, snaking deep within her like warm, live snakes, whose slithering bodies are full of hungry, ancient streams of lava.

She screams.

But no sound comes out.

And the snakes chase her across a wide-open plain that was once verdant but now whimpers with charred, flaking skin. The ground is cracked and from the jagged depths bubbles a stinking, hot, sulphurous darkness that whispers with a scorching voice: "We will destroy you, little girl. Come. We shall destroy you."

I scream.

But no sound comes out.

This is a dream, isn't it? Tell me it's a dream, Tove.

I reach out my hand across the sheet beside me but it's empty.

Janne, you're not there, your warm warmth.

I want you both to come home now.

Even you have gone, Daniel. Taken your cool warmth and left me alone with the dream and myself in this depressing bedroom.

I think it was a bad dream, but perhaps it was good?

2

Tove and Janne are eating bacon and eggs on a spacious balcony with a view of Kuta Beach, and not even the memory of the terrorist bombs remains.

Tove and Janne are tanned and rested, and their radiant smiles reveal shining white teeth. Janne, muscular, has already taken a morning swim in the cooled hotel pool. As he gets out of the water a beautiful Balinese woman is waiting on the edge with a freshly laundered and ironed towel.

Tove is beaming fit to match the sun.

Smiles even more broadly at her father and asks:

"Dad, what are we going to do today? Eat rice with honey and nuts in a Buddhist temple of ivory-white marble? Like the pictures in the brochures?"

Malin adjusts her Ray-Bans with one hand, and the image of Janne and Tove vanishes. Then she takes a firmer grip on the handlebars of her bicycle as she pedals past the Asian fast-food stall on St. Larsgatan just before Trädgårdstorget, thinking that if you only let your thoughts go, they can come up with all sorts of things, conjuring up images of anyone at all, making caricatures of even the people that you know and love most.

The self-preservation instinct. Let your subconscious make parodies of your loss and anxiety and jealousy.

It's no more than quarter past seven and Janne and Tove are in all probability on the beach now.

And Janne doesn't even like honey.

Malin presses the pedals down, picking up an almost imperceptible smell of smoke in her nostrils, the city tinted slightly yellow by her sunglasses.

Her body is starting to wake up.

But she feels a resistance. It feels like it's going to be even hotter today. She didn't even want to look at the thermometer in the kitchen window at home. The asphalt is oily under the wheels, it feels as if the ground might crack open at any moment and release hundreds of glowing worms.

A cycling summer.

Nothing's any distance away inside the city. At this time of year everyone who can cycles in Linköping, unless the heat just gets too much. She prefers the car, but somehow all the talk about the environment in the papers and on television must have got to her. Think of future generations. They have the right to a living planet.

At this time of day Malin is completely alone on the streets, and in the plate-glass windows of H&M in the square there are adverts for the summer sale, the words flame-red above pictures of a famous model whose name Malin realizes she ought to know.

SALE.

Heat on special offer this year. Stocks are way too high.

She stops at a red light near McDonald's at the corner of Drottninggatan, adjusts her beige skirt, and runs her hand over her white cotton blouse.

Summer clothes. Ladylike clothes. They work okay, and in this heat skirts are always better than trousers.

Her pistol and holster are concealed beneath a thin cotton jacket. She recalls the last time she and Zeke were out at the firing range, the way they frenetically fired off shot after shot at the black cardboard shapes.

The burger chain is in a building from the fifties, a gray stone façade with concave white balconies. On the other side of the street sits the heavy brown building from the turn of the century where the psychoanalyst Viveka Crafoord has her clinic.

The shrink.

She saw right through me.

Malin remembers what Viveka said to her during a conversation they had toward the end of a murder investigation.

"What about you, why are you so sad?" Then: "I'm here if you want to talk."

Talk.

There were already far too many words in the world, far too little silence. She never called Viveka Crafoord about herself, but had called several times in connection with cases where she wanted "psychological input," as Viveka herself put it. And they've had coffee several times when they've bumped into each other around town.

Malin turns around.

Looks back toward Trädgårdstorget, toward the flashy new bus stops and containers full of reluctant flowers on the patterned paving, the red-plastered façade of the building containing the seed shop and Schelin's Café.

A pleasant square, in a pleasant city.

A plastered façade, shielding insecure people. Anything can happen in this city, where old and new collide, where rich and poor, educated and uneducated are in fact constantly colliding with each other, where prejudices about those around you are aired like bedclothes. Last week she had been in a taxi with a middle-aged taxi driver who had a go at the city's immigrant community: "Spongers. They don't do a stroke of work, we should use them as fuel for the incinerator at Gärdstad, then we'd get some use out of them."

She wanted to get out of the car, show her ID, tell him she was going to arrest him for incitement to racial hatred, the bastard, but she stayed silent.

A black man in green overalls is walking across the square. He is equipped with a pair of long-handled pincers to save him having to bend over to pick up litter and cigarette ends. The bottles and cans have already been taken care of by Deposit-Gunnar or another of the city's eccentrics.

Malin looks in front of her, as St. Larsgatan forms a straight line out of the center of the city, only turning when it reaches the edge of the smartest district, Ramshäll.

Hasse and Biggan live there, Markus's parents. Close to the hospital, both of them doctors.

The light turns green and Malin pedals onward.

The beer and tequila from last night have left no trace in her body. Nor has Daniel Högfeldt. He crept out while she was asleep, and if she knows him at all he'll be in the newsroom now, cursing the lack of news, waiting for something to happen.

Malin cycles past the medical school, hidden behind leafy maples, and a hundred yards off to the right, at the end of Linnégatan, she can make out the Horticultural Society Park. Beyond the school the buildings thin out, making way for a parking lot, beyond which lies the Hotel Ekoxen, generally regarded as the best in the city. But Malin turns the other way, down toward the entrance of the Tinnerbäck swimming pool. Tinnis, as the pool is known locally, opens at seven, and in the parking lot by the entrance there are just two cars. An elderly red Volvo estate wagon and an anonymous white van, possibly a Ford.

She jumps off her bike, parks it in the stand beside the doors, and takes her bag from the rack on the back.

There's no one at the desk by the turnstile.

Instead there's a note on the smeared glass: THE POOL OPENS AT 7:00 AM. FREE ENTRY BEFORE 8:00 AM.

Malin goes through the turnstile. The sun is just creeping above the stands of the Folkungavallen Stadium farther down the road, hitting her in the face, and in just a few seconds the relative cool of morning is forced out by an angry heat.

Before her Malin sees the twenty-five-meter pool, the abandoned indoor pool, the bathing area in the lake, and the grass slopes surrounding it. Water everywhere. She longs for it.

The changing room smells of mold and disinfectant.

She pulls her red bathing suit over her thighs, feeling how taut they are, and thinking that her exercise regime is holding the years at bay, and that there can't be many thirty-four-year-olds in better shape. Then she gets up, pulling the bathing suit over her breasts, and the touch makes her nipples stiffen under the synthetic fabric.

She shakes her arms. Pulls the goggles out of her bag. Too warm in the station's gym these days. Better to swim.

She takes her wallet, pistol, and mobile and goes out of the changing room toward the outdoor pool. She walks past the showers. She doesn't want to shower even though she knows those are the rules, prefers the first water to touch her skin to be the water she's going to be swimming in.

No holiday until the middle of August.

Her colleagues are taking their well-earned breaks now, in July, most of them, apart from Zeke and the duty officer and Detective Inspector Sven Sjöman.

Johan Jakobsson is with his wife and children at her family's summer place by some lake outside Nässjö. Johan had a pained look on his face when he outlined his plans for the summer to Malin in the police station kitchen.

"Mother- and Father-in-law have built another two little cottages, one for us and one for Petra, Jessica's sister. With their own kitchen and bathroom, the whole works. Everything so that we don't have a legitimate excuse not to go."

"Johan. You're thirty-five. You should be able to do what you want."

"But Jessica loves it there. Wants the kids to have their own childhood memories of the place."

"Lots of arguments?"

"Arguments? Like you wouldn't believe. My mother-in-law is the most passive-aggressive person you can imagine. The victim mentality comes completely naturally to her."

Johan had taken a gulp of his hot coffee, far too large a gulp, and was forced to spit it out in the sink when he burned his mouth.

"Fuck, that was hot."

Just like the summer.

Malin steps out onto the narrow concrete path that leads down to the banked seats that in turn form a staircase down toward the pool, feeling her bathing suit cut in between her buttocks.

Börje Svärd.

His wife, Anna, who has MS, is in a respite ward at University Hospital. Three weeks away from the house she had furnished with her assured taste, three weeks in a hospital room, entirely dependent on strangers. But dependency is nothing new for her, completely paralyzed for years.

Börje himself on a much-longed-for hunting trip in Tanzania, Malin knew he'd been saving up for it for several years.

She also knew that he had left his dogs at a kennel up on Jägarvallen, and it was the dogs he chose to talk about when he gave her a lift home one Friday evening toward the end of June.

"Malin," he said, his waxed moustache twitching. "I feel so damn guilty about leaving the dogs."

"Börje. They'll be fine. The kennel in Jägarvallen has a good reputation."

"Yes, but . . . You can't just leave animals like that. I mean, they're like members of the family."

In the weeks before he left Börje's body seemed to shrink under the weight of guilt, as if it were already regretting going.

"Anna will be fine as well, Börje," Malin had said as they pulled up outside the door on Ågatan. "She'll be well looked after at University Hospital."

"But they don't even understand what she says."

She'd had the words "try not to worry about it" on the tip of her tongue, but left them unsaid. Instead she had silently put her hand on Börje's arm, and at the usual morning meeting the next day Sven had said:

"Go, Börje. It'll do you good."

Börje, who would usually have been annoyed by a remark like that, had leaned back in his chair and thrown out his arms.

"Is it so obvious that I'd rather not go?"

"No," Sven had said. "It's obvious that you should go. Go to Tanzania and shoot an antelope. That's an order."

Malin is down at the pool now, her nostrils full of the smell of chlorine. She walks down the long side toward the end where the starting blocks look like gray sugar lumps above the flaking black lane markers. Beyond the pool stand a line of tall elms, their leaves yellowing, and she's still alone at the pool; presumably none of the other people left in the city has the energy to get up so early?

Karim Akbar.

Police chief.

Not as controversial in his choice of holiday as his choice of career. He, his wife, and their eight-year-old son have rented a cottage outside Västervik. Three weeks' holiday for Karim. But not really a holiday. He's told Malin that he's going to write a book about integration based on his own experiences, while his wife and son take day trips and go swimming.

Malin already knows what the book will be about: the little Kurdish boy in the far-too-cramped flat in Nacksta up in Sundsvall. The father who commits suicide in his despair at being excluded from society. The son who takes revenge by studying law and becoming the youngest police chief in the country, the only one from an immigrant background. Articles in the press, appearances on television discussion programs.

Malin climbs up onto the starting block. She likes swimming in the middle of the pool, where she isn't troubled by the swell at the edges. She crouches down and carefully puts her towel and mobile on the asphalt, hiding her pistol inside the towel and pulling on her goggles before getting ready to dive in.

Degerstad would be back from his course up in Stockholm in early September. Andersson was still off sick.

Malin stretches her ankles, feeling her body get ready to split the surface of the water, as her unconscious checks off every muscle, organ, cell, and drop of blood from a list that is as long as it is quickly ticked off.

Muscles tensing. And off.

She doesn't hear the mobile phone ringing, angrily announcing that something has happened, that Linköping has been woken from its hot summer lethargy.

One arm forward, the other back. Breathing every fifth stroke, swimming eighty lengths of the twenty-five-meter pool, that's the plan.

She vaults at the end of the first length, enjoying the response of her body, the fact that the hours in the gym at the station are showing results, the feeling that she is in control of her body, and not the other way around.

Of course it's an illusion.

Because what is a human being if not a body?

Her body like a bullet in the water, the bathing suit like a red flash of blood. The surrounding buildings and trees as vague images when she breathes, otherwise not there at all.

She approaches the end, the first circuit of forty almost over, and she tenses her body for another turn when she hears a voice, a calm deep voice that sounds insistent.

"Excuse me, sorry . . ."

She wants to swim, doesn't want to stop and talk to anyone, answer any questions, wants to use her body and escape from all thought, from all . . . yes, what, exactly?

"Your mobile . . ."

Could have been Tove. Janne.

She slows down instead of turning, her hands on the metal steps of the ladder.

A distant voice between her quick breaths, a face dark against the sun.

"I'm sorry, but your mobile was ringing when I walked past."

"Thanks," Malin says as she tries to catch her breath.

"Don't mention it," the voice says, and the large, dark figure disappears, seeming to shrivel up in the sunlight blazing behind it. Malin heaves herself out of the pool, sitting on the edge with her feet still in the water. She reaches for her mobile over on the towel.

It's waterproof, a fairly basic model.

Zeke's number on the display.

A new message received.

She doesn't feel like listening to it.

Zeke answers on the third ring.

"Malin, is that you?"

"Who else?"

"The Horticultural Society Park," Zeke says. "Get there as fast as you can. You're fairly close, aren't you?"

"What's happened?"

"Don't know exactly. We got a call here at the station. See you at the playground up by Djurgårdsgatan as soon as you can get there."

The words take the chill of the water from her body. Sun and heat, the tone in Zeke's voice.

The cracks in the ground are opening up, Malin thinks. The time of glowing worms has arrived.

3

alin hurries to the changing room with her towel around her neck, the wet footprints left by her feet on the concrete of the steps drying before she gets there.

She tears off the bathing suit, giving up any idea of showering off the chlorine from the pool. She puts on some deodorant but doesn't bother to comb her hair. She pulls on her skirt, her white blouse, the holster and jacket, and the white sneaker-style shoes.

Through the turnstile.

Onto the bicycle.

Breathing.

Now.

Now something is happening.

What's waiting for me in the Horticultural Society Park?

Something has happened, that much is clear. Zeke's words before he hung up, quickly telling her about the call received at the station fifteen minutes earlier, put through to his desk from reception, how the gender-neutral voice at the other end of the line had been indistinct, upset: "There's a naked woman in the Horticultural Society Park, she's sitting in the summerhouse by the playground. Something terrible must have happened."

A naked woman.

In the largest park in the city.

The person who called hadn't said anything about how old the woman was, nor whether she was alive or dead, nothing about anything really. A patrol had probably got there by now.

Maybe a false alarm?

But Malin could tell from Zeke's voice that he was sure something serious was going on, that evil was on the move again, the indefinable dark undercurrent that flows beneath all human activity.

Who made the call?

Unclear. A panting voice.

No caller number had been indicated on Zeke's phone, or out in reception.

Malin heads for the gate to the park beside the Hotel Ekoxen, cycling past the entrance to the hotel bar. They mostly have busloads of German tourists at this time of year, and as Malin rides past the dining room she can see the elderly Germans swarming around the breakfast buffet.

Over by the park's open-air stage the large lawn is surrounded by fully grown oaks, and the park is a regular venue for high school seniors' drunken parties in the spring. Malin imagines she can still pick up the smell of alcohol, vomit, and used condoms. Down to the right is the summerhouse that was built on the site of the park restaurant that burned down long ago.

The white paint of the patrol car like a shimmering mirage farther up the park.

Cycle faster.

She can feel the violence now. Has been in its vicinity often enough to recognize the traces left by its scent.

The patrol car is parked by the little summerhouse at the foot of a small hillock. Beside the car is an ambulance. In the background Malin can make out white blocks of flats with walkway balconies, and through the trees she can just make out a yellow stuccoed building from the turn of the century.

She folds out the bike's kickstand.

Takes in the scene. Makes it her own.

Close to her there are swings made of car tires behind a green-stained wooden fence. There is a patch of sand with a climbing frame and three small spring-loaded rocking horses that look like cows. A sandbox.

Two uniformed policemen wearing outsized pilot glasses, beefy Johansson and rotund Rydström, wandering back and forth on the grass beyond the sandbox. They haven't seen her yet, seeing as she's hidden by the patrol car as she approaches.

Comatose.

They should have heard her. Or noticed the paramedics waving in greeting from the bench where they were sitting on either side of an orange, blanket-wrapped bundle. A thickset older man, she knows his name is Jimmy Niklasson, and a young girl, blond, around twenty or so.

She must be new.

Malin knows they've been having trouble finding women. A lot fall by the wayside on the physical tests.

Niklasson looks at Malin, worried.

The orange figure, the person between them on the bench.

Wrapped in a health service blanket, and they're holding on to her, her head is covered by the blanket, head bowed, it's like there's simultaneously something and nothing between them.

Malin walks slowly toward the bench.

Niklasson nods to her, the blond girl does the same.

Johansson and Rydström have seen her, shouting across each other:
"We think—"
"She's probably—"
"—been raped."

And when the words split the air and find their way across the playground and the park, the figure in the blanket looks up and Malin sees a young girl's face, its features distorted with fear, with the insight that life can present you with dark gifts at any place and at any time.

Brown eyes staring at Malin.

Seeming to wonder: What happened? What's going to happen to me now?

Dear God, Malin thinks. She's no older than you, Tove.

"Shut up," Malin shouts at the uniforms.

Where's Zeke?

The girl has bowed her head again. Jimmy Niklasson removes his arm from her and stands up. The new blond girl stays where she is. When Malin sees Niklasson coming toward her she wishes that Zeke had got to the scene first instead of her, that he could have dispensed the calming words that she will now have to give.

He's good at calm, Zeke. Even if he's also good at tempest.

Johansson and Rydström have come over as well, a wall of male flesh suddenly very close to her.

Rydström's gravelly voice:

"We found her over there, in the summerhouse, she was lying on the planks of the floor."

Johansson:

"We helped her up. But she was completely silent, we couldn't get any response from her, so we called for an ambulance."

"Good," Malin says. "Good. Did you touch anything over there?"

"No," Rydström says. "Just her. We sat her on the bench, exactly like she's sitting now. We gave her the blanket we had in the back of the car. They brought more blankets with them."

"Are there any clothes over there?"

"No."

"She's bleeding from her genitals," Niklasson says, and his voice is strangely high for such a large man. "And as far as I can tell, she's been beaten on her lower arms and shins. But she's remarkably clean, almost like she's been scrubbed."

"She smells of bleach," Rydström adds. "Her whole body is sort of white. The wounds on her arms and legs also seem to have been rinsed and cleaned up, very carefully."

"Get her into the ambulance," Malin says. "It'll be calmer for her in there."

"She doesn't want to," Niklasson says. "We've tried, but she just shakes her head."

"Does she seem to know where she is?"

"She hasn't said a word."

Malin turns to Rydström and Johansson.

"No one else was here when you got here?"

"No. Like who?" Johansson says.

"The person who called in, for instance."

"There was no one here."

Malin pauses.

"You two," Malin says. "Cordon off the crime scene. Start by the fountain down there and draw a ring around us here."

Malin sits down slowly on the bench. Careful not to invade the girl's space, trying to get closer to her with friendliness.

"Can you hear me?" Malin asks, looking at her gleaming white skin, the wounds on her arms like neat islands. The girl looks like she's been outside naked through a whole cold winter's night, in spite of the heat. There's an innocence to her white skin, as if she had danced with the devil on the edge of death and somehow survived.

The girl remains still, mute.

A faint smell of bleach in Malin's nostrils.

It reminds her of the pool at Tinnis.

The young paramedic on her other side is sitting in silence, and doesn't seem bothered that Malin hasn't introduced herself.

"Can you tell me what happened?"

Silence, but a very small sideways movement.

"Does it hurt?"

"Can you remember?"

"You don't have to be afraid."

But no reaction, no answer, nothing.

"Stay with her," Malin says, getting up. "Don't leave her alone."

Down by the fountain the two uniformed officers are attaching the cordon tape to a tree, and Niklasson is busy inside the ambulance.

"Can we take her to the hospital?"

The young paramedic's voice is soft and amenable, soothing.

"My name's Ellinor, by the way. Ellinor Getlund."

Malin holds out her hand.

"Malin Fors, Detective Inspector. You'll have to wait with getting her to the hospital, even if she ought to go straightaway. She might start to talk if she gets a bit more time here at the scene. I'm going to take a look around in there in the meantime."

A summerhouse shaded by a tall oak.

Sweat under her blouse.

The clock on her mobile says 8:17.

Already it's as hot as the fires of hell.

The summerhouse has its own microclimate. A strange, damp heat hits Malin as she steps cautiously into the open space. It must be a good five degrees warmer than outside even though there are no walls, it's more a collection of pillars than a room.

Unnaturally warm in here.

As if the atmosphere had gathered together some particularly troublesome molecules in one place, as if an invisible devil were dancing in the air.

She looks down at her feet. Takes care not to stand in any footprints. A pool of blood some distance away, some smaller splashes of blood around it, together they almost form the shape of a body.

What?

Blood that's flowed out of her.

A black shadow. What were you doing here at night?

You're no older than my Tove. You ended up here even though you shouldn't have.

No clothes, no traces of fabric that Malin can make out with her naked eye.

A mobile ringing, Ellinor Getlund's measured voice behind Malin. The voice coming closer. Has she left the girl alone?

Malin crouches down. Breathing. Runs her hand over the floorboards, careful not to touch anything that their crime-scene investigator and forensics expert, Karin Johansson, might want to look at.

Sees the blood on the railing above the place where the girl was lying.

Did someone throw you over the railing? Or did you climb over it yourself?

Children's voices in the background.

Ignore them. What are they doing here so early?

Malin gets up and walks over to the railing. Marks made by loads of shoes on the other side, footprints, bushes some distance away, some broken branches. A tree, a rough pine slightly farther in. Was that where you waited? Did you pull her into those bushes? Or did someone else leave those tracks? Entirely unrelated? Did it all happen in a completely different way?

Children.

Lots of them.

They're laughing.

Saying: "Police. Ambulance."

And then they scream, and scream again, and agitated women's voices echo through the park, then Niklasson's voice.

"What the hell?"

Malin turns around.

Ten preschool children in yellow tunics. They're howling now. Two teachers with surprised looks on their faces. A naked, beaten, wounded, but unnaturally clean girl moving toward them from the bench. The children sick with fear, as if they had suddenly infected each other with a terror virus in the face of the strange, scary sight coming toward them.

The children are now screaming out loud.

"I told you to stay with her!" Malin roars.

Ellinor Getlund heading after the girl, her mobile in one hand, the orange blanket, hastily plucked up from the gravel beside the bench, in the other.

The naked, glassy girl climbs over the fence around the swings, not caring about the wounds on her arms and legs, or the dried blood on the inside of her thighs. She walks across the sand. Sits down on one of the tires and starts swinging back and forth, a pendulum motion that seems to be an obstinate attempt to make time stop.

Her gleaming white body, the blood on her thighs somehow luminous.

Down by the fountain Rydström and Johansson are still fumbling with the cordon as if nothing had happened.

Where are you, Zeke? Malin thinks. I need you here right now.

4

Zeke standing cautiously beside Malin in the summerhouse.

He arrived just after they had got the girl down from the swing, wrapped her in the orange blanket, and sat her down inside the ambulance. She climbed in without objecting.

The preschool children have made a collective retreat from the park. Once their initial fear had subsided they seemed mostly amused by the funny lady swinging without any clothes on, and wanted her to carry on, and some of them were upset when Malin and Ellinor Getlund helped the girl down.

Malin explained to one of the preschool teachers that the playground was a crime scene, but that they would probably be able to use it again tomorrow. The woman didn't ask what had happened, and seemed mainly concerned with getting the children away from there as quickly as possible.

Zeke came running up the path from the fountain and the summerhouse. His clean-shaven head was nodding up and down, and the beads of sweat in the wrinkles on his forty-five-year-old forehead became more obvious the closer he got. Light-blue shirt, light-blue jeans, beige linen jacket. Black hiking shoes, far too heavy for this weather, but very official.

Malin couldn't help herself snapping as he stopped beside her, breathless. She was standing beside the car, and had just given Ellinor Getlund a severe reprimand.

"At a crime scene you do what the police officer in charge tells you, and I told you to stay with her."

Ellinor Getlund not backing down, asking instead:

"When can we take her? She needs to get to the hospital."

"When I tell you."

"But—"

"No buts."

To Zeke:

"And what took you so bloody long?"

"I ran out of petrol. As luck would have it I was only a couple of hundred yards from the Statoil station. I haven't run out of petrol for years. It's this damn heat."

"The heat?"

"It stops your brain working."

"True enough. I hope we don't miss too much in this investigation."

Malin told him what she knew, what she had seen in the summerhouse, then they went down there again together, and now Zeke is standing beside her in the unwalled room, his thin face full of doubt.

"We don't know for sure if she's been raped?"

"No, but everything points toward that, don't you think?"

"Yes . . ."

"And that it could have happened in those bushes."

Zeke nods.

"Or else someone hurt her somewhere else and released her here. God, it's hot in here. Weird."

"I'd like you to talk to her," Malin says. "See if you can get her to say anything. I've got a feeling that we're only going to be able to get her to talk here, nowhere else."

The back of the ambulance is open.

A figure wrapped in an orange blanket sitting on a stretcher, the young paramedic close, so close, as if she will never leave her. The girl has the blanket over her head, her head still bowed. The inside of the ambulance smells of hospital and disinfectant, tubes from oxygen cylinders run along the walls, and short cords with yellow corks hang down from the roof. A cardiac support machine is fixed to the internal wall.

Have you saved many lives? Malin wonders.

You can't save the girl in here now.

Can anyone?

Zeke climbs in first. Malin just behind him, gesturing to Ellinor Getlund to get up. They sit down on either side of the girl.

Zeke turns to face her, and asks:

"If you feel like lifting your head and looking at me, that's fine. If you don't, never mind."

The girl sits motionless.

"What happened here last night?"

"Can you tell us?"

Silence that lasts several minutes.

"Did somebody force themselves upon you here last night?"

Zeke runs a hand over his glistening scalp.

"If you don't want to say anything, you don't have to. But it would be good if we knew your name."

"My name is Josefin Davidsson," the girl says.

Then she falls silent again.

The ambulance heads off toward the fountain, the brake lights hesitant as the vehicle turns toward the gate onto Linnégatan.

Josefin Davidsson said nothing more. Just her name.

What happened?

What were you doing in the park?

Your clothes. Where are they?

Has someone washed you?

Who are your parents?

Where do you live?

Who was the person who made the phone call? Who saw you first? Unless . . .

Their voices increasingly desperate. Full of questions in the face of her silence.

"My name. Josefin Davidsson."

"What now?" Zeke says as the ambulance disappears from sight.

"Now we wait for Karin."

"Johannison?"

Malin can hear the derision in Zeke's voice. Thinks: Why do you dislike her so strongly, Zeke? Because she's beautiful? Because she's smart? Or because she's rich, and rich is the same as better?

"Bali. We're going to be staying at the Bulgari resort in Uluwatu," Karin Johannison says as she scrapes flakes of blood from the railing. "I'm taking my holiday in August, so we'll be there for a month, it's at its best then."

"Janne and Tove are there at the moment."

"Oh, how lovely. Where are they?"

"Some hotel on a beach called Kuta."

"That's the best beach. Terribly exploited though."

Malin considers how suntanned Karin is even though she's been working indoors at the National Forensics Laboratory all summer. She looks as indecently fresh and alert as she always does, her blue eyes radiating a positive shimmer, her skin glowing with care. Her dress, expensive pink fabric draped around her body, contributes to the impression of genuine class.

Just before, Karin fine-combed the bushes and the grass beside the summerhouse. Picked up litter that she put into small marked bags.

"I'll try to get fingerprints. But there could be thousands here, or none at all. Wood's difficult."

"I thought you could get prints from anything," Zeke says.

Karin doesn't answer.

"It might be like you said, Malin. That he attacked her over there in the bushes, and then dragged her here and bundled her over the railings. We'll have to see what the doctors say about her injuries."

"We don't even know if she was raped. Or if the perpetrator was male."

Zeke's voice is confrontational.

"Time to go back to the station," Malin says, wondering what's happened to Daniel Högfeldt. He or someone else from the *Correspondent* ought to have been here some time ago. But maybe their contacts in the force are on holiday. And maybe the call about the girl sounded too dull over the radio.

But he'll be here soon enough, Daniel. As surely as summer. The hottest story of the season has arrived, hotter even than the forest fire.

"Girl raped in Horticultural Society Park."

Beyond the cordon a group of curious onlookers has gathered. People dressed for summer, all of them wondering the same thing as them:

What's happened?

Zeke leaves the car; one of the uniforms can drive it back to the station. Malin fetches her bicycle and looks toward the summerhouse one last time before she and Zeke leave the park.

The sun has climbed higher in the sky, and now patches of light are falling into the circular space, the sunbeams seem to wallow in what has happened, trying to affirm it with their ever-changing interplay.

This is only the start, the sunbeams seem to be saying, this summer can still get even hotter, less forgiving. Just you wait, after us comes the darkness.

"Are you coming, Fors?"

Zeke's voice urgent and calm at the same time.

Finally a proper case to grapple with. And it's summer. He doesn't have any ice hockey to deal with.

Malin knows that his son, Martin, the big star of the Linköping Hockey Club, the pride of the city, is having a break from training for three weeks. Zeke hates hockey, but is so loyal to his son that he goes to every match during the season. But at this time of year there isn't even any ice inside the Cloetta Center.

The footpath out of the park runs between two blocks of flats, and is lined with flower beds, their plants wilting and losing their color in the heat. Out on Djurgårdsgatan a number 202 bus goes past on its way to University Hospital.

It's hardly six hundred yards to the police station, Malin thinks. Yet here, so close to the physical heart of the law, a girl has been attacked and raped.

All security is just a chimera.

Four girls in their early teens fly past them on their bikes. Bathing gear in their bike baskets.

On their way to cool down. To the pool out at Glyttinge, maybe? Or Tinnis?

Chatter and commotion. Summer holidays and something lurking behind a tree in the dark.

5

We're going swimming, swimming, swimming, you say, have you seen my armbands, Mum, have you seen my rubber ring, where's the rubber ring? I don't want to sink, Mum.

I hear you.

You're above my darkness but I don't know if you hear me, hear me calling: Mum, Mum, Dad, Dad, where are you, you have to come and you have to come and get me and who are all these people shouting about swimming, about rubber rings, about ice cream?

But I felt the drops.

They're lingering. What do the drops smell of? They have a different smell from how water usually smells. Do they smell of iron? Animal waste?

Your feet.

I hear them trampling on me.

Above.

And I think I'm lying down, but maybe I'm the one swimming, maybe the moist darkness around me is water. It must be water, I like water.

And now you're playing.

Where's my ball, Mum?

Shall I catch it for you? My arms can't. They're stuck by my sides and I try to move them, I try, but they seem stuck in whatever it is that surrounds me.

But why are you trampling on me?
I don't want you to trample on me.
Where am I?
Where are you, Dad?
I can swim, I can float, but I'm not getting anywhere.
I can swim. But I can't breathe.
My room is closed.

The nursery on the other side of the small park outside the crime team's meeting room is closed for the summer. There are no children using the swings or the red-painted slide, no three-year-old hands digging in the dry sand of the sandbox.

The heat is childless, the city in summer almost the same.

Instead there are two decorators inside the nursery school's windows. They're both up ladders, bare chested, and are rhythmically rolling pink paint onto one of the walls, much faster than it looks.

Happy colors.

Happy children.

Malin looks around the meeting room. Pale-yellow, fabric-textured wallpaper, a graying whiteboard on the short wall by the door. They got new chairs back in the spring. There was a manufacturing fault on the old ones, and the new ones, of curved wood with black vinyl seats, are astonishingly even more uncomfortable than the old ones, and in the heat the vinyl sticks damply to the cloth covering your buttocks. The police station's air-conditioning can't cope with providing a tolerable temperature.

The clock on the wall of the meeting room says 10:25. The morning meeting is severely delayed today because of the girl in the Horticultural Society Park.

How hot is it now?

Ninety-five degrees outside, eighty-five in here?

Opposite Malin sits a suffering Sven Sjöman. The patches of sweat under the arms of his brown checked shirt are now spreading toward his gut, which has grown even larger during the spring and early summer.

Be careful, Sven.

Heart attacks are common in the heat. But you're sensible enough to move slowly. I know that much. If you have one defining feature, it's that you're sensible. You're fifty-five years old, you've been with the police for thirty-three of them, and you've taught me all I know about this job.

Almost, anyway.

But most of all you've taught me to believe that I'm well suited to detective work.

You're the most talented officer I've ever worked with, Malin.

Do you realize what words like that mean, Sven?

Perhaps you do, otherwise you wouldn't say them.

Zeke next to her. Pearls of sweat under his nose and on his brow. Her own scalp feels damp, like after she's been to the gym.

"Well, we make up the sum total of the crime department's investigative unit this summer," Sven says. "So it's entirely up to the three of us to make sense of last night's events and work out what happened to the girl who says her name is Josefin Davidsson. Something else came in this morning. A girl by the name of Theresa Eckeved, fourteen years old, has been reported missing by her parents. I'll take responsibility as lead investigating officer for both cases."

"Oh dear," Zeke says. "There's a theme developing: girls."

First nothing happens, Malin thinks, then nothing happens, and then everything happens all at once.

"Missing," Malin says. "A fourteen-year-old? She's probably just run away from home."

"Probably," Sven says. "Theresa Eckeved's parents have told me what's happened. But we'll start with Josefin Davidsson."

"One thing at a time," Zeke says with a smile, and Malin can see that he has got some energy back in his overheated, summer-weary, hardworking gray eyes. The whole thing is a bitter paradox, the way violence and suffering provide them with work and to that extent make them happy. Should I be feeling this happiness? Malin thinks.

Gloom and happiness, she thinks.

If I mix those two feelings up, what do I get? One of the nameless feelings that you are bound to feel as a police officer at some point. One of those emotions that makes you feel guilty, that makes you doubt the nature of humanity, not so much because of what you see and hear, but because of what it does to you.

Rape.

That gets you moving.

Murder.

And suddenly you're bursting with energy.

"Josefin Davidsson is currently being examined by doctors up at University Hospital. They'll work out if she was raped, and they've appointed on-duty psychologists to give her support, and try to get her to talk."

"I checked," Malin said. "There are a hundred and twenty Davidssons in Linköping alone. We'll have to put everyone we've got onto calling them all if she doesn't talk and no one gets in touch."

"And we don't know who called to say she was out in the park," Zeke says.

"No. That could be tricky," Sven says. "The call probably came from a pay-as-you-go mobile. We all know how it is. It could have been a passerby who doesn't want anything to do with the police. Or someone involved in the attack. And none of Josefin Davidsson's family has contacted us yet," he goes on. "Not a peep. We'll have to organize door-to-door inquiries in the flats around the park. And when the doctors and psychologists have finished, you can try to question her at the hospital."

"Maybe she's older than she looks," Malin says. "Allowed to be at home on her own when her parents are away."

"Which leads us to Theresa Eckeved," Sven says. "Her parents have been to Paris and Theresa wanted to stay at home in their house out in Sturefors with her boyfriend."

Malin shudders when she hears the words *house* and *Sturefors*.

Sturefors.

The suburb of Linköping where she grew up.

Thousands of images come flooding back to her. How her parents used to skirt around each other instead of walking side by side. How she used to run through the rooms, in the garden, always with a feeling of not knowing where she was, that reality was something utterly different to what she was experiencing, and that every corner, bush, word, inference concealed a secret. A longing to be grown-up and the vain expectation that everything would look clearer then.

Her girlhood bedroom. Posters of Duran Duran.

Nick Rhodes.

"See them walking hand in hand across the bridge at midnight."

"Girls on film."

"But when they got home yesterday Theresa was gone, and when they called her boyfriend's parents it turned out that he'd been at the family's place in the country the whole time, without Theresa."

Markus.

Tove.

She may not exactly have lied at the start of their relationship, but she had concealed the truth. The lengths she went to to try and find her own place for a love she thought would make me angry. She didn't even trust me that much. Thought I'd try to make her see sense. And I did as well. Convinced myself I was protecting you, Tove, but I wasn't: I was only trying to stop you making the same mistakes I made. Bloody hell, I was twenty when I got pregnant with you, Tove. I couldn't bear to see you enter the same confused place where I was, the same sick, double feeling of love and of being backed into a corner. So I didn't trust you, thinking of myself, and you hid your first love from me.

What do you call that?

Failed motherhood. Nothing more, nothing less.

"Didn't they speak to her on the phone while they were in Paris?"

Zeke sounds tired again, sluggish hoarseness audible in his voice.

They must be regretting their trip, Malin thinks.

"Apparently not," Sven says. "The girl didn't answer her mobile, and she didn't answer the landline at home, but they didn't think that was particularly odd."

"No?"

"A bit touchy, evidently. Used to lose mobiles."

"And how long were they in Paris?" Zeke asks.

"They set off six days ago."

"So she could have been missing almost a week now?"

"And the parents don't have any idea where she could be?"

"Not when I spoke to them."

Sven Sjöman adjusts his shirt before going on.

"We'll prioritize the girl in the park, but you'd still better start by going out to Sturefors. Talk to the parents, calm them down, refer to the statistics, tell them she's likely to turn up soon."

Sven gives them the address.

Only a block away from the house that Malin grew up in.

The same district.

The same early 1970s dream. Pools in some gardens. Generously proportioned houses with wood and brick façades, mature fruit trees in neat, precious lawns.

She hasn't been out there since her parents sold the house and bought the flat by the old Infection Park. They're still in Tenerife, even though they usually come home for the summer. But, as her father explained over the phone: "This year we're staying on. Your mum's just started playing golf and is going on a course this summer. It's cheaper to do it now than in high-season in the winter."

"I'll water the plants, Dad. They're in safe hands."

In actual fact there were very few plants still alive in her parents' flat now, and it was far from certain that those would survive the summer. But what could they expect? It's been a year since they were last home. What are they really keeping the flat on for? Suddenly Malin wants to be there, longing for the chill she always feels there. It would actually be quite pleasant right now.

"And the media," Malin says. "What are we going to do about them? We can probably expect them to leap on the cases of Theresa and Josefin like bloodthirsty gnats."

"No doubt," Sven says. "But we'll lie low. So far we don't know that a rape has been committed, and it could be a while before they find out about the report of the missing girl, couldn't it? Maybe we'll get twenty-four hours' grace. And we might actually need the help of the

public, maybe with both cases. We'll have to see how things develop. Refer any inquiries to me. I'll take care of the jackals while Karim is away."

"He's bound to come in," Zeke says. "If things really heat up."

"No question," Malin says, then her phone rings.

Her mobile is in front of her on the gray tabletop, and the signal coming from it is angry, intrusive, as if it wanted to remind them that their conversation was nothing but theories, that it was time for a bit of harsh reality.

Malin looks at the number on the display.

Answers.

Listens.

"You'll have to take that up with Sven Sjöman. He's looking after press inquiries over the summer."

She passes the phone to Sven, raising her eyebrows with a sardonic smile.

"It's Daniel . . . Daniel Högfeldt from the *Correspondent*," she says. "He wants to know about the girl who was raped in the park and the missing girl from Sturefors, and if we suspect any connection."

6

A connection?

One girl is missing.

One girl has been attacked, possibly raped in the Horticultural Society Park. A long shot? Hardly. It's not impossible. Time, and their work, will turn up any connections if they exist.

But for now they're keeping an open mind, as the cliché has it. For now they're staring out at the asphalt of Brokindsleden through the windshield, the cycle path alongside the main road empty and the heat snakelike, scentless. The air seems to be utterly still, shimmering, low in oxygen. The wheat fields have been flattened by the heat, as if an immense hot fist had pressed the plants back into the ground and said to them: Don't think that your lives are possible, not this summer, this year will be a year of burning.

Zeke's hands at the wheel of the Volvo.

Steady.

Like his son Martin's hands on his hockey stick.

At the end of the season Martin received an offer from the Toronto Maple Leafs, but he turned it down. His girlfriend is expecting a child and wants it to be born in Linköping. And the team's main sponsors, Cloetta and Saab, joined forces and came up with a multimillion-kronor offer to persuade Martin to stay.

"Now the lad's rich," had been Zeke's comment. "And he'll get even richer if he moves to the States."

And it had sounded as if Zeke wanted Martin to move, as if he'd had it up to here with ice hockey and glory and praise and money.

"Ice hockey. What a fucking useless game."

Malin had asked him what he thought about becoming a grandfather.

"You must be excited, and proud," but Zeke had just muttered in reply. She had let the matter drop; once the baby was born he'd be beaming with joy, she was sure of that. The child would stroke his shaved head and say "prickle, prickle," and Zeke would love it.

Sturefors.

They are driving in silence, now approaching the edge of the small community.

Malin closes her eyes.

If the heat is scentless out there, what does the inside of the car smell like?

Air freshener and Aramis aftershave.

What do the gardens smell like now? What did they used to smell of?

Freshly mown grass.

A little girl's feet moving over the blades of grass, drifting forward. Alone in the garden. It smells of Dad. Mum. I hear her shouting, following me through the house, complaining, and how Dad backs down and I want him to stand up for me, contradict her, let me know that I'm good enough.

And how he stands there limply next to Mum, his mouth open as she shouts at me, how his own hesitant protests disappear back into his mouth as she stubbornly carries on.

The wind in my hair as I cycle past the houses, along the streets on my way to school. My feet beneath me, feet pounding the jogging track.

This is a competition, everything is a competition.

And one night when you thought I was asleep, when I was lying outside your door, I remember it now, only now, in this air-conditioned car, I remember what you said, you said: "She must never find out. This must stay a secret."

Mum's sharp voice. The tone of someone who has never found her place in the world.

Dad, what is it that I must never know?

The boys' football matches in the pitch behind the red-painted school building. The red shirts of the home team.

Bodies, warm. The floodlights on. Bankeberg SK, Ljungsbro IF, LFF, Saab. All the teams, the boys, the girls alongside, under the covers down in the cellar, what if someone comes?

Lilac hedges. Wooden fences, stained green. Families trying to be families. Children who are children. Who go swimming, and know that they're here to take over.

Sturefors.

Low blocks of flats and houses situated close to the Stångån River. Most of them built in the late sixties and seventies. Some built by the families themselves, by craftsmen planning their own homes, others bought by engineers, teachers, civil servants.

No doctors out here then.

But there must be now.

Doctors and engineers behind the tall, yellowing hedges, behind the fences, behind the yellow and white bricks, the red-painted wooden façades.

Uncut lawns. Trees that are starting to bear fruit, and by every house little flower beds with plants that have either withered completely or are shrieking for water. Abandoning the city for the summer is an obvious choice for most people in Sturefors. Not so much for the thousands of immigrants who live in Ekholmen, the mass housing project they passed on the way out here.

"You can turn off here," Malin says. "It's the next road down."

"So you know this place?"

"Yes."

Zeke takes his eyes off the road for an instant, ignoring the sign on a white brick wall warning of children playing.

The speedometer shows thirty, five above the speed limit.

"How come?"

Not even my closest colleague knows this about me, Malin thinks. And he doesn't need to know either.

I've no intention of saying that I grew up in a neighboring street, that I lived here from the time I came home from the Linköping maternity unit until I left home, in this well-to-do but increasingly insular Sturefors. I have no intention of talking about Stefan Ekdahl, and what we did in Mum and Dad's bed four months to the day after my thirteenth birthday. I have no intention of explaining how everything can be fine but sad at the same time. And do you know, Zeke, I have no idea how that happens, how that can be the case. And I have even less idea of why it might happen in the first place.

Janne.

We've been divorced for more than ten years now, but have never managed to let go of each other. Mum and Dad have been married since prehistoric times but may well never have got close to each other.

"I just know," she replies.

"So you're keeping secrets from me, Fors?"

"Maybe that's just as well," Malin says, as Zeke stops the car outside a white tile-clad house ringed by a low, white concrete wall.

"Theresa Eckeved's home. Feel free to get out, Miss."

A pool glitters in the background. Neatly trimmed poplarlike bushes of a variety Malin can't name surround the pool, and it looks like there's fresh compost in every bed.

Coffee and store-bought cakes set out on a teak table, comfortable blue cushions behind their backs. In the ceiling of the conservatory, just beside the built-in open fireplace, a fan is whirring, bestowing a welcome coolness. A bucket of ice sits next to the coffeepot.

"In case you'd like coffee *con hielo*," as Agneta Eckeved put it as she sat down at the table with them.

"I'll take mine hot," Zeke replied from his seat at the end of the table. "But thanks for the offer."

Then Sigvard Eckeved's words, as annoyed as they were anxious.

"I can't think why she'd want to deceive us."

And in those words is an awareness that he no longer determines much in his daughter's life, if anything at all.

The cakes smell sickly sweet in the heat, the coffee is too hot on the tongue.

Sigvard Eckeved's voice is high, but has a deeper after-tone as he tells them what they already know: that they have been in Paris and that Theresa's boyfriend was supposed to be here with her, but he has been at his family's place in the country outside Valdemarsvik with his parents, that Theresa's purse and mobile are missing, etc., etc. They let him finish, only interrupted by his wife's short corrections and explanations, her voice considerably more worried. Do you know something? Malin wonders. Something that we ought to know?

When Sigvard Eckeved has finished Zeke asks:

"Do you have any pictures of Theresa? To help us, and for us to send round to other police stations if we need to?"

Agneta Eckeved gets up, walking away from them without a word.

"She's just run away, hasn't she?" Sigvard Eckeved says once his wife has disappeared inside the house. "She must have. It couldn't be anything else, could it?"

"That's what we're going to find out," Malin replies. "But she'll turn up, you'll see. In statistical terms, the probability of that is almost one hundred percent."

Then Malin thinks: If she doesn't turn up, what will you do then with my encouraging words? But in that case my words here and now will be the least of your problems. But my words do more good now than harm then.

Agneta Eckeved comes back with a number of colorful packs of photographs in her hand.

She puts them on the table in front of Malin and Zeke.

"Have a look and take whatever pictures you want."

Everyone always says I'm a pretty girl.

But how can I believe them and trust that it's not just something they're saying, and anyway, I don't care about being pretty.

Who the hell wants to be pretty?

Pretty is for other people.

I'm grown-up now.

And you spoke to me in a new way that made me blush, but it was cold in the water so no one noticed anything.

Dirt.

Is it dirty here? And where do the pictures come from? How can I see them, I don't understand.

I've seen most of them before. They're from this year, just a few of all the ones Mum takes so manically of us as a family. Stop taking pictures all the time, Mum.

Just come.

Come and get me.

I'm scared, Dad.

The beach in Majorca last summer.

Winter in St. Anton, sun in a blue sky, perfect snow.

Christmas and Easter.

How can I see the pictures and hear what you're saying even though I'm not there? And the water? What water? And why is it so sludgy, so thick, like frozen clay when it ought to be nice and warm against my body?

Give me the rubber ring, Mum!

"She's a very pretty girl, isn't she?"

And then a female voice, a bit older.

Very pretty, don't you think so, Reke? Reke? Who's that?

I'm so tired, Dad. There's something slippery and sticky against my skin.

Why aren't you saying anything? I can see you at the table in the conservatory, how the sun reflected in the water of the pool throws patterns on your cheeks. But here, with me, where I am, it's dark and cold and lonely. Damp.

I'm not supposed to be here. I realize that much.

I don't want to be here. I want to be with you, I can see you but it's like you don't exist, as if I don't exist.

Don't I exist?

When I think about it I get scared in a way I've never been before. When I think about you, Dad, I feel warm.

But also afraid.

Why don't you come?

Malin chooses a picture that shows Theresa Eckeved's face clearly: small mouth, full lips, chubby teenage cheeks and lively, almost black eyes, medium-length dark hair.

No point asking what sort of clothes she had with her. What about how she usually dresses?

"Jeans. And a shirt. Never skirts, not ever. She thinks they're stupid," Agneta Eckeved says.

"In the pictures she looks almost girlish."

"Appearances can be deceptive. She's a bit of a tomboy," Sigvard Eckeved says.

"You don't have any suspicions about where she might be? Any special friends?" Zeke asks.

Both parents shake their heads.

"She doesn't have that many friends," Agneta Eckeved says. "I mean, she knows lots of people, but I wouldn't say many of them are real friends."

"We'd like phone numbers for her boyfriend and any friends that you happen to have numbers for," Malin says. "And anyone else who means a lot to her. Teachers, sports coaches, and so on."

"She's never really liked sports," Sigvard Eckeved says. "But there's a girl who used to come and swim here sometimes, some new friend who lived in the city. Do you remember her name, Agneta?"

"Nathalie. But I've no idea what her surname might be."

"What about a phone number?"

"Sorry, no. But her name was Nathalie. I'm sure about that."

"If you do remember, we'd like to know," Malin says.

"Does Theresa have a computer?" Zeke asks.

"Yes. In her room. She doesn't use it much."

"Can we take it with us? To check her emails and so on."

"Of course."

"Thanks," Zeke says. "That pool certainly looks very inviting," he says.

"You're welcome to have a swim," Sigvard Eckeved says.

"We have to work."

"It does look nice," Malin says. "Cool."

Stop the small talk.

Find me instead.

I'm missing.

I realize that now. That must be it. Otherwise you would have come, Dad. Wouldn't you?

Do you think I'm here of my own free will?

You believed he was my boyfriend. How gullible can you be?

But I want to tell you how it is.

I'm yelling, but you still can't hear me.

And the ringing, from the mobiles up there.

Stop trampling on me. Stop it.

"Yes, Fors here."

Malin is standing on the steps of the Eckeveds' well-kept seventies dream. She managed to fish the phone out of her bag and answer on the third ring. Zeke is beside her, with Theresa's Toshiba laptop under his arm.

"Sjöman here. You can go to the hospital, ward ten. The doctors have finished examining her. And she's feeling a bit better, she's even managed to tell them who she is."

"Josefin Davidsson?"

The heat like a glowing net around her brain.

"Who else, Fors, who else?"

"What have we got?"

"She's fifteen years old, lives with her parents in Lambohov."

As she clicks to end the call Malin looks through the green-tinted glass beside the front door, sees Sigvard Eckeved's silhouette pacing anxiously back and forth in the hall.

7

You came to us late, Theresa.

I was forty-two, your mum forty-one.

We did all the tests, and the doctors said that there might be something wrong with you, but out you came to us one late February day, like a perfectly formed reminder of all that was good in the world.

For me you are smell, feeling, sound, breathing in our big bed at night.

You creep in tight and what am I to you? The same as you are to me. We are each other, Theresa.

They say that having children is an act of handing over, showing you a way out into life. Giving you to the world, and the world to you.

I don't believe that for a moment.

You're mine.

I am you, Theresa.

Together we are the world.

Children are an elevation, about realizing emotionally that we human beings are one. The child is the foremost carrier of that myth.

One's own child, the person I am.

You're two years old, running across the parquet floor of the living room, language is developing, you flail and point, consuming the world, we consume it together. Even if I sometimes tell you off, you come to me, searching in me for the world.

You're four and a half and you hit out at me in anger.

Then you run through the years, further from me, but closer each time because you are leaving an impression within me.

You are twelve.

With love I creep into your room at night, stroking your cheek with my hand, breathing in the smell of your hair.

We're on the side of the good guys, I think then.

You, I, your mum, our dreams, and all the life we live together as one and the same.

The world is created through you.

You are fourteen.

Opinionated, stubborn, provocative, angry, but the embodiment of friendliness. You are the most beautiful person the world has ever seen.

I understand you, Theresa. Don't think I don't. I'm not stupid. I just don't want to move too fast.

We are the same feeling, you and I.

The feeling of unending love.

8

The dark-skinned cleaner sweeps his mop back and forth over the speckled yellow linoleum floor, shadows become sunlight, which becomes shadow as his never-still body moves across the sunlit window at the far end of the corridor of the hospital ward.

When the sun shines on it, parts of the floor seem to lift. A faint smell of disinfectant and sweat, the sweat emitted slowly by bodies at rest.

Ward ten.

A general ward. The seventh floor of the high-rise hospital building. Doors to some rooms stand open, pale pictures on graying, yellow-painted walls. Through the windows of the rooms Malin can see the city, sunburned and still, panting mutely, its enforced desolation.

Patients resting on their beds. Some wearing green or urine-yellow hospital gowns, others their own clothes. It isn't hot inside the hospital, the rumbling ventilation units are obviously adequate, yet it still feels as though listlessness reigns supreme here as well, as though the sick were getting sicker, as though those who have to work through the summer can't quite manage their allotted tasks.

A nurse materializes in a doorway.

Flowing red hair, freckles covering more than half her round face. She looks at Malin and Zeke with big green eyes.

"You're from the police," she says. "It's good that you got here so soon."

Malin and Zeke stop in front of the nurse. Is it so obvious? Malin thinks, and says:

"And the girl, Josefin Davidsson. Where can we find her?"

"Room eleven. She's in there with her parents. But first you need to talk to Dr. Sjögripe. If you go in here, she'll be with you shortly."

The red-haired nurse indicates the room she's just come out of.

"The doctor will be here in five minutes."

The clock sticking out from the wall in the corridor says 12:25.

They should have got lunch on the way. Malin's stomach rumbles with a gentle feeling of nausea.

They close the door behind them. Sit on wooden chairs in front of a desk, its gray laminate top covered with advertising folders and leaflets, yellow files. A window beside them looks onto a dark ventilation shaft. There are several anonymous files on the bookcase against the wall behind the desk.

Warmer in here.

Rumbling from the dusty, heart-shaped ventilation grille in the ceiling.

Five minutes, ten.

They sit in silence next to each other. Want to save their words, pull them out newly washed and clean later. For now, this silence fills a function. And what would they say?

What do you think about this?

We'll have to see.

Has she been raped, or did the blood come from somewhere else? And the smell of bleach? The whiteness? The cleansed wounds?

The door opens and Dr. Sjögripe comes in, wearing a white coat.

She's maybe fifty-five years old, cropped gray hair clinging to her head, making her cheeks, nose, and mouth look sharper than they really are.

A pair of reading glasses with transparent plastic frames hangs around her neck. The cheap sort, for a pair of twinkling eyes. Intelligent, aware, self-confident, like only the eyes of someone who has had everything from the very start can be.

Both Malin and Zeke practically leap out of their chairs. Anything else was unthinkable.

Sjögripe.

The most blue-blooded family in the whole of Östergötland. The family estate at Sjölanda outside Kisa is a significant employer, one of the largest and most profitable agricultural businesses in the country.

"Louise Sjögripe."

Her handshake is firm, but not hard, feminine but with a certain pressure.

Dr. Sjögripe lets them sit down before taking her own seat behind the desk.

Malin has no idea what position Louise Sjögripe occupies in the family, but can't help wondering. Doesn't want to wonder. Gossip, gossip, think about why we're here instead.

"Considering the circumstances, Josefin Davidsson is doing fairly well now," Louise Sjögripe says. The way she says the words makes her voice sound hoarse.

"What can you tell us? I'm assuming you conducted the examination?"

Zeke sounds slightly irritated, but not so as most people would notice.

Louise Sjögripe smiles.

"Yes, I examined her and documented her injuries. And I'll tell you what I think."

"Thank you, we'd be grateful, I mean pleased, if you could," Malin says, trying to look the doctor/aristocrat in the eyes, but the self-awareness they exude makes her look toward the window instead.

"In all likelihood she has been abused. She couldn't have caused the wounds on her arms and legs herself, and they weren't caused in self-defense. Those don't usually look, how can I put it, quite so regular. It's as if someone has inflicted the injuries with a sharp object and then washed and cleaned them carefully."

"What sort of object?" Malin wonders.

"Impossible to say. A knife? Maybe, maybe not."

"And the bleeding from the vagina?"

"Her hymen was broken by penetration, and the blood vessels on the inside of the vagina were damaged. Hence the bleeding. But that's normal with a first penetration, so it's likely that a relatively soft object was used, with a degree of caution."

Louise Sjögripe takes a deep breath, not because what she has just said seems to trouble her, but to emphasize what she's about to say.

"There are no traces of sperm inside her. But the perpetrator doesn't seem to have used a condom, because I found no sign of any lubricant. What I did find, however, were some very small, almost microscopic traces of something resembling blue plastic, as if Josefin Davidsson was penetrated by an object of some sort rather than a male member."

"And . . ."

Zeke tries to ask a question, but Dr. Sjögripe waves her hand in front of her face dismissively.

"I've already sent the traces to National Forensics. I know the routine. I've also taken blood samples from the blood on her thighs. Nothing apart from her own.

"And you don't have to worry. I haven't said anything about the girl's injuries to her parents. They're part of a crime, so I'll let you deal with that. I just discuss the medical situation with them."

Malin and Zeke look at each other.

"So she couldn't have caused the injuries herself?" Malin asks.

"No. That would be practically impossible. The pain would be too great. The penetration? Probably not."

"And the blood tests?" Malin wonders. "Was there anything unusual about them? Could she have been drugged?"

"Our initial analysis didn't show anything. But I've sent samples to the central lab for a more detailed examination, and that's when we'll find out if she had any foreign substances in her blood. But a lot of substances disappear quickly."

"What about the fact that she looked like she'd been scrubbed clean? She smelled of bleach."

"Someone's washed her very carefully, you're right. As if they wanted to make sure she was completely clean. There were no strands of hair or anything that could be linked in any way to the perpetrator by DNA testing, nothing on her entire body."

"Is it possible to isolate traces of any disinfectant that might have been used on her body?"

"Probably. I took epidermal samples from her back and thighs. Those have gone off to the National Lab as well."

"So how is she now? In your opinion? Is she talking? At the crime scene she hardly said a word."

"She's talking. Seems okay. And she genuinely doesn't seem to remember anything about what happened."

"She doesn't remember?"

"No. Mental blocks aren't unusual after a traumatic experience. And it's probably just as well. Rape is one of the worst curses of our times. This spreading absence of norms. The lack of cultural respect for another person's body, usually female. I mean, here in Linköping alone we've had two gang rapes in three years."

You sound like you're reciting an article, Malin thinks, and asks:

"When did she start talking?"

"While I was examining her. It hurt and she said *ouch* and then the words were somehow back. Until then she had been silent. She said her name and looked at the clock in the room. Then she wondered what she was doing in the hospital and said that her parents were probably worrying."

"Is there any way of getting her to remember what happened?"

"That's not my area, Inspector Fors. I'm a doctor, not a psychologist. A specially trained psychologist spoke to her about an hour ago, but Josefin couldn't remember anything. She's with her parents in room eleven. You can go and see her now. I think she can cope with a few questions."

Dr. Sjögripe opens a file, puts on the glasses hanging round her neck, and starts to read.

*   *   *

Room eleven is the embodiment of whiteness, lit by clear, warm light. Motes of dust drift through the air, dancing gently back and forth in the single room.

Mr. and Mrs. Davidsson are sitting on the edge of the bed on either side of Josefin, who is wearing a red-and-white flowered, knee-length summer dress and white bandages on her wounds, her skin almost as white as the bandages.

It could have been me sitting in their place, Malin thinks.

The three of them smile toward her and Zeke as they enter the room after knocking first. Josefin's cheerful voice a moment before:

"Come in!"

"Malin Fors, Detective Inspector."

"Zacharias Martinsson, the same."

The parents stand up. Introduce themselves.

Birgitta. Ulf. Josefin remains seated, smiling at them as though the previous night's events hadn't happened.

I've been like you, Malin thinks. Gone out on a warm summer's evening, all alone. But nothing bad ever happened to me.

Fifteen.

Only one year older than Tove.

It could have been you on the bed, Tove. Me and Janne, your dad, beside you, distraught, me wondering what monster had done this and how I could get hold of him. Or her. Or them.

"We're looking into what happened to Josefin," Malin says. "We've got a number of questions that we'd like to ask."

Nodding parents.

Then Ulf Davidsson speaks: "Well, we went to bed last night, me and Birgitta, without realizing that Josefin hadn't come home, and then this morning we assumed she was asleep in her room, and didn't want to wake her, and neither of us gave a thought to the fact that her bike wasn't outside . . ."

"I can't remember anything," Josefin interrupts. "The last thing I remember is setting off from home on my bike. I was going to the cinema on my own. The late showing of *X-Men 3*."

Her father: "Yes, we live in Lambohov. She usually cycles into town."

Malin and Zeke look at each other.

At the parents.

Knowing which of them will do what.

"Could I have a word with the two of you in the corridor while my colleague talks to your daughter?" Zeke asks.

The parents hesitate.

"Would that be okay?" Malin asks. "We need to talk to you separately. Do you mind if I talk to you, Josefin?"

"It's fine," Birgitta Davidsson says. "Come on, Ulf," she says, heading toward the door after a long glance at her daughter.

Malin sinks onto the bed. Josefin makes room for her, although there is no need. The same girl who was sitting on the bench that morning, on the swing, but somehow not the same.

"How are you feeling?"

"I'm okay. The wounds hurt a bit. The doctor gave me some pills, so I can't really feel it."

"And you don't remember anything?"

"No, nothing. Apart from leaving home on my bike."

No bicycle in the Horticultural Society Park, Malin thinks. Where's the bike got to?

"Were you going to meet anyone?"

"No. I remember that, because that was before I set off."

"Did you get to the cinema?"

Josefin shakes her head. "I don't know. All that is sort of gone, until I woke up here, when the doctor was starting to examine me. That's when I realized I was in the hospital."

She doesn't remember me, Malin thinks. Or the park this morning.

"Can you try to remember? For my sake?"

The girl closes her eyes.

Frowns.

Then she bursts out laughing.

Opens her eyes, saying: "It's like a blank piece of paper! I can sort of see that someone must have hit me, in theory, but it's like a big white blank, and that doesn't feel bad at all."

She doesn't want to remember.

Can't.

An organism protecting itself. Hiding away the images, voices, sounds in a distant corner of its consciousness, inaccessible to what we think of as thought.

But the memories take root there, chafe, hurt, and send out tiny, unnoticed little shock waves through the body, causing pain, stiffness, doubt, and anxiety.

"You don't remember how you got these wounds? Or anyone washing you?"

"No."

"And your bicycle, where did you leave it?"

"No idea."

"What make is it?"

"A red Crescent, three gears."

"You haven't been in touch with anyone over the Internet? Anyone who seemed odd?"

"I don't do that sort of thing. Facebook? Chat rooms? *Really* dull."

Banging on the wall from the corridor. Malin has been expecting it.

Zeke's words just a moment before:

"Your daughter has been attacked and a blunt instrument has been inserted into her vagina. Probably with force."

And Ulf Davidsson kicks the wall, clenches his fists, mutters something Zeke doesn't understand. Birgitta Davidsson is silent beside her husband, staring into the door.

Then her words.

"But she doesn't remember, so it's as if it didn't happen, isn't it?"

Ulf Davidsson collects himself, stands still beside his wife, putting his arm round her shoulders.

"No," he says. "It didn't happen."

*   *   *

The family on the bed in front of them.

Questions recently asked still hanging in the air. The answers float-ing around them with the dust particles.

"Everyone else is away for the summer, but we're staying at home this year."

"Telephone numbers of any friends we ought to talk to?"

"No, no special friends, really."

"Yes, we're staying in the city, saving up for the winter, we're going to Thailand."

"They don't want to hear about . . ."

"Any boyfriend?"

"No."

"Anyone else who could have had something to do with this?"

"Not that we can think of."

"No idea."

"No one in your closest circle of acquaintances? Family?"

"No," Ulf Davidsson says. "Our families don't live around here. And none of our relatives would do anything like this."

Two girls.

Theresa. Josefin.

And neither of them really seems to exist. They're like motes of dust in the summer city, invisible and nameless, almost grown-ups, insubstantial as the smoke from the forest fires.

Then a knock on the door.

It opens before anyone has time to say "Come in."

A sweeping mop. A huge black man in overalls that are too small for him.

"Have to clean," he says before they can object.

In the corridor, on the way toward the lifts, they meet a middle-age blond woman wearing an orange skirt that Malin guesses is from Gu-drun Sjödén.

Malin's finger on the lift button.

"That must be the psychologist," Zeke says. "Do you think she'll get anything?"

"No chance," Malin says, thinking that if they're going to stand the slightest chance of solving this, Josefin Davidsson will have to remember, or else a witness will have to have seen something, or else Karin Johannison and her colleagues at the National Forensics Lab will have to come up with something really good.

Hypnosis, Malin thinks.

Anyone can remember anything under hypnosis, can't they?

9

It's half past one.

Indoctrinated children all around Malin.

The dry, cool air finds its way down her throat and out into her lungs, shocking her body, triggering its defense mechanisms even though the experience is pleasant. Harsh colors making her eyes itch: yellow, blue, green. A clown, pictures, numbers, and an artificial smell of frying.

But it's cool in here.

And I'm hungry.

The tinted windows make the crashing daylight outside bearable, and I don't have to wear those damn sunglasses, they impose a filter on reality that I hate. But you have to wear sunglasses out there. The light today is harsh, like having an interrogation lamp aimed right into your eyes, the beams like freshly honed knives right into your soul.

McDonald's by the Braskens Bridge, on the side of the river facing Johannelund. Malin doesn't usually let the great Satan satisfy her hunger, but today, after their visit to the hospital, she and Zeke make an exception.

Kids with Happy Meals.

The walk from the hospital entrance to the car, parked in the sun

on the wide-open parking lot, made them doubt it was actually possible to be outside at all in heat like this. Then the car, it must have
been a hundred and fifty degrees in its stuffy interior, hot as a sauna,
with a protesting engine, a smell of hot oil and the air from the vents
first hot, then cold, cold, cold.

The restaurant half full of families with children. Overweight immigrant girls behind the counter jostling each other, giggling and di-
recting quick glances toward them.

"Isn't there any way of tracing the person who made the call about
Josefin?"

Zeke aims the question into thin air.

"Not according to Forensics. Pay-as-you-go. We'll have to leave
it as a question mark and move on. And hope whoever it was gets in
touch again."

Malin takes another bite of her Filet-O-Fish.

"And the bicycle?"

"Could have been stolen. Or it's just somewhere else. She could
well have been attacked in a completely different location, and moved
to the Horticultural Society Park. Impossible to know until she remembers. We'll have to get everyone to keep an eye out for the bike."

Zeke nods.

"Well, we can start by calling Theresa Eckeved's boyfriend," Malin
says once she's taken another bite of greasy American fish.

"You or me?"

"I'll call. You carry on eating."

"Thanks. Damn, this crap tastes really good when you're hungry.
Martin would go mad if he saw me eating this shit."

"Well, he can't see you," Malin says, pulling the piece of paper with
Theresa Eckeved's boyfriend's phone number from her pocket.

He answers on the fourth ring.

"Peter."

"Is that Peter Sköld?"

A gravelly teenage voice, sullen, sarcastic.

"Yes, who else? To the best of my knowledge, I'm the only person
with this number."

To the best of my knowledge?

Do teenagers really talk like that?

But maybe Tove would use that sort of phrase. A bit old-fashioned, affected.

"My name is Malin Fors. I'm a detective inspector with Linköping Police. I've got a few questions about your girlfriend, Theresa. Have you got time to answer them?"

Silence on the line, as if Peter Sköld is working out if he can avoid being questioned.

"Can you call back later?"

"I'd rather not."

Another silence.

"What about Theresa? Her parents called and asked if she was here."

A hint of anxiety in his voice.

"They reported her missing to us, and she told her parents she was going to be with you. But presumably you already know that?"

"I've been out in the country for a few weeks. We were going to meet up when I got back."

"But she is your girlfriend?"

"Of course."

The answer comes too quickly. Next question, pile on a bit of pressure, Malin.

"When did you last see her?"

"Before I left town. We had coffee in the shopping center in Ekholmen."

"She's very pretty, Theresa. How did you meet?"

"Sorry?"

"How did you meet?"

"She, I mean, we . . ."

Peter Sköld falls silent again.

". . . met at a dance organized by both our schools."

"What school do you go to?"

"Ekholmen."

"What year?"

"Starting my freshman year soon. I'm fifteen."

"And where was the dance?"

"Ekholmen. In our school hall. What is this? An interrogation?"

"Not yet," Malin says.

You're lying, she thinks. But why?

"So she really is your girlfriend, then?"

"I said so, didn't I?"

"And Nathalie? Do you know her?"

"You mean Nathalie Falck?"

"I mean Theresa's friend Nathalie."

"Falck. I know her. She's in the same year as me, in the other class. We're not exactly close friends, but I know her."

"And she and Theresa are good friends?"

"I suppose so."

"Have you got her number?"

"Hang on."

A bleeping sound on the line.

"It's 070 315 20 23. Look, I'm supposed to be going fishing with my dad, is this going to take much longer?"

Memorize the number.

Then:

"Why do you think she told her parents that she was going to be with you?"

"How the hell should I know?"

The father's voice on the phone now.

Impatient. Tired.

"So she's disappeared. I see. Well, the parents did sound worried. It's damn near impossible to keep control of kids these days. There was never any question of them spending the holidays together. We're out in the country. We like spending time together, just the family."

Are they really going out with each other?

Yes, he says they are. "But they never stay the night with each other and so on, that's what kids their age do, isn't it? But yes, they certainly spend time together, at least Peter often says so, but you know how it is, I don't really have the time or inclination to poke about in their private lives, so what do I know? She's been around our house once, I think, so I can't really say if they're together or not."

Poke about, Malin thinks. Do it. Poke about as much as you can.

Otherwise they might go missing.

And who knows if they'll come back?

Secret teenage lives.

My own.

Tove's.

"Good luck with the fishing," Malin concludes.

"Fishing? I never go fishing, I always buy mine from the fishmonger in town."

Noisy hamburger kids all round Malin as she calls the number she memorized a short while ago.

"Can we come and talk to you?"

"Sure, but I have to work."

Nathalie Falck. Studied nonchalance, an alert tone to her voice. Self-confident. Answered on the second ring.

What is that voice hiding? What secret?

Sven Sjöman's words.

An investigation consists of a mass of voices. Learn to listen to them, and you'll find the truth.

That's what you said, isn't it, Sven? Something like that, anyway.

Peter Sköld's voice. A liar's voice? Malin wonders.

"Nathalie, do you know Theresa Eckeved? Her parents have reported her missing."

"Yes, I know Theresa. So she's missing? She's probably just gone off somewhere for a while. She likes being by herself. And it's not that damn easy to be left alone, is it?"

"Strange practice, really, leaving a fourteen-year-old home alone. Completely normal here, but maybe punishable in the US where they think a serial killer is lurking around every corner."

"Where are you?"

"At work, in the Old Cemetery."

*   *   *

Zeke takes the key out of the Volvo and Malin can feel the fish burger in her stomach, fermenting and trying to send sour gas up from her stomach, but she holds it down, would really rather forget that they ate lunch at the great Satan.

They get out of the car.

The wall of the Old Cemetery could do with painting; peeling gray strips are hanging down toward the asphalt of the parking lot. Opposite there are blocks of redbrick housing built in the late eighties. The buildings are quiet, almost constricted and uncomfortable in the heat. A balcony door on the first floor stands open, and when Malin listens carefully she can hear the stereo inside. Tomas Ledin singing stupidly about love and sex, but even though she doesn't usually like it she likes it now, in this oppressive heat, because the music shows that there is still life in the city, and that an invisible hydrogen bomb hasn't wiped out everything except evil.

Behind the wall grow tall maples, their foliage still green, but with a pale, dry nuance. Headstones in rows beyond them, Malin can't see them, just knows they're there.

The graves are old, just as the name suggests.

The cemetery shed is some hundred yards away, behind the memorial grove where Malin sometimes comes.

Malin and Zeke are wearing their sunglasses, walking along one of the cemetery's raked paths, toward the figure up by the memorial grove that must be Nathalie Falck. She's short and muscular, a white vest stretched across her ample, recently developed teenage chest, as she leans on a rake. Plump teenage cheeks, a ring in her nose and short, spiked black hair.

They introduce themselves and Zeke takes off his sunglasses, to build up a rapport, or at least try to.

"Good summer job. Must have been hard to get?"

"Easy. And hot. No one wants to spend all summer pulling out weeds in the bloody cemetery. But I need the money."

Nathalie Falck kicks her Doc Martens boots in the grass as she says the word *money*.

Then they ask about Theresa Eckeved.

"So you don't have any idea where she might have gone?"

"No idea."

"When did you last see her?"

"About a week ago."

"What did you do?"

"Had an ice cream on Trädgårdstorget."

"Did she seem different? Did you notice anything odd, anything unusual?"

"No, not that I can think of."

Nathalie Falck is making an effort to speak in a deep voice.

Sweat on her forehead. Down Malin's back.

"Are you worried?" Malin asks.

"No. Why should I be?"

"She's missing."

"She can look after herself."

No anxiety in her voice, but her eyes? What are they saying?

"I'm just going to have a fag," Nathalie says.

"A bit of smoke doesn't bother us," Zeke says. "And I've always thought the eighteen-year age limit is silly."

The packet of cigarettes emerges from her camouflage shorts.

A gesture in their direction: Do you want one?

Hand gestures turning down the offer. Instead Malin asks:

"Are you good friends?"

"No. I wouldn't say that."

"So did you meet at the dance? Like Peter and Theresa?"

"What dance?"

"One of the joint ones organized by Ekholmen School and Sturefors."

"There've never been any dances like that. Wherever did you get that idea?"

Malin and Zeke look at each other.

"So how did you meet?" Zeke asks.

"In town. I don't remember exactly where or when."

In town.

Of course. Hundreds of youngsters drifting about in packs on Friday and Saturday evenings. Drifting, flirting, fighting, drinking.

On the third stroke it will be 10:00 PM precisely. Do you know where your child is?

No.

No idea.

"So you don't remember?" Zeke says. "Was it long ago?"

"Maybe a year or so ago. But I like her. We can talk about stuff."

"Like what?"

"Most things."

"And you and Peter are in parallel classes at Ekholmen School?"

"Yes."

"And you're friends?"

"Sort of. We talk at breaks. Have coffee sometimes."

"Do you know if Theresa had any other friends? Someone she might have gone to visit?"

Nathalie Falck takes a drag on her cigarette. Says: "Nope. But what do I know? Everyone has secrets, don't they?"

"She's hiding something," Zeke says as he starts the car. "It's obvious."

The car hot as a blast furnace again.

"So far everyone seems to be hiding something."

"A tough girl, that Nathalie. More like a guy."

"Not particularly feminine, I'll give you that."

"And Peter Sköld is lying through his teeth."

"Let's get Theresa's computer to Forensics before we do anything else," Zeke says. "There could be any amount of information on there. Emails. Websites she's visited."

"And Josefin Davidsson?"

"They should have finished the door-to-door now," Zeke says, putting his foot on the accelerator.

10

"The door-to-door in the area around the park hasn't turned up anything," Sven Sjöman says. "No one saw anything, no one heard anything. The few people who were home, that is. As we know only too well, the city's empty in July. And I'm afraid no witnesses have come forward, and our caller hasn't been in touch again, so we can't do much more except wait for Karin Johannison's report and the results of the more detailed tests, and see if the bicycle turns up somewhere."

The clock on the wall of the staff room in the police station, just inside the detectives' open-plan office, says five past five, the red second hand moving in rheumatic slow motion up toward the top, and the whole day seems flat and tired of itself.

Seeing as there are only the three of them, they're having their meeting in the staff room.

It's been a long day, Malin thinks as she watches Sven drink his coffee in deep black gulps. His mobile is switched off beside him, the message to reception abundantly clear: No more calls from the media. That was the first thing he said to Malin and Zeke when they got back to the station.

"They're completely mad. Since Högfeldt wrote that first piece they've been calling like crazy. I've spoken to *Aftonbladet, DN, Expres-*

sen, Svenska Dagbladet, and I don't know how many others. Both local television news teams have been here, wanting an interview."

"Summer drought," Zeke says. "They can get a lot of mileage from a violent rape and a disappearance at the same time. Throw in the forest fires and their summer is saved."

"Did you mention the bicycle?"

"Yes, I told the *Correspondent* that we're looking for a red, three-gear Crescent. They're publishing the details."

"When did Karin say the tests would be finished?" Malin asks.

"Tomorrow at the earliest. At least that's what she said when I called a little while ago. No fingerprints on the wood in the summerhouse."

"Christ, she's taking her time," Zeke says.

"She's usually always so quick," Malin says.

"Karin knows how to do her job. We know that," Sven says. "So, what have you two managed to come up with about Theresa Eckeved?"

"No one seems to have any ideas about where she could be," Malin says. "We've spoken to her supposed boyfriend and the only friend we've managed to get hold of, and they don't know anything either."

"Supposed boyfriend?" Sven says.

"Yes, we can't be too sure of that," Malin says. "These youngsters are hiding something from us. And the boyfriend's lying."

"So how do you plan to find out what they're hiding? And why he's lying?"

Sven is suddenly authoritative, as if he wants to know the answers now, and not hear a plan for the investigation.

"We're working on it," Zeke says. "This heat isn't helping."

"The heat's the same for everyone."

Then Sven softens slightly.

"Well, so far it's nothing but an ordinary missing person report."

"But she could have been missing for a week now. We really have to find more people who know Theresa and talk to them. And bring in the boyfriend, Peter Sköld, for questioning," Malin says. "He's at his parents' place in the country, near Valdemarsvik. We'll have to get his father to bring him in.

"And we've asked for a list of calls made from Theresa's mobile.

She hasn't taken any money out of her bank account since the day her parents set off for Paris; they've already checked."

"Did she have a computer?"

"Forensics has it."

"Good. Kids spend half their lives online these days."

Not Tove, Malin thinks. Not so far as I know.

"And the attack and rape of Josefin Davidsson?" Sven says. "What do you make of that? That has to be our main priority at the moment."

"We're going to check if any known sexual offenders in the area have been released from prison or any care facility recently. They could have become active again," Zeke says. "We'll have to look at old cases as well, see if there are any similarities."

"Good. What about gang rape, is that a possibility? Even if nothing at the crime scene suggests that?"

"We don't even know if she was attacked in the Horticultural Society Park at all," Zeke says. "As far as we know, she could have been attacked somewhere else entirely and just dumped there, couldn't she?"

"True," Sven says. "I forgot to say that the lab prioritized their detailed analysis of Josefin Davidsson's blood test. Completely normal. No sign that she'd been drugged. But there are a number of substances that disappear from the blood in a matter of hours. And the skin samples didn't give any clear results, apart from standard bleach and soap. The soap is probably from her clothes, and the bleach was used to clean her, so presumably the perpetrator was trying to erase any possible evidence. Karin's examining the microscopic blue fragments that Dr. Sjögripe found inside Josefin Davidsson."

"So, gang rape, any thoughts?"

Malin knows what Sven is aiming at with all his inferences and questions.

But he doesn't want to say anything, wants them to come up with it, because however you put it, it's going to sound racist.

In the end Zeke says it:

"We'll have to talk to Ali Shakbari and Behzad Karami."

Shakbari and Karami.

Guilty of having sex all night long with a hopelessly drunk girl.

But they weren't convicted of anything, and were released after their trial back in June.

"She agreed to it."

"She wanted to, for fuck's sake."

On the kitchen table of a flat in Berga?

"For fuck's sake, she was up for it. She's a slut."

Impossible to prove the opposite. And when Sven takes another mouthful of his coffee Malin considers official truths, and unofficial ones. How the entire police force and media know that practically all gang rapes are committed by two or more young men from immigrant backgrounds, but no one writes or says anything stating that truth outright.

Nontruths.

Politically uncomfortable.

And then the problem isn't there anymore.

And if it isn't there, it can't be discussed.

Which leaves a problem that doesn't exist and that therefore can never be solved.

And then there are girls like Josefin and Lovisa Hjelmstedt. That was her name, Shakbari and Karami's victim.

Girls like Theresa Eckeved.

Theresa's probably just gone off by herself somewhere.

Gone away.

Just like that.

When Malin sits down at her desk after the meeting her mobile rings.

Where is it?

There, in her bag.

"Hi, Mum!"

"Tove!"

Tove.

Malin can see her in front of her, the excitement in her blue eyes, her brown hair lifted by the breeze from the sea.

Are you both okay? she thinks.

I miss you even more now that I hear your voice.

But at the same time, it's good that you're not in the city.

It must be past midnight. What are you doing up so late? You ought to be in bed.

But Malin holds back. Wants to show her trust.

"How's everything there, then?"

"We went on a boat trip today. To a little beach."

"Was it good?"

"Yes, although the trip back was a bit boring, but I had a book with me. We've just been out to get some food."

"Is the food good?"

"It's all right."

"Loads of things cooked on skewers?"

It's as if the distance is making our conversation more superficial than our conversations usually are, Malin thinks. How the words can be just as trivial across the kitchen table in the morning, but they gain tone, context, and meaning from the fact that she and Tove are both there. As if all the intuitive contact disappears somewhere on the way between all the transmitters, cables, and satellites.

"Which book are you reading?"

"Several. But I didn't like *Madame Bovary*. It's really old-fashioned."

The sound of a xylophone in the background, a band playing in the hotel dining room?

"Is that some sort of orchestra I can hear?"

"They're playing in the dining room. Is it hot at home?"

"Boiling, Tove."

"It's not too bad here. Do you want to talk to Dad?"

"Why not."

"Malin?"

Janne's voice.

"Yes. So how are you both?"

"Fine. But it's hot. How are things at home?"

"Hot, unbelievably hot. I've never known anything like it."

"You should be here with us. It's nice here."

Bali.

Be there, Malin thinks, *just disappear from the heat here and those unfortunate girls?*

The way he disappeared to Bosnia, to Rwanda, to Somalia, anywhere that didn't involve the impossibility of their love. She has heard his voice a thousand times over crackling phone lines and felt her stomach clench and fill with a hot, black, anxious lump.

Sarajevo. Kigali. Mogadishu.

Janne's voice on those crackling lines, a message of what could have been, a greeting from a life that never was.

The same thing now.

"I read about the forest fires on the *Correspondent*'s website," Janne says. "They could do with me at home right now."

And she gets angry. Thinks: I could do with you now. But you, we, never realized it. You always gave in to your damn restlessness. Will you ever grow up enough to put your foot down and say that this is my place on the earth? It doesn't automatically follow that it's grown-up to build latrines in a refugee camp or drive a truckload of flour along mined roads. Being grown-up can mean staying put.

The anger dissipates as rapidly as it blew up.

"The others can cope, Janne."

"But it said that one fireman has been seriously injured."

"I miss you both," Malin says. "Give Tove a kiss from me. It's time she was in bed."

The *Correspondent*'s website.

The computer illuminates the bedroom, which would be completely dark without the flickering light from the screen.

The blinds closed tight, their jaws clenching to keep out the evening light.

Forest fires holding the area in their grip. One fireman injured when he tripped over on burning moss. Burns to his face and hands, that must be the one Janne read about. The pictures in the paper are dramatic, with firemen like little clay figures in front of a huge wall of flame, ready to set fire to them, burn them.

Daniel Högfeldt hasn't called her again, but he called Sven five times during the day.

He links the cases in one article. And writes about them in separate pieces as well.

"Summer Linköping is shaken after a violent rape in the Horticultural Society Park and the disappearance of . . ."

Linköping shaken?

Sleepy, more like. Drowsy with heatstroke.

The articles are short on detail. They're leaving things open for the time being.

Daniel and the media make their own valuations. For them the cases are one and the same, Theresa's disappearance no ordinary disappearance, the connection is good for them, even if Sven doesn't want anyone to talk about the connections and thus help conjure up an evil monster for summer Linköping.

She's just seen him on the local news. His eyes flicking to and fro, showing an uncertainty that Malin has never seen before, as if the camera were devouring him. "At this point we can't say for certain . . . we are continuing to investigate . . . no connection . . ."

Karim Akbar had called in from his holiday. Wondered if he ought to come in, look after the hyenas, as he put it to Sven.

Sven's reply:

"Take your son fishing, Karim. Write your book."

Then she reads an article about the heat wave. About a stream of deaths among elderly inhabitants in sheltered accommodations, how caretakers have found several elderly clients dead from heart attacks; how they can't cope with the heat or the dry air of the air-conditioning. One district nurse quoted as saying: "It's terribly hot in our patients' flats. They're having trouble drinking enough fluids and regulating their body temperature. And we don't even have time for our regular rounds when so many people are on holiday."

Malin turns off the computer and goes into the living room, stands by the open window, and listens to the buzz of conversation from the pub on the ground floor.

Go down?

No, not today.

Even if her whole body is screaming for a tequila.

Instead she goes into the bedroom, lies on the bed, and closes her eyes.

The harsh daylight lingers in the form of burning pricks of light on her retina, but from the darkness around her a figure emerges.

Malin sees Nathalie Falck in the cemetery, her mouth is moving but it's not Nathalie's voice, it's Peter Sköld's over the phone.

Two youngsters united in a lie.

But they're old enough to know that they have the right to silence, that if they just stay quiet they can make the police's job practically impossible.

Someone who stays silent can get away with pretty much anything. Language is the greatest enemy of the guilty.

Malin opens her eyes again.

She hears the voices from the pub, livelier than any she has heard so far today, but she can't make out any words in the chatter. She closes her eyes. Feels Daniel's body against hers, his weight. Maybe I should . . .

No.

Sleep instead.

Tired as hell.

In a room in the University Hospital Josefin Davidsson lies under a thin white sheet, willing her conscious mind to remember what her body remembers, what has happened to her. Her parents are still sitting in armchairs by the window, looking out over the flickering lights of Linköping, also wondering: What happened in the Horticultural Society Park? Or somewhere else? What secrets are concealed by the scorched grass and bark and leaves, the night and the darkness? At the same time they long to be far away, at home in their perfectly ordinary beds.

I want to remember, Josefin thinks, but I don't remember anything.

Do I want to remember? What happened still exists, even though I can't remember it, doesn't it?

Soon I'll be able to go home.

I shall lie on the porch and try to remember, I shall whisper to myself: remember, remember, remember!

The earth above me, does it have any memories?

I know why I'm here now.

Where I am.

I'm Theresa.

It must be night up there. I can't hear any voices of people swimming.

And I'm sleeping here, aren't I?

How did this happen?

Why am I sleeping here?

What are my dreams now?

Tove's voice is in the room, in the dream.

"Look after yourself, Mum, I'll be home soon."

From a hiding place deep within Malin's sleep, the voice says the words she wants to hear.

"I'll be home soon."

What would I be without you, Tove?

Without both of you?

And then Tove is standing there by her bed, holding her arms out to her, and Malin is going to embrace her but then Tove is almost gone again, her gangly body is transparent now, like a scarcely visible hologram, something vague for her memory and sense of loss to cling onto.

Come home, darling.

Don't disappear from me. Promise me that.

11

I t must be some homeless badger moving about at the dark edge
of the forest.

The pines and birches are swaying, on parade, as a faint nocturnal wind sweeps in from the Baltic, across the skerries and rocks of
the archipelago.

What are you digging for?

Is there something buried under the ground? Or are you just trying
to find your way back to your set, to the meandering tunnels you call
home?

A black-and-white striped back. A scrabbling sound. What is it,
hiding in the forest?

Karim Akbar is sitting on the porch steps of the cottage his family is renting for three weeks. St. Anna's Archipelago, Kobbholmen,
your own rowboat out here from the jetty in Tattö, and then the great
Swedish stillness. Hotter than ever this year.

Seven thousand kronor a week.

Swedish, more Swedish, most Swedish. The charcoal is still glowing after the evening's barbecue. A jetty of their own, with a view
from the wooden planks out across the narrow channel that leads to
open sea. Inside the cottage his family, wife and eight-year-old son,

are sleeping. This is paradise for him, and he ought to be sleeping by her side now, but does she want him there?

Sometimes he wonders. It's as if their life, and he himself, isn't enough for her. As if she wants something else. She doesn't say so in words, but with distance, or perhaps merely an absence of presence whenever he approaches her.

But I shan't get any physical peace now, Karim thinks. I want to bring order to what's happening in the city.

The girls.

One disappeared. One lost.

And then Sven Sjöman's face on the television screen. His brow wet with sweat, his hair a mess.

Daniel Högfeldt's voice:

"Do you think Theresa Eckeved is still alive?"

And the way Sven's opinion on the matter was clear from the look in his eyes, not the same as the opinion his words expressed.

"We are taking it for granted that she isn't dead."

"For God's sake, Sven, we are taking it for granted that she's alive!"

News.

Cameras.

This is a good profile-building opportunity, Karim thinks. But the house out here is nice, restful, and maybe I'm tired of all the pictures, the words?

When did that happen?

Hasn't even started writing his book.

Can't be bothered to be politically correct, and in that case it's better to let the pen lie.

The badger shuffles through the forest.

I want to get to the girls. Something's under way. Something dark. And I want to be there when it emerges into the light.

The kebab is rumbling around his stomach, the charred edges of the lamb trying to find a way back up.

Janne woke up early when he had to dash to the toilet.

That evening's restaurant had been the worst so far.

Greasy rice, bad meat, but Tove seemed to like her calamari. She's sleeping now, they each have their own narrow bed on a white stone floor. The aluminum railing of the balcony is still warm from the day's sun, and the sea is a hundred yards away, along a road lined with pubs, restaurants, souvenir shops, and temples. The Balinese in their colorful fabrics seem unconcerned at the exploitation, the air thick with incense as they march past in their religious processions that he doesn't understand the first thing about.

But that's what civilization looks like here, and the early Balinese morning is mild. The wine he drank with dinner has made his system unsettled, and he can't get back to sleep.

The hotel restaurant is dark.

The pool too.

Faint music from a bar that's still open, but not so loud that he can't hear Tove's breathing, and he thinks that she breathes just like Malin in her sleep, slow and steady, but every now and then the rhythm is broken by something like a whimper, not anxious or troubled, but relieved, as if something within them was finding its natural tone.

The nocturnal heat quite different from Africa.

Tropical night in the rainy season. There's nothing like it.

When the rain crashes down and you can feel the fungus growing on your skin, the way the splashing of the raindrops can't hide the evil that's after you, moving through the leaves, the insects, the trees.

There's always something that comes between people.

Religion.

Like in Bosnia.

Tribal loyalty.

Like in Rwanda.

And always politics, money, ambition, and game playing.

And often people like me. The willing cleaners. The ones who show up in the immediate wake of the catastrophe.

Things that have happened, recently and long ago. They collide, one way or another, in a moment of history, and then everything changes direction. An explosion of violence and you just have to deal with it.

A warm wind on his face.

Africa.

Cold wind.

Balkans.

A raw, damp cold that he will always carry with him.

Her voice on the phone just now, the poor, crackling line. The same tired performance as so many times before, their words, the things they say without saying anything at all.

What have I done?

Malin.

What the hell have we done? What are we doing?

It's time to stop messing about and to start playing the game seriously.

Janne goes in from the balcony. Lies down on his bed next to his daughter. Listens to her breathing.

Malin is dreaming of a cold wind whistling through tightly packed ground. Of a tiny little creature whimpering and trying to find its way into her hands.

She dreams of an open field made of sky and fluffy clouds.

She dreams that she's swimming in the sea with Tove and Janne, and alongside them swims a fourth person, faceless but not frightening, more like the incarnation of everything good that a person can be, if only in a warm summer's dream.

Sven Sjöman's wife Sonja looks at her husband. The way his stomach seems to spill across the mattress, the increasingly deep wrinkles on his face, and she listens to his snoring, the way it seems to get louder with each passing year, with every pound added to his stomach. But one minor miracle: She accepts the snoring, it has become a part of her, her life, them.

She usually wakes up at three o'clock or so.

Lies there quietly beside him and looks out through the drawn curtains, how the garden outside, its shapes, assume different guises according to the season.

The darkness of summer is relative.

The trees, apples and pears and plums, are clearly visible, not even imagination can turn them into anything but trees.

She usually pretends to be asleep when he creeps out of bed to go down to his woodwork room in the basement. She knows he wants to think that she's asleep, that he'd never leave her alone in bed if she let him know she was awake.

He bought a new lathe in June.

There're going to be a lot of bowls. He's started selling them in the craft shop at the castle.

In August they're going to Germany.

Sven reluctant, increasingly resistant to long journeys as the years pass, while she is keener.

"We should go to Australia. Go and see how Joakim's doing."

"Nineteen hours on a plane? The lad'll be home for Christmas. Isn't that enough?"

Driving down to Germany.

Minor roads.

Hotels where no one else ever seems to have stayed.

Sven.

They've been married more than thirty years.

She sees his anxiety in his sleep, the girls, all the terrible things she read about in the paper, all the things he refuses to talk about.

Zeke Martinsson has woken up, is in the kitchen of his house in Landeryd, waiting for the coffee machine.

The smell of coffee, of waking up, of a new day spreading through the room.

The clock on the stove says 5:23.

He almost always sleeps right through undisturbed, waking up early and fully rested.

The house is hot.

Must be ninety degrees. His wife wanted to buy an air-conditioning unit for the bedroom, but this heat can't last much longer, and then that would be ten thousand down the drain. But what's ten thousand?

Martin's going to earn millions. Just from playing a bit of ice hockey. Has already done so.

But everything's good if it isn't bad.

Brain surgeons earn nothing compared to ice hockey players. And nursing assistants?

The whole thing is just one big joke.

And their girls. Theresa and Josefin. What's happening?

Those bastard gangbangers in Berga. Stupid kids with a completely sick imported view of women. They bring out the worst in me.

And Peter Sköld. Nathalie Falck.

What are they hiding?

Zeke pours himself a mug of coffee. Sips at the hot drink, feeling his body wake up simply from breathing in the vapor through his nose. He puts the mug down on the kitchen table, goes out into the hall, opens the front door.

The garden is still. Flowers, bushes, trees. Like dark, frozen figures.

Dad spent ten years in Åleryd Geriatric Hospital before he was allowed to die. Stiff, locked inside himself by a Parkinson's disease that no medicine, old or new, could do anything about. Like a denuded tree in a garden.

Zeke creeps out in nothing but his underwear.

No neighbors at home, or up, if they happen to be home against all expectation. He opens the mailbox, puts his hand in, and pulls out the *Correspondent.*

Looks down in the box for advertising flyers but it's empty, just a few earwigs creeping into one corner.

He holds the paper up to the sky, at such an angle that he can make out the headlines in the dawn light, see the picture on the front page.

Pictures of Theresa Eckeved.

From the same sequence as the pictures they got from her parents yesterday.

Girl missing for a week . . . parents pleading for information . . .

Zeke folds the paper.
Coffee.
Must drink more coffee.
Make my brain pure and clear.
Today holds something important in store for me.

12

Peter Sköld has blond highlights in his hair, and he's so thin, almost painfully skinny, and his father, Sten, a man with determined green eyes and a sharply chiseled face, looks at his son with a pained expression when he crosses his bare legs as he sits down on the chair in the staff room at the police station.

Neither of them seems tired, even though they must have set off early that morning from their place in the country.

And Malin sees it at once.

Peter Sköld is aware of the significance of silence.

Why?

Because you have things that belong only to you, don't you, Peter?

Malin sits down and Zeke goes over to the coffee machine.

"Coffee, anyone?"

But father and son decline and Malin, who has already kick-started the day with three mugs, also turns down his offer.

"Thanks for getting here so early."

The clock on the wall says twenty past eight.

"It only takes an hour or so to get here, more or less," Sten Sköld says. "And now that Theresa's gone missing it's the least we can do."

Malin looks over at Peter Sköld.

What's that I can see in his face?

Fear? Cynicism? Silence.

"So are you a couple, you and Theresa?" Malin asks.

The answer comes quickly. Peter Sköld's slender hand through his hair.

"Yes."

Zeke sits down at the table with a steaming-hot mug of coffee.

"You don't seem to spend much time with her," Sten Sköld says to his son.

"Like you'd know about that? We're together."

"Did you notice anything different the last time you met?" Malin asks.

"No, like what?"

"That dance you mentioned, where you met for the first time. There have never been any dances like that," Malin says.

Peter Sköld's eyes flit about before he looks up at the ceiling.

"Okay, we met in town. I didn't want anyone to know I was the sort of kid who hangs out there sometimes."

"But you're allowed to be in town, Peter."

"Am I? That's not how it seems. Listen to me: We *are* together. But we didn't meet the way I said. And I've spent the summer holiday in the country."

"Yes, he has," Sten Sköld says, a new firmness in his voice.

"So you're not meeting another friend when you say you're going to meet Theresa?"

Malin throws the words at Peter Sköld.

"And who would that be, then?"

"You tell us."

"There's nothing to tell."

"Are you sure?" Zeke says. "Completely sure?"

"What exactly are you getting at?" Sten Sköld asks.

Peter Sköld smiles.

"I haven't got anything else to tell you."

"And you don't know if Theresa met anyone else when she said she was going to meet you?" Zeke asks.

"We're together, I told you."

"You don't seem particularly worried that she's missing."

"I am. I am worried. I just show it in my own way."

"Your own way?"

Peter Sköld sinks back in his chair, pushing his hair back from his forehead.

You little shit, Malin thinks. Fourteen years old? Fifteen? And already so . . . yes, what?

His eyes. Malin looks into them.

Shame. There's shame in those eyes. And fear. I ought to be giving you a hug, but you've made that impossible now.

"Okay, so tell us everything you know that might be of interest to us," Malin says.

"Well . . ."

"Hang on a minute," Sten Sköld says. "Is my son suspected of anything?"

"And Nathalie Falck?" Malin asks.

Peter Sköld smiles again, seems to consider his options before saying:

"A school friend. Nothing more. We like the same sort of music, the three of us."

"What sort of music?"

"Anything new," Peter Sköld says. "I really haven't got anything else to say. Can we go now?"

"Theresa is missing. A girl called Josefin has been raped," Malin says. "Tell us what you're hiding. Now. Do you know Josefin?"

"I don't know any Josefin."

"My son has already said he's told you what he knows," Sten Sköld says, standing up. "We're going now, Peter."

"He hasn't told us everything," Zeke says.

Once father and son have left the police station Malin and Zeke sit down at their desks.

"He's not telling us everything," Zeke repeats.

"Maybe you wouldn't either if you were him."

"Do you think his dad was holding him back?"

"No. That father knows his son. I don't think he was all that keen for Peter to say anything else."

"What do you think he knows, Malin?"

"Something, Zeke. Something."

Teenage worlds.

Tove's world.

The way she didn't tell Malin about Markus to start with. How Malin had been hoping that their lives would somehow get more similar the older Tove got, that they would have more things in common.

Has that happened?

No.

Although.

No. Don't lie to yourself, Malin.

I don't know if Tove is keeping secrets from me. God knows, I certainly annoy her. Sometimes, Malin thinks, I can see that she almost despises me and the life I lead.

Unless that's something inside me instead? Am I being too hard on my daughter?

That must be it.

It must be.

Sven Sjöman slumped in his chair at the end of the table in the meeting room, his furrowed cheeks burning red from the heat and perhaps a night of too little sleep.

It is 9:00 AM exactly.

The morning meeting starting on time this Friday morning.

Beside him is Willy Andersson from Forensics.

In front of Andersson, Theresa Eckeved's bulky white computer is whirring away. The Internet cable hangs limply toward the floor yet still seems to have something to say to them.

Zeke and Malin are standing behind Willy Andersson, looking at the screen, and Malin thinks that he's done a quick job, whatever he's found.

"Well?" Zeke says.

"She doesn't use the computer very much," Willy Andersson says.

"I haven't found any pictures, just a couple of school essays about biology, and I can assure you that they aren't of any interest."

Andersson.

Is he capable of working out what's of interest to us? Malin thinks.

Biology essays.

Yes, he probably is.

"What else?"

Malin can hear the expectancy in her own voice.

"She empties the memory cache regularly, so I haven't been able to track her surfing habits very far back. The information might be on the hard drive, or maybe we could get it from the service provider's servers, but that'll take time."

"How long?"

"Weeks. Information wiped from the cache is left as fragmentary traces on the hard drive. It takes time to build up any sort of comprehensible picture from them. And at this time of the summer the service providers won't be terribly keen on going through their server logs."

"But?"

Malin can tell from Willy Andersson's voice that he's found something else.

"From what I have been able to find in the memory cache and web browser, I can see that she has a Facebook page."

Willy Andersson clicks to open the page.

Theresa Eckeved's face.

Innocent. But also hard.

No notes. Only a few friends: Peter Sköld, Nathalie Falck. Only one who leaves comments: a certain Lovelygirl. Nothing more than an alias.

"Hello darling!"

"You're so beautiful."

"Suck me."

"Can you find out who this Lovelygirl is?" Malin wonders.

"She's a registered user, but she hasn't got a page of her own," Willy Andersson replies. "I can get in touch with Facebook and see if they can give us any information that could help us identify her."

"Anything else?"

Sven sounds almost pleading, but there's a note of relief in his voice. A Lovelygirl, something to go on.

"She's got a Yahoo! email account as well," Willy Andersson says. "But I can't get into it."

"Is Yahoo! likely to be any quicker than Facebook?"

"I doubt it. I'll try them both, and we'll see."

"Get onto it," Sven says. "And make sure they know why it's urgent."

"Nothing on Myspace? YouTube?"

Malin remembers the videos on YouTube a year or so ago of a teenage girl being raped and abused. It turned out to be her best friends torturing her.

Peter Sköld. Nathalie Falck. Torturers?

"Nothing on Myspace. I haven't checked YouTube, but I can do some searches today."

"Get onto it," Sven says again. "Get onto it."

"And Peter Sköld and Nathalie Falck haven't got their own pages either?"

"No, not as far as I can see," Willy Andersson says, getting up, and his thin, beige cotton trousers hang limply around his skinny legs.

Andersson.

Forty years old.

Looks more like fifty.

"Good work," Sven says.

"It was pretty straightforward," Willy Andersson says as he unplugs the computer and puts it under his arm.

"I'll be in touch," he says, and then he's gone, and only the heat and the sound of the door closing linger in the meeting room.

"So, you two. What are you up to?"

"We're going to see Behzad Karami."

And a silence descends on the room. A quite specific silence that Malin recognizes and likes, the silence in an investigation where the thoughts of the officers coalesce around an idea, a line of inquiry worth following up.

"Lesbians," Sven says. "Could there be a lesbian angle to this case? That Lovelygirl on Facebook certainly gave the impression of being homosexual."

"And Nathalie Falck is pretty masculine," Zeke says, and Malin thinks that he's being prejudiced, but deep down she agrees. She can feel the suggestions in the room.

"So, there could be a lesbian angle. Keep it in the back of your minds," Sven says.

"Maybe Nathalie Falck knows who that Lovelygirl is?" Malin says.

"Okay, time for the gangbangers," Zeke says, standing up. His eyes full of expectation.

A code.

We need a damn code for the lock.

It's just after half past nine. They're standing in the shade under the porch in front of the door of a run-down block of flats. The once-yellow brick of the façade has faded to ochre, and the surrounding grass and flower beds look like no one cares or is paid enough to look after them. Cigarette ends, cans, broken green bottles.

Malin can see herself in the glass of the door, her face improbably long and her skin somehow glowing.

Berga.

Only a few miles from the center of the city, and just half a mile from Ramshäll.

Another world.

Unemployment.

Immigrants.

And the usual: single mothers trying to raise their children to be decent people, as best they can with underpaid jobs that swallow up ten hours a day.

Absentee fathers are no myth here.

Most of the inhabitants of Berga are probably at home, even though it's summer.

Two blocks away from where they are now standing Malin found one of her old school friends, dead from a drug overdose. In a small one-room flat on the first floor, her first year with the Linköping Police, when she moved back with Tove after graduating from the Police Academy.

A smell had been coming from the flat.

The neighbors had reported it.

And she and a colleague had gone around, and he had been lying on the floor beside the bed, the place an absolute dump, and he stank and his body must have swollen up, but by the time they arrived it looked almost shriveled.

Jimmy Svennson with three *n*'s.

He used to be quite a charmer. Pothead turned junkie turned dead.

What's the smell now?

Scorched summer.

"What are we going to do about the door, Malin?"

"Wait until someone comes."

"You mean . . ."

"I was joking, Zeke. A little morning joke," and Malin pulls her key ring from the inside pocket of her pale-blue jacket, sticks the skeleton key in the lock, and twists.

"This sort of lock's easy."

Zeke looks at her admiringly.

"I have to say, you're bloody good at that, Fors."

The stairwell smells of mold and the lime-green walls are in serious need of a coat of paint.

No lift.

They're panting by the time they reach the third floor.

"Bet you he's asleep," Zeke says as he presses the doorbell beside Behzad Karami's door.

They ring again and again.

Malin calls Behzad Karami's mobile number, there's no landline listed.

There must be a terrible amount of ringing inside the flat.

She was stoned.

Then the voice on the mobile, with just a faint trace of an accent in his Östergötland Swedish even though Karami was already eight years old when he moved here.

"Do you know what time it is, you bastard?"

"This is Malin Fors. Police. If you open the front door, the ringing will stop."

Zeke's finger on the bell.

"What?"

"Open the door. We're standing outside."

"Fuck."

Over the phone Malin hears a body moving, then there's rattling behind the door, Zeke's finger ringing constantly now, and the sound of the doorbell getting louder and louder the more the door opens.

"Good morning, Behzad. So you've gone and messed things up for yourself again, have you?"

Zeke's voice full of distaste as he lets go of the bell.

Behzad Karami's face puffy with sleep and possibly alcohol, and who knows what else? Tattooed torso, powerful shoulders, a necklace of animal claws and teeth around his neck. Nineteen years old, his big, black, shiny BMW parked closer to the center.

On the other hand.

After a spell in youth custody he was never found guilty of anything. And we couldn't get him for the rapes, and maybe his "business" is going well? What do I know? Malin thinks.

"We'll come in," Zeke says, and before Behzad Karami can protest Zeke has pushed him aside, stepped inside the hall, and on into the single room.

Behzad Karami hesitant.

Branded since he sat in jail while they investigated whether or not the gangbang of the drunken Lovisa Hjelmstedt could be classed as rape or serious sexual assault.

But the case collapsed.

She agreed to it, and witnesses had seen her dancing with Behzad Karami and Ali Shakbari at the club, seen her leave with them of her own accord, even if she was so drunk by then that she could hardly walk.

"Not done any cleaning for a while, Behzad?" Zeke says. "But a mummy's boy like you probably can't manage that, eh? Keeping things clean?"

Behzad Karami standing in front of Malin in the living room. His back is covered by a showy fire-breathing dragon.

"I clean whenever the hell I feel like it. It's none of your business, you pri . . ."

"Say it," Zeke snarls. "Make my day. Finish what you were going to say."

"Zeke, calm down. Sit down on the bed, Behzad."

The rough wallpaper is full of scorch marks and stains, and on the bed is a torn pink sheet. The blinds are pulled down over the view of Berga's rooftops. A huge flat-screen television is screwed to one wall, and the stereo and speakers take up most of the free floor space. The tiny kitchen is oddly clean, as if it had recently been used and scrubbed very, very thoroughly.

Behzad Karami sinks onto the bed, rubbing his eyes, says: "For fuck's sake, couldn't you have come a bit later, what the hell do you want?"

"A girl was raped yesterday. She was found in the Horticultural Society Park," Malin says.

"Don't suppose you know anything about it?" Zeke says.

And Behzad Karami looks down at the green linoleum floor, shakes his head, and says:

"We didn't rape Lovisa, and I haven't raped anyone else either. Get it? When the hell are you going to get it?"

His voice.

Suddenly afraid.

Behind the muscles and tattoos he's just a boy, yet also a man who feels ashamed when people around town whisper behind his back, judged by the public court of a provincial city.

"That's him, the one who raped . . ."

"Bloody animal. That's what they're like, those . . ."

"Where were you the night before last?"

"I was at my parents'. We've got family over from Iran. Check with them. Seven people can tell you I was there until five o'clock in the morning at least."

"And after that?"

"Then I came back here."

Josefin who remembers nothing. Was she attacked before or after the cinema? What time?

"You came straight back here?"

"I just said so."

"Why should we believe you?" Zeke says, patting Behzad on the head.

"What about Ali, do you know what he was doing then?"

"No. No idea. Are you going to fuck about with him as well?"

Malin can see Zeke getting angry, how he's trying to stop himself hitting Behzad Karami. Instead he says in a loud voice:

"So you didn't go down to the Horticultural Society Park after the party? Didn't hide there waiting for a girl to go past?"

Malin takes a step back, out into the hall. She goes into the little kitchen, a completely different world from the rest of the flat: cupboard doors gleaming white, albeit worn.

She runs her hand over the draining board, smells her hand, lemon-scented detergent. She opens a cupboard, finds an unopened bottle of bleach.

She can hear Zeke roaring in the living room.

Knows that Zeke's anger can be so terrifying that it forces out truths, admissions of guilt where you least expect them.

"You're mad, you fucking pig."

Zeke's eyes black as he comes out into the hall and finds her in the kitchen.

"We're done here," he says. "Aren't we?"

"Not quite," Malin says, and goes back in to Behzad Karami.

He's sitting on the edge of the bed, breathing heavily.

"The kitchen. How come it's so clean?"

"Mum did it the day before yesterday."

"One last thing: Do you know where we can get hold of Ali?"

"Try his dad's flower shop on Tanneforsvägen. Interflora. He's helping out over the summer."

The car's air-conditioning is straining.

Malin at the wheel.

Zeke singing along loudly to the choral song filling the car.

Sundsvall church choir sings Abba.

"The winner takes it all, the winner takes . . ."

Zeke's voice isn't as gruff when he sings as when he talks. Malin has learned to put up with the music, partly because she has begun to see the point of singing in a group, but mainly because she can see what the music, and the sense of belonging, does for Zeke, the way he can switch in a matter of minutes from an adrenaline-pumped alpha male to a cheery, tuneful, almost harmonious man.

They're heading toward Tannefors.

Past the deserted skateboard ramps at Johannelund, the scorched yellow grass of the forgotten little fields between the river and the blocks of flats, then they cross the Braskens Bridge. Down to the left the mismatched buildings of the Saab factory huddle in the heat.

Aeronautics industry.

Actually a weapons industry.

But the pride of the city, nonetheless.

Because that's what Linköping is like, Malin thinks. Self-conscious, almost arrogant, wanting to be smart and a little bit exceptional, an exquisite little metropolis in the big wide world. A reluctant rural town, a provincial city with delusions of grandeur, but without any real self-awareness or sense of style. Which is why it's hard to think of a more provincial provincial city than Linköping.

"What are you thinking about, Malin?"

"The city. How it's actually pretty okay."

"Linköping? Has anyone said otherwise?"

As Zeke's question hangs in the air Malin's mobile rings, the call cutting through the car and into their ears.

"I'm done with the tests, Malin. I've analyzed what the doctors at University Hospital found inside Josefin Davidsson."

Karin Johannison's voice.

Ice-cold, self-assured in the heat.

"We're on our way," Malin says. "We've just got to get something out of the way first."

13

Most of the drops turn to steam, wiped out before they have time to land on the countless potted plants standing on the shelves beneath the florist's limp red awning. The noisy whirr of the humidifier bores into Malin's brain, but fades away when they step into the damp cool of the shop.

The tall, dark man behind the counter immediately assumes a watchful, hesitant posture; he recognizes them, Malin's sure of that.

Malin shows her ID.

The man nods but doesn't say anything.

"We're looking for Ali Shakbari."

"What's he done now?"

The man sounds resigned, but also annoyed.

"Probably nothing," Malin says. "But we need to talk to him."

The man points toward a door with a plastic window.

"My son's in the stockroom. You can go through."

Ali Shakbari is standing at a bench screwed into white tiles, trimming some red roses. The whole room has a strange, pleasant perfume. When he catches sight of them he grows afraid, the look in his brown eyes oddly watery. You want to run, don't you? Malin thinks.

"Ali," Zeke says. "How are things?"

No answer, and Ali puts the pruning shears down on the bench slowly, his thin, sinewy body in perfect shape under his white cotton overalls.

"What were you doing the night before last?"

"What do you mean?"

Defiant now.

Malin explains about Josefin being found in the Horticultural Society Park.

"And you think I had something to do with it?"

"We don't think anything," Malin says. "So, what were you doing?"

"Dad and I were cleaning the stockroom. We didn't finish until 3:00 AM. It's so fucking hot that it's easier to work at night."

"It's true."

Ali's father is standing in the doorway to the stockroom, holding the door open and radiating authority.

"Then I drove him home. He was home by about three thirty."

Malin looks around the stockroom.

Every inch of the room is sparkling clean, well ordered.

Too clean? Malin thinks before picking up one of the red roses from the bench.

"These are lovely," she says.

"Finest quality," Ali Shakbari's father says.

There are two sorts of people in the world. Hunters and the hunted.

So far in this investigation those roles haven't been fixed.

Are we the ones being hunted, drifting like motes of dust on the hot breeze? Malin thinks. So far we haven't reached the point where we're doing the stalking. Not yet. But maybe now, as a result of what I can see under the glass, in the hot light of the four lamps placed around the small but powerful microscope. The answer may lie in this blue substance, a blue truth.

The fragments are so tiny that they're hard to focus on.

The edges of the tiny blue fragments almost jagged.

A windowless laboratory in the basement of the National Forensics

Lab, which smells of chemicals and disinfectant. A humming noise from a fume cupboard.

Zeke's heavy breathing beside Malin, Karin's voice in her head:

I know what it was, Malin. What the doctors found inside her.

"What you're looking at is fragments of paint," Karin says. "The sort of paint that's normally used to color plastic."

The blue fragments blur in front of Malin's eyes. Floating.

Is the truth moving about somewhere down there?

Or something else?

A first clue.

A blue color, dead particles moving, as if they had been buried alive under the glass.

Malin raises her head from the microscope and looks at Karin.

"What could the paint have come from, what sort of object?"

Zeke sounds impatient, irritable because of July's never-ending hot weather, or possibly just because Karin is in the room.

Karin's voice is mild:

"It's impossible to say, it could be any one of a thousand things."

"Such as?"

"Such as a garden hose, the handle of a cheap mop, a salad server, a lamp stand, a toy spade."

Malin, Zeke, and Karin fall silent.

Josefin Davidsson penetrated without knowing it.

Theresa missing. Hints of lesbian activity on her Facebook page. Lovelygirl.

Does all of this fit together?

Nathalie Falck. Almost like a man. What do men have that women don't?

What's the voice?

Here and now.

Malin listens to the room. Something is taking shape in front of her eyes.

What are the girls in this investigation saying? Theresa, Josefin, Nathalie?

"Such as a dildo," Malin says. "A dildo."

And she doesn't know where the words come from, but they're there in the room.

"Sure, such as a dildo," Karin responds. "Not at all impossible."

"How do we go about looking into this?" Malin says, turning to face Karin. "Is it even possible to get any closer than guesswork?"

"Manufacturers keep records. We can start by checking the most likely products, I mean the sorts of thing this paint could have been applied to. Such as a dildo."

"What do you think, Malin?" Zeke asks.

"I don't know. But a dildo doesn't seem unlikely. Her vagina wasn't really injured, just penetrated. As if the object had been designed to do that."

"But surely it's possible to cause damage with a dildo?"

"Yes, if you're hardhanded. But then, you can cause damage with anything."

"My experience is that the vagina almost always shows serious damage when hostile penetration occurs with an object that isn't designed for the purpose," Karin says. "It could very well be a dildo. You can get both hard and soft models."

"You're an expert?" Zeke says.

"No," Karin says. "But that much I do know."

And then the realization of where the paint came from, that it was scraped out from within Josefin. Malin comes to think of Maria Murvall, the young girl who was raped in the Tjällmo forests several years ago and now sits mute in a mental institution. The crass words in the report about her shredded innards, her body lying on the bed of her room in Vadstena last winter, when Malin visited in connection with another case.

Probability, Malin thinks. Forces herself back to concrete facts.

Thousands of things and their language, listen to the language of these things instead, to what they're saying now. The air-conditioning in the room splutters, a slow coughing sound spreading through the ventilation pipes before it falls silent and almost at once a debilitating heat starts to take over the room.

"God, how stupid," Karin says. "Now it's broken and who knows

how long they'll take to fix it in the middle of the holidays like this, if there are any of them working at all."

"They're probably working," Zeke says.

"A dildo," Malin says. "That makes sense, even if our perpetrator could in theory have used pretty much anything."

She says nothing about her earlier thought about a lesbian connection. But surely lesbians often use dildos? Or is that just prejudice? No, one of her classmates at the police academy had proudly shown her her collection and given her detailed descriptions of dildo technique.

Zeke nods in agreement, no trace of doubt in his eyes.

"I was thinking that I could get Forensics to check dildo manufacturers," Karin says. "See what sort of paint they use. It might take a while, but you'd be surprised how much even the strangest businesses know."

Then Karin leans forward and puts her eye to the microscope, saying:

"It really is a beautiful shade of blue, isn't it? Clean and pure, like spring water."

Outside the heat has taken a firm grip on the air, and the wind, insofar as there is any, is hot, dragging through already parched treetops. The smoke from the forest fires is pungent on the air, the wind must be coming from Tjällmo today.

The fires keep getting worse. This morning an elderly couple had to be evacuated from the house they've lived in for sixty years.

The light seems to attack your eyes, any sunglasses that let you see anything at all are helpless against it. And she could really do with clear vision right now, to see all the connections that are scraping away at her consciousness like little shards of metal.

Malin and Zeke retreat to the lobby of the National Forensics Lab and its relative cool, where they sit down on one of the red Lammhults sofas, panting, unable to summon the energy to walk the hundred yards to the police station.

"Shit," Zeke said. "I didn't think it could get any hotter."

"Oh, it can," Malin says. "And this damn light. Even the thought of it gives me a headache."

"So, a dildo?"

"I don't know, Zeke. Maybe."

Zeke runs a hand over his shaved head.

"So who uses dildos?" he says.

Malin thinks, not answering Zeke's question, preferring to leave it open and let Zeke see the connection for himself.

"Someone who's been chemically castrated? Someone suffering from impotence? Someone who just feels like it? Lesbians?"

"Lesbians," Malin says, lingering over the word to let Zeke realize what she means.

"So that's what you're thinking?" Zeke says with a smile. "Lovelygirl on Theresa's Facebook page. Nathalie. And Josefin? Do you think she's lesbian as well?"

"No. But the perpetrator could be. A definite line of inquiry, anyway."

Zeke nods.

"So who else would use a dildo?"

"I can't think of anyone else."

"Maybe some unlucky bastard who's lost his crown jewels altogether?"

"You reckon?" Malin says.

"How can we know? Or else the scum in Berga have come up with a new way of humiliating women," Zeke says.

Malin stares in front of her.

Sees how Ali Shakbari and Behzad Karami filled Josefin Davidsson with cheap wine, then took turns raping her on a sofa with a blue-painted dildo. Sees them laughing, exhibiting the very worst of masculinity, even though they're scarcely more than boys.

That's racist, Malin thinks.

Shrugs off the image of the boys.

Malin and Zeke sit in silence beside each other on the sofa. Breath-

ing in the air, cool and dry, looking out at the heat, at the way it's making the air in the police station parking lot vibrate and snake.

Tove and Janne in Bali, cooler than here.

It's ten past nine and Malin is sitting at her kitchen table, eating cereal. She's so tired she couldn't even be bothered to slice a banana.

Hot in the flat.

No air-conditioning.

She raised the dildo idea with Sven over the phone, he thought it sounded like a lead worth pursuing, and said that he'd get some uniforms to check places where you could buy blue dildos on the net, in parallel with Karin's work: "That's how people buy that sort of stuff these days, isn't it?"

Daniel Högfeldt.

She thought for a while that there could be something more than just the physical between them, and maybe there is, but mostly it's this: the way their paths cross, day after day, until they meet up in his or her flat. But not tonight, he's still in the city, Malin knows that much, and not in this heat, this isolation. Her own sweat is enough, and exhaustion is making every muscle wither and buckle, and she's missing Tove and Janne so badly that it's on the point of turning into grief.

Her mobile rings.

It's in the living room.

Malin puts the spoon down, gets up, hurries through to find it. Guesses that something's wrong.

Karim Akbar's number.

"Malin here."

"Malin, what the hell do you think you're doing? Just because there's been a rape, you start harassing local immigrants?"

How could he know?

"We . . ."

"No excuses, Malin. Take a look at the *Correspondent*'s website, it's all there in black and white."

"Hang on, Karim, calm down."

"And now every single bloody media organization in the country is calling me for an opinion."

Karim's in his element.

Malin can't work out if he's genuinely angry or just pretending to be, actually happy to get some media coverage in the news drought. All his articles and appearances are controversial, but politically safe in the attitude toward integration that he represents. What's Karim's long-term goal? A ministerial post? But he doesn't even belong to a political party.

Her computer is on in the bedroom.

Click, click, click.

The *Correspondent's* website.

A photograph of Ali Shakbari and Behzad Karami standing outside the blocks of flats in Berga.

Headline:

"No Evidence: Police Harassing Immigrants."

The caption to the picture:

"We had nothing to do with the rape in the Horticultural Society Park, but the police are hassling us just because we're immigrants."

Daniel's tabloid angle:

"The Correspondent *has tried to obtain a statement from representatives of the Linköping Police today, but no one was available."*

A blatant lie to fit the story.

And you've been in my bed?

And doubtless will be again.

"Are you still there, Malin?"

There must have been a two-minute silence on the line, quite unlike Karim.

"I'm here, Karim. It was just an idea, one of many leads, you can see that, can't you?"

"I can see that."

"And they were the suspects in the Lovisa Hjelmstedt case."

"I know, Malin, but surely you can see how bad this looks?"

"Enjoy the attention," Malin says.

Karim laughs, but his laughter is hollow and tired.

14

The phone is on the table in front of Malin.

It's glowing.

Who the hell does Karim Akbar think he is, sticking his nose into their work?

It is not the job of a police chief to micromanage an investigation, but Karim has never really been able to stick to the boundaries, and an unspoken pact has developed among the detectives in the crime unit: Let Karim do what he likes, and we'll get on with our work. Because Karim isn't short of good qualities, and he actually has complete confidence in his officers. And he's good for the police in Linköping, his fondness for the media has focused attention on the work of the police in the city, and this attention has been rewarded with an increased budget from higher up.

Everything, Malin thinks, lying back on the sofa, absolutely everything can be traced back to this bloody mediatocracy, celebrity culture, the rapturous elevation of the mediocre, the uninteresting, into a form of religion. Our souls have no peace, Malin thinks, so we take an interest in Nothing:

Hair colors.

Skirt length.

Who's fucking who.

Celebrity weddings, divorces, collagen injections, sex scandals . . .

Well, thank God Tove doesn't care.

Karim.

Friends with the minister for integration. They share the same view of immigrants: make demands, be tough, but woe betide anyone else, any nonimmigrant, if they should happen to say something negative—then the air grows thick with verbal detonations.

Malin takes a deep breath of the air in the flat, the smell of a long hot summer where evil has started to make its move.

Sometimes she imagines evil as a shapeless black beast moving through vegetation and city alike. Who the beast is waiting for, who it might be, are as yet unknown.

She switches off the television.

Gets up.

Goes out of the flat.

Vague ideas of what she wants.

The pub downstairs is open, the clattering air-conditioning audible out in the street.

Call Daniel? Shout at him? Fuck him? Make use of his damn cock. Drink herself senseless. But there's nothing worse than having to work with a hangover, and they have to work tomorrow, even though it's Saturday.

Call Zeke and see if he fancies going for a beer?

Call Helen from the local radio station; it's been ages since they met up.

In the sky above her a third of the moon is glowing against a thousand pale stars, and she can see them stretching out their hands to each other without ever quite reaching.

"Zeke here."

He answers on the third ring.

His voice gruff, as if he's just woken up.

"It's me, I was just wondering if you fancy a beer and a chat about the case. I can't relax, what do you think?"

Thinks: I sound manic.

Lonely?

No question.

Just as I am.

"Malin, it's half past nine, you ought to be in bed getting your strength back for tomorrow. We've got a lot to do. I was on my way to bed, so no beer for me. We have to work tomorrow, you know that."

"Did you say half past nine?"

"Exactly, Fors."

Silence on the line.

"But you can come out here if you like. We can have a chat. Gunilla can make us some tea and sandwiches, we've got Kinda gherkins."

Zeke's wife.

Niceness and normality personified.

A pharmacist at the chemist's on the main square.

Too nice.

"Thanks, but no thanks, Zeke. I don't want to intrude. See you first thing in the morning."

"Good night, Malin."

She's left standing on the sidewalk with her phone in her hand.

Shall I go into the pub?

In again and up to the flat?

Call Tove, Janne?

Her skin is crawling, and not because of the heat.

Damn this thirst. This urge. I know it doesn't do a bloody bit of good.

Then in her mind's eye she sees Josefin Davidsson in her hospital bed. Her face contorted with nightmares, with suppressed memories.

Shortly afterward Malin is walking across Trädgårdstorget, perfectly aware of where she's going. The evening is slipping slowly into night, and the square's only open-air terrace is empty, a dark-skinned waiter is collecting the ashtrays, there are no glasses to clear on any of the tables.

She walks along Drottninggatan, past the imposing residential blocks. Cars pass: a green Volvo, a white pickup.

The black iron gate of the Horticultural Society Park beneath her hand, still warm from the day's scorching sun, but not hot enough to burn.

Malin opens the gate and steps into the park, quite alone now, presumably no one dares to come here at this time of day now, after what's happened.

Naked.

Raped.

Preschool kids approaching.

I don't remember anything.

The beast, it could be here, Malin thinks as she moves slowly deeper and deeper into the park, past the well-tended flower beds and the fountain, the greenhouses along the fence, and then the summerhouse, the playground, the almost-silent stream, a slight trickle of water, insignificant yet still full of voices, of hidden memories.

She can see the balconies on Djurgårdsgatan.

The thankless door-to-door inquiries.

No trace of the red bicycle, even though the uniforms have been down every possible route she could have taken into town.

Not many people left in the city, but even so, she must have screamed. Someone ought to have woken up. Did they move you here, Josefin? And, if so: Where were you before then? Where were you taken?

Malin skirts around the summerhouse, fingering the tape of the cordon that has already been pulled down, and closes her eyes, seeing someone chasing a naked, wounded, scrubbed-clean young girl back and forth across the grass, how she's tied up, gagged, how someone pushes a piece of blue plastic in and out of her, and how her memories close ranks, saying: Stop, no admittance! Grass beneath her body, hardly any dew in the heat, his, her, their bodies over you, muscles pressing you down with full force, the grass a bed you'll never, ever be able to leave, ever be able to get up from.

Was that it?

Josefin Davidsson.

Maria Murvall.

Theresa Eckeved missing.

A connection?

Josefin.

You wandered about until you were found, but you're still here with us.

And you're free, yet somehow not.

Theresa.

Are you still here? Where are you?

I can hear a voice.

I don't recognize it. But it's asking me where I am.

I want to know where I am. Because if I know where I am, I can get away from here, get away from the cold and the dark and the lonely and find my way home.

Everything is black now.

And cold.

So please, ask where I am again. Let your voice be an audible beacon to show me the way out of fear and this dark dream.

Ask again, please.

Ask.

"Theresa, where have you gone?"

Malin says the words out loud as she pauses beside the summer-house.

Birdsong.

Faces. Peter Sköld, Nathalie Falck, Behzad Karami, Ali Shakbari, other faces without clear features, the one who made the phone call, others, and still others.

Have to talk to Nathalie again.

Who is Lovelygirl? Maybe she knows.

Malin crouches down.

Fumbles in the grass with her hand.

A badger rooting about.

Who are you, who would do something like this? What sort of despair are you in? What happened to you, to make you capable of doing this to Josefin? What do you want to tell me? Has a smoldering snake from hell been released into your verdant paradise? Maybe the inferno is here, now and forever. And why so clean? What did you want to scrub away? Or scrub into being?

Time clusters together. The ground, memories, give way, the truth fleeing to protect its bearer.

How? Malin thinks.

How can I get you to want to remember, Josefin?

The stench of cremated forest.

Of cremated insects, animals, moss.

The forest now a penal colony for the wretched.

The stench of glowing worms teeming out of fire-ravaged ground. It's strong in Malin's nostrils, and if she could fly, glide over the plain and Lake Roxen and the forests around Tjällmo she would see the fires twinkling far below her. She would see the burning points of light and wonder if they were magma, or the truth, or brutality that has decided to seep out, as if some breaking point has been reached.

She would see the girls drifting and crackling like fireflies in the darkness.

15

Saturday working.

No question now, when their summer has taken a turn into unimagined, dark, Dante-esque circles.

They have to work. None of their colleagues will be called in from their holiday unless it's strictly necessary.

The smell of charred wood and extinguished lives is even more apparent in the morning.

But not intrusive, just different, almost pleasant, like a fire lit by the characters in one of Tove's old picture books, a fire for children to warm their frozen hands around.

No wind today, and for the time being at least the light is merciful, Malin thinks as she sees the flags hanging limply against their poles in front of the entrance to the police station, the large parking lot behind her almost empty, just a couple of cars with police markings ready for the hunt.

Malin drags herself through the heat.

Tired today.

Even at five to eight the heat is debilitating and she is sweating under her white jacket and T-shirt. She's wearing a skirt again, couldn't stand the thought of trousers, even if she hardly ever wears a skirt for work, it feels too feminine, too weak, too much like a statement. Her world is a masculine world. Whatever any feminists on the National Police Board might like to think.

So she usually wears trousers.

But not in this sort of heat. Not today.

She read about the forest fires on the *Correspondent*'s website over breakfast. A photograph of the blazing forests covered the first page, and other pages detailed the efforts of the fire brigade to put the fires out. Several hectares were alight. The fires had taken hold in the drought and wanted more, had become dependent on territory, on life. Fire crews from Linköping, Norrköping, Motala, and Finspång were all battling in the dusty forests.

Janne wishes he was there.

Fire would be better than Bali. He wants to plow all of his longing into work, into firefighting, saving others instead of trying to understand himself, me, Tove. Us.

And then her investigation.

A page to itself.

A picture of a dildo with the text: *"Police suspect attacker used blue dildo."* Prejudices. Karami. Shakbari. Speculation about Lovelygirl.

How the hell did word of the dildo leak out?

Karin Johannison? Sven Sjöman? Maybe Sven, under pressure from some journalist.

Oh well, it was out now.

The door of the police station glides open automatically. Ebba is sitting behind the reception desk, in early.

Says: "Good morning, Malin."

Malin nods in response.

Zeke and Sjöman are at their desks, even though the morning meeting isn't due to start for another hour.

Always this meeting, whenever they're working. No matter whether it's overtime or not.

They're both studying various documents, but they still notice her arrival, looking up at her almost simultaneously, and Zeke says:

"Malin, so you thought you'd show up!"

Zeke happy to be in ahead of her for once.

"Malin, welcome!"

Sven, wearing a creased pair of white linen trousers, is evidently also pleased to see her.

When she sees the look on Sven's face, Malin decides not to mention her visit to the Horticultural Society Park last night, although she had been planning to, she knows that Sven likes it when you try to get the feel of a crime scene afterward.

"Did you go for that beer, Malin?"

No, Malin thinks, but I had a stiff tequila when I got home.

"You're looking a bit tired."

Zeke crowing, grinning, friendly, almost paternal.

They start their morning meeting before nine.

They don't bother with the meeting room again, one of the round tables in the staff room will do, there are hardly any uniforms or civilian staff to disturb them today.

Sven looks more tired than usual, and Malin wonders where his new tiredness comes from, thinking that it must be the heat. She notices the fine sawdust on his hairy lower arms. The dust clings to his skin in little lumps and Malin thinks, Sven, you must have been up early this morning, working away in your basement, and maybe that's just as well, what with these forest fires and sluggish investigations.

As if he could hear her thoughts, Zeke says:

"That's one hell of a blaze in the forests. It's just getting worse and worse."

"Eighty firemen," Sven says.

"And the fire's heading for Lake Hultsjön," Malin adds, and silence falls in the staff room as the three of them sip coffee from their caffeine-stained porcelain mugs.

"Okay, let's get going," Sven says. "We've got a recently released rapist in the area whom we ought to check out. A Fredrik Jonasson living in Mjölby, thirty-two years old. Evidently he lives with his mother. Attacked a woman outside her flat. Attempted rape and violent assault."

"Mjölby can deal with that," Zeke says. "Are we going to check other sex offenders as well, or just the ones that have been released recently?"

"We'll start with this," Sven says. "We haven't got the resources to do more right now, but I'll make sure we have a list."

"What else?" Malin says. "How are we going to deal with Behzad Karami and Ali Shakbari? We need to check Behzad's alibi. Can we get some uniforms to talk to the people who are supposed to have been at the party? Have we got enough people for that? Or are we going to have to pull in someone from their holiday?"

"Slow down, Fors," Sven says. "We've got no evidence at all against Shakbari and Karami."

Karim must have spoken to him, but Sven would never hold back a line of inquiry just because Karim put pressure on him. Or the press.

"Have we got enough people?" Malin asks again. "Can we bring in anyone from Motala? Mjölby?"

The holidays were sacred, otherwise none of them would ever get any time off.

"We can spare a couple of uniforms," Sven says. "They can check his alibi."

"Which ones?"

"Jonfeldt and Bulow."

Good guys, Malin thinks. Young, single, but not gym bunnies, not the riot-squad type. More like future detectives.

"Do you really think they're involved in this?"

Zeke sounds dubious.

"Who knows?" Malin says.

Thinks: I've heard their voices in this case. Remembers Sven's words: *Listen, Malin. Listen to the voices of the investigation.* Recently he's elaborated on this: *You have to listen if you're going to learn anything, and if you learn something, you can get close to the truth. So close that you can touch it.*

"No news about Theresa either," Malin says. "Assuming nothing new came in last night? Unless Peter Sköld or Nathalie Falck has volunteered any new information?"

"Complete silence. On all fronts," Sven says. "She could have been missing a week now."

Then Sven changes tack.

"What about the lesbian angle?"

Zeke no longer hesitant. Malin dubious now, though.

"Just because we suspect that a dildo might have been used doesn't mean that we have to track the movements of every lesbian in the city, does it? Because there's some hint of a lesbian relationship on Facebook?"

"No one's suggesting that," Zeke says. "But it's a line of inquiry that's worth following up."

"In that case I'd like to talk to Nathalie Falck again," Malin says. "Alone."

Zeke nods.

"Makes sense," he says. "She didn't seem to like guys like me much."

Sven mutters "Yes" before adjusting the belt of his linen trousers and saying:

"Nothing new from Andersson in Forensics. Presumably he hasn't found anything else, and he can't have heard back from Facebook or Yahoo! yet."

Then Sven takes a deep breath before going on.

"I checked where local lesbians hang out these days. There's evidently some sort of club in Norrköping, Déjà Vu Delight. According to my sources, they haven't got a club in Linköping."

"I suppose the market's too small," Zeke says. "All the dykes probably run off to Stockholm as soon as they get the chance."

"Or even farther than that," Malin adds.

"What about the National Federation for Gay and Lesbian Rights? Is it worth contacting them?" Zeke says.

"They don't have an office in the area," Sven says. "You'll have to check out that club, Malin. Take a look, see what you can find out."

"You mean, go and ask if there's anyone who uses dildos and has ever exhibited any violent tendencies?"

Sven doesn't answer.

"Surely this is taking it too far, considering what we've actually got?" Malin says. "Can't we leave them alone in their own club? I might have a contact I can chase up."

Sven stays silent.

"You're right, Malin. Check your contact," he says eventually, then clears his throat and says: "So what other theories have we got? Ah yes, whether or not anyone has lost his penis? That sort of thing is confidential, and a bit of a long shot."

He says this without sentimentality, Malin thinks. As if it were just a nuisance to anyone who's had this happen to them.

"I'll check a few of my contacts anyway," Malin says, and she can see a frown develop on Sven's forehead.

"Don't try taking any illegal shortcuts now, Malin."

She doesn't answer.

Thinks: Would we ever get anywhere if we didn't take the occasional dodgy shortcut?

And Theresa? Where are you?

Am I under water? Is that green, brown, black wet stuff around me algae, water lilies? Are those pike teeth nibbling at my legs?

What does this dream want with me? Or am I really awake?

But if I am, then surely everything shouldn't be black?

Am I blind?

Have my eyes burned out, but they can't have, because they don't hurt. They're intact, yet somehow not, and I try to blink but nothing happens, and why, Dad, why haven't you come to shut my eyelids for me? Or are they shut? Or is just one of them open?

I want to close my eyes now. Get away from this place, all of this, and all the sounds, words I can't understand, they're like the devil's language, the backward speech on some worn-out heavy-metal record.

Turn off the voices.

Let go of my arms.

Let me move my arms and legs and feet and eyelids.

What do the voices want? The ones I can hear beneath me, no, above me, my hearing a space rising through the dream.

16

Soporific paperwork and unresolved discussions about the case after the morning meeting. Malin didn't have time to call her contacts.

They've come into the city center, and now the oxygen seems to be abandoning the air altogether under the parasols covering the tables outside the Gyllenfiket café, but at least the light is bearable in the shade.

There are two customers apart from Malin and Zeke, an elderly couple drinking coffee and eating slices from a whole loaf of coffee bread. It is almost half past four, and the heat has culminated in needle-sharp sunlight, and the scented particles from the forest fires have found their way across the city once more.

Iced coffee.

Con hielo.

They sip in silence, taking it in turns, and over by the windows of the Gränden shopping arcade a pigeon struts to and fro in front of a branch of Intersport. Inside the windows the beach balls and blow-up mattresses look more and more deflated by the second.

"Can you smell it?" Zeke wonders.

"Yes," Malin says.

"Do you think they can stop it?"

"They're bound to."

I'm stuck.
In this green, brown, black.
In damp plastic.
I don't want to be blind.
No burning ants are going to crawl inside my open eyelids.
Why? Tell me why you haven't come to take me home, Dad?
I want to wake up now. I've never had this sort of dream before.
I want to wake up, Mum. Dad.
I want to.
Not be blind.
Wake up, wake up, wake up.
But how?
Tell me, how can I wake up?

Zeke nods.

"Take a look around, Malin. You could almost imagine we were on our own in the city. Just us and our prey."

"My head feels like it weighs a couple of thousand pounds in this heat," Malin says. "It just doesn't seem to want to think."

"Does your head ever want to?"

"Very funny, Zeke."

"I saw a documentary on television last night," Zeke says. "Some wildlife program. About some bloody spider that mates with its own offspring."

"Sounds like a good way for a species to wipe itself out."

"Somehow it still led to a sort of evolution," Zeke says. "Spiders with close-set eyes."

A young woman walks past with a Saint Bernard dog on a lead, the dog's huge body swaying back and forth. It looks ready to pass out.

"Zeke, I was thinking of having a word with Nathalie Falck this evening."

"Why not? Just be careful."

Malin breathes in the summer air, feeling the heat in her lungs.

They go their separate ways at Trädgårdstorget, and when Zeke has disappeared from view Malin pulls out her mobile.

Senior Consultant Hans Stenvinkel sinks onto the uncomfortable chair in his hot office in ward nine of the University Hospital.

A five-hour operation just finished.

He was trying to save the leg of a motorcyclist who had crashed into a tractor outside Nässjö and been flown to Linköping by air ambulance. Time would tell if the young man would be able to keep his leg—the damage had been extensive, the leg split open from the knee to the hip, but the vascular surgeon had done his best.

Is that sweat dripping from my brow, or water from washing after the operation? Bloody hell, Hans thinks just as the phone rings.

Malin's number.

What does she want?

The mother of his son Markus's girlfriend, Tove. The tense but pleasant and evidently brilliant detective inspector. The distant, troubled, but after-a-couple-of-glasses-of-wine relaxed woman. Hasse has often thought when in her company that it's as if she doesn't really like doctors.

"Hans here."

Her voice at the other end of the line isn't as alert as usual and he can hear the sound of traffic in the background.

"This is Malin. Tove's mum."

"Hi, Malin. How are you coping with the heat? Haven't melted yet?"

"Half of me has just dissolved onto the sidewalk."

Hasse chuckles. At least she's got a sense of humor.

"How's Tove getting on in Bali?"

"She's having a great time."

"Markus is at our summer cottage outside Torshälla, but he'll be home when Tove gets back."

"I was thinking that you might be able to help me with something, Hasse."

"Okay. Fire away, Malin."

"I could do with finding out if there's anyone in the city who has lost his penis."

"I beg your pardon?"

"Lost his—"

"Sorry, I heard you, Malin."

"It's to do with the rape of that girl."

"The one who was found in the Horticultural Society Park?"

"Yes."

"The information you're after is confidential, Malin."

"I know."

"Sorry, Malin, I can't help you. It's illegal to reveal the details of anyone's medical notes."

"I know that too, Hasse."

*   *   *

He sounded shattered, Malin thinks, tired, when I asked. Those long operations must be draining. Malin puts her mobile in the front pocket of her skirt, during the day its pale-blue fabric has gained some light-brown stains and Malin wonders if you can get jeans that would be thin enough to put up with in this heat.

The pub downstairs is as tempting as ever. Crazy to live in the same building as a pub.

Sitting at the bar, alone, along with everyone else.

Getting happily, hazily melancholic.

Drink a chilled beer, its bitter, sharp coolness, the alcohol going to your head and filling its nooks and crannies with miraculous emptiness.

But no.

Not now.

The key in the door of the flat.

A stale smell, clothes and everything else just one big mess.

Malin stops, looks at herself in the mirror.

Heat wrinkles?

Whatever, they're certainly new, those little lines in the skin around her eyes.

I'm thirty-four, Malin thinks. And I still don't recognize my own reflection, I still don't know who I'm looking at.

They come to her again. Like summer ghosts.

Janne.

Tove.

And Daniel Högfeldt.

And she is consumed by a sudden painful sense that life is over, even while she's slaving away at it.

17

H er voice fills the bedroom. She's talking about the girls.
It doesn't really matter what she says.

It's the movement of her voice, its vitality, that's the important thing.

The presenter on local P4. Her friend.

Helen Aneman must be working evenings now, unless she works at pretty much any time of day.

"And to all you girls out there in Linköping. Please, take it easy. Whatever you're doing, don't go out alone. We don't know what this summer has let loose."

Then Helen introduces a track and Malin lies on her bed with the blinds closed, listening to her friend's voice in the relative darkness.

She sounds sexy.

Alone, but not tragic, as if she were waiting for someone to come to her in the studio and take her away.

Her Prince Charming? Well, why not?

The music starts. A hard-rock track. The words of the lyrics mean nothing. Malin is jerked back, gets up, slamming one hand down on the radio's Off switch.

Sven Sjöman called half an hour ago, just after nine o'clock.

"You're going to see Nathalie Falck?"

"I called her. We're meeting up in a little while. She sounded reluctant, to say the least."

"It's good that you're working, Malin."

"So you don't think I've got anything better to do?"

"No, actually I don't, Fors."

The defiance in Nathalie Falck's dark eyes.

The lies beyond the defiance.

Or truth withheld.

Nathalie agreed to meet her after some persuasion, but maintained in a razor-sharp voice that she had nothing to add.

Chosen location: the cathedral.

"I can meet you in the cathedral at ten. I go there sometimes."

"Is it open that late?"

"They don't lock the doors before eleven in the summer. Some new accessibility thing. And it's cool in there."

And now they're sitting in one of the brown-painted wooden pews toward the front, near the modern painted altarpiece, and above their heads gray stones of different shades reach upward to form an arch, stones that have spent centuries trying to disprove the law of gravity.

Nathalie is wearing a black vest and skirt. She radiates a courage and determination that Malin wishes she could have had as a teenager.

"What do you want to know?" she asks without looking at Malin.

"Yes, what do I want to know? Why don't you tell me? I'm sure you haven't told us everything that might be of interest to us. Nice skirt, by the way."

"Don't try to manipulate me. It isn't a nice skirt. H&M crap."

"Who's Lovelygirl?"

Malin looks for a reaction in the girl sitting beside her.

Nothing.

"I don't know any Lovelygirl."

"It's an alias on—"

"I've seen it on Theresa's Facebook page. Don't know who it is."

That came a bit too quickly, Malin thinks.

"You're sure?"

No answer.

Nathalie huddles up, as if to say: thus far, but no further.

Malin falls silent. Lets the church's faint knocking sounds take over for a few short moments.

"Is it hard being different?" she asks eventually, and she can see Nathalie Falck relax.

"Do you think I'm different?"

"Yes. It shows. In a good way."

"It's not hard. It's just different."

"Theresa is missing, Nathalie. You have to tell me what you know."

And Nathalie Falck turns her round face toward Malin, looks her deep in the eyes.

"But I don't know anything else. I know Theresa, but I don't know everything about her."

Her pupils contract. A sign of lying.

But are you really, actually lying?

"What about Josefin Davidsson, do you know her?"

"You mean the girl in the park? Oh, come on! I'd never even heard of her until I read about her in the paper."

By the entrance to the cathedral, some seventy-five yards behind them, someone turns a rack of postcards.

"Why do you come here?" Malin asks, recognizing her own visits to the memorial grove up in the Old Cemetery, and thinking that Tove would never come here of her own accord, the library is her place.

"I like the way it's so peaceful. And big. There's room for me in here, somehow."

"It's certainly big."

"What do you think has happened to Theresa?" Nathalie Falck asks.

"I don't know," Malin answers. "Do you?"

Then Nathalie points to the altarpiece, at the angular, painted figure of Christ.

"Do you believe in the Virgin Birth?"

Malin doesn't know how to react to the question.

Virgin Birth?

"I mean," Nathalie Falck says, "what's the point of innocence when everything pure and beautiful always ends up dirty? Is it actually possible to talk about such a thing as fucking innocence in the first place?"

It's just after midnight when Malin lies down on her bed for the second time that evening. It's just as hot and lonely as the rest of the flat.

She has the radio on.

Helen Aneman is talking about the heat and the forest fires, how one of the firemen from Mjölby who was taking part in the effort to put it out had been surrounded by flames on a gravel track and had been seriously injured.

"He's in University Hospital right now, and I think we should all spare a thought for him and his family."

Then music.

"Into the Fire."

Bruce Springsteen's epic about the firemen who headed straight into the burning World Trade Center to save others. The wonderful thing about human beings: how we can instantly drop our responsibilities for family, friends, acquaintances, and sacrifice our lives for someone completely unknown to us, our neighbor.

"May your strength give us strength."

How the possibility of sacrifice makes us human.

"May your hope give us hope."

And she has read that the firemen who survived said that they never hesitated, never felt any fear, nor any sense of duty, just a feeling of being one and the same as those in need.

"May your love give us love."

If people are reincarnated, let those firemen come back.

Then the song ends and she turns off the radio.

She shuts her eyes. Waits for sleep and dreams, but instead her thoughts race around her skull.

Nathalie Falck. Lovelygirl. What is it that Nathalie isn't saying?

Can't do any more there. Let time do its work. Josefin. Her closed memory.

Norrköping and Linköping have lesbian women in the fire brigade, Janne has told her, but who are they? Maybe they could tell her something?

It's a cavalcade of prejudices, this investigation.

Immigrant youths gang-raping young girls.

Lesbian firefighters, police officers.

They had a quick discussion after the meeting, about the obvious facts: that there were plenty of dykes in the force, but that Petreaus was the only open homosexual in Linköping.

"Let sleeping dogs lie," Sven said. "Petreaus is on holiday. Don't get her mixed up in this."

"You're right," Zeke said. "All hell would break loose."

Reality, unreality.

When did you last have your hair cut by a male hairdresser who wasn't gay?

Which was more or less how Zeke could have put it.

Nathalie Falck.

She wants to look tough, but deep down she seems scared, shy, as if she's spent the whole of her short life running, trying to get to grips with who she is. But perhaps that's what we all do, Malin thinks. Try to get to grips with life, and most of us just about manage to keep our heads above water. It's so much easier to run away from the pain and rush instead into the embrace of comfortable well-being.

The tequila is at the top of the cupboard above the fridge.

Her body is twitching for alcohol. Her stomach, heart, soul are whispering: Warm us, sedate us, make us soft. Combat the heat with the heat of strong liquor. That's who you are, Malin.

She breathes in the warm air.

A faint, faint smell of burning wood. Thinks of the firemen:

"Up the stairs, into the fire."

18

Words unspoken.

They drift through the room like dead souls.

Intimations. But of what?

I never had any brothers or sisters, Malin thinks as she walks through her parents' flat by the old Infection Park.

It's just after eight o'clock, Sunday morning, the city even more desolate than on a normal morning. I'm the last person on earth, Malin thought as she walked to the flat. All the others have burned up. She left her bike at home, wanted to get her body going by walking, stick one angry finger up at the heat.

She wants to water the plants before the morning meeting they agreed to have at half past nine, the need for overtime self-evident now: They can't lose a second in this investigation. Up earlier than necessary in spite of the lack of sleep in the heat. In spite of the large shot of tequila she drank in two burning gulps.

Weakness in the face of desire. It's always desire that gets out of control, it doesn't matter what sort it is.

The flat.

Four rooms and a kitchen, on the third floor of a house built just after the turn of the last century. Four rooms full of furniture from the house in Sturefors, of memories, of intimations of disappointments, unfulfilled dreams and lies, but also of a negotiated love, her parents' own particular love.

We stick together. But we have no respect for each other, we hate each other's bodies, we each have no interest in the other, in their words, opinions, dreams, longings, but we shuffle along side by side with our secrets and lies, and as long as we do that then we still have something. Don't we?

Like hell you do, Malin thinks.

She and Janne. How they really didn't have in common any of the things you're supposed to have in common. No interests. No hopes. But they had something that must have been there right from the start. An obvious love, as if together they manifested each other's humanity, the fundamental goodness, faith, and warmth that must always, always be the ultimate truth.

Every day and reality.

Sorrow and pain.

Day after day they saw how their love wasn't enough, how it clung on but fell apart, and not even Tove could hold them together.

A nameless catastrophe. And Janne was on his way to Bosnia along with the Rescue Services Agency. A fucking note on the table.

In our hour of need we stick together.

And he disappeared, and she took Tove with her to Stockholm.

Love can remain but become impossible. The feeling that something very real between them still remains.

She curses that feeling. That's a before-tequila feeling, the very worst of all. Or the next worst.

Unbearable.

Maybe I need something to believe in, Malin thinks.

You'll water the plants, won't you?

Dad's mantra over the phone.

These rooms do something to me, Malin thinks, even though they've never been mine, they're closed and open at the same time.

Is there a secret? Or is that just what I feel?

Never just a feeling.

Watering the plants.

The watering can has been Malin's lot since her parents moved four years ago. She and Tove haven't been to visit them, and they've only been back three times.

"We won't be home this summer, Malin."

"Okay."

"You'll do the watering, won't you?"

She's had that question a thousand times from her father, and a thousand times she's said yes.

But most of the plants are dead now.

She's put the survivors in boxes on the floor beside a shady wall in the living room, trying to spare them from the sun and the worst of the heat, even though the flat must produce a terrible static heat during the day that turns chlorophyll pale.

Big pots.

Dry soil, dampened by the watering can.

She can feel her parents' love in the flat, not their love for her, but for each other. Love as a deal, a sensible arrangement, a way to shut out the world.

Why? Malin thinks. Why do I feel such loss among these things?

She didn't call Janne and Tove yesterday, and they didn't call her.

She's sitting on one of the worn wooden benches on the hill leading down from her parents' building, fingering her mobile.

The fire brigade. Lesbians. The alien world of teenagers. Thousands of years between each generation.

Janne.

She fingers the keys as an unbearable ray of sunlight breaks through the foliage of the trees and she edges closer to the building.

Smoke in the air, just a hint, the fire is evidently spreading toward Lake Roxen. Is Lake Hultsjön going to burn? Really? Can a lake evaporate?

"Janne here."

He sounds lively. Restaurant noises in the background.

"Is that you, Malin?"

"It's me. How are you both?"

"Good, we're having lunch. There's a guy who grills fish for you. Tove loves it."

Fish.

She doesn't usually love fish.

"And you, how are you getting on?"

"We're struggling with that rape case I mentioned. That's one of the reasons I'm calling."

Silence on the line.

"So how can I help?"

Malin gives a brief outline of the case, about the dildo and the lesbian line of inquiry.

"So you want to know if I know anyone in the fire brigade who might be able to talk to you and tell you a bit about the lesbian community in Östergötland?"

"Pretty much."

"No prejudices there, then. What about your own ranks?"

"Sensitive, Janne. But what the hell are we supposed to do, there's a fucking rapist on the loose, a really vicious one at that. And another girl's gone missing. God knows where she is."

She explains briefly about Theresa Eckeved, and how they really haven't managed to come up with anything at all.

Another silence.

"Janne, it could have been Tove."

He says nothing at first, then:

"Talk to Solhage down at the station. I'll talk to her, she's okay, and she's working the whole of July."

"Thanks, Jan. Can I talk to Tove?"

"She's just gone up to the room, can you call back a bit later?"

When Malin has ended the call she turns her face to the sun, hoping to get some color in her tired features, let the rays wipe out those horrible wrinkles, but after just a few seconds the heat is too much for her and she gets up from the bench, thinking:

No one can control the passage of time, not me, and not you out there somewhere, whoever or whatever you are.

*   *   *

Malin walks up to the police station, careful to stay on the shady side of the street. Her legs are dragging behind her body, her sandals heavy on the pavement, which feels almost sticky under their soles.

Thinking, as her feet move forward in turn:

Exclusion leads to hate, and hate leads to violence.

Sexual exclusion, not chosen voluntarily.

It's mostly young people who choose to stand aside, or believe that they're choosing exclusion. No truly adult person chooses to stand on the sidelines, or at least very few. The passage of time brings with it the realization that belonging is everything. You, me, we.

What do I belong to?

The divorce was the biggest mistake of my life, Malin thinks. How could we, Janne? In spite of everything, everything, everything.

Five hundred yards away Daniel Högfeldt is sitting at his desk, and has just printed out thirty, maybe forty, articles from the past twenty years about rapes in the city and the surrounding area, the results of a search in the paper's digital archive.

He's laid the articles out on his desk, they cover the whole surface and side by side they make a frightening sight, the city seems to contain an active volcano of sexual violence against women, most of it within the family, but also cases that for some reason seem worse; of insane, starving men attacking women in the city's parks, and occasionally men too, come to that, there's one case of male rape down in the park by the railway station. Most of the cases seem to have been solved, but some must still rankle with the police: Maria Murvall, the case Malin is so hung up on, and the well-documented case of the woman who was raped and murdered outside the Blue Heaven nightclub. And more besides.

Shall I write an exposé about the unsolved cases? Daniel thinks. Shall I poke about a bit, read up on them all and write a gruesome series about Linköping's recent history of rape as diverting summer reading?

Something will come out of it.

But what?

In terms of statistics Linköping is no worse than anywhere else, but it's no better either, which is a fact that would give its inhabitants' very well-developed sense of self-worth a serious kick.

One thing is certain.

There is violence and sexual hunger to write about. Violence and hunger to match this infernal heat.

Then Daniel closes his eyes for a few short seconds, the word *heat* makes him think of Malin, and he wonders what she's doing at the moment. But no clear image resolves itself, and he opens his eyes and thinks: I'll drop these unsolved cases, but one day I'll go even further back and see what hellish stories this dump is trying to hide.

But for the time being I have to concentrate on what's happening here and now.

Malin's white blouse is stained gray with sweat, she thinks that she must have another one in her locker in the changing room, otherwise she's stuffed.

The police station up on the hill, the solid stone buildings around it, ochre-colored cubes tormented by the sun, tired of the dust rising from the parched, bitter ground. Behind her the University Hospital, one of the few places in the city that's still a hive of activity.

Solhage.

She was one of the stars of Linköping FC's women's team until they got serious and started buying players from all around the country. After that she couldn't even get a place in the squad.

Must have been a bitter blow.

Best to give Janne a bit of time to call her before I get in touch.

But if you can handle being a woman in the pathetically macho world of the fire service, you can probably deal with being left out of a football team.

Not long till the morning meeting.

Once we've been through the state of the investigation I'll give Solhage a ring.

19

"It was actually quite a relief to give up football."

"So you weren't bitter?"

"Not in the slightest, I was tired of all that kicking, and it was all starting to get pretentious. I mean, commentators on television talking about analysis and drawing little lines to show how someone runs. I mean, analysis is supposed to be saved for world affairs, isn't it?"

Malin laughs.

The masts of the yachts in the lock are sticking up above the stone edge like poles, swaying back and forth and giving the illusion of a dying wind, only there is no wind. In the background Malin can see the yellow wooden façade of the lockkeeper's cottage, and opposite her, in the shade of the parasol outside the canalside hostelry in Vreta Kloster, sits Viktoria Solhage, smiling, a warm smile that softens her thin face framed by long blond hair.

The morning meeting hadn't taken long.

She told them about her meeting with Nathalie Falck.

Otherwise there was nothing to report, nothing new from Karin and Forensics. Their colleagues in Mjölby had checked up on their sex offender, Fredrik Jonasson. His mother could give him an alibi.

They agreed that Malin should talk to Viktoria Solhage alone. Woman to woman.

The phone call to Viktoria Solhage. She hadn't sounded at all put out.

"Let's meet at the canal hostelry at quarter past ten. I get Sundays off. I live out in Ljungsbro, and it's a nice bike ride along the towpath. But I haven't got long. I have to head up to the fires later, we've all been called in."

Now the former football star is sitting in front of Malin and talking about the end of one part of her career and the start of the next. Viktoria Solhage was the first female firefighter in the city. She was controversial, and Malin remembers what Janne said when she was appointed: "Okay. She passed the tests. But how do I know if she'll be able to carry me if I pass out in a sudden burst of smoke?"

She's probably stronger than ninety percent of the men in the service, Malin thinks as she looks at Viktoria Solhage's bulging muscles.

"Pull, for God's sake, can't you see that we're going to hit the edge?"

"I am fucking pulling!"

Voices from one of the boats in the lock.

Coffee and ice cream in the shade of a parasol, it would have been lovely if the temperature wasn't already ninety-five degrees in the shade.

"Janne called, like I said. I was annoyed at first, but what the hell, the important thing here is that no more young girls get raped, isn't it?"

Viktoria Solhage screws up her nose, then her face becomes expressionless as she waits for Malin's questions.

"What do you think," Malin says. "Is there anyone in the city's lesbian community who seems to carry a lot of aggression?"

"A lot of aggression? I daresay we all do, but that much . . ."

Viktoria Solhage shakes her head.

"Dyke is synonymous with aggressive to you lot, isn't it?"

Malin feels herself blushing. Wants to put her sunglasses on and look away.

"No, but you know how it is," Malin says.

"How is it? Tell me."

Malin gives Viktoria Solhage a beseeching look before going on:

"There's no one with particularly problematic baggage? Any child-hood traumas that you know about? Anyone who was raped?"

"No, most people keep that sort of thing to themselves, don't they?"

"But?"

"Well, sometimes things can get a bit rough in bed, like they can for anyone. If only you knew. And sure, some girls fight with each other when they're drunk, competing to see who can be toughest."

"Does anything ever get reported?"

"No, we mostly keep things to ourselves. Maybe if someone went way over the line, but even then most of us would keep quiet. But everyone's like that, aren't they? No one calls the police unless they have to."

"Why do you think that is?"

"As far as we're concerned, I know why. The police don't give a damn about what a few dykes do to each other, Malin Fors. There's a deep mistrust of the police, you ought to know that."

"But you can't think of anyone who's been in a bad way, anyone who's been unusually violent?"

Viktoria Solhage looks down into her coffee cup.

Takes a deep breath.

You want to say something, Malin thinks. But Viktoria Solhage hesitates, turns to look at the canal and the lock, and the gates that are slowly closing again.

"Can you imagine being stuck in a little ditch like that all summer?"

"You were about to say something, weren't you?"

"Okay."

Viktoria Solhage turns to face Malin.

"There is one girl," she says. "She seems to be dragging a lot of shit around, and there's gossip about her being particularly violent. There's a hell of a lot of rumors about what she went through as a child. If I were you, I'd probably take a look at her."

"What's her name?"

Viktoria Solhage looks down at her cup again. Then she pulls out a pen and paper from her handbag, writes down a name, address, and phone number.

"Look," she says, pointing at the canal. "There they go."

Malin turns round.

Sees the yachts in the next section of the canal, heading for the lock that leads to the little lake halfway down toward Lake Roxen.

"Once they're out in the Roxen," Malin says as she turns around again, "they'll be free of the ditch. Good for them, eh?"

Viktoria Solhage smiles.

"The canal isn't called the divorce ditch without reason."

Malin puts the piece of paper in the front pocket of her trousers.

"Thank you," she says. "One last thing. Does the name Nathalie Falck mean anything to you?"

Viktoria Solhage shakes her head and says:

"Promise me one thing, Malin. Don't let this business turn into something that reinforces the image of lesbians as macho idiots."

"I promise," Malin says.

"In Stockholm, at any rate in the center of the city, people are very tolerant about the way other people want to live, but out here in the country it's different. Most people have never even met anyone that they know is homosexual. You can imagine how much fun it would be if the city got the idea you were hunting a lesbian killer."

"I've got something we should follow up."

Zeke's voice hoarse over the mobile.

Malin has just waved goodbye to Viktoria Solhage, who disappeared along the towpath up toward Ljungsbro, and is now cursing her stupidity. The place where she left the car is no longer in shadow, and the sun is now baking its dark-blue frame.

It must be at least a hundred degrees in there.

And the damn light is cutting right through her sunglasses and seems to have made giving her a headache its only goal.

"What did you say?"

As she says the words a dust cloud drifts past, making her cough.

"I've got something we should look into."

"What?"

No answer, instead: "Did you get anything from Solhage?"

"A name. We'll have to check her out. And you?"

"I got a text message from an anonymous sender."

"We get those every day."

"Don't try to be funny, Malin."

Then Zeke reads aloud from his mobile.

"Check Paul Anderlöv. A very unfortunate man."

Silence.

So Hasse did it: ignored the law on confidentiality.

She hadn't thought that he would.

"Who do you think sent it?" Malin asks.

Zeke snorts.

"That's something neither you nor I want to know. But I'm not stupid, Malin."

"So you know what it's about?"

"Yes. Like I said, I'm not stupid."

The Volvo is hotter than a sauna.

A very unfortunate man.

Bloody hell, Malin thinks. Is this right? Shouldn't he be left in peace?

One naked, wounded girl on a swing, one girl missing. Reality a gray, yellow, charred mess.

Malin is in her car on the way back to the city.

Outside the windshield the plain is still like a mirage conjured up by slowly smothered flames, as if a shimmering blue sky, stretched far too thin, has set fire to the fertile farmland that stretches all the way to the luminous horizon. The heat is hammering the ground with absolute confidence.

The open fields are drooping under the vault of the sky and the rye and corn are slowly burning up beneath the sun's rays, the rape is curled toward the ground, pale yellow, whimpering as if every golden leaf were gasping for air and were just waiting to be buried with the worms.

They're the only thing moving out here on the plain right now.

Glowing worms that have spilled out of the volcanic cracks shaken forth by evil. Zeke is waiting in his car outside the house in Ryd. His engine idling, the air-conditioning on full-blast.

The yellow-brick building near the center is only three stories high, yet still seems to contain the misery of the whole country in concentrated form, with its satellite dishes beside the windows, its cluttered balconies and outdoor spaces and general air of abandonment. The paths between the buildings are desolate, but the flats inside are teeming: refugees, drug addicts, social outcasts, the lowest-status workers, people excluded from society.

But there are two worlds here.

Some of the blocks contain student flats: people with dreams, their lives ahead of them, and beyond some tall oaks Malin can just make out Herrgården, the science students' bar and bistro.

Malin nods to Zeke through the side window, and he opens the door and gets out.

"So this is where the unfortunate Paul Anderlöv lives?"

"This is where he lives," Zeke says. "How do we explain how we found out about him?"

"We don't," Malin replies.

20

The thing about pain is that it's an eternal curse, because it wipes out time. It bestows an intimation of death and a stench of carrion upon a present which seems never-ending.

The physical pain disappeared long ago.

But psychological pain?

Medication.

But it doesn't help, and nothing gets better with time, no, everything gets worse, the pain is always new and each time it is more assured, more arrogant.

I am pain, Paul Anderlöv thinks as he hears the doorbell ring.

And he gets up from his armchair, turns down the volume of *Days of Our Lives* on television, and makes his way out to the hall. Once again, he is struck by the fact that his body seems to have disappeared, become limp and saggy instead of hard like it was before.

Fourteen years since it happened.

But it could just as well have been yesterday.

Malin holds up her ID toward the unshaven man in the doorway, his face simultaneously sunken and swollen, his cropped hair thin on his scalp.

"We're from the police. We'd like to ask a few questions," Malin says. "Are you Paul Anderlöv?"

The man nods.

"Can we take it out here?" he goes on to say. "It's a mess inside, and I don't really like inviting people in. Has there been some sort of trouble in the neighborhood?"

"We'd prefer to come in," Zeke says in a voice that doesn't leave any room for discussion.

And Paul Anderlöv backs down, showing them into a sparsely furnished living room with messy heaps of newspapers and motoring magazines. There's a noticeable smell of smoke, vodka, and spilled beer, and in the corners there are dust balls the size of sparrows.

Malin and Zeke sit down on a pair of chairs by the low coffee table.

Paul Anderlöv sinks into an armchair.

"So, what do you want?"

He's trying to sound tough, Malin thinks, but he just sounds resigned and tired and his green eyes are uncertain, tired beyond the limits of tiredness, and he's sad in a way that Malin has never seen anyone sad before.

"Have you heard about the rape in the Horticultural Society Park?"

When he hears the word *rape* it's as if all the air and water and blood disappear from Paul Anderlöv's body, as if he realizes why they've come. His head sinks down toward his chest and he starts to shake and whimper. Malin looks at Zeke, who shakes his head, and they both realize that they've crossed a boundary, the boundary that justifies intrusions into people's lives in the search for the truth.

Malin gets up.

She sits down next to Paul Anderlöv on the sturdy arm of the chair, but he pushes her away.

"Go to hell," he says. "After all, I've been there long enough."

Paul Anderlöv collects himself, seems to pull himself together, makes coffee, puts away a pair of white dishwashing gloves as he asks them to take a seat in the kitchen, with a view of the civic center in Ryd.

"I'm not so stupid that I can't work out the way you're thinking," he says. Resignation in his voice, but also relief. Perhaps because he knows that they're going to listen to him.

"I read about the dildo and I understand perfectly well, and I'm not even going to comment on the fact that it's idiotic and superficial and simplistic. But I understand your thinking. Could he be sexually frustrated? Mad?

"Well, I'm not mad. Sexually frustrated? You bet I am, what do you think it's like living like this, you should see what I look like down there," and Zeke looks involuntarily away from Paul Anderlöv and out of the window, but the shabby brick and paneled façade of the civic center give little comfort and he notices a spider outside the window, and an almost invisible web stretching from one side of the frame to the other.

"Anyway, how did you find me? Actually, I don't even want to know. Maybe it was through Janne, your ex, Fors, I know him. We were in Bosnia together, in ninety-four. We've had a few beers together, talking about our time in the field, or rather: I talk about my memories to him. He's as quiet as a broken car stereo."

"Janne hasn't said anything about you."

"Oh, so it wasn't Janne? No, I didn't really think it would be."

Paul Anderlöv starts talking, and they listen.

"It happened on a mountain road outside Sarajevo. I was one of the IFOR troops, and it was the sort of shitty, gray, rainy day when it was practically ordained that something was going to fuck up. It was that sort of day, and it did get seriously fucked up; the jeep hit a mine that had been buried outside a village called Tsika. I remember an explosion, a great sucking explosion, and then I was lying in the road some twenty yards from something burning, and I could hear someone screaming and screaming and screaming, loud enough to bring down the mountains, and then I realized I was the one doing the screaming. Everything down there was just black, no pain, just black and empty.

"Two men died.

"One lost a leg.

"And then there was me.

"I'd happily have changed places with one of the others.

"And now you show up, a couple of fucking cops, and what the hell do you know about anything? You know nothing."

They let the silence do its work.

Then they ask the questions that have to be asked.

The cretinous, asinine questions.

From haze to clarity, as the poet Lars Forssell wrote, Malin thinks. From clarity to haze.

"What were you doing on the night between Wednesday and Thursday?"

"Have you ever met Josefin Davidsson?"

"Can anyone give you an alibi?"

"So you still have the desire even if the ability is gone. Did your frustration make something snap?"

"So you weren't in the Horticultural Society Park?"

"But you do like teenage girls, then?"

Paul Anderlöv's eyes are fixed to the IKEA clock, the same sort I've got in my kitchen, Malin thinks. But the second hand still works on yours.

Paul Anderlöv doesn't respond to Zeke's insinuations.

Relinquishes the day to the unending ticking of the clock.

"Why do I feel like a complete bastard, Zeke?"

The heat envelops them, forcing sweat from their pores, the sunlight reflected in the cars around them.

"Because you are a bastard, Fors. A case like this one turns us all into bastards, Malin."

"The price of truth."

"Stop philosophizing."

Boundaries crossed, moved.

"Lunch?" Zeke says. "I could murder a pizza."

*   *   *

Conya on St. Larsgatan.

Best pizza in the city. Big, greasy, unhealthy.

The owner usually lets them off paying when he's there.

"Police, free of charge."

Like an American cop film. Zeke loves it. Corrupt? Maybe a little, but the owner refuses to let them pay.

One of the many hardworking, frowned-upon immigrants in this city, Malin thinks as she takes a bite of her Capricciosa.

The piece of paper Viktoria Solhage gave her is on the table in front of her.

The name on it:

Louise "Lollo" Svensson. An address, a phone number.

"Louise," Zeke says. "Could a Louise have Lovelygirl as a nick-name?"

"Maybe. Maybe not. Don't you think?"

"Lovelygirl," Zeke says. "A healthy dose of self-irony?"

"It's a long shot, Zeke, to put it mildly," Malin says, feeling how the pizza is making her feel fatter and greasier with every passing second.

"Lovelygirl," Zeke says once more. "Isn't that what all men want, really? A Lovelygirl?"

"Yes," Malin says. "I suppose so."

"Bloody good pizza," Zeke says, giving a thumbs-up in the general direction of the open kitchen.

The man standing by the pizza oven smiles, picking out ingredients from small plastic tubs and burying some of them in tomato sauce on a freshly spun base.

21

I've been lying here, fettered to time and this cold darkness for far too long now.

Where are you, Dad?

Just tell me, you're not coming. Not now. Not ever. Or maybe sometime far, far in the future. I don't want to be stuck here that long.

It's horrid here. And I'm so frightened, Dad.

So just come.

Take me away from the voices.

Voices.

Like worms on top of me.

I've heard your fawning, bloated noises for ages now.

Your voices.

You're happy about something.

Why?

I have no idea why you sound so happy, because here, here with me everything is damp and cold and the dream never seems to end. But maybe this isn't a dream? Maybe it's something else?

Swimming! Swimming!

Is that what you're shouting?

I love swimming. Can I join in? Can we go swimming together? I've got a pool in my garden at home.

Am I in the pool now, with my eyes shut?

A dog is barking, but everything's dark, so dark, and if I didn't know it was impossible I'd free myself from my muscles, my body, and then the being that is me would drift off.

But that isn't allowed in this dream.

No.

So instead, your happy cries. Up there? That's right, isn't it?

Earth and sand and a wet chill, a damp plastic chill, the grains close but not actually inside.

Is this a grave?

Have I been buried alive?

I'm fourteen, so tell me, what would I be doing in a grave?

Swimmers.

More than usual on a Sunday.

No entrance fee to the beach at Stora Rängen, you just leave your car farther up and walk over the meadow where Farmer Karlsman has been kind enough not to put any bulls this year.

He did that one summer a few years back, before the kiosk was here. They wrote about it in the *Correspondent*. But the farmer didn't back down that year.

The visitors are so carefree, with their families, children and women and men all enjoying the heat and the dubious cooling effect of the warm water, protecting their skin with expensive sunblock, their eyes with even more costly glasses.

And now, Slavenca Visnic thinks, now they're queuing at my kiosk, waiting impatiently for me to open up. Just hold on a bit, you'll get your ice cream. The children so happy to be getting ice cream, you can't buy more happiness than that for seventeen kronor.

Just hang on, be grateful that I'm here at all.

Aftonbladet? Expressen?

Sorry, no newspapers.

Who are you really, you who society has left behind, you who don't have anywhere else to go? We share that fate at least. In one sense, anyway.

Slavenca puts the key in the door of the beach kiosk, tells the crowd in front of the shutters to calm down, I'm about to open up, you'll get your ice cream in a minute.

Beyond the people, almost naked, she can see the water of the lake, sees them strutting in the sun, thinks that the reflections make the surface of the water look like transparent skin. And the big oak tree over there by the lake. Always so secretive.

Her kiosk at the Glyttinge pool is closed.

Spoiled youngsters who don't want summer jobs. Future ministers of leisure.

Sometimes she thinks that the whole of Sweden is one big leisure committee consisting of people who've always had it too good, who don't have the faintest idea about sorrow.

Then she opens the shutters.

An ugly kid, eight years old or so, a girl, is at the front of the queue.

"A Top Hat," she says.

"I'm out of those," Slavenca says, and smiles.

A dog is barking down by the oak, on the patch of ground where the grass has somehow vanished and been replaced by bare earth.

The dog has just peed up against the tree, but now he's frantic.

Standing at attention, marking that there's something there, something hidden that needs to be found.

He barks and barks and barks.

His paws digging, digging, digging.

I can hear noises, barking.

Slowly, slowly they drag me out of my dream, up, up. I want to wake up now, I want to wake up.

But I'm not going to wake up. Am I?

Am I going to wake up, Dad?

I'm stuck in something much worse, much stranger than sleep. But how did I get here?

Someone has to tell me, tell everyone, tell Mum and Dad. They must be worried; I don't usually sleep this late. And what are those other noises? It sounds like digging, and someone, a woman's soothing voice saying: "Okay, Jack, okay. Come here now," and the barking turns into whimpering, and someone says: "Okay, stay there, then, stay there."

Slavenca is taking a break from the relentless selling of ice cream, ignoring the next customer, leaving the surprised woman to stand there glaring into the kiosk, at the fridge full of drinks.

Don't be in such a rush, she thinks. If it gets even hotter you'll buy more ice cream and drinks.

She's put her prices up and people complain about her charging twenty kronor for a Coke, seventeen for a Popsicle.

Okay, so don't buy them, then.

Bring your own drinks with you.

But if the ice-cream company hears about her raised prices she won't be allowed to sell their products anymore. So what, there are other suppliers. Anyway, I ought to be in the forest with the other volunteers, tackling the flames.

And that dog over there.

He shouldn't be barking like that, shouldn't be there.

He's frantic, as if there's a bitch in heat buried by that tree.

Mad dogs. Mad men. Desire can lead to anything.

And that ugly girl who was first in the queue, she's looking down into the hole the dog's digging.

What on earth does she think she's going to see?

The wet and the dark are getting thinner, and that dog barking is getting louder, the voices have died out behind the barking and am I waking up now? The light up there, and the digging, and then my view is clear, but fuzzy, grainy, as if there were soil or sand in my open eye.

Am I free now?

Can I go home?

And I see a black dog, its nose and teeth, and he's barking excitedly and I want to get up, but my body doesn't exist.

And the dog disappears and instead there's a girl, the same age as me, no, younger, and her face changes, distorts, and I see her mouth form a scream and I want to tell her to stop screaming, it's only me, waking up at long last.

My body does exist, but do I?

Slavenca rushes out of the kiosk and down toward the girl and the dog, people are rushing over, all the bathers, and the scream is contagious, yes, even the water and the trees and the cows up in the meadow seem to be screaming.

"Out of the way," Slavenca says, then she's standing on the edge of the hole, looking down.

A girl's open eye beneath thin plastic, blue, curious.

The life gone from those eyes long before.

You poor thing, she thinks.

She's seen a lot of eyes like that, Slavenca, and all those mute memories come back to her now, lifeless memories of a life that never happened.

PART II

In the Eyes of Summer Angels

ON THE WAY TOWARD THE FINAL ROOM

You were left to rest and wait close to purifying water.

Murdered, but perhaps not yet dead.

I know that rebirth is possible, that innocence can come back. It didn't work with you, my earthbound angel, but it will work with someone else, because how else are the spiders' legs to disappear, how else can I put a stop to the rabbits' claws tearing away deep within me?

Our love couldn't evaporate, no matter how much pain the hot summers brought with them, no matter how much the tentacles crept over our legs.

This city has masses of trees, parks, and forests. I am there among the black, silvery trees. You are also there somewhere. I just haven't found you yet.

I want to get there now, feel your breath on my cheek. I want to have you here with me.

So don't be scared.

No one will ever be able to hurt you again.

22

The blue and white tape of the cordon. The steaming water of the lake in the early-afternoon light, like the bare skin of the people standing in the shadows of the trees on the slope, on the other side of the tape, watching the police officers with curious, hungry eyes.

The uniforms are fine-combing the ground down toward the shore where Malin, Zeke, and Sven Sjöman, together with Karin Johannison, the duty forensics officer, are carefully freeing the body from the soil and transparent plastic. It's unnaturally white, scrubbed, its cleansed wounds like the craters of dark, red-blue volcanoes in a dead human landscape, the grayish skin recently touched by hungry worms for the first time.

"Careful, careful." Karin's words, and they are careful, slow, keen to preserve any evidence that might be left in the location where the body was found.

Mingling with the bathers are the journalists, from local radio, television, from the papers, from the *Correspondent*. Daniel Högfeldt isn't there, but Malin recognizes the young female temp who interviewed her for a piece of coursework she was doing about crime reporting at the journalism college back in the spring.

Where's Daniel?

He doesn't usually miss something like this.

But presumably even he gets Sundays off. And if that's true, good luck to him.

The muffled sound of digital cameras.

Eyes eager to get closer, to document events so that they can be sold on.

Malin takes a deep breath.

Is it possible to get used to this heat?

No.

But it's better than freezing cold.

Can nature self-combust as a result of events caused by human beings? Attack us in protest at all the stupid things we do to one another? In her mind's eye Malin can see the trees on the meadow, the oaks and limes, tear their roots from the earth and furiously beat everyone to the ground with their sharp branches. Burying us with our wicked deeds.

The sweat is dripping from Zeke's brow and Sven is panting, his heart-attack gut juddering up and down above his belt as he squats on the ground with a blank expression on his face.

"It has to be Theresa Eckeved," he says. "It looks like she's been wrapped in ordinary transparent garbage bags."

"No chance of tracing them," Malin says.

The girl's face scrubbed clean under the plastic, her body naked, as white as her face, almost entirely uncovered now, also scrubbed clean. There's a deep open wound in the back of her head, and wounds as big as saucers on her arms, stomach, thighs, all cleaned and somehow trimmed at the edges, like neatly tended flower beds, blue-black, nurtured.

"It's her," Malin says, noting the stench of decay, no smell of bleach here. "I recognize her from the photographs. It's her, no doubt about it."

"No doubt at all," Zeke agrees, and Sven mutters:

"Just because it's hot as hell, surely the whole world doesn't have to go to hell."

Malin looks at the body.

"It's like someone's cleaned her really, really carefully," Malin says.

"Like someone wanted to make her, the wounds, as clean and neat as possible. Like with Josefin, only even more so."

White skin, black wounds.

"Yes," Zeke says. "Almost like a ritual."

"She doesn't smell of bleach."

"No, she smells of decay," Zeke says, and Malin thinks: You're no older than Tove, what if it was you, Tove? What would I have done then? And then she sees herself sitting on the edge of her bed with her service pistol in her hand, raising it slowly to her mouth, ready to let a bullet explode her consciousness forever.

Fear. You were scared, weren't you?

You must have been scared.

How did you get there in the ground?

"That's what we're going to find out," Malin says, and Zeke and Karin and Sven all look at her.

"Just thinking out loud," Malin says. "How long has she been here?"

"Considering how damp the skin is from the plastic it was wrapped in, and how the body has started to bloat in spite of the earth on top of it, I'd guess three days, maybe four. It's impossible to say for sure."

"Three days?" Zeke says. "She could have disappeared up to six days ago."

"I can't say right now if she was moved here after she died," Karin says. "I'll try to figure that out."

"So she could have been held captive somewhere for a couple of days," Sven says. "And then moved here."

"Someone might have seen something," Zeke says.

"You think so?" Malin says. "This is a pretty remote spot if you're not here to go swimming."

"People, Malin. They're always on the move, you know that as well as I do."

Malin sees herself in the Horticultural Society Park the other night.

Did you see me then? You who did this?

You who are doing this, you're trying to put something right, that has to be it. It must have been dark when you dragged the body down here, the trees bearing witness as you buried her in the ground. And why so close to the water where most people are? Maybe you wanted us to find her. What is it that you want from us?

"How did she die?" Malin asks, as an unexpectedly cold wind blows past her legs and out across the lake.

"I don't know yet," Karin replies. "The head injury was probably the cause of death, but as you can see there are clear strangulation marks around her neck."

"Sexual violence?"

"No clear signs of penetration. But I'll have to examine her more closely."

Karin.

Smart, not to say driven, but her view of the dead is like an engineer looking at a machine.

"It'll be hard to find any forensic evidence," Karin says. "There must have been hundreds of people who came here to swim over the past few days. Any footprints or other evidence has probably disappeared by now."

"Unfortunately that's all too likely," Sven says. "But the scene can probably tell us a fair bit about the perpetrator, if we just give it some thought."

The perpetrator?

Malin thinks, You're so sure about things, Sven. Just as sure as I am that that gut of yours is going to be the death of you if you don't do something about it soon.

"What do we think about a connection with Josefin?" Malin asks.

"They're probably linked," Sven says. "Both girls scrubbed clean the same way. But we can't be absolutely certain. Karin, you'll have to check for traces of paint."

I can see you and hear you, all you strangers, and I understand that you're talking about me, but I don't want to listen to your wretched words.

Wounds on my body.

Sexual violence.

Perpetrator.

Penetration?

No.

Captive, captive, dead.

Dead.

A blow to the head.

And who's dead? Not me, I'm fourteen years old, do you hear? You don't use words like dead *about someone who's just fourteen years old. I've got many years of life ahead of me, at least seventy, and I want those years.*

I want them back.

Give them to me, Dad.

I refuse. Refuse.

I feel no pain and if I did have those wounds that you're talking about then surely I'd be screaming?

But my voice.

It can't be heard, but is audible nonetheless, and the words are different, it's as if I've grown up in this dream and woken up with a new register.

Register?

I'd never use that word.

Let me be! Don't touch me!

Let me sleep, dream myself away, let me be. What are you doing with me?

All the awful things I've been dreaming.

Go away, now.

Let me carry on sleeping.

I can see a face.

A woman's face, it's a thin, pleasant face framed with blond hair that blends into the pale green of the trees, the blue of the sky.

She's looking at me.

I want to get up, but it's like I don't exist. Don't I exist? But if I didn't exist, then you wouldn't be talking about me, would you?

Malin crouching down over the girl.

One eye open, the other closed, almost pleading for sleep. The body still, almost pressed into the ground. Bruising around the neck.

The scrubbed body.

The neat, trimmed wounds.

Just like Josefin Davidsson in the Horticultural Society Park.

Sven may still have a few doubts, but it must be the same person, the same people, behind this. From now on these cases are one and the same.

Soil under the girl's nails, the only trace of dirt.

You wanted to get away from here.

Didn't you?

The girl in the pictures in the house in Sturefors.

Now here. A scared father trying to keep calm. An anxious mother giving them the photographs. And then what?

I promise you one thing, Theresa: I won't give up until we've got him.

Or her.

Or . . .

The mantra within Malin like a prayer, and she looks away from the girl's single open eye and up at Sven. He's making a plan, drawing up an internal checklist of how to move forward with this, everything that needs to be done and mustn't be forgotten. Calling in off-duty officers, going door-to-door around every house within a two-mile radius, questioning all the people on the beach, today, yesterday, and the day before, appearing in the media and pleading with anyone who might have seen something, the removal of the body, the wait for Karin's report, informing the parents . . . telling them this unbearable news.

Malin knows whose job that will be. Sometimes they have someone with them when they break news like that, a priest or a counselor, but often they do it themselves. And who knows how long it might take to rustle up a priest in the dog days of summer?

Tove in Bali.

I won't think about that.

Burdens.

And then Malin looks at Theresa again.

Her scrubbed-clean mouth lies open, as if she had been suffocated with deoxygenated air, as if someone wanted to stop her words getting out, or maybe just demonstrate the importance of oxygen, that it means everything, that the earth, from which we come, is all that we have.

On the other side of the cordon people are starting to move away once the uniformed officers have made a note of their names and asked the preliminary questions, and a few of them gaze longingly up toward the shuttered ice-cream kiosk.

Sometimes, Malin thinks, a police investigation is all about the art of the impossible.

Up in the meadow a cow is lowing, as a gathering breeze stirs the grass. The smell of smoke from the forest fires doesn't reach here, but Malin can still sense the crackling in the air, how millions of intimations have been set in motion.

"Malin!" the summer temp journalist calls after her as she heads off toward the meadow. "What have you got for me?"

"No more than you can see for yourself," Malin says without stopping.

The journalist is wearing a large pair of sunglasses, and they make her look stupid.

"Was she murdered?"

Damn stupid question.

"Well, she didn't bury herself."

Two of the people from the beach, a man and a woman in their thirties, are standing by the kiosk, in front of the brightly colored poster of the various ice creams, pulling their jeans on over their bathing suits.

Malin goes over to them and they give her a look that says that they'd rather be left alone, and the man says:

"We've already said what we saw, that we came here to go swimming, and then some mutt found her."

Mutt?

A cartoon word.

"One question, about the kiosk," Malin says. "Is it usually open? Do you come swimming here often?"

She hates it when this happens, when the questions fall out of her in the wrong order, but often it leads to decent answers, there's something disarming in the uncertainty revealed by clumsily posed questions.

"We come swimming here every so often," the man says. "The only problem is that the kiosk is normally shut, apparently because the woman who runs it has several others and can't get the staff."

"The woman?"

"Yes. I think her name's Slavenca, from Bosnia or somewhere like that. She can be pretty unpleasant when she feels like it, almost like she doesn't want any customers. She was here earlier, she disappeared just before you lot showed up."

"Thanks," Malin says.

Down by the body Karin Johannison is working against the clock, trying to get finished before darkness falls, but there are still several hours' work ahead of her and her recently arrived assistant. Malin knows that they have a floodlight in their Volvo. But maybe they won't have to set it up tonight. The summer night will smile on them, a gentle smile that will make their work easier, their careful search for details and clues on the body and in the vegetation around it that could lead them all closer to the truth.

Karin looks up at Malin.

Waves.

Her eyes are tired, they've lost a little of their obvious sparkle, maybe they're already in Bali, those eyes.

Bali.

Island of beauty and violence.

A place where rebirth is possible.

23

The house where I grew up.

The bricks seem to be dripping off the façade in the heat, uncovering memories, intimations.

And lies.

But which lies?

Zeke at the wheel, focused.

They aren't going faster than the prescribed twenty-five, and the hedge around Malin's childhood home is drooping more than before, as though it's made up its mind to give up in the heat of summer.

No one at home in the house.

Who lives there now? What are their memories?

I circle around those memories, Malin thinks. They're still inside me, like electrical will-o'-the-wisps, timeless flares in my consciousness, in all that is me, my actions and somehow my future as well.

What am I so scared of?

I'm both trapped by and running from everything that once was, refusing to let go because I think that those days can explain something to me today.

Air it all out.

Throw out all those old clothes. They aren't coming back.

Mum and Dad in Tenerife.

With every passing day Malin is more and more convinced that her parents are hiding something, and now, now, in this moment as they drive past her childhood home in Sturefors to notify a couple of unsuspecting parents of a death, she feels it more clearly than ever. Her past conceals something, and without finding out what that secret is she will never be whole.

And then the house is gone from view. Withdrawn into memory.

The Polaroid picture of the dead Theresa Eckeved is in her pocket. It's her, Malin is certain of it.

Zeke before they got in the car:

"You'll have to show them the picture, Malin, I'm not doing it."

She's no older than Tove, and even though Malin tries to force away the image of her daughter, even though she keeps her eyes open, Tove's face keeps taking the place of the dead girl's in the picture.

Go away, away, Malin thinks, but to no avail.

You are all girls.

You are the only girl.

I'm going to get the bastard who did this. I'm going to understand.

Her finger on the doorbell, sweat on her brow. Zeke a step behind her, his sunglasses in his hand now, his eyes ready to show sympathy.

Tove, there once more.

Sounds behind the door.

What sounds?

The heavy steps of someone who has realized that the ultimate disaster is approaching? The point where life stiffens and changes into a sluggish, bitter-tasting mess where happiness is nothing more than an intellectual exercise.

I'm happy. I can do this.

And the door opens.

The man in front of her fully aware of the situation. The woman behind him, her mouth slightly open, her frightened blue eyes almost blistered by an evident lack of sleep.

There you are again, Tove, even though all of my attention ought to be focused on these two people in front of me. If I have one task in the world, it is to look after you. That's the only one that seems obvious to me. And now, now that you're a stubborn teenager, it's clear that you don't want me to look after you, apart from taking care of the practical details.

I will never stop looking after you, Tove.

I can't.

Sigvard Eckeved opens the door wide, steps aside, and his shoulders slump and his wife vanishes in the direction of the conservatory in a vain attempt to flee the truth, because it is the truth, their truth, which has come to their home, and they both know it.

"Come in," Theresa's father says. "Have you made any progress, got some more questions? Do you want coffee? Agneta," he calls into the house, "can you put some coffee on? We're bound to have some ice, so we can get you both iced coffee. You can't help wondering if this heat is ever going to let up."

Malin lets him talk.

She and Zeke sit down on chairs on one side of the white sofa in the living room. The pool sits invitingly behind them. And Agneta and Sigvard Eckeved understand what Malin and Zeke's positioning means and sit down on the sofa, not leaning back, leaning forward instead in an almost exaggerated show of interest, as if this exaggeration could hold the nightmare at bay.

"We've found a young girl out at the beach at Stavsätter," Malin says.

"It can't be Theresa," Agneta says. "She'd never go swimming there, the pool . . . but I suppose she did used to cycle out there sometimes . . ."

"The girl was murdered, and I'm very sorry to have to tell you that I think she's your daughter."

Theresa's parents, the people in front of them, sink back into the sofa, the air somehow sucked out of them, and the woman whimpers when Malin takes the photograph out of the pocket of her blouse and puts it on the dark, polished, oak tabletop. Outside in the garden a crow is cawing anxiously, and a leaf falls from a bush, rippling the still surface of the pool.

"Can you tell me if this is Theresa?"

She can feel how Zeke is forcing himself to stay in his seat, how he wants to rush out of the house, out into the garden and run away from the summer-still roads of this little housing development.

But he stays seated.

Confronting the present.

All the nameless emotions drift through the room like dark spirits and coalesce into just two words: *grief, pain.*

Agneta Eckeved turns her head away; if she doesn't look at the picture then it doesn't exist, and everything it represents doesn't exist either, and Sigvard Eckeved leans forward, sees his daughter, her closed eyes and her pale-yellow skin transparent from the absence of oxygen. She isn't asleep, he'll never stroke his daughter on the cheek as she sleeps and quietly whisper, *I'll be here when you wake up, I'll be here for you no matter what, no matter what pain this world throws at me, I'll be here for you.*

Instead just this photograph on the table.

Death.

The end.

"It's Theresa," he says, and Agneta Eckeved turns her head even farther away from the photograph and Malin can just see tears trickling down her cheeks, large, clear, justified tears.

"It's her," Sigvard Eckeved says.

Malin nods.

"Okay, now we know for sure," Zeke says.

Malin takes the picture from the table, holding it in her hand, somehow it doesn't feel right to put it back in her pocket, just like that. Just putting away the picture of the dead girl, out of sight of her parents.

Then Agneta Eckeved says:

"Put it away, the picture, will you? Just do it."

Malin puts the picture away.

Sigvard Eckeved stands up.

Says: "I'll see if the coffee's ready."

Then he stops and his body starts to shake.

*   *   *

The childhood home.

The white bricks.

The sound of cars.

"What happens now?"

Sigvard Eckeved's question, once he's composed himself.

Malin knew what he meant, but chose instead to tell them about the formalities, that the coroner would have to examine the body before they could release it for burial, that they could see her if they wanted to, but that it wasn't essential for them to go through any further formal identification.

Sigvard Eckeved listened to her until she had finished.

"You misunderstood me," he said then. "I mean with us, what's going to happen to us now?"

24

Mum, Dad.

I can see you in the house and you're sad. But I can't hear what you're saying, why are you so sad? What's happened? If you're worried about me, don't be, in a way it's like I've just popped out for a bit.

But I think I might be ill.

That I'm asleep.

That I'll come home when I wake up.

Mum's lying on the bed, and you, Dad, you're walking up and down in the conservatory, it must be hot in the sun.

You had a visit just now, I saw the woman, she was here with me a little while ago, looking at me so strangely, why? She put a photograph on the table at home, but I didn't want to look at it.

Someone took a picture of me. I heard the sound of the camera.

I'm in an ambulance.

Am I ill?

I'm in a plastic bag, but it doesn't feel as claustrophobic as before. I'm in the back, the bit where they put people who aren't well. I can see myself lying there, how is that possible? I'm drifting, Mum, Dad, I can be in several places at once in this dream.

I'm alone, and I must be very ill, because how else could I be having this sort of dream?

Mum, Dad.
I'm alone and scared.
You, or someone else, must come and help me.
But don't be sad.
I miss you so much, and that longing will never end, wherever you or I end up.

"That was that."

Zeke doesn't look up from Brokindsleden, and she knows him, knows he wants to do something now, something active, wants to get on with something concrete so that he doesn't go "crazy as a mad dog," as he usually puts it.

"What are we going to do now?" Malin asks.

"Let's go and see Louise Svensson. Where does she live? You had it on a note."

From the front pocket of her jeans Malin pulls out the piece of paper Viktoria Solhage gave her.

"Viktoria Solhage said she liked to play rough."

"Let's go. Where does she live?"

"I think the address is some farm outside Rimforsa."

"Good, we'll head out there now, before Sjöman has time to call a first meeting about the case."

She wants to say: "But, Zeke, is this right, we've got nothing on her, wouldn't it be better to leave her in peace?"

But she doesn't say those words.

"Let's get to grips with this bull dyke," Zeke says.

His shaved head beside her, hard, impenetrable, like the look in his gray-green eyes when someone's upset him.

"What about Peter Sköld and Nathalie Falck? Do you think they'll be upset when they hear what's happened?"

"I'm sure they will be," Malin says. "Maybe now Nathalie Falck will tell us what I think she knows."

"What do you think she knows?"

"Something."

"It's not easy to know what," Zeke says, and Malin thinks of Peter
Sköld, his father, and what seemed to be a shared silence between
them.

Zeke has turned up the volume of the choral music.

The forest, pines and firs, embracing them, the road a path through
darkness, only opening up after several miles, when they emerge into
a clearing that contains an empty, scorched yellow meadow where
the grass has grown tall before withering in the heat and collapsing
back onto the soil. Beyond the meadow the road disappears into the
forest again, then opens out once more onto a rough, unplowed field.
Beyond the field is a red-painted, two-story farmhouse flanked by
two barns whose wooden façades are worn and dusty and should have
been painted years ago.

The whole of the world's longing for rain seems to be concentrated
on this place.

They park on the gravel in front of the farmhouse.

Three Alsatians rush up to the car, their barks loud when the music
shuts off abruptly, the dogs jumping up at the windows, baring their
teeth, and Malin can see the saliva running as they protect their territory.

Then a voice, a gruff woman's voice through the noise of the dogs.

"Easy now, easy."

And the dogs obey the command in the voice, backing away, and
Malin sees the woman, maybe close to six feet tall, dressed in dirty
green overalls and a little cap from the farmers' union that hardly covers her cropped hair.

Her eyes are black.

Angry.

How old is she? Forty-five? Fifty?

As Malin opens the car door she thinks, Life has really fucked with
you, hasn't it? And now you're getting your own back.

*   *   *

The woman in front of them in the farmyard seems to grow in the harsh light.

Louise "Lollo" Svensson, farmer, living alone out in the middle of the Rimforsa forests at Skogalund Farm, with just her dogs, a few pigs, and some caged rabbits in one of the outbuildings for company.

Malin and Zeke show their ID. The dogs growl over by the porch steps, ready to attack at any moment.

"And what do you want?"

"Your name," Malin says, "has cropped up in an investigation, and we'd like to ask you some questions."

Lollo Svensson steps closer to them.

The dogs show their teeth.

"What fucking investigation?"

"The one concerning the girl who was found raped in the Horticultural Society Park. And this morning a girl was found murdered at the beach at Stavsätter."

"So one of my sisters has been talking, then? Talking crap about me? Doesn't surprise me. Most cunts are no better than your average fucking dick."

"I'm not at liberty to say—"

"I get that, dear lady constable. So what do you want to ask?"

"What were you doing on the night between last Wednesday and Thursday?"

"I was here at home."

"On your own?"

"No, I had them with me."

Lollo Svensson gestures toward the Alsatians.

"But they can't tell you what we were doing, can they?"

"There's no one else who can confirm that you were at home?"

Lollo grins at them.

"Do you know Theresa Eckeved?"

"No."

"Do you know a Nathalie Falck?"

"Not her either. Never heard the name before."

"Lovelygirl? Does the name Lovelygirl mean anything to you?"

No noticeable reaction.

"Lovelygirl? I don't know any Lovelygirl."

"So you like to play rough," Zeke says. "What does that mean? Playing rough with young girls? Is that it?"

For God's sake, Zeke, Malin thinks, but she knows what he's doing, lets him get on with it.

But Lollo Svensson doesn't let herself be provoked.

"I haven't got anything to do with any of that."

"Do you like tying people up, maybe cut them a bit, whip them? Is that the sort of thing you like, Louise?"

"You should probably leave now if you haven't got any more questions."

"And you brought a young girl back here and things went a bit wrong, with the dildo, was that it? Or else she ran off when you were done, is that what happened?"

"You should probably . . ."

Lollo Svensson takes three steps back, as if to mark her withdrawal, as if to say: "I've said what I've got to say, now you're on your own."

"I've got to see to the pigs," she says. "The pigs can't look after themselves, they're weak, really weak, really pathetic, actually."

"Can we take a look round the barns? Inside the house?"

Malin waits for an answer.

"You're crazy, Inspector Fors. Like I'd let you in without a warrant? What a fucking joke."

"Do you know a girl called Josefin Davidsson? Or a Theresa Eckeved?"

Malin's voice dry and sharp. Her blouse is sticking to her body, and God knows how hot Lollo Svensson must be in those overalls, and suddenly her large, solid frame slumps before their eyes.

"I . . ."

"So you had a bit of rough sex with them out here," Zeke says. "After you'd brought them out here, lured them out here. What with? Drink? The dogs? Horse riding? Have you got horses?"

No answer.

"Do you normally use dildos on your girls?"

And when Malin hears Zeke say the word *dildo* she is filled with a sense that they are missing something obvious in the way they've been thinking about the dildo.

But what?

Lollo Svensson turns around and takes the dogs with her into the farmhouse, and Malin and Zeke are left standing beside the Volvo in the farmyard, inhaling the smell of summer forest and silence, of a loneliness so obvious that it makes the summer seem cool.

25

The car bumps unhappily along the gravel road.

"What do you think?"

Zeke's voice calmer now, not theatrically agitated or provocative anymore.

The forest is closing in on the car, hundreds of shades of yellowish green, pained, begging for rain.

"I don't know," Malin says. "I never cease to be amazed at what the forests around this city contain."

She recalls last winter's excursions, in connection with the case of Bengt Andersson and the Murvall brothers, and she can still feel the debilitating cold, how it sucked the air from her lungs as she forced her way through the trees toward the sound of death and evil deep within the forests around Hultsjön.

"No, they're full of surprises."

"Have we got enough for a search warrant?"

"Probably; we won't need much considering what's happened. It might even be enough that she refused to let us in."

"I'm curious to see what's inside that house," Malin says.

Young girls.

Their bodies, dead and alive, floating like unfettered manatees in endlessly bubbling water.

Get us up, help us, move us on.

Tove far away on the other side of the world, in paradise, but one with a snake—the Islamic extremists and their violence.

Away with the image, don't think about her now.

Janne.

Running along a beach with his heart thumping in his body. Always leaving.

"I want to know what's hidden inside that house," Malin says.

"Me too," Zeke says. At that moment Malin's mobile rings.

Karin Johannison's name on the display.

On the floor of Karin Johannison's room a humidifier is fighting for decibel supremacy against a portable air-conditioning unit. The humidity is fighting an uneven battle against the cold, but together the two machines make Karin's room the most bearable that Malin has been in for ages, even though there are no windows, and in spite of the mess of books and reports and files and journals all over the desk, the shelves, and the floor.

Malin and Zeke are sitting on the two rib-backed chairs Karin has for visitors, while she leans back in a futuristic black designer office chair, which she almost certainly bought herself with her own money, just like the humidifier and the air conditioner.

"Nice chair," Malin says.

"Thanks," Karin says. "It's an Oscar Niemeyer, I got it off the Internet from South America, some site in Brazil."

"Did you buy those contraptions there as well?" Zeke asks. "They sound like they come from the third world."

Karin ignores Zeke's insult and moves on to what they've come for, switching to her professional persona:

"Theresa Eckeved had been penetrated, subjected to sexual violence. I couldn't find any sperm, just traces of the same paint as inside Josefin Davidsson. In all likelihood, we're talking about the same perpetrator."

"But it's good to support the poor, isn't it?"

Zeke couldn't stop the words once they were on their way out of his mouth, and Malin can see in his eyes that he regrets them and is feeling foolish, and Karin continues to ignore Zeke, pretending that he hasn't spoken.

She goes on:

"She's been carefully washed, and if she was scrubbed clean it was done carefully. I've found traces of bleach on her skin. Just like Josefin Davidsson.

"The wounds have been cleaned, maybe with surgical spirit, maybe bleach, and the perpetrator has tidied up the edges with an extremely sharp implement, possibly a scalpel, but it's impossible to say for sure. What was used? Rough knife? A big spike? Something brute, like an animal tooth. No, but what?"

"Like Josefin Davidsson's wounds?" Zeke wonders.

"Those were just cleaned," Karin says. "These have been trimmed at the edges."

"Trimmed?"

"Yes, trimmed. The wound to her head wasn't fatal. Nor any of the wounds to her body. She was strangled. The soil under her fingernails was identical with the soil on the beach, which suggests that she was murdered there."

"So she wasn't moved there?"

"Probably not."

"So she could have gone there with the perpetrator?"

"What do I know, Malin?"

"Her mum mentioned that she used to cycle up there sometimes," Zeke says. "Maybe Theresa was just taking an evening swim?"

"How long was she in the ground?" Malin asks.

"A week, I'd say. Maybe a few days more. It's impossible to say for certain."

What were you doing out there? Malin thinks. It must have been late, and you were alone.

Evil is on the loose.

God help us.

God help all the girls who are still in Linköping this summer.

*   *   *

"Do you know where the traces of paint came from?"

Zeke's clear and focused now, his antipathy toward Karin set aside, stashed away somewhere inside himself.

"No idea, but it's the same object, no doubt about that. I haven't been able to identify the source of the paint, though. It's not one of the more common ones used in Sweden. But you're chasing the same perpetrator, you can be sure of that."

"Forensics has started looking at different makes of dildos."

"Good," Karin says. "There are any number of them. As far as I'm aware."

"Anything else?"

"No traces of sperm, no hair, no skin, no strands of fabric, nothing, nothing, nothing," Karin says, unable to hide her dissatisfaction and annoyance that she can't give them anything more, anything concrete to go on, anything to latch on to in their hunt for whatever is on the move out in the city.

"Shit," Malin says.

"You'll get him," Karin says.

"If it is a him," Malin says.

The smoke from the fires in the Tjällmo forests is noticeable in the parking lot in front of the police station and the National Forensics Lab where Karin works.

The forests north of Ljungsbro are burning now, and the fire is spreading. There are extra bulletins of both local television news programs about the advance of the flames.

Are the fires deliberate?

Who started them?

Why have fires broken out in so many places at the same time?

Zeke gets into the driver's seat of the Volvo.

Malin pauses by the door, hears him curse the heat inside the car, and closes her eyes, trying to follow the smell of the fire up above the city, seeing in her mind's eye how the heat presses the few people left, little more than dots, toward the asphalt, and she follows her thoughts out over the plain, the scorched fields and the blue of Lake Roxen, and she sees the fires, the way they're eating and jumping their way through the forests, leaping recklessly from treetop to treetop in an explosive dance, destroying pretty much everything in their path, but also creating the possibility of new life.

And Janne, wanting to be back home with the rest of his crew, wanting to put on his protective clothing and head out into the boiling, smoke-fogged darkness to save whatever can still be saved.

"Malin, are you going to stand there all day?"

Soot, Malin thinks. Dirt. How long do firefighters have to scrub their faces after a day like this?

"Malin!"

She jerks herself free of her thoughts and gets into the heat of the car.

I'm dead.

There's no point fighting it.

The plastic, in spite of its dense darkness, is like plastic wrap around me, it can't hold me here any longer. It never could, really, but somehow it feels safe. I understood my freedom when I was suddenly there with you, Mum and Dad, where I could see your despair, when I wanted to tell you that I'm here, in spite of everything, and that it's sort of okay, even if I'm still scared and worried and sad that my life ended up being as short as it was.

But what does time matter?

Easy for me to say.

Mum and Dad.

I know that time will drag for you. There's nothing that makes time drag more than pain.

And your pain will never pass.

It will change color over the years, marking your bodies and the way you're judged by the world.

You will become your grief, Mum, Dad, and maybe there's some com-
fort in that. Because if you are your grief for me, then you are also me, and
if you're me, then we're together. Don't you think?

I want to comfort you, Dad.

Somehow I'll find a way to let you know that I'm okay, as soon as I
think I am.

Only one person can ease my anxiety, and she knows it.

I rise up toward the sky.

The heat that torments you all doesn't exist for me. The heat isn't even
a smell here.

I drift down toward the Volvo, look into Malin Fors's face. She doesn't
know it, but with each passing day the look in her blue eyes grows a bit
more tired, but also a bit more certain.

Only the sadness is constant.

And the fear that she tries so vainly to hold at bay.

On the way to the prosecutor, one of the ones on duty over the summer, not particularly happy to be called in to the office on a Sunday
evening. The same prosecutor who earlier rejected Sven Sjöman's offer
to relinquish legal responsibility for the preliminary investigation,
saying that they would have to hold on to that responsibility themselves until they had made some progress.

Malin had spoken to Sven over the phone, and he had given
them permission to proceed: "Search the house, but you and Zeke
shouldn't go alone, who knows what she might do if it turns out
you're right."

Sven had also said that "at long last and far too fucking holiday
late" they had got hold of the list of calls made from Theresa's mobile,
and that she had called Nathalie Falck a lot, Peter Sköld occasionally,
and no one else except her parents. "She seems to have been a bit of
a loner," Sven said. They hadn't heard anything from either Yahoo! or
Facebook, and Forensics was still working on identifying the dildo. A
quick search on the net had come up with more than nine hundred
manufacturers.

Malin thinks about Josefin Davidsson. About the hypnosis that she hasn't had time to sort out. Must get round to doing that.

The prosecutor.

A recently appointed young man named Torben Eklund.

Malin looks through the windshield.

But instead of the city she sees her face, her eyes, the look in them, and she wonders what happens to that look with the passage of time, and then she gets scared, feeling a chill run through every vein and capillary, an ice-cold and sharp sting of stardust. That isn't my face in the windshield, she thinks, it's Theresa Eckeved's face, and Malin knows what she wants, what her lifeless white skin, her clear, radiant, colorless eyes want.

Her mouth is moving.

What happened?

Who?

What, how?

I am putting my trust in you, Malin Fors, to bring me some peace.

Then the face is gone, replaced by Malin's own familiar features. The face and features that are somehow just as they are.

Josefin Davidsson pulls the thin white sheet tighter around her body, not wanting to see the bandages and think about the wounds, but knowing that they're there whether she likes it or not.

She notices the chemical smell of the hospital room, and the pain she can't remember the cause of. But she realizes that that memory, buried somewhere deep within her, is important.

She could have gone home on Friday. But she wanted to stay over the weekend, and they let her. The doctor understood when she said that she liked how peaceful it was here.

She's watched television out in the day room. Read on the newspaper websites, the *Correspondent* and others, that they've found a girl's body at a beach out near Sturefors.

I have to get to my memories, Josefin thinks, and the sky outside the window is growing pale, late-afternoon blue and empty, just

26

A blue and white police car behind them.

Evening is falling slowly over the road and the forest seems to regain some of its lost verdure, a false nuance, the color of a blunt knife.

They're leading the way in the Volvo, three uniforms in the car behind: two factory-farmed recent graduates, lads with bulging muscles and an attitude that suggests they can sort out all the crap society might throw at them. Malin can never understand how that sort of bloke ever gets past the admissions board, but presumably they know how to give all the right answers. She's seen the websites for people wanting to join the police: This is what they want to hear. And sure, the answers fit and if you're smart it can work. The third uniform is an old hand called Pettersson, now working part-time because of a bad back, and sometimes Malin can see that he's in some discomfort, his fingers tensing as he channels the pain from his nerves out into his fingertips so that he can go on.

She can't remember the new recruits' names, can't be bothered to learn them, because who knows how long they'll be staying? They probably want a transfer to Stockholm, Gothenburg, or Malmö, where the real action is.

The farm in the clearing.

Has she guessed that they're coming?

like her memory. But it's there, they did it in biology, memories are like electricity, and a person can remember everything that's ever happened to them under the right circumstances.

But do I want to remember?

Am I scared that he or she or they are going to come back?

No.

I'd be dead if that was what they wanted.

The hospital cotton is soft, so soft, and she shuts her eyes, drifts off to sleep even though the room is full of the brightest light and bubbling life.

"No problem. I'll sign a search warrant straight away."

Torben Eklund's voice as neutral as his office in the courthouse on Stora Torget, his gray face thin but still bearing an inexplicable double chin.

"How's the investigation going?" he asks.

"Forward, slowly," Malin replies.

"We have extremely limited resources over the summer," Torben Eklund goes on. "That's why I've decided to leave responsibility for the preliminary investigation with the police."

"That suits us fine," Zeke says.

Lawyers, Malin thinks. What in the world would make anyone want to become one of them?

Torben Eklund is the same age as me, but already middle-aged.

A black-faced clock on an unpainted brick wall, the white hands showing 5:25.

Then it hits her.

Maybe in the eyes of young girls I'm already middle-aged. And after that comes death. Doesn't it?

Has she cleared things up?

Away?

Zeke's voice over the radio to the others:

"Fors and I will go and knock, you get out and wait by the car. Understood?"

Silence. No barking.

Where are the dogs?

Then a yes from Pettersson.

"Good," Zeke says as the car comes to a halt in the farmyard.

They get out.

A watchful silence.

They head for the porch steps.

Malin has the search warrant in her hand.

Has she taken refuge in the forest?

What's in there?

In those closed rooms?

Malin looks over her shoulder.

They're standing there, waiting but ready, almost hungry, Pettersson and the new recruits in their hot, dark-blue uniforms. The heat is still oppressive, but the sun has disappeared behind the barns, making it bearable.

"A torture chamber," Zeke says. "What if she's got a fucking torture chamber in there?"

Malin's clenched fist against the white-painted wooden door.

No one coming to open it.

Someone aiming a weapon at them from somewhere inside?

Maybe. It could happen. Malin thinks the thought momentarily, remembers reading about American cops going out to desolate farms only to get shot, thinks of the officer who was shot and killed by a psycho in Nyköping. Malin knew him, he was in the year below her at the police academy, but they weren't exactly close.

Another knock.

More silence.

Just the slight rustling of a wind-free forest, from life in motion around them.

"She must have gone," Zeke says. "Unless she's hiding in there."

"We'll have to break the door down," Malin says.

"Check if it's locked first."

And Malin slowly reaches out her hand to the door handle, pushes it down and the door swings open, as if someone had left it open for them, as if someone wanted them to go in.

A hall with rag rugs and a stripped pine bench on bare pine floorboards.

Well kept, Malin thinks. Cared for.

And silent.

She steps into the hall. Zeke behind her, she can feel his breath, warm, and she knows that he's giving a sign to the others to spread out around the house and that one of them will watch the door behind them, ready to rush in if anything happens, if there's any noise.

The kitchen.

Thoughtfully renovated, it must date from the forties, floral tiles and new rag rugs. The gentle evening light is falling in narrow streaks through a net curtain. The coffeemaker is on, the coffee freshly made, the oven is on, and there's a smell of newly baked buns. Malin sees a tea towel on the countertop over a baking rack, the bulge suggesting coffee bread, sweetly scented.

"What the fuck is this?" Zeke says.

Malin hushes him and they carry on into the house, to the living room, where the television is on, an episode of the old children's classic *Seacrow Island,* that Malin doesn't recognize. Here again there is a sense of time standing still.

A computer on a desk.

They go up a creaking staircase to the upper floor. The walls are covered with tongue-and-groove paneling, on which Lollo Svensson has hung tinted lithographs of open fields and tractors. The bedroom, the only room upstairs, has whitewashed walls and light streaming in through a bay window, rag rugs on the scrubbed floor, everything looks sparklingly clean, as if she uses cleanliness to try to keep something away, or perhaps invite something in.

"She's here," Zeke says.

"She's here somewhere," Malin says. "I can feel it. She isn't far away. There's something here, something."

And Malin goes back down the stairs, opens the door leading to the cellar, and the smell of domestic heating oil gets stronger with every step they take.

An oil-fired boiler, shiny and green, in an equally clean room. Cleaning products on a shelf. No bleach.

A door, a steel door ajar, as if it led to a shelter.

Malin points at the door.

Zeke nods.

Malin opens the door, expecting to see Lollo Svensson hanging from the ceiling, surrounded by contraptions from a medieval torture chamber in complete contrast to the room upstairs, a contrast to the idyll that this old, homely farmhouse actually is.

Then they see her.

She's sitting on a chair behind a Ping-Pong table covered with colorful wooden toys, dolls, and stuffed animals. She's wearing a thin, pale-pink dress.

A doll's house on a shelf. Moving boxes stacked against whitewashed concrete walls.

Lollo Svensson smiles at them, a different person now, her hard facial features soft, resignation manifested in the body that Malin recently thought might harbor the soul of a murderer.

Could it?

Your body? Harbor the soul of a murderer?

"I knew you'd come back," Lollo whispers. "So I came down here and waited. Waited for you to come."

The soul of a murderer, Malin thinks. We all harbor one of those.

27

The forest seems to be breathing for Linda Karlå.

But with sick lungs.

Only now, in the evening, is it cool enough for running, even if it's still too hot for most people. The running track in Ryd is deserted apart from her, her feet in new white Nike running shoes drumming on the sawdust trail, the electric lighting above her not lit, she doesn't know if they turn the lights on in summer, at this time of year it stays light late when there are no clouds in the sky.

Maybe it's stupid to go running alone in the woods considering what's happened. Before the police have caught the culprit. Who knows what could be lying in wait?

But she isn't scared.

Air in her lungs.

Her breathing somehow enclosed within her body, her brain.

Her heart is racing, yet somehow controlled, as if she can direct the most important muscle in her body by sheer willpower.

She runs at least fifteen miles each week. All year round, and she runs the Stockholm marathon and one abroad: When it feels rough in the winter she thinks about Tokyo, New York, London, Sydney, letting the trees become skyscrapers and crowds, her forty-one-year-old body is strong, so strong.

It would be dangerous for someone less well trained to go running in this heat.

But she can handle it.

She actually thinks the Ryd track is too flat, it might be worth taking the car out to the hills of the Olstorp circuit.

Pressure in her chest.

Onward, Linda, onward.

The trees.

The sawdust.

The lights. The tree up ahead.

Its trunk unnaturally thick three feet above the ground.

Is it really a tree? A body? Behind the tree. Something waiting. For me.

Malin is standing in Lollo Svensson's kitchen, waiting, listening. Trying to understand, because in Lollo's words there is a hint of the feelings that will lead them in the right direction in this case.

The uniforms are back by the car out in the farmyard again, restless now that they've realized that the anticipated drama has become a yawn.

Malin and Zeke gave them the task of searching the barns and smaller outbuildings, but they didn't come up with anything, just snuffling pigs and rabbits in cages and a load of clutter that must have been left behind by the farmer who sold the place to Lollo Svensson. The dogs were asleep in a fenced run, almost drugged by the heat, or something else. No signs of violence, of evil, just things, abandoned things, unfettered by memories, of no value except as pieces of a puzzle for the archaeologists of future civilizations.

"I want to be left in peace," Lollo Svensson says. "That's why I bought the farm. Can you understand that?"

She's sitting on a rib-backed chair at the kitchen table. Back to her cocky, blunt, unpleasant butch self again. The gentle individual they found downstairs among the toys in the basement vanished the moment they came back upstairs.

A human wall, Malin thinks. A gray dressing gown over the pink dress. What's happened to her? To you? How did you end up like this?

Malin sees herself in the kitchen.

Snooping about in the dark. In the most private things. In the pain. And she knows she's good at it, and she knows she likes doing it.

Damn you, Fors.

How did you end up like this?

"I didn't have anything to do with the attacks on those girls. Are you going to talk to the whole fucking women's football team now as well, then? There are supposed to be loads of dykes there, aren't there? Go and talk to them!"

"What about the toys in the basement? How do you explain those?" Zeke doesn't succeed in concealing his curiosity, a desire to understand that stretches far beyond their investigation.

"I don't explain them at all. They're toys from when I was small. I get them out sometimes. Nothing odd about that."

Linda Karlå is standing still on the sawdust trail. There's something close by. But what?

Something is moving in the forest, even though everything's still. Is that a crawling sound? A person? The smell of decay, or purity? Thoughts fly through her head and on into her heart and stomach, forming themselves into fear.

No.

I'm not scared.

The forest is big, it's making her small and alone even though it's no more than a few hundred yards to the yellow blocks of flats and houses over in Valla on the other side of Vallavägen.

No movement over by the tree. But there's someone there.

I'm sure.

And then she thinks of the girls again, the one they found murdered, the one they found raped and disoriented in the Horticultural Society Park, and she's struck by how foolhardy it was of her to set out alone on a running track, now that real evil has shown its face in Linköping.

How stupid can you be, Linda?
A movement.
A person on the track?
Heading toward me?
Sweat on my white vest. My breasts hard under the sports bra.
I'm so scared that I can't move.

Zeke is rocking from foot to foot in one corner of the farmyard.

No dildo. No sex toys at all.

The evening is still debilitatingly hot. Lollo Svensson is inside the farmhouse, watching them through the kitchen window, can't seem to get rid of them soon enough. In the dull light the barns look crooked, almost ready to collapse under the weight of the mournful evening sky.

The dogs have started barking over in their run.

The car with the uniforms is disappearing down the gravel drive, soon no more than a misplaced noise from the dense forest, a pulse through old leaves and desiccated moss.

"She's mad," Zeke says. "Do you think she's Lovelygirl?"

"We'll have to see what Forensics finds on the computer."

"But is she mad?"

"Because she likes looking at her old toys? I'm not sure. But she's certainly different," Malin says. "Who knows what sort of crap she's been through? And what wouldn't a person do to survive?"

"Can we find out?"

"Do we need to?"

"Do we want to?"

"I don't think she's got anything to do with this," Malin says.

"Me neither," Zeke says. "But she still hasn't got an alibi."

My heart.
Where is it?
There, holding all of my fear.

It's about to burst beneath my ribs.

Linda Karlå is running, her shoes conquering yard after yard of the trail, as the forest twists around her.

Is someone chasing me?

It sounds like something enormous is slithering after me, as if the tree roots are lifting from the ground and trying to trip me up, burrow through me with a thousand sharp, calcified nodules, then hide me under a thin layer of soil, consuming me slowly, but I can run so fast.

Faster now.

The sound of hooves. Hooves?

She runs.

Finally the vegetation opens up.

The parking lot.

Her car on its own. No one following.

She throws herself into the residual heat of her SEAT.

A deer?

Something else was watching me out there as well.

I'm sure of it, Linda Karlå thinks as she starts the car and drives away.

But what?

The sound of hooves disappearing into the forest. The darkness that was snapping at her heels.

28

Stora torget is vibrant with artificial light from the big open-air bars and the surrounding buildings. Mörners Inn, Stora Hotellet, Burger King, their chairs and tables set out on the sidewalk and paving stones, the first of these boasting tall canopies that turn its customers' conversation into indistinct chatter, a sound full of expectation and happiness.

It is just past ten o'clock.

A lot of people even though it's a Sunday.

The air is still warm, but people are daring to venture out, eager for the condensation running down the outside of a well-filled glass. There is a rumbling sound from down on Ågatan, the whole street full of bars, and in the winter, spring, and autumn there's always trouble there at weekends. The *Correspondent* has printed acres of coverage about pub-related violence, but at the same time people need to let their hair down and the concentration of the location is manageable for the police. We know where things are likely to kick off, Malin thinks as she looks across at the seating areas.

Probably no one I know there.

And if anyone I do know should happen to be there, I don't want to meet them.

Zeke dropped her off outside the flat, and under the cold water of

the shower she felt how much she missed Tove, Janne, Daniel Högfeldt; she wanted to call him and tell him to come over, drive out
some of what she's seen today.

Let him work off some of her frustration.

But he didn't answer and instead she lay down for a while on Tove's
bed, pretending to watch over her daughter who is on the other side
of the planet, in paradise, not far from crazy bombers.

And Tove's scent, caught in the sheets.

And Malin began to cry.

Sad in a simple and obvious way about the way everything had
turned out with her and Janne, with her and herself, and the un-
mentionable thing that the psychoanalyst Viveka Crafoord had
glimpsed just by looking at her. But then Malin did what she always does. Forced herself back, the tears, all the sorrow, then got up
and left the flat. Some types of loneliness are worse than anything
else.

All the customers in the terrace bars. The chink of glasses. The
twirling waitresses. There is still life in summertime Linköping, even
if this heat, this evil, are doing their best to drive any sense of joy into
the ground.

Shall I sit down here? Among everyone else?

She stands still, letting the evening enter her body.

Evil. Where does it start?

In front of her the square transforms into a volcanic landscape, as
hot, glowing magma seeps out between the paving slabs in destructive
black streams. Evil, a human undercurrent that history sometimes
gathers up into an eruption, in one place, one person, in several people. You can become evil, or come close to it, sometimes so close that
you can feel its breath, and then you realize that it's the breath from
your own lungs hitting you in the face. Malevolence, fear, the way
Janne once told her after drinking too much whiskey that he thought
that war lay at the heart of human nature, that we are really all longing
for war, that God is war and that violence is only the start, that the
whole fucking world is just one vast act of abuse, a pain that will only
end when humankind is wiped out.

"We want war," Janne said. "There's no such thing as evil. It's just a made-up word, a pathetic attempt to give a name to the violence that's bound to happen. You, Malin, you cops, you're just fucking tracker dogs, you sniff about, trying to keep something utterly fundamental at bay."

The magma is oozing, flowing around the feet of the people drinking beer in the square of this small city in this small, small corner of the world.

Here I stand.

I have to embrace violence, love it the way that I understand love. Evil is scentless, soundless, is has no texture, yet at the same time it is every smell, every sound, and all the experiences of the world that a person can feel against their skin.

A buried girl.

A boy kicked to death after a party.

A thirty-three-year-old student blown into a thousand pieces on a bus.

A bomb buried in the sand of a beach in paradise.

I refuse, I refuse, I refuse to believe you, Janne.

But you've seen war.

Maybe a beer in the square?

No.

Your society isn't mine.

Not tonight.

I'm Batman, Malin thinks. Damaged goods, yet trying to watch over something.

She carries on along Hamngatan, up toward the Hamlet bar. A hint of smoke from the forest fires reaches her nose. They're still open, and she takes a seat at the bar, feeling safe there, surrounded by the decades-old wooden paneling.

Only her and a few of the closet alcoholics at a table in the corner.

The beer is cheap here.

"Evening, Inspector," they call.

She nods in their direction as her beer appears in front of her.

"And a tequila, double," she says to the bartender.

"Sure thing, Malin," he says with a smile. "One of those evenings?"
"You've no idea," Malin replies. "No idea."

Daniel Högfeldt has switched off his phone, his articles about the
murder ready for tomorrow. He's gone into one of the paper's conference rooms and is resting his body in one of the uncomfortable chairs.

Wants to be alone.

His body somehow demanding silence.

He thinks about Malin.

Where are you now?

We're two unhappy souls moving around each other in this city,
and sometimes we meet and play a static game. For a while he mistook
their game for love. But not any longer. He knows, or believes that he
knows, exactly what he wants from Malin Fors. And what she wants
from him. A conduit to relieve a mass of sexual energy, and that's why
they work so well together in bed: They want the same thing and they
both know that the harder they play, the better.

But sometimes.

When she's fallen asleep beside him and he's lying there looking at
her, he wonders.

Is she the one he's been waiting for?

His?

No, don't lay yourself open to that sort of disappointment. He
doesn't know much about her, but she has several photographs of her
ex-husband, Janne, in her flat. He seems to be able to calm her down.
Like her daughter.

Where are you now, Fors?

Daniel gets up.

Starts walking about the room restlessly, as if to combat the feeling
that time is passing far too slowly.

There's burning in her dreams.

It sometimes happens when she's been drinking. Cold flames eating her legs, trying to pull her into the darkness, whispering: We'll destroy you, Malin, destroy you, even if you listen to what we've got to say.

What do you want? What do you want to say?

Nothing, Malin, nothing. We just want to destroy you.

There are snakes in the dream, and animals with hooves, and when she wakes up she remembers the dreams clearly, their constantly changing images, impossible to sort out.

There's a boy in the dreams.

Malin doesn't know who he is, but she forces him away, as if she had some sort of conscious consciousness even in the dream. That's the darkest of dreams, like the one Janne has when he dreams about the children in Rwanda, the ones who'd had their hands cut off, the ones he fed in the hospital of the refugee camp. Their eyes. Six-, seven-, eight-year-old eyes full of wisdom about how life would turn out, about how it could have turned out.

And then the voice of the flames:

So you think you can destroy us?

Pride, vanity, avarice, a bonfire of all of those, Malin.

And she wakes up and screams at the voice of the flames, "SHUT UP, SHUT UP," and she's still drunk and can feel the beer and tequila dancing through her body, remembering how she wove her way across the square down toward St. Lars Church, trying to read the inscription above the side door, and the way the words disappeared before her eyes, but she still knew what they said: "Blessed are the pure in heart, for they shall see God."

Then what?

Awake all night, thinking about Tove, longing for Tove, daydreaming about Janne's familiar body, their original love, and completely wet down there when she finally got to thinking about Daniel Högfeldt.

Horny.

In the way you only get from alcohol, and she caressed herself and came without a sound once she'd disentangled herself from the sheet covering her body.

Can I sleep now?

But sleep wouldn't come. Instead it was as if the orgasm lingered within her, making her heart race, and she pulled the sheet over her again, up over her face, and as the morning light gradually dawned beyond the blinds she played dead, turning herself into Theresa Eckeved, trying to feel her fear and despair, trying to feel her way toward what had happened, what had caused the volcano to erupt this time.

Her body felt alive.

Her blood was magma in her veins.

She was longing for more alcohol.

Then she thought about Maria Murvall. Lying in her room in Vadstena Hospital. About the evil that had put her there.

The same evil?

Her brain felt pickled.

The threads of the case spinning around.

A dildo? Blue?

A lesbian? Lollo Svensson. A sex offender? A damaged man? The football team? Prejudice, prejudice, prejudice. Peter Sköld. Nathalie Falck. The person who made the call about Josefin Davidsson?

Silence. Intimations, prejudices.

But what else are we supposed to go on? And what about Behzad Karami and Ali Shakbari out in Berga? Sodding bloody family alibis. One of the boys, or more than one, could have crossed a boundary and worked out that you liked it. The owner of the ice cream kiosk?

A thousand possibilities.

Drifting dust thrown into the air, needing to be gathered together to form a clear, black jewel.

The city demands it.

The papers.

The victims and their families.

And me.

But is there only one truth?

And with that thought her consciousness succumbed to sleep, and she slept dreamlessly for an hour before she woke up and a new day of the investigation into the tragic girls of Linköping could start.

29

The last remnants of the previous evening's alcohol seem to disappear as Malin's body pierces the water of the Tinnerbäck pool. Cooler.

The water ought to be cooler, but it would probably cost too much to keep the temperature lower in a summer as hot as this one. Four lengths will have to do, she can feel her body complaining at the effort, how it wants to rest but at the same time enjoy the relative cool.

Better than the boiling-hot gym at the station.

Her body wakes up.

You could go mad not being able to go swimming in a summer like this. A couple of lifeguards with long-handled nets are fishing out prematurely fallen leaves from the pool. Malin looks at the lifeguards as she dries herself with her worn pink towel.

She skimmed the *Correspondent* before she left home.

Six pages about the murder of Theresa Eckeved, statements from Karim Akbar, pictures of the scene of the murder, of her parents' house, but no statement from them. Photos of Theresa, her body wrapped in plastic, her passport, private pictures. Daniel Högfeldt had had help with the articles from wily old Harry Lavén.

The headline on the front page: *"Summertime Death."*

Beneath it: *"Evil on the Loose in Linköping."*

She was convinced Daniel had written the headlines himself. He must have worked like a madman yesterday, not wanting to take her call, realizing that she wouldn't want to talk about the case but wanted something else instead.

Cock.

How harsh even the thought of the word sounds.

Malin gathers her things and heads off toward the changing room, feeling the clear, almost scarily blunt smell of chlorine, somehow cleaner than everything else.

You're right, Daniel, she thinks. It's come to the city:

Summertime death.

Reporters from what seems like every newsroom of any significance in the country have come to the city, flocking outside the entrance of the police station, journalists clutching notepads, recording devices, photographers with their extra eyes, cars from Swedish Television and TV4, summertime death a summertime dream for those with papers to sell.

Malin forces her way through the sweaty huddle of reporters, sweaty herself after the bike ride up here, avoiding Daniel Högfeldt as he throws her a longing look and waves, calling: "Have you got anything for me, Malin? Have you got anything to go on?"

But Malin ignores him, ignores all of them, some faces familiar from previous cases.

In the entrance she is met by Karim Akbar, dressed in a faultless pressed beige cotton suit and a pale-blue shirt that contrasts neatly with the slightly darker tone his skin has turned after all that sunbathing in Västervik.

Malin isn't surprised to see him, but nor is she pleased. She knew he wouldn't be able to stay away when there was a top-drawer media storm in the offing.

"Malin," he says. "Good that you're here. I felt I had to come in and manage the press conference, and keep an eye on the investigation."

"Welcome home," Malin says. "But the investigation's under control. You know that Sven's one of the force's most experienced preliminary investigators. Aren't you supposed to be writing a book over the summer?"

"Forget the book, Fors. The press conference is at nine o'clock. They'll have to wait outside until then."

"Do you know what you're going to say, Karim?"

"It's quarter past eight. We'll have to take a meeting right away. Martinsson and Sjöman are already here. Why are you . . ."

Karim stops himself.

Looks Malin deep in the eyes, right into her tiredness, and lets what he was about to say drop.

Instead:

"How's Tove getting on in Bali?"

Malin smiles: "Fine, last time I spoke to her. Thanks for asking. But it'll be good to have her home again."

"I'm sure it will," Karim says.

And Malin knows that he wants to say something about the Islamists on the island, knows that he practically loathes them for making life difficult for anyone whose appearance suggests that they could be Arabic.

It is exactly half past eight.

The air-conditioning in the meeting room is grumbling unhappily, the four of them sitting round the table, the blinds in the windows facing the playground pulled down to keep the light out.

Four officers.

A Monday morning, after a weekend at work for three of them. Tiredness is creeping up on her, in spite of the adrenaline that an important case always releases.

One police chief, one preliminary investigator, and two inspectors, far too few for a case of this significance, and all four of them know it; and they know that holidays will be canceled or colleagues from neighboring districts called in. Or there's another option.

Sven Sjöman is the first to speak:

"There are far too few of us to handle this, we know that. My suggestion is that we call in National Crime, to save us interrupting our colleagues' holidays or calling in people from other districts."

"Not National Crime," Karim says, and Malin knew that was what he was going to say. "I've checked with Motala, Mjölby, and Norrköping. We can have Sundsten from Motala and Ekenberg from Mjölby. Norrköping is understaffed as it is, so they can't let us have anyone. But Sundsten and Ekenberg will be here today, tomorrow at the latest. Börje's in Africa and Johan's away with his family, somewhere in Småland, I believe."

"Ekenberg," Zeke exclaims. "Do we really want that idiot here?"

Malin knows what Zeke means. Waldemar Ekenberg is infamous for being completely reckless in his work, and he's also infamous for getting away with it in all the internal investigations that followed. But he isn't without his admirers and supporters in the force: Waldemar Ekenberg certainly gets things done when they need to be done.

"We have to take the people that are available," Sven says. "I shall be keeping an eye on Ekenberg personally."

"And Sundsten? Who's that?"

"Some bright young thing. He spent a year in crime in Kalmar before moving to Motala. Supposed to be pretty smart."

"Good," Zeke says. "We need all the help we can get."

"You're right there," Malin says.

"The more I think about these two cases," Zeke goes on, "the messier everything gets, sort of hazy. It's a bit like looking at a fire, and just when you think you've fixed your eyes on a flame, it's gone."

Sven takes a deep breath, which makes him cough badly, turning his already red face a shade darker, and Malin gets worried that this heat is about to mess with Sven's already hard-pressed heart.

"So," Karim says. "What have we got and what do we know? Can you give me an update?"

"Malin?"

Sven hasn't recovered from his fit of coughing.

"We have two crimes," Malin says. "Although we're basically convinced we're dealing with one and the same perpetrator.

"On Thursday morning Josefin Davidsson was found, disoriented, in the Horticultural Society Park, raped with something which seems likely to have been a blue-colored dildo. She had a number of wounds, probably inflicted by a knife. Her body was scrubbed clean with bleach, and the wounds carefully washed. She's still in University Hospital and doesn't remember anything about what happened, or what led up to it. The sexual nature of the crime led us to check out a recently released sex offender, but he has a solid alibi. A door-to-door of the surrounding flats hasn't given us anything. No one saw or heard anything. And no witnesses have come forward. The presumed use of the dildo led us to look into the possibility that the perpetrator is female, possibly from the city's lesbian community, where the use of dildos could be fairly widespread. This line of inquiry led us to Louise 'Lollo' Svensson, who refused us entry to her home, which is why we applied for a search warrant—the search was carried out yesterday. And produced absolutely nothing. She suggested in passing that presumably now we were going to talk to, quote, 'the whole fucking women's football team.' Forensics is checking her computer at the moment to see if there's anything to go on there, for instance if she's the person behind Lovelygirl on Theresa Eckeved's Facebook page."

Malin falls silent.

Hesitates.

Says nothing about the line of inquiry that led her and Zeke to the unfortunate Paul Anderlöv. Never mind. He should be left in peace.

Instead she goes on:

"How we got to what we know is in the reports, although of course I'm protecting the identity of my sources. We've also checked out Ali Shakbari and Behzad Karami. But they've got alibis as well, albeit provided by their families."

"I already know that," Karim snaps, evidently annoyed all over again at the suggestion of prejudice in this line of inquiry.

"I'm just trying to update you, Karim," Malin says calmly. "So that you can make a splendid statement, sorry, truthful statement to the journalists."

"Let her carry on," Zeke says.

"Then yesterday Theresa Eckeved was found murdered at the beach at Stavsätter. She had been buried, wrapped in ordinary transparent garbage bags, but a dog belonging to one of the bathers still managed to catch the scent. From a quick preliminary investigation Karin Johannison at National Forensics says that Theresa Eckeved was also abused with what seems to have been a blue dildo, which is why we're fairly convinced that these cases are linked. The cause of Theresa Eckeved's death was strangulation, but she had also received a blow to the head from a blunt object. She appears to have been killed at the beach. And she was scrubbed clean as well, according to Karin's analysis, using bleach, just like Josefin Davidsson. And her wounds were pedantically clean, trimmed with a very sharp, and very precise object, possibly a scalpel."

"So we've got a lunatic on the loose in the city?"

Malin is taken aback by how blunt Karim is being; he doesn't usually use such straightforward language.

"Looks like it," Zeke says.

"A person," Malin says. "Don't use the word *lunatic*. A damaged, sick individual."

And she thinks of the girls' wounds, how they are similar yet different, as if they illustrated an almost tentative approach to violence.

"A scalpel," Karim says, breaking her train of thought. "So who would have a scalpel?"

"Possibly a scalpel," Malin says. "A scalpel is clinical, clean, like chlorine. Possibly. You can buy them from any chemist."

"Do we need to give Josefin Davidsson any protection?" Karim goes on to ask.

"If the killer wanted her dead, he would probably already have made sure of that," Sven says. "She didn't seem to be in any fit state to escape, or to have actually done so."

"We'll have to check with her parents," Karim says, before going on: "The pair of you have made a lot of progress."

"Yes, you have," Sven agrees.

"But we haven't got anywhere."

Zeke drums his fingers on the table.

"Zeke, she was only found yesterday," Sven says.

"Theresa, yes, but we've had longer to work on Josefin Davidsson. And we still don't even know who called us about her."

And a silence spreads through the room, they all know that the first minutes, hours, days are the most important in any case, that an investigation becomes elusive with time, slippery, and can easily slide from the grasp of even the most experienced and talented detectives. If the truth remains hidden, it changes the lives of everyone involved forever, in small but clearly perceptible ways.

"Reinforcements are on their way," Sven says, "so we can pick up the pace. I suggest that we let Sundsten and Ekenberg check the alibis of all known sex offenders in the area." He goes on: "I've got the list ready. And we can get them to go door-to-door around the parents' house out in Sturefors. See if that turns up anything. Malin, Zeke? What are you going to do?"

"We thought we might have a word with the owner of the ice-cream kiosk. We couldn't get hold of her yesterday, or, to be more accurate, she disappeared before we had a chance to talk to her."

"Good. Talk to her and see where it leads. What about the other people on the beach?" Karim encouraging, almost imploring.

"Nada. *Niente,*" Zeke says. "And no other witnesses have come forward. Not one single tip-off. This whole city is in a fucking coma."

"Did she usually go swimming there?" Sven asks.

"Well, they've got their own pool," Malin says, "but Theresa's mother did say that she sometimes cycled out there."

"Maybe she went for an evening swim?"

Malin nods.

"How do you think we should play this with the press?" Karim asks.

He's asking us for help with the press. That's a first, Malin thinks.

"We can't say anything, in case we jeopardize the inquiry," Zeke says.

"We have to give them something," Sven says.

"Tell them we're working on the theory that the murder is connected to the girl who was found in the park. But not how or why we suspect that."

210

Mons Kallentoft

Malin can hear that she sounds sure of her opinion as she speaks, even though she isn't at all.

"Okay, that's what we'll do," Karim says.

"The football team," Sven says. "The women's football team. Give their coach a call. After all, Louise Svensson did mention the team. That has to mean something. And the suggestion of homosexuality in teenage girls. We need to follow up that line of inquiry."

Malin makes a face.

"She just said it in passing. She was being ironic. And my source didn't say anything about the women's team."

"Call her," Sven says. "Call anyway."

"What's his name again, the coach?" Zeke wonders.

"Her," Sven says. "Something like Pia Rasmefog. Danish, evidently."

Karim looks like he's thinking. Not about calling Pia Rasmefog, but something else.

"Nervous about facing the hyenas?"

Zeke, smiling.

"You know that's my natural element, Martinsson."

Karim almost alarmingly self-assured.

30

"Does it really make sense to call Pia Rasmefog? Isn't that just prejudice?"

Malin is sitting at her desk in the open-plan office.

"You mean, is it prejudiced to look at the women's football team because the attack and the murder both seem to have some sort of lesbian involvement?"

Zeke at his desk a few feet away, by the window looking out onto the parking lot. Cars shining in the light.

"I don't think it is, Malin. Because even if Lollo Svensson only mentioned them in passing when we searched her house, we still have to check it out, just to make sure. And Viktoria Solhage used to play football, so the team has cropped up more than once in this investigation."

"Sure, but it was still just something Lollo Svensson said in passing."

"Everybody knows that dykes play football."

"Can you hear what you sound like, Zeke? You sound completely bloody mad."

"But am I wrong?"

"You call, Zeke. The number's 140 160."

*   *   *

The phone rings three, four times before someone answers Zeke's call.

His face is tense, and Malin is curious to hear how he's going to approach Pia Rasmefog with his questions. She's read interviews with the Dane in the *Correspondent,* and from what she's read, she's a tough nut who doesn't let anyone get the better of her.

"Yes, hello," Zeke says, and Malin can hear that his voice is hoarser than usual, the tone is higher, and he's nervous, unsure of how to approach Rasmefog.

"This is Detective Inspector Zacharias Martinsson from the Linköping Police. I'd like to ask you a few questions, is now a good time?"

His choice of words milder than usual.

"Great. Well, you see, the women's football team has cropped up in the investigation into the murder of Theresa Eckeved . . . How? . . . Well, I'm afraid I can't reveal . . . no, no particular player, just in general . . . yes, perhaps . . . but . . . yes, of course, it might seem prejudiced, but please, calm down . . . this is actually a very serious crime that we're investigating," and then, suddenly, Zeke takes charge of the conversation, and Pia Rasmefog appears to understand that they have to ask, seeing as 'the women's football team' has cropped up in the investigation, albeit only on the periphery.

"Is there any player that you believe could have a tendency toward violence? More than anyone else. . . . No? Anyone who's been behaving differently over the last few days? . . . Not that either? Nothing that you think could be of interest to us?"

Zeke takes the phone from his ear, the conversation is evidently over.

"Fucking furious. She didn't even answer the last question."

Karim Akbar absorbs the light from the photographers' flashes, as the camera's clicking lenses call out: "You exist! You're special!"

Sullen and angry journalists in rows in front of him, dressed lightly in the summer heat, yet still in that typical, scruffy, bohemian journalist style that Karim hates.

He hasn't given them much, and Daniel Högfeldt and that hot-tempered woman from *Aftonbladet* in particular are critical of the silence.

"So you can't answer that question?" Daniel Högfeldt almost shouted. "Because you don't want to jeopardize the investigation? Don't you think the general public in this city has a right to know as much as possible seeing as there's a murderer on the loose? People are frightened, that much is obvious, so what right do you have to withhold information?"

"There's no suggestion that we're withholding information."

"Are the cases connected?"

The woman from *Aftonbladet*.

"I can't answer that."

"But is that one of your theories?"

"It's one of a number of possibilities."

"So what's your theory?"

"I'm afraid I can't answer that."

"Is Louise Svensson a suspect in either case?"

"No, not at the moment."

"So the search warrant wasn't called for?"

Karim closes his eyes. Waits a couple of seconds, then hears a new voice:

"But you must have something to go on?"

He opens his eyes just as one of the journalists says:

"According to our information, she's a lesbian. Do you suspect a sexual connection of that kind?"

"No comment."

Worse than usual today, more excitable that ever before. Suddenly he wants to get away from the podium, back to the jetty of the house in Västervik. He has to give them something just to get them to shut up.

So he says the words, and the moment they leave his mouth he knows it was a mistake.

"Our investigation has led us to look into the LFC women's football team."

"Why?"

"Do you suspect a lesbian connection?"

"I can't . . ."

"Is it just prejudice within the police force that has led you to turn your attention to the women's team?"

"Any particular player?"

"How do you think this will affect the general attitude toward women's football?"

Questions flying at him like bullets, like jagged shrapnel from something exploding.

Shit, Karim thinks. Then he shuts his eyes for a moment again, thinking about his family, his eight-year-old son, who learned to swim just last week.

The kiosk at the beach outside Sturefors is closed.

The tape of the cordon around the oak where they dug up Theresa Eckeved's body as recently as yesterday is still taut, and there are very few bathers; one family with two small children. They're sitting on a blanket down by the water, apparently unaffected by what has happened, by what to Malin seems to control and own this entire place, its air, its sounds.

Slavenca Visnic.

The owner of this kiosk, another one at the beach in Hjulsbro, and one outside the pool at Glyttinge: The county council provided them with that information. She runs all three as a trading company. But today the kiosk is closed, and Malin can understand why.

"I wouldn't have opened up either," she says to Zeke as they pace uneasily up and down in the morning heat in front of the kiosk, taking care to stay in the shade of the trees, sweaty enough already. Zeke's white shirt is stuck to his body, and her beige blouse is faring no better.

"No, people are staying away."

"Let's go to Hjulsbro. She might be there."

There was a mobile number on the license documents. But no answer when they rang.

"You go back to the car," Malin says, and Zeke looks at her, nods, then heads up the slope toward the meadow, where the heat seems to be creating a new sort of stillness, natural yet somehow frightening, as if the heat were making every living creature go into hibernation.

Malin goes down to the tree, bends over, and steps under the tape of the cordon.

The hole in the ground.

No glowing worms, but still a feeling that the ground could open up at any moment, spewing out destructive masses of livid, liquid fire.

Theresa.

She isn't here, but Malin can still see her face.

One eye open, the other closed. The strangulation marks round her neck. Her cleanly scrubbed white body and the dark wounds like lost planets in a shimmering, irregular cosmos.

And Malin wonders: How did you get here? Who would want to do this to you? Don't be scared. I never, ever give up.

Promise me that, Malin Fors, promise that you'll never give up trying to find the person who committed this ultimate act of abuse.

I'm trying to touch your warm, blond hair, but my fingers, my hands don't exist where you are, even if I can see you quite clearly from where I'm drifting in the sky just above you.

The girls.

Me. Nathalie.

Peter. You know so well what we had together. But you don't realize what it means, not yet. Dad never understood, didn't want to see, perhaps, what I was, am.

The same thing for you, Malin, with your dad, yet not quite. You blame your mum, thinking that she was in the way, muddying and diminishing his concern for you.

Maybe.

But it could be something else. Couldn't it?

You're far below me, Malin.

But still near.

But you're a long way from one thing, Malin: certainty.
So don't give up.
Because even if I know what happened, only you can convey the story
to Mum and Dad, and show them the truth.
Maybe the truth could help them?
It doesn't really make much difference to me anymore.
Maybe I am the truth now. The only pure, clear truth that a person needs.

The wind is blowing through the leaves of the oak, rustling them. It's a warm wind. But where are the connections, the threads twining together that can lead me, us, in the right direction?

The water of the lake almost seems to bubble in the heat. Boiling and stagnant, deadly poisonous yet still endlessly tempting: Jump in, and I'll drag you down to the bottom of the lake.

What were you doing out here?

Not an intrinsically evil place, not really.

Malin sinks to her knees beside the hole, the former grave.

She touches the ground with her hand.

It turns her fingers brown. And the sun reflects off the water of the lake, which looks unnaturally clean in the cutting heat. The reflections are like lightning in her eyes, like sharpened knives in her retinas, but she doesn't want to put on her Ray-Bans, wants to see reality just as it is.

Her blouse is sticking to her back.

"Hello!" A man's voice. "You probably shouldn't be in there."

The man over on the blanket.

Law-abiding.

But he's showing you respect, Theresa.

Malin stands up.

Pulls out her wallet from the front pocket of her denim skirt.

Holds up her ID.

"Malin Fors. Police."

"I hope you get the bastard," the man says in her direction, his eyes staring somewhere up toward the pale green of the meadow.

31

The kiosk by the beach in Hjulsbro is closed as well. Even though it would surely have been possible to rake in some serious money on a day like this. There must be at least a hundred people lying on the slope down toward the river and the fast-flowing, gray-black water. The noise from the power station farther downstream cuts the air, the turbines running on full, sending out a faint metallic smell into the air.

A summer for swimming.

Small children paddling in the enclosed safe area this side of the jetty. Overconfident teenage boys diving far out into the flow and struggling to get back; their gangly, unfinished bodies scare Malin, they reek of potency.

"That looks good," Zeke says, as he crouches at the top of the slope in the shade of a fir tree.

"I wonder if it really cools you down. It must be eightysome degrees in the water."

"Yes, and how clean is it?"

"All this sweating makes you obsessed with cleanliness," Malin says, as she rubs a small leaf between her fingers, soft and almost cool on one side, rough and warm on the other.

The kiosk outside the Glyttinge pool turns out to be closed too. The privately owned pool is a very successful investment in a summer like this one, and behind the fence Malin and Zeke can hear the noise of the bathers, their shouts and yelps, their happy laughter.

Behind them Skäggetorp, and Ryd not far away.

It's not so strange that the pool is busy. In those areas, where the poor and the immigrants live, people are spending the summer in their flats.

"We'll try Slavenca Visnic at home. Maybe she isn't well?"

"It's still odd," Malin says. "All three kiosks are closed. This is the time of year when they make their money. And if she isn't going to be there herself, she ought to have employees, don't you think?"

"The same thought did occur to me, Malin."

"There's something weird about it."

"What's weird is this heat, Malin. Shall we take a dip? To clear our heads?"

"Have you got anything to wear?"

"Skinny-dipping's good enough."

"I can see the headline in the *Correspondent:* 'Naked Detectives in Glyttinge Pool.'"

"Mr. Högfeldt would like that," Zeke says.

"What do you mean by that?"

"What do I mean?"

"Yes."

"I don't mean anything, Malin. Relax."

Slavenca Visnic's flat on the ground floor of Gamlegården 3B in Skäggetorp is deserted as well.

The smell of the forest fires is very noticeable here, closer to the blaze, and the smoke seems to have filtered between the low, white-brick blocks of flats.

No one answered when they knocked on the door in the stairwell. No sounds from inside the flat, and now they're standing in the little garden, looking through the blinds into a gloomy room where only the furniture stands out: a sofa, a table, a couple of armchairs, and an almost empty bookcase, set out on what looks like oak parquet flooring.

"Does this woman actually exist?"

"Doesn't look like it," Zeke replies.

"Maybe she's gone away. Abroad. Or just for the day."

"Yes, but now, and with three kiosks?"

"We'll have to check her background. The Migration Board ought to know something. I'll get one of the uniforms onto it," Malin says.

Then her mobile rings.

Sven Sjöman.

"A woman who was out running on the jogging track in Ryd yesterday evening has called. Said she felt like she was being watched, that someone was lying in wait, stalking her. If you've got time, go and talk to her."

"Sure. We're done here."

A name.

An address down on Konsistoriegatan, in the center of the city.

Linda Karlå offers them chilled apple juice in the kitchen of her tastefully furnished two-room apartment. The flat is in a building dating from the thirties: beige stucco, well kept, one of the oldest housing cooperatives in the city, with astronomical prices to match.

They sit with their drinks around the kitchen table, and Linda Karlå apologizes for taking up their time. Zeke explains that they're interested in anything that could be connected to the murder and the other attack.

"I was out running," Linda Karlå says. "I run a lot. Not all that often in the forest in Ryd, and I don't know why, but I suddenly got the feeling that someone was watching me, waiting for me deeper in the woods. I didn't see anyone, but there was someone there. It could have been a man. Or a woman. I know I was being watched, and when I ran there was someone following me. There was a sort of snaking sound, at least that's what I thought at the time. But I'm fast, so I made it to the parking lot."

"You didn't see anything?" Malin asks.

She makes sure that her voice sounds interested.

"No. But there was someone there. I just thought maybe you'd like to know. Maybe he, whoever did it, lives in Ryd?"

"Maybe. If it is a he. And if it was him."

"Well, it terrified me, anyway."

"Best to stay away from the forest in Ryd for a while," Zeke says. "Go running on open streets until we've sorted this out."

Linda Karlå looks relieved.

Almost surprised that they're taking her fears seriously.

"It's really much nicer to go swimming at this time of year," she says. "There are so many good pools in the city."

Outside the building, on the way back to the car, Zeke asks: "So what do you make of that?"

"Yes, what the hell do I make of that?" Malin says.

It's just after two o'clock when they get back to the station. They grabbed lunch out at IKEA in Tornby, the warehouse full of people trying to escape the heat and pick up some summer bargains from the great Ingvar, purveyor of fine design to the masses.

Karim Akbar is standing, looking wretched, in front of the computer at the desk he's had set up for him in the open-air office, in addition to the large office he has upstairs.

"What's up with him?" Zeke says as he wipes the sweat from his brow and pulls his shirt away from his chest.

"God knows," Malin says. "Do you think it's got a bit cooler in here? They must have got the air-conditioning going again."

"Perfect," Zeke says. "Can't be more than seventy degrees."

Karim waves them over to him.

Two windows open on the huge computer screen.

Aftonbladet and the *Correspondent*.

They've both put the football angle on their front pages.

"Lesbian Killer?" is *Aftonbladet*'s headline, above a picture of the team. The article starts: "According to Police Chief Karim Akbar, the investigation is now focused on Linköping's top-flight women's football team . . ."

The *Correspondent:*

"Crime and Prejudice?"

"What has led the police to turn their attention to the team is as yet unclear . . ."

Both sites include quotes from Pia Rasmefog.

She's furious that the team is the focus of this sort of attention without any concrete evidence being presented, that it seems to be because the crime appears to have a lesbian angle, and that one of the most widespread prejudices in society right now is that women's football teams are always full of lesbian players. Still worse, according to Pia Rasmefog, is the suggestion that lesbian players would be extraviolent, which is an insulting but widely held misapprehension.

"This just shows how rigid the police are in their thinking, on a number of different levels," she tells *Aftonbladet.*

"Holy shit," Zeke mutters. "How did you manage that, Karim?"

"We made one call," Malin says. "As a result of someone mentioning the team in the course of our inquiries. But we aren't focusing on them at all. What on earth did you say at the press conference?"

Malin turns toward Karim, expecting him to look embarrassed and angry, ashamed at his obvious mistake, but instead he just looks defiant.

"I said that the team had cropped up in the investigation."

"Why did you say that?"

"They were pressuring me and I wanted to give them something, and stupidly that was what came out. But on the other hand: Maybe something will come of all this fuss."

Sven Sjöman comes over to them.

He can't suppress his smile when he sees the screen.

"We could issue a retraction?" he says.

"No damn retractions," Karim says. "Just let it go."

Karim's skill at manipulating the media has always impressed Malin in the past, his ability to find just the right place under the spotlight.

But this . . .

What a ridiculous blunder.

It makes us look like something from the Stone Age.

Like the riot squad hitting gays over the head.

I think you're going to, you think I'm going to, I believe you're going to do it, you do it, then I do it too . . .

The things we ruin with our words. Prejudices laid bare, confirming and empowering evil.

This heat is making all our brains overheat, Malin thinks as she walks back to her desk. Our brains are boiling so hard that they don't work anymore.

She looks at Karim from a distance.

His trim frame, clad in a cotton suit, huddled on his office chair, radiating a new sort of tiredness that she's never seen before, as if he's fed up with this whole media game, with the ridiculous little exchanges of information and opinion, as if he's just longing for clarity, for black and white.

Good luck, Karim, Malin thinks. It's millions of years since the world was black and white, now it consists of millions of colors, most of them hideous and scary, but many of them heartbreakingly beautiful, reasons to feel gratitude for every new day on the planet.

Then her phone rings.

"Fors."

"This is Viktoria Solhage. I've just seen on the Internet. You can imagine how disappointed I am. Can't you?"

"Viktoria. I—"

"There's already more than enough prejudice, Malin Fors. I trusted you."

"Viktoria—"

Click.

Silence. Nothing more.

Just the thought that everything was going to hell.

32

The air-conditioning doesn't reach all the way down here, not even the ventilation seems to be working, and the small windows out onto the yard may be open but the air they're letting in is so hot that it doesn't seem to contain any oxygen.

The gym in the basement of the police station.

One of Malin's favorite places in the world.

Has to come down in spite of the heat.

Has to come down, even on a day like today when the gym is reminiscent of one of the outer circles of hell, and the freshly painted yellow walls are turning fiery orange because the salt of her sweat is clouding her sight.

Ten minutes on the treadmill just now.

Her white vest soaked through.

She thought she was going to faint.

Thinks about Nathalie Falck. Wants to talk to her again, but what could she say that wasn't said last time? Time must be allowed to do its work. Time they don't have.

One dumbbell in each hand, thirty-five pounds, up and down, up and down, fifteen reps, then rest.

The muscles in her upper arms are long and sinuous and stronger than they look.

I'm so exhausted in this heat that I feel like throwing up, almost. She's done it before, thrown up in the vomit-green bin by the door of the gym.

Usually alone down here.

Most of the others use gyms down in the city.

But Malin likes the sense of being underground. Sometimes Johan Jakobsson keeps her company when he has time between school runs and feeling guilty about anything and everything. She can see how family life is draining him, how he's starting to get wrinkles in his once so boyishly smooth forehead.

Tove.

I'm thirty-four.

I wouldn't mind, I ought to have more wrinkles in my forehead. Even if I don't like the ones I've got.

Shit.

I'm going to exercise away all the crap that this summer has brought with it.

Tove.

Home soon.

Janne. How can I miss you so, when it's more than ten years since we last lived together?

I see you from a distance.

Your shortcomings pale, have paled over the years, haven't they? Away from each other, we've grown together. Can love work like that?

Her lie about not being able to drive them to the airport. Skavsta, Ryanair to London, then a direct flight to Bali with some British charter airline.

Their farewell in the hall back home in the flat twelve days ago is like a scene in a film now, soundless, scentless. She and Janne reserved toward each other, all three of them oddly quiet, as if years of longing and loss suddenly became apparent there in the hall and the looming distance between them.

What could have been.

She hugged and kissed Tove, Janne, then the usual farewell phrases, the feeling that new ones were called for, a sort that people had never said before.

What do we do now?

That's what she thought, and she noticed Janne's clumsiness when he opened his mouth, saying:

"You should have come too."

And at that moment she wanted to hit him, jump on him and beat the shit out of him, while at the same time wanting to sit on an airplane, resting her head on his shoulder, Tove asleep by her side, the two of them awake in a comforting, whispering simplicity.

But instead she said:

"Janne, for God's sake. You know that's impossible," and she could feel that she had said, whispered, screamed those words a thousand times before, that they had become their mutual invocation, a sort of truth simply because they had been spoken and thought enough times, and Tove shouldn't have to hear this tired crap.

Tove horribly aware beside Janne, horribly conscious of the subtexts.

What are we doing to you, darling child?

They had left the flat, Janne's friend Pecka blowing his car horn impatiently down in the street. An agitated farewell. A bad omen.

And she had gone straight to bed.

No. She had gone straight to Daniel Högfeldt's flat.

Let him hold her tight against the chrome frame of his Mio bed.

Then he banged the sorrow out of her.

And it was nice.

Malin walks past the main hospital building on her way out of the police station.

She spent a long time in the gym, then talked to Ebba in reception for half an hour, about the heat and teenage daughters, Ebba has twins, sixteen years old and a real handful.

Then Malin had spent hours sitting at her desk, thinking, still sweating, catching up on her paperwork, reading the Migration

Board's file on Slavenca Visnic, which had been emailed to her by the young uniform Zeke had given the job to earlier in the day.

That was quick, she had thought when she saw the email in her inbox. And then she had read the file on the screen, how Slavenca Visnic arrived in Sweden from Bosnia in 1994, after her husband and two children, four and six years old, were burned alive when their house in Sarajevo was hit by incendiary grenades, how she had been captured by Serbian troops when she tried to escape the inferno of the city. How they raped her for two weeks, how day and night lost all meaning, how she managed to escape, but refused to say how, wandering through the forests and along the roads at night until she reached Dubrovnik, where she had somehow managed to make her way to Italy and finally showed up in Ystad in the far south of Sweden.

Pregnant.

Abortion, eighth week, carried out in Norrköping.

Malin had noticed at once that the time line didn't fit.

The dates when she must have been raped by the Serbs, the date of the abortion.

At least twenty-four weeks between them.

Something alive.

Something killed.

So that something else can live.

A picture of Slavenca Visnic, long dark hair, sharp features, tired and angry eyes. But determined.

Is it you? Malin had thought then. Is it you? She thinks now, as she looks up at the windows of the hospital, points of light against the growing darkness of the evening sky.

She carries on.

Heavy steps.

Down toward the Horticultural Society Park, toward the trees of the park, and their darkness.

Malin walks along the path leading down to the summerhouse where Josefin Davidsson was found naked and disoriented, moving slowly, undressing herself in her thoughts and trying to capture what might have happened.

You want young girls. You scrub them clean. What do you want from the girls? Their innocence? Why one dead, one alive? Did she run away from you? Josefin? The wounds you inflict are clean, and, on Theresa, even neatly trimmed. You want things to be as good as possible, is that it?

Fear and loneliness.

I don't want to be here.

Swings, not moving.

The sound of the city in slow motion, sleepy. The smell of the forest fires still noticeable, but weaker tonight, the wind in the other direction.

Something blue.

Then a cracking sound from up in the trees, is there someone there? Is someone watching me? A bird of prey, perhaps?

Malin turns round, a black shadow is moving rapidly toward her.

What the hell?

What the hell's happening?

Run away.

It's moving.

I'm floating, shouting in your ear, but you hear nothing.

I disappear.

Don't want to see hear know about this.

But we'll soon meet again.

If you don't listen to me, we'll soon meet again.

Sofia Fredén was reluctant to accept the job of dishwasher at Frimis, the old Freemasons' hotel and club, didn't want to spend the summer working. But it was absurdly well paid, and easy to get to by train from Mjölby, the station just a stone's throw from the hotel.

Now she's tired after a long shift in the heat and humidity.

And she walks without thinking, with her brain somehow shut off, through the very darkest part of the Railway Park down toward the station, the lights of the city are close, nothing can happen to her here, and in her ears she has the earplugs of her iPod, music downloaded from the net, Jens Lekman's bombastic music, and it makes her feel slightly less tired.

She walks past the grove of rowan bushes and maples and a large oak tree.

Singing along.

And Sofia Fredén doesn't hear something start to move in the bushes behind her, doesn't hear something approaching, just feels the force of an arm being wrapped around her from behind, and a second later she's lying between four tall rowan bushes, on shitty, urine-stinking ground, deep within the darkness of the city, trying to save her own life.

The deer vanishes. When the creature noticed Malin it turned and ran off toward the stage over by the Hotel Ekoxen.

Malin's heart is still pounding from the adrenaline.

She goes inside the summerhouse. Sits down on one of the wooden benches, trying to piece together the fragments of the case she's carrying inside her.

People, places.

But they form nothing but a gray, shapeless mass, and a shiver of anxiety runs through her body, a shimmering whiteness that takes root deep in her diaphragm.

It's a good sign for Linköping that deer dare to venture so close to the center.

But something more than just deer is in motion, they're not alone tonight.

There are two of us now, Malin.

But Sofia Fredén doesn't yet know about her predicament.

I'll try to help her as best I can.

But I'm afraid my fear means that I can scarcely look after myself.

Please, Malin, kill off my anxieties. That's one of the things that we human beings are supposed to do for each other.

I know that now, as I drift up here.

33

The clock on the Tekniska Verken building says 5:42.

Already bloody light.

The black bicycle is weaving back and forth over the asphalt, the quickest route from the house out in Stångebro is past the Cloetta Center, through the tunnel under the railway, and up through the Railway Park.

Hungover.

But I'm Superman, thinks Patrik Karlsson, as he pedals on toward the tunnel.

The party last night. They had a barbecue in his garden, his mum and dad away in the country, and now he's on his way to his summer job at Frimis as a breakfast waiter.

Boiling eggs.

Laying tables.

Don't put out any little marzipan tarts if there are German tourists staying in the hotel. They take about a hundred each.

It's hotter in the tunnel, but it only takes a few seconds.

Up past the station building.

The Railway Park.

Buildings from the turn of the last century all around, showy apartments, ten large rooms, doctors' homes, he knows because he

had a girlfriend there once, a nice doctor's daughter called Corne-
lina.

What a fucking name!

Wonder if Sofia's working the dishwasher today.

Past the bushes. And those trees that his mum always thinks are so
beautiful.

But.

In the small clearing between the trees, in the dim light, there's
something there. There shouldn't be anything there.

Patrik Karlsson stops.

Lays the bike down on the grass.

He feels sick from the wine box last night. But sicker still from
what he sees.

His body lurches as he approaches.

There's a body in there, in the clearing.

Turn round.

Can't.

The body is naked, white, looks almost scrubbed, despite the blood
from the wounds.

The face.

The eyes, wide open. Gray blue white, far from alive.

Sofia.

From the dishwasher.

She won't be working the dishwasher today, Patrik Karlsson thinks,
before he lets out a stifled, involuntary scream.

"It's happened again."

Zeke's voice more tired than Malin has ever heard it before. Tired
in a new way, not despairing but almost indifferent, and that scares
Malin even more.

She's seen that indifference in some older officers, and prays that
neither she nor Zeke ends up like that, but not Zeke, never Zeke; that
somehow innate sense of engagement in his hard, green eyes could
never fade. Could it?

And he says it again.

And Malin, sitting up naked in bed on a sheet wet with sweat, doesn't want to absorb the words, and hopes they've found a living girl disoriented in a park, or anywhere, but she can hear from Zeke's voice that this isn't the case.

She was practically dragged from her dreamless sleep by the ringing of the phone.

It's happened again.

They found Josefin on Thursday, Theresa on Sunday, and now, two days later, it's time for another girl. Dead?

"How bad?"

"As bad as it could be."

Malin clenches the fist that isn't holding the phone.

"This is fucking well not going to happen again."

"You're right there," Zeke says. "It's time we got this bastard now."

It's only two hundred yards from Malin's flat to the latest crime scene.

She makes her way there along the shady side of St. Larsgatan. Dragging her feet, doesn't want to see what she knows she's going to see.

No smell of smoke, the wind must be coming from a different direction again today. But Malin can still sense it somehow, the smoke, she can detect its resonance, a new tone settling over the city.

The heat.

The implacability of this summer.

Fear.

The awareness that something malevolent is on the loose.

Stay indoors, girls. Don't go out. Go in groups, only in the light, be on your guard, cheat death, it could be anywhere, anywhere at all.

Violence like a suffocating arm around Linköping, this city of knowledge, a snake twisting around its proud industries, IT companies, university, and hospitals, around its inhabitants, each one more remarkable yet also more scared than the last.

Fear is a parasite, expressing itself in violence, which will slowly, slowly consume the city's joy in life. Unless, Malin thinks, we put a stop to this now.

She walks past the *Correspondent*'s offices on St. Larsgatan.

Daniel almost certainly down in the Railway Park already.

Frimis.

Zeke said that both the victim and the lad who found her had summer jobs there.

The hotel's façade like a faded medieval castle. And in there was where those ridiculous Freemasons held their meetings. Karim is a member. And Zeke's son, Martin, has given a talk to the old men about what it's like being a top sports star.

Malin wants to think about anything at all apart from the sight that greets her when she turns the corner down toward the park: two patrol cars, uniformed police officers, cordons, journalists, and photographers.

Low-growing bushes in tight clusters around the gravel paths.

An attractive grove of what, rhododendrons?

No, rowan bushes, maples, an oak.

Karin Johannison inside the grove.

Malin can just make out the red and orange flowers of a lovely dress that she's seen Karin wear before.

Karin is crouched over the body.

"Her name's Sofia Fredén."

Malin can hear the tiredness even in Karin's voice. Not indifferent or despairing, more like sympathetic and involved, in a way that she's never heard Karin before.

"Another one," Karin says as she stands up and looks at Malin, her eyes full of sympathy as well, but also anger.

"Another one," she repeats.

And Malin nods, looks down at the body, its eyes closed, and the scrubbed skin is glassy, almost transparent white, with deep gashes across the chest, neat in spite of the blood, but not the same as the injuries to Theresa or Josefin. The blood that's poured from the wounds makes the body look oddly peaceful; the contrast between the white skin and the red has that effect.

A smell of bleach is in the air.

"It almost looks like she's glowing," Malin says. "Have you got any thoughts about the wounds? They're different from before. And there's more blood."

"The wounds?" Karin says. "Yes, they're different. They look like they were made by some sort of claws. A small bird, a guinea pig, maybe a rabbit or a cat. As to why there's more blood? Maybe the killer didn't have time to wash her or wait for the wounds to stop bleeding. We are in the middle of the city, after all."

In Karin's voice there's none of the superiority that's usually there, and it makes her more pleasant, humble.

Rabbit claws.

Are you still finding your way? If you can just get it right, then all this will sort itself out, all your wishes will be fulfilled?

The cages at Lollo Svensson's farm.

"It's like he or she is still trying things out," Malin says to Karin. "Seeing as the wounds look different each time."

"Maybe, Malin. But what do I know?"

In the distance she can hear Daniel Högfeldt's voice:

"Malin, is it the same perpetrator?"

And Karin answers his question, albeit quietly, to Malin.

"Particles of blue paint in the vagina, the body scrubbed clean, strangled. I can guarantee you that we're dealing with one and the same perpetrator."

Malin looks Karin in the eyes. She blinks slowly in response.

"It could have been one of us, Malin, if we were younger."

"What about the lad who found her?"

"He's sitting in the Volvo with Zeke over in the parking lot."

Patrik Karlsson is sitting terrified in the backseat of the car.

Seems to believe that they're going to think it was him.

"We don't think you had anything to do with this, Patrik. Not for a second."

The air-conditioning in the car is roaring, one of the commonest and most welcome sounds of the summer.

"We've already checked your alibi," Zeke says. "And we know that you worked together. Right now we're just wondering if you can tell us anything about her that we ought to know?"

"I only spoke to her a couple of times."

His soft teenage cheeks move up and down.

"She was always busy with the dishes. Used to say she wished she'd taken the job in the café at Tinnis instead, where she worked last summer."

Tinnis.

What wouldn't I give to go swimming right now?

"I didn't really know her. Sure, I thought she was pretty. But like I said, I was on my way to work and just happened to go past on my bike."

Sofia, Malin thinks.

Just on her way home from work.

Did she just happen to walk past the perpetrator?

"Do you know where Sofia lived?"

"In Mjölby. She must have been on her way to catch the train."

"Mjölby?"

Malin closes her eyes.

We're way behind, she thinks.

34

It's the sort of day when she feels like drinking one, two, three, four beers for lunch, then carrying on drinking all afternoon with the help of a large bottle of tequila. But it never happens, because she never gives in to that sort of impulse. Instead: delayed morning meeting at the station.

An intent Karim Akbar at the head of the table, the whiteboard behind him giving off a dull glow, lit up by the daylight seeping in through the gaps in the lowered, tilted Venetian blinds.

Sven Sjöman is sitting to the left of Karim, bags under his eyes, his bulging stomach tight under a washed-out yellow cotton shirt, and Malin knows he's suffering in the heat, knows it's much harder for him than other people to get through days like this. She noticed him getting more and more tired during the spring, but didn't want to ask why, didn't want to vocalize what was obvious, not wanting to think about what would happen if he went off on sick leave or if his heart somehow packed up.

Mentor.

You've been my mentor, Sven.

His mantra: *Listen to the voices of an investigation, Malin. Hear what they're trying to tell you.* Which she has gradually, over the days, weeks, months, and years, translated into: *See the images, feel the intimations, notice the patterns.*

Zeke opposite Sven.

Ready to pounce again, his back straight, ready to deal with whatever shit gets thrown at him. Nothing can break me! A hungry look in his eyes, nothing to hide, an unveiled human being.

Their colleagues from Motala and Mjölby are taking part in the group meeting for the first time.

Sundsten. Per.

A younger, child-free version of Johan Jakobsson, slim and sinewy, sitting there with an open face beneath flaxen hair, wearing a crumpled white linen suit. A guileless but watchful look in his eyes, a sharp nose curving slightly toward his thin lips. He looks intelligent, Malin thinks.

Waldemar Ekenberg.

Long and faithful service.

A malformed police officer with an infamous weakness for excessive force. Cigarettes have left deep lines in his face and he's thin, looks older than his fifty years. His hair is a lifeless gray, but the look in his gray-green eyes is still strangely vibrant: We're going to get this bastard.

Karim begins:

"Karin Johannison has confirmed that the traces of paint match the other victims. We'll be getting a more detailed forensic report later today, tomorrow at the latest. So, we're dealing with the same perpetrator. Or perpetrators."

"Well," Waldemar Ekenberg says, and his voice is thin and rattling. "We can hardly expect to find the perpetrator among her close acquaintances. There don't seem to be any natural connections between the girls, do there?"

"Hardly," Zeke interjects.

"I've had time to get a good look at the case now," Per Sundsten says. "It's like we're dealing with some sort of shadow. Someone who exists, yet somehow doesn't."

Sven nods.

"What do you think, Malin?"

The expectation that she's going to say something wise, something that takes them a bit further.

"There's a pattern here. I just can't see it yet. Have Sofia Fredén's parents been told?"

Theresa Eckeved's mother sinking to the hall floor, screaming.

Her father, some of his wits still about him, his whole being radiating the realization: I'm only at the start of this nightmare.

"Persson and Björk in Mjölby have taken care of that," Waldemar Ekenberg says. "They're good, they'll do it as well as anyone could. It's an impossible task. And they'll be questioning Sofia's parents about her as well. Just the essentials."

Task.

Malin tastes the word, twists and turns it, the way it creates distance in an attempt to make this most human encounter bearable.

Then a quick overview of the situation from Per Sundsten.

The latest door-to-door inquiries around the houses of Sturefors had turned up nothing, and the convicted sex offenders that he and Ekenberg had had time to check out all had watertight alibis. Ten people on the list, five checked. "We'll carry on with the others today. But I don't really expect it to give us anything."

"We haven't got ahold of the owner of the kiosk yet," Malin says. "Seems to be away. All three kiosks are shut, in the middle of high season."

"The fuss with the football team has died down," Karim says. "That's one advantage when things move so fast, no one has time to linger over things that don't matter. But it was clumsy of me."

A team-building confession, a bit of rhetoric for the officers on the case. One tiny little mistake, but you'll forgive me, respect me again. Won't you?

I respect you, Karim. You're a better police chief than most.

Sven speaks up.

"Still nothing from Yahoo! or Facebook. Evidently they're very restrictive when it comes to giving out information. Yahoo! claims they need an American court order. Facebook hasn't even replied. And Louise Svensson's computer was completely clean. She could have cleared it out, seeing as she was expecting us to turn up."

Sven takes a deep breath.

"We're still trying to identify possible manufacturers of the dildo, but so far we haven't got anything concrete."

Then he rubs a hand over his head.

"How do you suggest we proceed?"

Sven is head of the preliminary investigation, but it feels as if responsibility for the case is fluid, snaking to and fro across the room like hot, hot tar, so hot that no one wants to burn their fingers on it.

The air-conditioning unit groans.

Shudders.

And falls silent.

"Shit! Just when it had started working at last! Things are going to heat up again," Zeke says.

And they all wait for Sven to make a proposal, lead them further, and he starts to speak.

"Sundsten and Ekenberg. You take the door-to-door around Frimis, and talk to Sofia Fredén's colleagues at the hotel. Malin and Zeke, get hold of the kiosk owner, and maybe you could check if Josefin Davidsson has remembered anything by now? Just some quick questions? And we'll have to hope that a witness turns up, someone who saw or heard something, or that they come up with something about Sofia Fredén in Mjölby that can move us on. Otherwise we'll just have to wait for Forensics to give us something. Well, those are the lines I see ahead of us. Anyone else?"

Silence round the table.

"Right then," Karim says. "Let's get to work."

"A shadow."

Zeke standing beside Malin's desk. Trying out the word.

"Something like that," Malin says. "A shadow of a person. Or a person driven toward utter transparency."

"Or a lack of transparency," Zeke says.

"Then there are the different sorts of wounds that were inflicted on the girls," Malin says.

"Seems almost like a sort of curiosity about violence," Zeke says.

"Cleanliness. All that scrubbing."

"As if the killer wanted to purify them."

"Is Josefin Davidsson still in the hospital?"

"We'll have to check. Otherwise she's probably at home."

Zeke waits by Malin's desk as she rings.

Waits until she hangs up and says:

"She's at home."

"Do you think she'll be able to remember anything now?"

"No," Malin says. "But we'll give it a try."

Malin thinks of Maria Murvall, who must be able to remember being attacked in the forest, but who has squeezed her whole being into a corner, letting her consciousness act as the basis for a life that's been stripped down, a life that's really no better than most animals'.

Is that what evil can do to a person?

Apparently.

Then Malin's phone rings.

Ebba in reception.

"There's someone who wants to talk to you, Malin. Says he wants to be anonymous, he's got a very strong accent. Says it's about the girls."

"Put him through."

The voice, the accent, the prejudices that arise at once. He sounds, even though Malin doesn't want to think it, stupid, speaking in scarcely intelligible Swedish:

"You know that fucker Behzad Karami, he hasn't got a fucking alibi, his family is just lying, he was somewhere that night, and last night too, I know. You have to check him again, they're lying to you. He often does strange things at night, he just disappears."

How can you know that? Malin thinks, and says:

"What's your name?"

No number on the display, the man, or rather the youth, is probably ringing from a public phone.

"I don't have a name."

"Hang on—"

Click.

Malin turns toward Zeke. A questioning look in his eyes.

"Behzad Karami just reappeared in the case. We should check him out again."

"Okay, but where do we start? With Behzad Karami, Slavenca Visnic, or Josefin Davidsson?"

Malin throws up her hands.

"Which one do you think would have air-conditioning at home?"

"Let's start with Josefin," Zeke replies. "Besides, Visnic is proving rather difficult to get ahold of, to put it mildly."

35

"Doesn't Karim live out this way?" Zeke asks, wiping the little beads of sweat from his upper lip. They look like tiny burn blisters.

"Yes, they've got a house here somewhere," Malin replies, thinking that Josefin Davidsson was incredibly lucky to get away with her life.

They park by the school. Josefin Davidsson lives with her parents in one of the row houses in Lambohov.

The red-painted wooden houses are small, unassuming family dreams, clinging together, with neatly tended front gardens and hedges that have grown tall over the years since the houses were built.

"I think Karim's son goes to school there," Malin says as they walk slowly toward the houses. They stop outside number 12, go into the little garden, and ring the bell, but hear nothing from inside. So Malin takes ahold of the ring hanging from the mouth of the gilded lion adorning the green front door instead, and just as she knocks the door opens and Josefin peeps out through the gap.

"Hello. Oh, it's you. What do you want?"

"We'd like to ask you some questions," Malin says. "We want to see what you remember. Or if you can remember anything else?"

"Come in."

Josefin opens the door.

She's wearing a loose, pale-pink dress that hangs limply about her body, her hair wet after what Malin assumes must have been a shower. The bandages on her arms and legs are dry and clean.

She walks into the house ahead of them, leading them past a kitchen with white cupboards and on into a living room where two burgundy-colored Chesterfield sofas sit facing one another. In the background is a patio with a hammock and plastic garden furniture. The room is hot and smells faintly of smoke and sweat and freshly made caramel.

Malin and Zeke sit down beside each other and Josefin settles down opposite them. You look older here at home, Malin thinks, as if the ornate furniture and cheap Wilton rugs are stealing life from you.

"I can't remember anything," Josefin says. "And, really, why would I want to?"

She knits her hands in her lap, they turn white and she turns away to look at the garden.

"Are your mum and dad out?" Malin asks.

"They're at work."

She looks back at them.

"They could be here, get compassionate leave if you'd rather not be alone."

"Then they'd get less money. And they'd probably rather work."

"You don't mind being left on your own?"

"No, I don't remember anything, so what would I be afraid of? That it could happen again? That's not very likely."

The person who hurt you, Malin thinks. I'm afraid of them, and so should you be. You should be afraid, but you're sensible, what good would being afraid do? The chance of the perpetrator coming after you is small, and if he or she wanted you dead, then you wouldn't be here.

"Why did you go to the cinema on your own?" Malin asks. "People usually go with a friend, don't they?"

"I like going on my own. Talking just spoils the experience of the film."

"Okay. Try to remember. What did you do that evening, what happened? Try to get an image, a word, a smell, anything at all, in your head. Please, just try."

Malin tries to sound as persuasive as she can, but there's an under-
tone: Remembering is possible. And it would help us.

And Josefin shuts her eyes, concentrating, but soon opens them
again and looks at Malin and Zeke with a sigh.

"Sorry," she says.

"What about your dreams?" Malin asks. "Anything from them?"

"I never remember my dreams," Josefin replies.

On the way out Malin stops in the hall, looking at her face in the mirror. Through the door on her left she sees Josefin put a saucepan of
water on an old Cylinda stove.

Without knowing why, Malin goes into the kitchen and puts her
hand on Josefin's shoulder.

"How are you going to spend the summer?" she asks, and Josefin
starts and turns around.

"I'm going to take it easy. I was supposed to be working in the
kiosk at the pool in Glyttinge, but I resigned after just three days. I'd
rather have the time off instead."

Malin stiffens.

"So you know Slavenca Visnic?"

Josefin laughs.

"I don't think anyone knows that woman."

"She was supposed to be working for Slavenca Visnic, but resigned
after just three days."

Malin is trying not to sound too excited about the connection.

"Bloody hell," Zeke says. "Bloody hell!"

"And she had an idea about where Slavenca might be, didn't think
she'd gone abroad."

"Where, then?"

"She might be up at the fires. As a volunteer. Apparently she spoke
of nothing but the forest fires when they started working together,
said they probably needed help."

"I read in the *Correspondent* that there are about a hundred people helping out at the edge of the fires. With blankets and so on."

"That would make sense. Her family died in a fire in Sarajevo. A grenade attack on the building they lived in."

Janne.

He worked for the Swedish Rescue Services Agency in Bosnia. She knows he saw all manner of horrors down there, but he's never really talked about it.

Silence.

Memory loss.

They're more than just cousins.

Siblings, maybe.

The road leads into the smoke.

There are cars lined up along the edge of the forest road leading into the inferno, into the fire. The edge of the fire is just north of Lake Hultsjön, so they drove through Ljungsbro and took the Tjällmo Road up through the densely grown forest, the same road they drove back on during the winter they were working on the Bengt Andersson case.

Neither of them mentioned this as they drove across the desiccated, tormented plain and the dust flew up across the road in thick veils.

Instead Zeke put on his beloved German choral music, deep chanting from some choir that has put new words to a Wagner opera.

High volume.

Dystopian, Malin thought. Perfect for a bad horror film.

The noise was only turned down when she called Sundsten and asked him to follow up on Behzad Karami.

"We'll sort it. We've finished the door-to-door around the Railway Park and Frimis. No one saw anything. But most people are asleep at that time of day."

Then she called Sven Sjöman and told him about the new connection.

"Good. At last."

Then they were approaching the fire, veils of smoke drifting over the car, the once-blue sky now gray and angry, and they could feel the heat gradually rising inside the car, a heat that made them want to turn back and flee before their skin started to scorch, boil, char, as their brains pictured catastrophic scenarios for their bodies. The smell was getting stronger and stronger, a burned world, the stench of flesh burned alive and the plaints of trees being consumed by greedy flames.

They turned off onto the gravel road they're now driving down, seeing as that was where the bright-red fire engine they were following turned off. Above them a helicopter is circling with a water scoop, and then it heads in over the fire, disappearing from view. People with soot-stained faces, their eyes hidden behind goggles, walking along the road.

"What sort of car has she got?" Zeke says, his hands firm on the wheel, the car heading slowly toward the core of the fire, burned-out trees around them, dust and ash swirling through the air.

"A Fiat van, according to the registration office, white."

"Haven't seen one like that yet."

An ambulance parked in a small side track, two firemen standing beside it, inhaling what must be oxygen from large yellow canisters.

And this is the inferno you can't wait to get back to, Janne.

People with blankets in their hands. Beating them on the ground where the smoke is rising. Farther ahead they can make out flames through the trees.

"There've never been fires like this in Östergötland before," Zeke says. "They're battling to stop it coming back to life again. Did you know, a fire blazing at its worst can jump more than fifty yards from treetop to treetop? Almost like an explosion, and that's when it gets really dangerous. That's when firemen get trapped, circled by the fire."

So far no one has been killed, no firemen, and no volunteers.

Just let it stay that way, with only the creatures of the forest losing their lives.

They meet a fire engine, one of the smaller ones, and Malin recognizes two of Janne's colleagues in the front seat but can't remember their names. They recognize her and nod.

"Tough guys," Zeke says.

"I guess so," Malin says.

The line of parked cars breaks up, fewer volunteers here, firemen from five districts running to and fro in the forest, moving in and out of the burned vegetation. And then they see it, the white Fiat.

"Bloody hell," Zeke says.

"The number matches," Malin says.

And they park close to the Fiat, open the doors of the Volvo, and the noise and the heat from the inferno, almost invisible ahead of them in the forest, hits them, the air full of a prickling smell of sulphur and burned meat, the sound of the fire a dark whistling, as if God himself were trying to sound the alarm.

The heat almost unbearable.

Summer plus fire equals sauna.

"Not even a Finn could put up with this," Zeke says, as if he could read Malin's mind.

"Fuck, no. It must be at least a hundred and fifteen degrees up here."

Cries and shouting from the fire, two low banks of smoke separating, and a woman, the same height as Malin, with soot-blackened clothes and a filthy, smeared face emerges between two charred maples.

"Slavenca Visnic, I presume," Zeke says.

"At your disposal, I guess," the woman says.

36

They rarely come at night, the explosions, but occasionally they do, ripping the children from sleep, and I have to hold Miro's little three-year-old body close to mine, Kranska in her dad's arms, her frightened eyes staring at me, as if I could save her if the will of God directed the Serbs' grenades at our flat, our house.

Distant explosions, getting closer.

Making the floorboards creak.

My son's warm skin against mine under the blanket, I can feel it through his pajamas, just like I can hear his heart racing, and the rhythm reminds me of my own inadequacy, because he knows that not even his mum can cure real fear. All four of us are sitting in bed together, sleep is impossible, but we're breathing together, our breath mingling and becoming one, and even though the war raging out there is merciless, elevated to the status of a religion, we still believe that nothing can touch us, that we're safe in our cocoon, spun of love and dreams, our home.

One day at the market.

The rifles on Sniper Alley missed me on the way home.

But an incendiary grenade had struck the roof of the building, burrowing down two floors and exploding in the flat below ours, and the flames must have consumed you quickly from beneath and the whole building was a blazing torch when I returned. People held me, their hot hands hard against my body and I wanted to go in, in to you, because I knew you were burning in there, and I wanted to burn with you.

Not even the slightest trace of you was left.

Nothing.

The phosphorous fire of an incendiary grenade really is that mercilessly hot. I slept on the charred remains of our love and our dreams, I slept there one night, trying to remember your smells, your sounds, faces, and voices, the way your skin felt, but all I could feel was the stinging smell of fire and ash, all I could hear was the sound of rifle fire and howitzers as they continued their mournful song.

I woke the next morning with cold rain beating against my bare neck. I walked right into the forest, not caring if I got shot or caught up in the front line, and the clouds hung over the hills and captured me after a few miles.

Their touch, the men's touch, didn't exist, no matter what they did to me, and what they planted inside me was a monster, nothing more.

I lay on a floor and everything that wasn't light was dark, the world yellow-black, yet still completely colorless.

I wanted them to kill me.

But how could they do that? I was already dead. And in my dreams your faces, your voices would come.

Go, Mum, go. Your path isn't finished yet. And I loved and hated you because I was alive, because you came from your new place just to tell me that.

I wanted to be with you, weave a new cocoon of impenetrable, everlasting love. I wanted to weave warm threads of love around your three hearts, to bring them back, to make them beat forever.

37

"Who'd live in a fucking dump like this?"

As Waldemar Ekenberg says this he yanks open the door of a block of flats in Ekholmen.

In the car on the way there:

"So how are we going to play this?"

Per Sundsten can hear the influence of English on his Swedish, hates the way his language is tainted by American cop shows.

Waldemar's voice smoother now, focused.

"There's no point pussyfooting around with Pakis like them. They've got a low pain threshold, so we just apply pressure."

"Apply pressure?"

"Yeah, you know."

Per knew. His older colleague's racist vocabulary, his generalizations about the people they were on their way to see, all of this upset him, but he said nothing, this wasn't the time to worry about that sort of thing, the crimes so serious that everything else could wait, and sometimes they were obliged to step onto the wrong side of the law to uphold it, it's been like that in every culture, in all ages, ever since Hammurabi inscribed his eye for eye, tooth for tooth.

I'm not naïve, Per thinks, just not as cynical as the man he had realized that Waldemar was during the course of the day.

In itself, there was nothing wrong with cynicism.

But the prejudices. You could get by fine without them. Everybody has a dirty streak, as Per likes to put it, no one's entirely blameless, no matter what their background or skin color.

The block of flats in Ekholmen where Behzad Karami's parents live.

Graffiti on the walls, badly sprayed tags on peeling paint.

And this was where Behzad Karami is supposed to have been at a party on the night that Josefin Davidsson was attacked. His parents live on the first floor, no lift.

Sundsten and Ekenberg ring the doorbell.

A pause.

A chain on the door.

A woman's face through the gap.

Waldemar is panting beside Per, out of breath from the stairs, says "POLICE!" as he holds up his ID.

"Let us in," he says, and his voice leaves no room for doubt, and the door closes and then opens again.

"I bet you're growing potatoes in the living room," Waldemar says, and laughs. "Either that or cannabis, eh?"

In the living room there's a large, black leather sofa along one wall, heavy curtains, deep-red velvet, hanging by the windows, garish paintings of Tehran on the patterned brown wallpaper.

"Looks like a brothel," Waldemar says to the dark-skinned man sitting on the sofa. Per thinks that the man looks ready to be bullied, must know why they're there, but also that he's been lying, trying to deceive them. Per can see the lies in the tension in his face, the look in his eyes, not anxious, just restless, the way a liar's eyes look. He has a pleasant face, his features serene in spite of his large nose and what look like acne scars on his cheeks. He isn't a large man, and the home gives the impression of being well kept, cherished, and Per imagines that Ekenberg has noticed the same thing, and that that's where he's going to focus his violence.

"Sit down, why don't you?" Waldemar says to Karami's wife in a thick Östergötland accent, and she sinks down, and her thin body, swathed in shiny dark cloth, seems to disappear into the sofa.

"Well, then." And without further ado Waldemar picks up a vase from the top of the television and throws it at the wall, sending shards of porcelain across the room, over the faces and clothes of the Karamis.

The woman cries something unintelligible in Arabic or Persian or whatever it is.

The man:

"What the hell are you doing?"

And Waldemar picks up a family photograph, drops it on the floor, and crushes it with the heel of his heavy shoes.

"Shut up!" he shouts. "You don't get away unpunished if you lie to the police."

"Am I supposed to have lied to you?"

Per is standing silently in the doorway, wants to intervene, tell Waldemar that that's enough, to pull himself together, this isn't how we do things, but he can see from Karami that he's close to breaking, that he's fond of his possessions.

"Your son," Waldemar yells. "He wasn't here the night Josefin Davidsson was raped, as you claimed! I bet there wasn't even a family party going on at all. So where was he? What was he doing? NOW!"

A samovar flies into the radiator under the window onto the balcony, a clanking sound as the thin metal breaks.

"Do you think I'd betray my son? He was here. We had a party."

And Waldemar overturns the coffee table with a force that shocks Per, then he's in front of Arash Karami, striking him across the nose and causing little trickles of blood to pour from both nostrils.

"Do you really imagine I haven't had to deal with worse than this? Well? This is nothing."

Karami's words are scornful when he's collected himself again. He spits at Waldemar, his eyes full of deep loathing.

And Waldemar strikes again, then again, and Per is about to jump in and stop him when the wife starts yelling on the sofa, in heavily accented Swedish.

"He wasn't here. We had a party, but he never came. We don't know what he does, but he never comes here anymore. Find him, and tell him to come home more often."

Waldemar calms down, stopping just before dealing a fourth blow.

"So you don't know what he gets up to?"

The Karamis sit in silence, Arash Karami's left hand pressing the bridge of his nose, trying to stem the flow of blood.

Neither of them answers Waldemar's question.

"Do you know what? I believe you. You haven't the faintest idea what your Paki son does, because he does some completely fucked-up stuff. Doesn't he? Christ, you can't even raise your own kids properly."

Waldemar heads toward the door, Per takes a step back, says in a calm voice:

"You realize there's no point reporting this. There are two of us who can confirm that Arash put up a struggle when we tried to take him to the station for questioning."

The wife is sitting in tears on the sofa, and Arash Karami doesn't even deign to look at them.

"Fucking towelheads," Waldemar says. "Lying to the police."

Outside the building, in the relentless heat from a sun that seems to have gone mad, Waldemar says to Per: "That went well, you playing good cop, me bad cop. And we didn't even plan it in advance."

Really bloody well, Per thinks, suddenly feeling sick.

But.

They got what they wanted.

Per feels his face getting hot, the same feeling as when his mother found out he'd been stealing from her purse when he was little.

Brutality.

In the course of his few short years as a police officer he's seen it all too often.

38

How does anyone survive what Slavenca Visnic has been through without losing their mind?

Abuse running like a poisonous thread through history. Does violence stem from abuse? Is time really a sort of volcanic ground which regularly erupts into violence? Huge explosions, with smaller intermittent sighs.

Maybe, Malin thinks, as she watches Slavenca Visnic's Fiat van disappear among the cars along the gravel road through the ash-covered forest.

Slavenca Visnic hadn't been surprised to see her and Zeke appear in the forest, and had been completely open with them, as if she had nothing to hide, as if the fact that one of the victims had been found near her kiosk in Stavsätter and another victim had worked for her was in no way compromising.

Once Slavenca Visnic had said hello to them she washed herself with water from a grayish-white container that she had brought with her, scrubbing the soot from her face with strongly scented detergent as Malin and Zeke waited. Slavenca Visnic was demonstrating with her actions that she worked to her own agenda, and neither Malin nor Zeke protested. Malin coughed as the smoke irritated her eyes and nose. Once the dirt was gone from Slavenca Visnic's face you could see that she must once have been beautiful, but that was long ago now, as experience and work had aged her prematurely.

"I realized that you'd want to talk to me," Slavenca Visnic said once she'd finished washing and had put on a clean T-shirt. Firefighters and volunteers were running past them, dragging hoses and steaming blankets. Helicopters were still circling overhead, and the relentless sound of the rotors made them raise their voices.

"You know," Slavenca Visnic said, "it's like the fire comes from under the ground, like the flames and embers are bubbling up from the center of the earth."

Malin noted that she spoke almost without any trace of an accent, thinking: You must have fought really hard for that.

Slavenca Visnic took a drink of water from her water bottle.

"Thirsty?"

"No," Zeke said, before going on: "You know why we're here?"

"I see the papers and the Internet, I listen to the news. I'm not stupid."

"Theresa Eckeved was found buried at the beach where you've got one of your kiosks. Josefin Davidsson, who was found raped in the Horticultural Society Park, worked for you at the start of July."

"I can understand why the connection would interest you," Slavenca Visnic said, wiping some beads of sweat from her forehead. "But there's nothing behind the connection. Nothing at all."

"Have you got alibis for the night between Wednesday and Thursday last week, and the night between Saturday and Sunday?"

Malin wanted to see if a direct question would rouse any reaction.

Slavenca Visnic laughed.

"No, I'm always alone in the evenings, but I got home late from the fires, so someone can prove where I was then, but not during the night. You can't think I had anything to do with this?"

Fresh laughter.

Almost mocking, as if Zeke and Malin knew pathetically little of the evil that Slavenca Visnic had encountered in excess.

"What about last night?"

"I was at home, sleeping. I've shut the kiosks for the time being. I want to help fight the fires. And it's impossible to get staff. No teenager wants to spend the summer standing in a kiosk selling ice cream. They're spoiled, the whole lot of them. Just look at Josefin Davidsson, she gave up after just three days, and that left me without anyone for Glyttinge."

"Did it annoy you when she gave up?"

Zeke's voice practically neutral.

"Stupid question. Everyone can do as they like. Can't they?"

"Within the bounds of the law," Zeke replied.

"I heard about the latest murder on the radio," Slavenca Visnic said. "And I can tell you straight that you won't find any connection with that girl."

"You like fire? Is that why you want to help out here?"

Malin's turn to be provocative.

"I hate fire. I want to eradicate it."

Flattery, Malin. That makes them talk.

Another of Sven's mantras.

"I know what you've been through," Malin said. "And I admire the fact that you're standing here now. That you've built up your own business."

"I didn't have a choice."

"You didn't notice anything suspicious out at Stavsätter? Anything at all?"

"Nothing. Until that dog started digging her up."

"You were there then," Zeke said. "Then you vanished. Where did you go? Most people would have stayed."

"I couldn't bear all those upset people. And I've seen dead bodies before. It was better to open up in Hjulsbro instead. The girl in the ground didn't exactly make people want to buy anything."

Slavenca Visnic more friendly now. "As I'm sure you can understand. When I work, I just want to sell as many ice creams as I can."

"You didn't see anyone behaving suspiciously on the beach at Stavsätter?"

Slavenca Visnic thought about it.

"No."

"And you can't tell us anything about Josefin Davidsson? Did you have an argument? That was what she implied."

"She probably thought I argued with her. I'm sure she was taking ice cream and sweets, maybe she was giving them away to her friends. I lost a lot of stock on the days that she worked, even though there weren't many people about then. If you remember, they had a problem with bacteria in the pool? The *Correspondent* made a big deal of it. They had to shut the pool for a few days."

Malin tried to remember the article, but it must have passed her by.

"So she got the sack?"

"Let's put it this way: I was pleased she resigned, even though she was the only person I had for the Glyttinge pool."

"Did the fact that she was stealing make you angry?"

"No, not at all. That sort of thing just happens."

"And there's no one who can give you an alibi?"

Malin asked again, she knew where she wanted to go with the question, and Slavenca Visnic gave her a long, weary look, as if to show that she knew what game they were playing.

"I have no husband. No children. I lost my family a long time ago. Since then I've made up my mind to look after myself. Other people just mean a whole lot of disappointment, Detective Inspector."

Slavenca Visnic closed the back doors of the Fiat.

Turned to face them.

"If you haven't got any more questions, I think I'll head off now. Make the most of the busiest time of day at the Glyttinge pool."

"Blue," Malin says. "Does the color blue mean anything particular to you?"

"I like white," Slavenca Visnic replied. "The purest color."

Slavenca Visnic is standing by the hotdog kiosk in Ljungsbro, eating a cheeseburger. She realized how hungry she was as she was driving away from the forest, past Vreta Kloster golf club.

The hot food and hot air are making her sweat, but she doesn't

mind the heat; anyone who lived through the wartime winters in Sarajevo knows what real cold is, and would never complain about a bit
of heat.

The town is quiet around her. Everyone's probably gone to the
beach.

The cops could think what they liked about her. They think they
can put everything right; the woman, Malin Fors, in particular gave
the impression that she wants to put everything right.

And then I show up in their investigation.

Connections.

The lifeline of their work.

It had to happen sooner or later, Slavenca Visnic thinks, feeling the
melted cheese sticking to her teeth as her stomach fills with food: the
ridiculous privilege of being able to eat your fill when you're hungry,
a privilege that few people in this country could ever understand or
appreciate.

The girls.

Things like that happen. Spoiled little girls can get their fingers
burned. Who knows why anyone does what they do?

War, it's everywhere, and it never ends.

All you can do as a human being is to try to create a reality for
yourself that you can live with.

Slavenca Visnic throws the last of the burger in the bin by the
kiosk counter. Gets in her car and drives away. Outside the big supermarket the newspaper fly sheets are all talking about the same thing.

"Summertime death strikes again!"

That's what the Correspondent's *fly sheet says about the fate that
got me.*

*Our summer angels, that's what the radio presenter with the warm
voice calls me, us.*

I didn't want to believe it at first.

*But then you came, Sofia, gliding toward me, around me, in a thou-
sand different ways at once, and you told me that you doubted it at first,*

*that fear and other feelings, many of them nameless, meant that you re-
fused to accept your situation at first, that you wanted to scream: not me,
I'm too young, I haven't had a chance to live, and now I want to scream it
too, now as we drift here together above the burning forests.*

The smoke and fires.

The burning treetops are a volcano.

*The machines and people and animals are like little pinpricks of de-
spair down there, fragments of life trying to stop the flames taking over,
trying to force the destructive power back into the meandering badgers'
tunnels under the ground.*

Is their struggle succeeding?

*Malin in the Volvo heading along the road down there on the surface,
down toward Ljungsbro, out onto the withered plain where soon all plant
life will have shriveled into soft fossils of what could once have been verdant life.*

You seem to trust her, Theresa.

If you trust her, then so do I.

*You said it had got easier for you now, now that there are two of us.
But for me everything is still so hard, even if I seem to have been less distraught about my state than you.*

*We drift side by side, wingless, but it still seems to fit, somehow, this
idea of us being summer angels. Unquiet angels, not your standard book-
mark angels, but girls who somehow want to get back what was taken
away from them.*

We're clean now, aren't we?

*I like words. The way they're mine now. And I like drifting in a world
that can be free of memories for as long as I like, as long as I manage
to keep my thoughts away from those hands, those white hands as they
squeezed my neck, and the scrubbing that I could still somehow feel, and
the smell of bleach, the fear I had time to feel before everything disappeared, only to reappear again, albeit in a far more unfathomable way.*

I want to remember who I was, who I could have become.

Older.

I am.

But never will be.

*   *   *

"Zeke. Hypnosis can make you remember things, can't it?"

His hands have a firm grip of the steering wheel as they drive past IKEA and the retail warehouses out at Tornby. She reaches for the stereo, turning down the choral music. The people in the parking lots are moving slowly in the sun, but are still heading determinedly toward the air-conditioning of the shops.

"So they say. But I've never heard of us ever using that method. It sounds a bit dodgy, if you ask me."

"But this isn't a joke. It could work."

"I know what you're thinking, Malin."

"We only have access to five percent of our memories, at most," Malin says.

"Have you been watching the Discovery Channel again?"

"Shut up, Zeke."

He grins at her.

"Hands on the wheel, eyes on the road."

"Aye, aye, Captain," Zeke says. "I'll try to remember that."

39

"So, you little black-haired worm," Waldemar Ekenberg says as he pushes Behzad Karami up against the wall of his one-room flat. "Did you really think you'd get away with lying to the police? One of your so-called friends has ratted on you. What were you doing last night? The night between Wednesday and Thursday, the night between Saturday and Sunday? You raped and murdered them. Didn't you?"

Behzad Karami still cocky.

Still convinced he can handle this.

But you're in the shit, Per Sundsten thinks. He's going to beat everything he wants to know out of you.

"Did you get a taste for little girls when you gangbanged that fourteen-year-old last winter? Huh?"

"We didn't—"

Waldemar pushes Behzad Karami back, thumping him against the wall again.

Then his voice softens:

"Don't try that with me. You know you raped those girls. Did you get a taste for it? And then it went wrong? And you ended up killing—?"

His voice gets louder with every word and then he punches Behzad Karami in the stomach. He folds in half like a switchblade.

Behzad Karami gradually collapses down the wall, and Waldemar takes a few steps back, his pupils enlarged from the adrenaline.

"I need a piss," he says. "Keep an eye on this sack of shit for me."

Behzad Karami gasps for air, finds it, and takes five deep breaths before turning to look imploringly at Per.

Don't look at me, Per thinks. I can't do a thing to stop him, I don't want to, because what if he's right?

"It would be best if you just told him what you were doing," Per says in his very gentlest voice. "Christ, he even scares me. And he never gives up."

"He's mad."

"Come on. Tell us. Then everything will feel better."

"Will you believe me?"

"That depends."

"On what?"

Behzad Karami is panting, but the color has returned to his face.

"On whether you're telling the truth."

"You wouldn't believe me if I told you the truth."

"I suppose you'll just have to try us."

Per looks down at Behzad Karami, bent, but not yet broken.

"Try us," Per says, and then Waldemar is back in the room again.

"So, the little shit has found his senses again, has he? Good. I'll just have to see to it that he loses them again."

"Do what the fuck you like."

"I'm going to," Waldemar says, then kicks hard twice at Behzad Karami's left shoulder, and Per sees the shoulder dislocate under the yellow and red T-shirt, and the scream that rises to the ceiling of the room and squeezes out through the window is full of primal pain, a scream of self-preservation crackling out from the core of the brain, out through the larynx and tongue.

"So it hurts, then," Waldemar whispers into the ear of the whimpering, recumbent Behzad Karami. He puts his arm on his shoulder, gently, and presses down slightly, and Behzad Karami screams again, not so loudly this time, and Per can see from his whole bearing that he's close to collapse.

Why resist?

Because that's your role?

Because you did it?

"Wait, I'll tell you, I'll show you my secret."

Behzad Karami is sitting on the sofa with his left arm twisted backward, over the back of the sofa.

Waldemar behind him.

"Don't make a fuss, you little shit."

And Waldemar pulls Behzad Karami's arm back, and there's a clicking, meaty sound as the shoulder pops back in, and the scream that comes from Behzad Karami's mouth is as primal as before, but this time contains the relief of an entire body.

"Fucking wimp."

Waldemar grins.

Per wants to get out of the flat, go home, wants this day to be over, but it isn't over, not yet, not by a long way.

The warm, gray-black water of the Stångån River.

The fish sluggish, lethargic down there, maybe they can feel their flesh changing form as the temperature of the water rises, Per Sundsten thinks.

Nowhere to flee. And if the heat is almost making the water stop being water, then what do the fish do? Float up to the surface, lifeless, swollen guts upmost, the shiny silver of their scales dulled by the murky liquid.

The football pitches of Johannelund, their netless goals waiting for a cooler season, until someone feels like kicking a ball again, it's too hot now, impossible, dangerous.

"If I show you, you have to believe me. I've got nothing to do with any of that shit."

Behzad Karami in handcuffs in the backseat of the car. They're on their way to the allotments in Johannelund, down by the river. That was where he wanted to take them, refusing to explain why.

"Nothing to do with any of that shit."

The words echo in Per's head as they walk along the well-tended gravel path that weaves between the allotments. The water sprinklers are working overtime, trying to keep the grass lawns green, and save the currants and gooseberries as best they can. The allotment owners are hiding in the shade of parasols or under the porches of their colorful little cottages.

That shit.

If you reduce murder and violence to shit you can handle it, and that means you can live with whatever you or someone else has done. Live with the fact that we human beings occasionally choose to treat our fellows in that way.

Waldemar calm.

Behzad Karami asked to be let out of the handcuffs up by the car, and Waldemar agreed to his request.

"If you run, I'll shoot you."

His voice ice-cold, and Behzad Karami nodded.

"Not that I have any idea what you want to show us here."

Waldemar more skeptical with every step.

"You'd better have something for us."

"I've got something for you," Behzad Karami says as he speeds up. "We're heading to the last plot, down on the left."

Hot, Per thinks as he treads along a sunny section of the path. Unhealthily hot, and Ekenberg is sweating alongside him, yet still largely unaffected by the heat.

An old man of steel.

Made by a dark, one-track steel that's no longer manufactured.

Then Behzad Karami opens the gate to the last allotment on the left. The grass is less well kept, the cottage an untouched white-painted shack, apparently uninhabited.

They go into the small plot, and Per notices the pedantically well-kept flower beds, the bushes, they look like raspberry canes, and they're planted in perfect rows, no mature fruit yet.

"There."

Behzad Karami points at the bushes.

"What do you mean, 'there'?"

Per wants to get his question in before Waldemar loses his grip.

"I was here those nights when you wanted to know what I was doing."

It's going to blow, here it comes, Per thinks, Waldemar's going to go mad. But instead he sighs, and there's no violence.

"These are my blackberry bushes. I grow blackberries, when I was little back in Tehran my grandfather used to take me to the souk with him and eat blackberries. I wanted to grow my own, it makes me feel better, sort of. A good feeling in my stomach. Like when I was little with Grandfather, just the two of us."

"So you were here watering them?"

Per skeptical.

"No, guarding them."

"Guarding them?"

"Yes, otherwise the deer eat the berries before they're ripe. I was sitting in the cottage, on guard. They jump over the fence and eat the berries."

"You were on guard?"

"Yes."

"Alone?"

"Yes."

"And you haven't told anyone about this?"

"No."

"Why not?"

"I bought the allotment with my own money."

"But why couldn't you tell anyone?"

"That I'm growing blackberries? My mates would think I'd gone mad, that I was queer or something."

"Queer?"

"Everybody knows that only queers grow things."

They watch Behzad Karami's back as he disappears along the path up to the parking lot.

"I believe him," Waldemar says.

"But it still isn't a proper alibi."

Then they go from allotment to allotment, asking if anyone saw Behzad Karami in his shack, and several confirm that they've seen light from the cottage in recent nights, but they haven't been able to tell if it was him inside.

Behzad Karami showed them the cottage before they let him go.

Hardly any furniture, just an IKEA bed in one corner, no mattress or sheets or pillow, just a gray blanket neatly folded at one end. The bare yellow floorboards covered in burn marks from cigarettes, the air inside as dense and suffocating as a freshly gutted elk's stomach during the autumn hunt.

"Blackberries," Per says as they get back to the car. "Can it really be that simple?"

"Everyone knows that," Waldemar says. "Arabs are crazy about blackberries. It's because they can't drink and don't get enough pussy."

40

"Mum?"

Tove's voice from thousands of miles away, the sound like a mirage in Malin's inner ear, loss which time and distance are making more like grief with each passing minute.

"Mum, are you there?"

The living room closes around Malin, the weather forecast promising heat, heat, heat. Don't want you to call, Tove, don't want that, can't you and Dad get it into your thick heads, into your wonderful, cherished hearts, I don't want you to call several times a day?

"I'm here, Tove. I'm here."

And Malin slumps onto the sofa, turning down the volume of the television with her free hand.

"Mum, is everything okay?"

I'm the one who's supposed to ask that, Malin thinks.

"Yes, everything's fine, darling. How are things with you?"

Wants to say: You're flying home tomorrow morning. I'll pick you up. But she lets Tove talk.

"We went to an elephant farm today, outside a city in the middle of the jungle called Ubud."

"Did you have a ride?"

"We both did, Dad and me."

"And you're back at the hotel again now?"

"Yes, we've just got back from a fish restaurant. It's already one o'clock in the morning. We went swimming today as well. It wasn't too windy, so the yellow flag was out. The undercurrents aren't so dangerous then."

Undercurrents.

Dangerous.

They've been in Bali two weeks, but Tove is already talking as if she's lived there half her life.

"Take care when you go swimming."

"Of course I take care. What do you think?"

"I'm just worried, Tove."

A deep sigh from the other side of the world.

"There's no need, Mum. We won't have time to go swimming again. Do you want to talk to Dad?"

"If he wants to."

Crackling on the line, calls in the background from someone who must be Janne, then breathing, long breaths that she knows all too well, which for a second send a warmth through her body, a resigned, sad, but still excited warmth.

Janne.

You bastard.

Why, why couldn't we make it?

"Hi, Malin."

His voice, what does she want from it? Solace? Context. Even though the voice can't give her that.

"How are you both?"

"Paradise exists, Malin. Here."

"I believe you. So you're not looking forward to coming home?"

"Not exactly."

"You went for a ride on elephants?"

"Yes, you should have seen her. Beaming with joy as she bounced along."

Enough, Malin thinks. No more now.

"How are the fires?"

"We were out there today," Malin says. "It looks pretty bad, not under control yet. But there are a lot of volunteers helping out."

"Our flight leaves bloody early tomorrow morning," Janne says.

"I know," Malin says. "And you're still up so late," wanting to say: I miss you so much my heart feels like it's withering away. My loss is turning into grief, Janne, a strange grief for the living, and every human being can only cope with a fixed amount of grief before they die, and mine is close to overflowing. But instead she says:

"Make sure you check in on time."

"Okay. We'd better get to bed now."

"Bye."

A click on the line.

Silence. Warmth.

Solace and context. What can give me that?

Malin had planned to wait until tomorrow, but rings Viveka Crafoord now.

"Come on over. You've got half an hour. We can put off lighting the barbecue for a bit."

Viveka Crafoord.

Psychoanalyst.

She wants to treat Malin, free of charge, but the very thought of Viveka's paisley-patterned chaise longue frightens Malin. She can't bear the thought of touching even the edges of her sadness, let alone its innermost core. So instead there's a bit of vague talk about her parents in Tenerife whenever she and Viveka bump into each other in the city and go for coffee. The fact that she doesn't miss them. Their apartment. Her mother's cheap rugs and ability to dress up her own life, making herself look more important than she is. Viveka polite, listening with interest, but convinced that Malin is just skimming the surface, and is stubbornly and suspiciously holding shut all the doors that lead inside her.

"And what do you think Janne thinks?"

Viveka had asked.

"About what?"

"Well, about the way you talk to him, for instance?"

"I've never given it much thought."

Viveka's country cottage is in Svartmåla, a sought-after, middle-class village some six miles south of the city.

Malin had trouble finding the house, meandering around the idyllic cottages in the Volvo, unwilling to stop and ask the way.

Then she came to a little turning down toward the lake, its shimmering water ice white and fiery pink beyond pines and firs.

A simple green mailbox bearing the name CRAFOORD in the shade of some tall maples.

Malin turned off, and couldn't help smiling as she pulled up in front of the obviously bespoke, architect-designed house with its two irregular floors, lots of glass, gray-stained wood. The house looked like a prototype for the sort of tasteful, costly-but-restrained architecture that people who are used to having money love. Viveka's house must be the most exclusive in the area. And with the best location, right on the water, presumably with its own jetty and beach.

"A microclimate," Viveka says, leaning back in the teak bench. "Don't ask me how it happens."

They're sitting at the back of the house, on an airy terrace with a view of the lake, Stora Rängen. Perennials and rhododendrons are crowding in on Viveka's husband, Hjalmar, as he stands at the barbecue with his broad back to them some ten yards away, on green-stained decking laid over gray Öland stone. It's undeniably cooler on the terrace, maybe five degrees lower than anywhere else, as if the greenery and water in the vicinity somehow magically lowered the temperature.

Just like the summerhouse in the Horticultural Society Park, Malin thinks.

But in there it was hotter.

Malin was right, below a granite outcrop is a motorboat tied up at a jetty, and two designer aluminum chaises longues on a man-made beach. Malin breathes in the smell of marinated pork sizzling on the hot grill. Bean salad on the table in front of them. She runs her arm over the teak armrest of her chair, its oiled, polished finish making her feel calm.

What does your husband do? Malin wonders. But she doesn't ask Viveka.

She just thinks how nice this huge man with the gentle face is. Then she looks into Viveka's face, hardly any wrinkles even though she must be fifty-five or so, no traces of grief, the signs of a good life. And Malin is struck by how little she actually knows about her. Do they have children? Then there is the fact that she has been welcomed out here in spite of the reason for her visit.

"So what do you think about what I said on the phone?"

She had explained about the case she was working on, and of course Viveka had read the paper, seen the news on television. "I'd like to hear your thoughts about the perpetrator."

"Let's eat first."

And shortly after that a dish of plump sausages and pork chops appears on the table, and they talk about the heat and drink a robust, sweet red wine that suits the meat perfectly. Just one glass for Malin, and Hjalmar becomes nicer with every word, and he explains that he works as a management consultant, freelance after many years with McKinsey in Stockholm.

And then the meal is over as quickly as it began and Hjalmar withdraws: "There's a match on." And Viveka throws out her arms, saying: "He's mad about football."

And Malin realizes that darkness has fallen over the terrace and that the only light over the lake is the glow of the moon, and the hopeful lights of a few houses on the far shore.

The approach of night seems to whisper to them, and Malin lets Viveka talk:

"I'm sorry, Malin. From what little I know, it's impossible for me to say anything specific. I did a course on profiling when we lived in Seattle, and I'd guess you're dealing with something of a loner who has a complicated relationship with his mother. But that's almost always the case. He lives in Linköping, probably grew up here, seeing as he seems to feel safe in the places where he commits these acts and leaves his victims. And he's obsessed with cleanliness and making his victims appear pure. But you've already worked that out for yourself. But why this obsession with cleanliness? Something to do with virginity? Who knows? Maybe this individual feels sullied somehow. Violated. Sexually. Or some other way. Maybe he's trying to recreate a form of innocence."

"Anything else? You say he, but could it be a woman?"

"Possibly. But it's probably a man, or a masculine woman. Maybe themselves the victim of abuse. There's always that possibility."

"And the wounds?"

"The fact that they're different might suggest that the perpetrator is finding his way by trial and error. As if he or she wants to come up with some sort of formula."

"That thought had occurred to me as well."

"If I were you, I'd start looking into the histories of people who've cropped up since things started to heat up. The key to this is in the past. As to why this is happening now, only they can know that. That's if they even know."

Malin's mobile rings.

She looks at the display. Wants to take the call, but leaves it, brushes it aside. Viveka doesn't comment on her behavior, and merely says: "He probably has a job, but few friends."

"Thanks, Viveka," Malin says.

Then she brings up the real reason she's there.

"If I wanted to question a witness under hypnosis, would you be prepared to be responsible for it?"

"Of course I would, Malin."

For the first time Malin sees Viveka look excited, expectant.

"As long as the witness agrees, I wouldn't have a problem with it."

They sit in silence.

Some broken laughter across the water, and the sound of splashing.

"Take a swim," Viveka says. "You can borrow a suit from me. You can stay the night. In the guest cottage. Hjalmar makes really good scrambled eggs for breakfast."

Malin thinks for a moment.

The number on her phone.

"I'd love a swim. But then I have to get home."

And the memory of the warm water of Stora Rängen courses through her as one hour later she is lying in Daniel Högfeldt's bed and feeling his hard, heavy, rhythmic body above hers, how he thrusts, groans, thrusts, thrusts hard and deep inside her, how she becomes water, no feelings, memories, or future, directionless drops, a body that is a still night of dreams worth dreaming, an explosion that is sometimes the only thing a human being's trillions of cells need.

If only to be able to put up with themselves.

41

His skin.

It's glowing as if it's been oiled in the thin dawn light forcing its way in through the gap at the bottom of the roller blind. When she came to him last night she didn't say a word, silently pushing him toward the bedroom, and now she is leaving just as soundlessly, getting dressed in his hallway, silently so as not to wake him.

Because what would she say to him?

That was nice?

Do you want to go to the cinema?

A romantic dinner, just the two of us?

He's lying there, just a few feet away, but he's still present within her as a feeling, a closeness, yet also distance.

A dildo.

A double distance. It must be like being filled with something that has nothing to do with human life, it must be the perfect tool for someone who wants movement, yet who also wants to stay where they are.

Malin leaves Daniel Högfeldt's flat, creeping through the hall, convinced he's awake somewhere behind her.

*   *   *

I hear you leave, Malin. Let you leave.

The bedroom is hot and the damp of our bodies is still in the sheets, the sweat under me both yours and mine.

Trying to get you to stay would be impossible. What could I say? Would I even be able to sound like I meant what I said? You're too complicated for me, Malin. Too many contradictions, far too smart.

Obvious and straightforward.

Like a pane of glass on a summer's day.

And a bit stupid, but with a good heart. That's the kind of woman I want. Unless the truth is the exact opposite. That I want you. But I don't know how to say it. Either to you, or to myself.

Home, shower, drink coffee, change clothes, miss Tove, Janne, enough regret to make her sick, and before she knows what's happened Karim is standing by a whiteboard summarizing that state of the investigation into the attack of Josefin Davidsson and the murders of Theresa Eckeved and Sofia Fredén.

Tove's coming home tonight.

I want to focus on that, Malin thinks. But it will have to wait.

The morning meeting, nine o'clock as usual.

The detectives in the room tired, their faces somehow furrowed by the summer heat and the violence, the human actions that it's their job to get to grips with. If not to understand then to make reasonably manageable, and contextualize them for both the public and themselves.

"The press is going crazy," Karim says. "They're crying out for information about the case, but we can't let ourselves be influenced by that. So, where shall we start? How are things going with the various lines of inquiry?"

"We questioned Behzad Karami and his parents yesterday," Waldemar Ekenberg says. "The anonymous tip-off was right. They were lying about the family party. Behzad claims he was standing guard over his blackberry canes in an allotment down by the river, and I think he's telling the truth, even if there are no witnesses who can state categorically that he was there. But they've seen lights on in the small cottage on the allotment on the nights in question."

"What about you, Sundsten?"

Sven Sjöman pants as he says the words, his face deep red.

"It seems to make sense."

"Seems?"

"We can't be absolutely certain. But the likelihood is that it's the truth. We're waiting to hear who made the call claiming that Behzad was involved. We really need to talk to them."

"So how are we going to get hold of them?"

"With difficulty. But Telia is trying to give us the location the call was made from. It was on their network, and we might be able to draw some conclusions based on people we know who are acquainted with Behzad. They're pretty familiar faces to you here in Linköping, after all."

"Good. What about the list of known sex offenders?"

"We got hold of three more of them yesterday. All in the clear."

"And nothing new about the person who called in about Josefin Davidsson?"

"No," Malin says. "That feels like a thousand years ago now."

"In all likelihood it was just a passerby who didn't want anything to do with us," Sven says, before going on:

"Okay. Well, the news from Mjölby is that the interviews with Sofia Fredén's parents and close friends haven't turned up anything. Sofia seems to have been an ambitious young woman, good at school, never involved in anything stupid. And Forensics hasn't come up with anything from the crime scene. But we'd guessed as much, hadn't we? Whoever is doing this is pedantically clean and careful. There were traces of bleach on Sofia Fredén's body. And the traces of paint found in her vagina are identical to those found in the earlier victims. And the cause of death was strangulation. Forensics is looking at her computer, and the lists of calls to and from her mobile are on their way."

Sven lets his words sink in.

Nothing is easy in this case, they're not getting anything for free.

"And still nothing from Facebook or Yahoo! They seem to be mainly concerned with protecting the confidentiality of their clients."

"There's nothing we can do to pressure them? What about the courts?" Zeke wonders.

"We could certainly make a legal request. But they could always appeal. And it's hard to know where the information would be. Who do you hold responsible for a server on the Cayman Islands?"

Sven changes the subject.

"As far as the dildo is concerned, Forensics has ruled out three hundred and fifty models. That's if it even *is* a dildo."

"What about Sofia Fredén's wounds?" Zeke asks. "Has Karin been able to say exactly what caused them?"

"Animal claws. But apparently it's impossible to say which animal."

"Louise Svensson keeps rabbits on her farm," Malin says. "And rabbits have claws."

"Loads of people in this city have rabbits and other animals with claws," Sven says. "And you can buy those necklaces of animal claws at any market."

Malin nods.

"I know, it was a long shot."

"Anything else?"

Sven turns to face Malin and Zeke.

"We spoke to Slavenca Visnic," Malin says. "And there's a connection between her and two of the girls. She has no alibi, but we haven't got anything concrete."

Malin explains the connections, that Theresa was found near one of the kiosks and that Josefin had worked at another one, which could mean something to the case, or could just as easily be coincidence, even if that would be unusual.

"It makes me uneasy," Malin says.

"Synchronicity has driven loads of officers mad," Per Sundsten says. "Connections that exist but which turn out to be completely meaningless. So where do we go with that?"

"We'll bear it in mind, but we carry on working without any preconceptions."

"Hard-core police work," Zeke says. "That's what counts now."

"I'd like to talk to Theresa Eckeved's friend Nathalie Falck again,"

Malin says. "It feels like she's not telling us everything we ought to know. Maybe she'll talk now, seeing as things have got worse. I don't think we'd get anything more from Peter Sköld, her supposed boyfriend."

"Talk to her," Karim says. "From where we are now, we've got nothing to lose."

"And we've just received the file about Louise 'Lollo' Svensson from the archive," Zeke says, and Malin gives him an angry glance, wondering why he hadn't mentioned it.

"Calm down, Malin," Zeke says. "No need to get excited," and the others laugh, and the laughter relieves the tension in the room, making the sense of hopelessness less tangible, as they seem to clamber one circle higher away from the investigative hell they are all in.

"I only got them five minutes before the meeting. Otherwise I would have shown you first."

Zeke usually gets annoyed when Malin goes off on her own track, and on the rare occasions when he has done so she gets unreasonably cross, cursing him and behaving like an unfairly treated child.

"I wouldn't dare do anything else," and now they're all laughing again, at my expense, Malin thinks, but there's warmth in their laughter, a pleasant warmth, not like this tormenting summer heat. And Malin thinks they could do with this laughter, she needs it, needs to hear that someone isn't taking this so incredibly seriously.

"Shut up, Zeke," and by now even Sven is laughing, until Zeke clears his throat and seriousness settles across the room once more.

"Evidently her mother accused her stepfather of abusing her, but the case never got anywhere. She must have been twelve at the time, if these dates are right."

"Not surprising," Malin says. "Just think, this sort of crap always comes up." Then Malin thinks about what Viveka Crafoord said: that the perpetrator could well have been the victim of abuse. Isn't that always the case? One way or another. That one act of abuse leads to another. The trail goes as far back through history as human life itself.

"Okay, but we can't question her again because of that," Sven says. "We've leaned on her enough as it is, and there are almost as many sordid backgrounds and family histories as there are people."

Karim looks focused, and Malin can see the thoughts racing through his head. The image of his own father must be in there, committing suicide in his despair at his failure to find a place in Swedish society, the father who died bitter in a way that you, Karim, would never allow yourself to be, and Malin thinks of the cliché her mother always used to trot out at the slightest failure or disappointment: "It's not what happens that matters, it's how you deal with it."

Then the words of the philosopher Emile Cioran come to mind: "Nothing reveals the vulgar man better than his refusal to be disappointed."

Are you the most disappointed person in the world, Mum?

Tenerife.

But back to the present.

"Hypnosis," Malin says. "I'd like to question Josefin Davidsson under hypnosis," and now it's Zeke's turn to look angry, questioning: What's this? I knew you were thinking about it, but we could have discussed it first.

"We all know that it's possible to remember things under hypnosis that you don't otherwise remember. I'm friends with Viveka Crafoord, the psychoanalyst, and she's offered to conduct an interview with Josefin under hypnosis, free of charge."

Waldemar Ekenberg laughs.

"Well," he goes on to say. "Sounds like a good idea."

"This mustn't get out to the press. They'll say that we're desperate," Karim says. "And we don't want that."

"Discretion is assured," Malin says. "Viveka works under an oath of confidentiality."

Zeke has got over his sudden annoyance.

"Will her parents agree?"

"We don't know until we ask."

"And Josefin?"

"Ditto."

"If it happens, and if it works, it could help us move forward," Sven says.

"It could be the breakthrough we need," Karim says.

"So what are we waiting for?" Waldemar says. "Get the girl to the fortune-teller!"

And Malin doesn't know what to say, can't decide if the hard case from Mjölby is joking or means what he says. A joke to smooth things over:

"Hocus-pocus," Malin says, getting up from her chair. "Okay, I'm going to go and stick some pins in a voodoo doll, Waldemar, so watch out."

Ekenberg comes over to her desk after the meeting.

What does he want? Malin thinks.

"Fors," he says, "you look happy."

"Happy?"

"Yes, you know, like you've just been fucked. Where do you go if you want to get a fuck in this town?"

And once again Malin doesn't know what to say, or do, hasn't felt so surprised since she was three years old and took a drink from a cup of hot water, thinking it was juice.

Shall I punch him on the chin?

Then she pulls herself together.

"You sack of shit. There isn't a woman in this city who'd touch you even with gloves on. Get it?"

Ekenberg was already on his way out.

Grinning to himself, Malin thinks.

Don't let yourself be provoked, we've got more important things to deal with.

But he was right.

She could still feel Daniel Högfeldt inside her.

Would like to suppress the smile spreading over her lips.

42

"That's absolutely out of the question."

Josefin Davidsson's father, Ulf, is sitting on the burgundy sofa in the living room of the row house in Lambohov, moving his toes anxiously back and forth over the mainly pink rug. His suntanned face is round, his hair starting to thin, and his wide nose is peeling.

"Hypnosis," he goes on. "You read about people getting stuck like that. And Josefin needs to rest."

His wife, Birgitta, sitting beside him on the sofa, is more hesitant, Malin thinks. She's evidently trying to read the situation, trying to follow her husband so as not to annoy him. Their roles are clearer now than the first time she met them at the hospital. They declined the offer of protection for Josefin, saying she needed peace and quiet more than anything else. Birgitta Davidsson is a neat little woman in a blue floral dress. So neat that she dissolves in your khaki-clad presence, Ulf. Doesn't she?

Zeke from his seat beside Malin:

"The psychoanalyst who would conduct the hypnosis, Viveka Craford, is very experienced."

"But do we really want Josefin to remember?"

Ulf Davidsson's words less adamant now.

Malin pauses, answers no in her mind, it would be just as well for your daughter if she didn't remember, she'll be fine without any conscious memory of what happened. But she says:

"It's vitally important for the investigation. Two girls have been murdered, and we have no witnesses. We need all the help we can get."

"And you're sure it's the same man?"

"Absolutely certain," Zeke replies.

"It doesn't feel right," Ulf Davidsson says. "Too risky."

"You're right, darling," Birgitta Davidsson says. "Who knows how she might feel if she could remember?"

"We have no idea when the murderer is going to strike again," Zeke says. "But sooner or later it will happen. So asking these questions under hypnosis is absolutely—"

Zeke is interrupted by a thin but clear voice from upstairs.

"Isn't anyone going to ask me? Ask me what I want?"

A look of irritation crosses Ulf Davidsson's face.

"We're your parents. We'll decide what's best for you."

"So you'd like to be questioned under hypnosis?"

Josefin Davidsson comes downstairs and sits in an armchair, the white bandages covering her wounds a sharp contrast to her bright-red summer dress.

"I would."

"You—"

"It's not going to happen."

"But, Dad, I—"

"Be quiet."

And the room falls still, the only sound the vibration of a bumble-bee's wings as it tries to get out through an open window, but keeps missing, again and again, flying into the glass instead with a short bumping sound each time.

"We're trying to find—"

"I know what you're trying to find. The devil himself could be out there for all I care, because you'll have to find him without upsetting my daughter more than is absolutely necessary."

"You're such a damn hypocrite, Dad," Josefin says. "When I told you that you could probably get compassionate leave to be here with me, you both took it. And went straight off to the golf course."

"Josefin!" her mother cries. "That's enough!"

"I'm begging you," Malin says.

"Me too, Dad. I'm going to do it, no matter what you want."

In the space of a second Ulf Davidsson suddenly looks fifteen years older, as if he's staked out any number of principles and opinions over the years, but has always had to back down in the end.

"It's the right thing to do, Dad. And if I remember something that helps them catch the killer, you'll be a big hero."

"You don't know what you're asking for," Ulf Davidsson says to his daughter. The look in his eyes is clear, but sad. "You don't know what you're asking for. But okay. If hypnosis is what you want, hypnosis is what you'll get."

On the way back to the parking lot.

The sun like the ice-blue core of a gas flame in the sky, the sort of light that sunglasses have no effect against. The ground seems to be sweating, even though it's so dry Malin imagines it could spontaneously combust. There's also the smell of the forest fires, tickling her nose and making her whole being feel slightly anxious. Phrases of gratitude in the house they've just left.

"Thanks. You're doing the right thing."

Reassurance:

"It isn't dangerous. It will be good for her to remember."

Practicalities:

"We'll be in touch when I've spoken to Viveka Crafoord. Hopefully this evening. Tomorrow at the latest. We'll be in touch, make sure we can contact you."

And now Viveka on the other end of the line, in her house out in Svartmåla.

"I'm just back from a dip in the lake."

Daniel Högfeldt's body.

The waters of Stora Rängen.

The key is in the past.

"She's agreed to be hypnotized. And her parents have given their consent."

"When?"

"Whenever suits you."

"Where?"

"Same thing."

"How about seven o'clock this evening in my clinic?"

"Perfect. As long as nothing else comes up."

Nathalie Falck is standing with a rake in her hand, its spray of teeth like a dying treetop against the blue summer sky, almost white with the heat.

They're standing among the graves at the far end of the cemetery, from where they can see the roof of the supermarket in Valla, and hear the cars out on the main road, forcing their way through the dense air.

"I use a grass rake for the gravel," Nathalie says. "It's easier than using the other sort."

"It's looking good," Malin said, gesturing toward the gravel path leading to the chapel where they hold the burial services. "You're very conscientious."

"Yes, I suppose it's unusual to be conscientious."

Zeke silent by Malin's side, in the shade of an old oak, the flowers on most of the graves scorched and crisp, prematurely withered in the cruel heat.

"I can see you looking at the flowers. But we can't water them fast enough. Not in this heat."

Malin nods.

"It is hot," she says. Then she asks: "You haven't told us everything, have you?"

"How can you know that?"

"Just a gut instinct. Two girls of your age are dead, murdered, so it's time to talk."

"I haven't got anything to tell you."

"Yes, you have," Malin says. "We both know that."

Nathalie Falck shakes her head lightly.

"No."

"Okay," Zeke says. "What were you doing on the night between Monday and Tuesday?"

"I was at home. Mum and Dad can tell you."

"Two girls," Malin says. "Theresa. Aren't you upset that she's dead?"

Nathalie Falck shrugs her shoulders, but Malin can see her eyes slowly fill with tears. Then she pulls herself together.

"Okay," she says.

"Okay, what?" Zeke says, and Malin can feel him trying not to sound angry and aggressive.

"Calm down, Zeke. Let her tell us."

Nathalie Falck takes a few steps into the shade before sitting down on the grass by the oak tree.

"I read in the paper that you searched Lollo Svensson's house. But the article didn't say everything. You ought to know that I had a thing with her, well, I went with her, just like Theresa did. I presume that's what you want to know, if you didn't already know."

Malin and Zeke are staring at each other.

So maybe that was what Theresa was doing when she said she was with Peter Sköld? Is that what he wouldn't tell them?

Louise "Lollo" Svensson.

So, you're back in the case again.

And are you Lovelygirl as well?

"Is Louise Svensson the same person as Lovelygirl on Theresa's Facebook page?"

"Not as far as I know."

Lollo.

A hot fog drifting into the meandering byways of the case, taking shape, disappearing, sweeping on, and taking shape again.

A shadow.

"Bloody hell," Zeke says.

"And it didn't occur to you that we ought to know this?"

"Well, yes."

"But you still—" Malin stifles her words, swearing inwardly. All this silence they have to fight against, all this life that has to be kept secret, to elevate it somehow, as if all this damn silence were holy water.

"But now you know," Nathalie Falck says with a smile. "I just didn't think it was anything to do with you. It's private."

"How do you mean, 'went with her'?"

"Had sex with her out at her farm. She'd give you money. And in case you're wondering about Peter Sköld, he's got a boyfriend in Söderköping. He was spending time with him whenever he said he was with Theresa. And Theresa was with me instead."

"Were you and Theresa a couple?"

"No. Not my type."

Not "your type," Malin thinks.

"We had sex a few times, every now and then," Nathalie Falck says. "But only as friends."

Zeke's words to Sven Sjöman:

"Get a patrol car out to Lollo Svensson's farm outside Rimforsa, and bring her in for questioning straightaway. She had a sexual relationship with Theresa Eckeved."

Pause.

The hot, clammy interior of the car as he opens the door in the cemetery parking lot.

"I know, Sven. We can always hold her on corruption of a minor."

Don't be too hard on her now.

See her as the person she really is.

Lollo, there's nothing wrong with her. Unless perhaps there is? Something wrong with her?

I remember her hands on my skin, the way she gave me money afterward, the taste of her swollen, moist crotch, and her words, whispering: Theresa, Theresa, Theresa, and the words turned to cotton wool among the flowery sheets, to the forest outside her window, to the dark expanse of the sky adorned with hopeful stars.

And she gave in to my tongue, and I had nothing against that, because I had so much to learn about the body that I no longer have.

Angels.

Like me, like Sofia.

Are we the eternal virgins?

Is she Lovelygirl, Malin?

Or is Slavenca Lovelygirl?

You'll have to work that out on your own.

So listen to Lollo, try to understand why she does what she does, why she is the way that she is.

I can feel your excitement, Malin.

The way you think you've caught a scent of the truth.

Imagining that it will help you.

That hope is driving us both, isn't it?

43

Waldemar Ekenberg is sitting at his temporary desk in the crime unit's open-plan office. His longs legs, clad in green linen, are up on the desk and he's drumming a pen against the arm of his office chair. Opposite him Per Sundsten is randomly surfing various news websites and bringing himself up to date with what's being written about their murders.

Expressen: "City of Terror."

Aftonbladet: "What the Killer Is Like."

Dagens Nyheter: "A Swedish Serial Killer?"

The *Östgöta Correspondent:* "The Linköping Killer: Man or Woman?"

He skims the articles, nothing new, nothing they don't already know, interviews with people in the city, young girls swimming at Tinnis.

"We're scared. We don't go out at night."

"There's a really weird atmosphere in the city."

"I've got a fourteen-year-old daughter. I worry whenever she goes out."

Per lets the screen saver click in on his laptop, pictures of a beach in Thailand.

God, what wouldn't I give to be there now? At that moment he sees Sven Sjöman heading toward their desks; from a distance it looks like he's shuddering as he makes his way through the office. Am I going to end up like that? Per thinks: so tired, and sort of slow? Sven's body might be tired, but the look in his eyes is all the more alert, and Per can see that Sven has something important for them.

Two strangers, Sven thinks as he heads toward Per and Waldemar's desks. Outsiders, even though they belong to the same force. The man of the future and the brute, the rumors that precede them both, Ekenberg a rotten egg who's been lucky enough to get away with it.

Sven has seen a lot of men like Ekenberg during his years in the police. He's always tried to keep away from them, or, as a senior officer, to get rid of them.

The ends do not justify the means.

Unless perhaps they do? In a case like this?

Sven recalls the girl's body in the Railway Park. Her eyes white and blind, like a sightless deer, polished stones that have lost their shine, their beauty.

Sven stops at their desks, two pairs of eyes staring at him, one pair, Per's, still seem to be somewhere else, but Waldemar's exude concentration on the task at hand.

"We've heard from Telia. The call has been localized to Mariavägen in Vimanshäll. There's a Suliman Hajif living there, he cropped up alongside Karami in the gang rape case last winter, although he was never a suspect. The likelihood is that the two of them have fallen out somehow and Suliman just wants to make life difficult for Karami."

The two outsiders have stood up.

"We're on our way," Waldemar says, and Sven sees his eyes turn black, the pupils expanding in anticipation of something that Sven would prefer not to express in words.

"Take it easy now. Be careful."

Per nods.

"Who knows," he says. "We might be getting close."

*   *   *

Ten minutes later they pull up on Mariavägen, outside a small, white block of flats, two stories surrounded by a garden with unkempt apple trees.

The heat and light pounce on them as they get out of the car.

"Sunglasses on," Waldemar grins.

The air-conditioning just had time to get going, turned up to maximum, and now a difference in temperature of some twenty-five degrees lets the heat get a stranglehold on them, driven on by the light.

They approach the house along a gravel path almost completely covered by weeds.

"Do you reckon he's home?"

"Probably," Waldemar says. "These lazy bastards usually sleep all day and do their dirty work at night."

"Listen, let's take this a bit more calmly, okay?"

Waldemar doesn't reply, pressing the buzzer for another flat, not Hajif's.

No answer.

Four flats.

"Do you know the postcode?"

"Sorry, no idea. We can call in and find out."

Flat number two, no answer, and, from behind, Per sees the muscles in Waldemar's back tense under his jacket as he takes aim at the door and slams into it with full force. The door gives in and Waldemar tumbles into the stairwell but stops himself from falling.

"Now he knows we're on our way."

"Don't you just love bad landlords? That door should have been replaced years ago. Come on, quick."

And they rush up the stairs to the first floor. No doors have opened to see where the noise came from.

Nothing but emptiness and silence and a gray-speckled stone floor and shabby pale-blue walls. Hajif's front door is painted pink.

They ring the bell.

Sounds from inside the flat.

No peephole.

Steps approaching the door, then disappearing.

"He's on his way out," Waldemar says. "He's going to run."

And once again he throws himself at a door, and this one too flies open without putting up much resistance, and in the narrow, messy hall stands a young man with a well-toned upper body and black hair in a ponytail. His dark eyes glare at them in surprise as he pulls on a pair of white sports underwear, his cock, pierced with a cock ring, visible, half erect.

"Listen, Paki, we need to talk to you. Nothing to get worked up about," Waldemar says, and Suliman Hajif pulls up his underwear, runs back into the flat, toward an open balcony door at the back of the building.

"Get him!" Waldemar yells, and Per rushes after Suliman Hajif, throwing himself at his legs just as he steps out onto the balcony, and the young man falls forward, headfirst, into the solid gray balcony railings, which give way and his body is dragged out, down, and he screams as he flails above the drop, the yellow grass twelve feet below.

"You're not going to fall," Per says as he fights to keep hold of Suliman Hajif on the balcony. He tries with all his strength to pull him up; he could break his neck in a fall like that, and then what good would he be?

Waldemar's hand on one of Suliman Hajif's feet.

They pull together, and up he comes, lying on his stomach and putting up no resistance as Waldemar cuffs him and drags him onto the white-lacquered wooden floor in the living room.

"What the hell was that all about?"

Per is panting, catching his breath, and slaps Suliman Hajif on the back.

"We just want to talk to you."

"Well, maybe not just that," Waldemar says.

He's pulled open the doors of the built-in cupboards. Per turns around, sees piles of magazines, the inside walls of the cupboards covered with porn pictures, serious, hard-core stuff, women shackled to racks, women being whipped.

Sex toys neatly lined up.

Masks.

Whips.

Chastity belts.

And there, in splendid isolation on the bottom shelf of one of the cupboards, a blue dildo. The paint flaking off its strangely transparent surface.

44

I nterview room one.

The dark-gray ceiling seems to be falling in on the even darker walls, a voice recorder on a black tabletop, Zeke and Malin on one side of the table, Lollo Svensson on the other, dressed in a white T-shirt with the words BITCH POWER. Her face and the look in her eyes radiate defiance, and she hasn't asked for a lawyer.

Malin thinks, feels, how best to open this lock. Is there any way? She thinks that it's probably impossible, before saying:

"So, you like young girls?"

Lollo Svensson glares into Malin's eyes, full of hatred now, but not toward me, Malin thinks, toward something else, and she thinks: If we can find the core of that hatred we can find the killer, the core of that hatred could be the core of this evil, this violence.

"Young girls. How come?"

Zeke scratches his shaved head, says:

"Do you want to look after them?

"And then things got out of hand with Theresa and Sofia, but Josefin managed to escape? Is that it?"

Lollo Svensson stiff, her mouth a thin line, her lips stuck together with age-old glue.

"Do you want to be nice to them? Have you got a special flat you take them to? Or a building somewhere on the farm? Nathalie Falck has been out to the farm. Was Theresa out there as well?"

Lollo Svensson clasps her hands.

Beads of sweat on her forehead, her top lip.

How can anyone be so angry?

And Malin asks:

"Why are you so furious, Louise? What happened to you?"

"None of your fucking business, Inspector."

"What about the report your mother made, the one in our archive? Nothing about that? Nothing you want to tell us?"

"No, Mum made that up."

A hissing voice, uneven sound levels on the recorder, cold white strings around Malin's heart.

"And the rabbits on your farm," Zeke says. "Do you normally pull their claws out?"

"What a fucking sick question. I keep rabbits because I like them."

"Did you and Theresa email each other about where to meet?" Malin asks. "Via her Yahoo! address?"

"No."

"Did you leave messages on her Facebook page?"

"I don't know anything about any fucking book of faces."

Fury in Lollo Svensson's voice.

"Lovelygirl? Is that you?"

"I've already answered that question once."

"Take it easy now," Zeke says. "How many times did you and Theresa have sex?"

"Am I under suspicion for something?"

"We've got proof of corruption of a minor. Nathalie Falck has told us that she had a sexual relationship with you before her fifteenth birthday. And you know that we know you had a sexual relationship with Theresa Eckeved as well."

"And?"

"And what?"

"What about the others? Have you found any connection between me and the others?"

"Why don't you tell us?" Malin says. "Tell us."

"How did you meet Sofia?"

"I've never met Sofia Fredén. Never."

"And Theresa. Did you use a dildo? A blue one?"

Malin and Zeke are aware of the find in Suliman Hajif's flat. Sundsten and Ekenberg are with him in the next room, putting pressure on the little shit. Who knows, maybe the case is solved now? Karin and her Forensics team must be ecstatic about the dildo. Now they probably won't have to dig out the right dildo from hundreds of possibilities. If it could even have been done. Maybe the truth will emerge on the other side of that black, depressing wall.

Suliman Hajif's eyes are full of fear.

You're scared now, you little shit, Waldemar Ekenberg thinks.

And you're right to be.

Because I don't mean you well.

Interview room two is identical to interview room one, albeit its mirror image, and in the corridor outside you can switch between the two rooms, looking in on the confessional spaces through glass windows that appear as mirrors inside the rooms.

"You raped and murdered Theresa Eckeved and Sofia Fredén. Josefin Davidsson managed to escape. We know it was you, we've got the dildo, the one which in all probability was used in these crimes."

Per Sundsten's voice amiable, factual.

"It will feel better if you confess. Easier."

"And all that fucking porn. You need treatment, Suliman."

"I didn't have anything to do with all that crap. I want my lawyer."

"He can come later on," Waldemar says. "We have the right to conduct a first interview with you on your own."

"What were you doing on the night between Wednesday and Thursday?"

"I've already told you, I was at home taking it easy on all the nights you're interested in. It's too damn hot to go out."

"But no one can prove that, Suliman."

The muscles in his arms are bulging under his beige custody shirt, at least two sizes too small.

"And the porn?"

"Hell, I like porn, and I like pushing dildos into girls. Fuck, I can get it up three times, at least, but they still want more after that."

"Where did you buy the dildo?"

"None of your fucking business."

"You ratted on Behzad Karami. Why?"

Even Waldemar's voice is factual.

"He did it."

"Probably not. And how would you know? Perjury is punishable by two years in prison."

"He goes out at night. So it must be him. It could be, anyway."

"What's gone wrong between the two of you?"

"None of your business, pig."

Waldemar gets up, takes two steps around the table before he pretends to stumble, and in his fall he manages to drag Suliman Hajif with him, and his nose hits the black tabletop with a loud cracking sound.

"Damn, this floor's slippery."

Suliman Hajif screams with pain, blood pouring from his nose, and Per expects to see Karim Akbar or Sven Sjöman come rushing into the room to put a stop to this, but no one comes, and instead Suliman is left sitting opposite them as the blood dripping from his nose stains his custody shirt.

"We're expecting the forensics report on the dildo any time now," Waldemar says, back on his chair again. "And then we'll know. So you may as well confess."

"I've got nothing to confess."

Waldemar gets up again.

Suliman Hajif jerks back, raising his hands in self-defense.

The passageway between the interview rooms is dark and cool and damp, and the recessed halogen bulbs in the ceiling cast a pleasant glow. Karim and Sven are following the interviews with Suliman Hajif and Lollo Svensson at the same time, letting Ekenberg carry on as long as he doesn't go too far over the boundary.

"What do you think?"

Karim's face is open, wondering. With every case he has become more humble, more open in his attitude to his detectives' work. As he has gained confidence in Malin, Zeke, Börje Svärd, and Johan Jakobsson he has relaxed, adopting a softer style of leadership than the one he had when he arrived: the omniscient boor.

Maybe he has realized that the work of investigation is in part a game, where curiosity and complete openness are a must if you want to see results. Maybe he has realized they really do have to work together to accomplish the tasks they are charged with? Or else he has understood that they are on their own, that they are on the front line against evil, that they have to look out for each other if they are to survive.

"I don't know what to think," Sven says. "Forensics is checking the dildo right now, and going through his flat. Karin Johannison is on duty, and she's usually pretty quick. We're also checking his computer. But that could take longer."

"And Louise Svensson?"

"She's about as damaged an individual as I've ever seen. And I've seen before what that sort of damage can lead to."

"But do you think she did it?"

Sven doesn't answer, but says:

"Maybe we should have a word with her mother. Find out a bit about her background."

Inside interview room one Lollo Svensson suddenly spits in Malin's face, but Malin keeps her cool and merely wipes the saliva away.

Obliged to continue the line of questioning.

A strong voice in this investigation.

Once she has wiped away the wet slime Malin says:

"So asking about your dad is a sensitive issue. Sorry, I didn't know."

"What's he got to do with this?"

Her voice controlled now after her furious outburst at Malin's last question.

"The report I mentioned. Something happened when you were a child. Your dad, did he hurt you?"

"Did he?"

Zeke trying to sound understanding, sympathetic, and he succeeds.

"I'm not talking about that. I've spent my whole life trying to forget about it."

Lollo Svensson calm now, as if she's found a new personality somewhere inside.

"Who can we talk to?"

"Talk to Mum."

Viveka Crafoord's words, her voice:

The key to this is in the past.

"And how do we get hold of her?"

A name. An address.

"Do you have to find out?"

"We have to look into everything."

"I admit to having sex with those girls. But I was nice to them. Gentle. Friendly. And I gave them money afterward. More than they expected."

"You don't expect us to believe you, right? How many blue dildos can there be in this city?"

Waldemar is sitting down again, after thumping Suliman Hajif's head on the table for a second time.

On his way back to his chair he looked in the mirror, at the face that seems to be withering away, aging away from him, a little more each day. A face wearing a mask, and whatever is behind the mask burned out long ago as a result of giving in to instinct, giving in to the most basic urges.

Violence. Sexuality. The same thing. Aren't they?

Waldemar knows: He's given in to violence.

And he knows that he will never have the energy to do anything about it.

He's not suited to therapy.

"I didn't have anything to do with this shit."

Suliman Hajif sniffs, holding his shirtsleeve to his nose to stop it bleeding. He sobs, and says:

"I'm innocent."

Waldemar leans toward the recorder:

"Interview with Suliman Hajif concluded. Time four seventeen."

Malin on her own in the toilet.

She's finished peeing, but still she sits there, feeling the clammy seat against her buttocks.

She shuts her eyes, thinking.

Suliman Hajif will be held until Forensics has finished, until the dildo has been compared to the earlier evidence. And then? Twenty years in prison, in a secure hospital? Or back home to surf for more porn?

They let Lollo Svensson go home.

She had admitted to what they already knew about her, but apart from that they had no evidence against her, and, as Sven said in the passageway outside the interview room once both interviews had been concluded: "There are limits to how much we can subject a person to with so little evidence. But we'll be keeping an eye on her."

"I want to talk to her mother," Malin says.

Sven dubious.

"Do we really want to upset an elderly lady because her daughter's name has cropped up in a murder investigation?"

"We need to find out what happened. It might lead to something. Viveka Crafoord said—"

Sven.

The way his face crumpled as he gave in to her.

"Okay. Zeke and Malin. Go and talk to her mother. Straightaway.

We need to look under that stone while it's still warm. Look back in time."

Sven didn't realize how oddly he had expressed himself.

"What about the hypnosis?" Malin had asked. "We're supposed to be doing that at seven."

"Can we do it later?"

"It'll be too late then."

"Yes, it will."

"And I'm picking Janne and Tove up from Nyköping after midnight."

Sven's face then, she would have given her year's wages for that look, how happy he seemed on her behalf, how he seemed to understand her anxiety and the way her loss had slid over into an inexplicable sense of grief.

Malin gets up from the toilet.

Pulls down her skirt.

Looks in the mirror.

Pale, in spite of all the sun this summer.

Tove and Janne.

Soon.

Soon you'll be home again.

45

eke raises the can of Coca-Cola to his mouth and drinks before taking a huge bite of his flatbread roll. The prawn salad trickles like thick magma down the outside of the bread. Down by the river beside the Scandic Hotel two black Saab limousines stop, and men in black suits get out and are guided into the hotel.

Zeke and Malin are standing at the hot dog kiosk by the fire station, near the roundabout leading out to Stångebro. Eating, recharging their batteries before their interview with Lollo Svensson's mother, and Malin before her drive to Nyköping later that evening.

"See them over there?"

Zeke points at the men in suits.

"Bound to be representatives from some damn company or government here to look at another weapons system."

"Maybe they're here to buy JAS fighters?"

"I doubt it. No one wants that plane. It cost billions, and it's already obsolete."

"I daresay you're right."

The owner of the kiosk, a swarthy man in his fifties, is brushing down his grill and doesn't seem to be listening to their conversation.

"All that advanced stuff they do out at Saab, who knows where the hell it ends up, and what damage it does."

"But it does good here," Malin says. "Loads of jobs."

The kiosk owner evidently has been listening to their conversation, his voice sharply accented:

"Excuse me. I overheard. My wife," he says from behind the counter, "she died in a missile attack in Fallujah. No one knows who fired it. Maybe there was something from Saab in the explosion, but what difference does it make? Saab, or someone else. Everyone makes their own decisions about what job they want to do."

Zeke throws the last of the roll in the bin by the door.

"Would you sell hot dogs to men like that?" he asks the kiosk owner.

"I'll sell hot dogs to anyone who's prepared to pay."

They walk past the fire station toward the block of flats.

No red fire engines outside the polished glass doors.

Janne's workplace.

He loves the station. It's as much his home as his house near Malmslätt.

"God, it's sticky today," Zeke says. "Don't you think it's humid as hell?"

Malin doesn't have time to reply before her mobile rings. She clicks to take the call without checking to see who the caller was.

"Malin!"

Dad's voice.

Not now.

But when else?

"Dad!"

Zeke grins beside her.

"How are you both?"

"It's really lovely down here."

"It's hot as hell up here."

"You should see how green the golf courses are, and there are no problems getting a round."

"Tove and Janne are having a good time in Bali."

"Malin. How's the apartment?"

"I haven't had time to go."

"But . . ."

"I was joking, Dad, the plants are fine. How's Mum?"

"Oh, the same as usual, I suppose."

They've reached the door to the block of flats. Zeke presses the intercom, sweat dripping onto his wrist. Malin sees her reflection in the glass of the door, a vague image impossible to bring into focus.

"Did you want anything in particular, Dad?"

The first time he's called in over a week.

"No."

So why are you calling? Malin thinks. Seeing as you're evidently completely uninterested in anything that's happening to me and Tove.

A buzzing sound from the door.

"Dad. Good to talk to you. But I'm on my way into a meeting."

"Don't worry, Malin. I'll call again another day."

A minute later Malin is standing in a lift that's shaking its way up through the building floor by floor. She can see her face clearly in the mirror in the lift, how the heat seems to be bringing out more wrinkles.

Parents, she thinks. What the hell are they good for?

"Everything has its price."

Svea Svensson's voice hoarse after many long years of smoking, her face shrunken with wrinkles, hair gray, in thin strips above her green eyes, eyes watchful but well meaning, as if the pupils are hiding a desire to let go of the secrets held in the electrical byways of the brain.

Her flat is on the top floor of the tallest block at the start of Tanneforsvägen.

Period furniture crammed into the living room, baroque chairs made in the fifties, an Empire-style sofa, Wilton carpets and prints of Johan Krouthén paintings on silvery-gray wallpaper, porcelain ornaments and a carriage clock that has just struck six.

Through the small windows of the living room they can see the Östgöta plain spreading out beyond the rooftops of the city as it un-

furls toward Ljungsbro. They can make out the hot waters of Lake
Roxen, almost see the steam rising over on the horizon, how it envelops the tormented, scorched fields in a fleeting, invisible mist that
hides the obstinate remnants of life that are still clinging on.

The pillars of smoke from the forest on one side have gathered
into an angry black cloud that doesn't know which way to go in the
absence of wind.

It looks like the world is standing still, Malin thinks, just as Svea
Svensson repeats:

"Everything has its price. If life has taught me anything, it's that."

Zeke and Malin are each slumped in a baroque chair.

Svea Svensson on the sofa behind the coffee table, her mouth moving, the words shaping a history that should never have needed to be
told, but which is nonetheless all too common.

Zeke:

"Can you tell us about Louise's life as a child?"

"Is it important?"

Malin:

"It's important."

"I'll start at the very beginning. If that's all right? Before she was
born. Back when I was a little girl?"

"Start wherever you'd like to," Zeke says, and the words start pouring from Svea's mouth, as if they had missed the sound they made.

"When I was seven years old my father left my mother and me.
We lived on my grandfather's farm, Övraby, outside Brokind, in one
of the old outbuildings. My father was a traveling salesman and one
day he didn't come home, and Mother found out that he had a new
woman in Söderköping. We were short of money, so Mother took a
job as a cook on an estate twenty miles away, down toward Kisa. I
stayed behind with my grandparents, and I remember that time as the
happiest days of my life. Then Mother met a new man. He had a shoe
shop in Kisa, lived in a flat over the shop, and Mother and I moved in
there. After just three nights he came into my room, I can remember

his cold hands pushing the covers off me, and it happened again and again, and one night Mother appeared in the doorway while he was doing it, and she looked for a while before carrying on to the toilet, as if nothing had happened.

"Do I blame her?

"No.

"Where would we have gone? Grandfather had had a stroke, the farm was gone.

"So he had his way, the shoe-shop bastard, and I left when I was seventeen, I ended up in Motala, in the kitchen at the factory, and I met a man in the Town Hotel.

"He was a traveling salesman, just like my father, although he sold industrial chemicals, and he got me pregnant, and I gave birth to Louise. And when she was eight years old he left us alone with the flat in Motala. He'd got a new woman in Nässjö.

"We lived on our own for a few years, just the girl and me. Then I met a new man, just like my mother had done, Sture Folkman by name. He bought and sold agricultural produce and we moved into his house down by the canal in Motala.

"Louise never said anything.

"I've often wondered why she didn't tell me what was going on.

"We'd been living there for three years when I found out what he was doing at night, what his cold hands were doing at night, what he was doing with his body.

"Where could we go?

"But I didn't let him have his way.

"I hit him on the head with a saucepan and we waited all night at the bus stop in the rain, Louise and I. It was a cold October night and the bushes and trees in the gardens around us turned into monsters, silhouettes of the devil's children.

"In the morning, just after it was light enough to make out the real shape of the bushes and trees, the bus came. It was heading for Linköping, and I've never been back to Motala since, and I've never seen the bastard since then. And my first husband, Louise's father, drowned while he was out fishing.

"I blame myself, you know, Inspectors.

"I let my child down, my girl, and no matter what pain a person has suffered themselves, you must never turn your back on a child. And that's what I did by not seeing.

"We ended up in a hotel room near the station. I reported him to the police, but there was nothing they could do. The nice ladies in the social security office sorted out a flat for us, and I got a job in a café and Louise started school. But even so, ever since then everything has somehow always been too late.

"I never let any man come into my home after that."

Malin is pacing up and down beside the bed in her flat, freshly showered and wearing just her pants and bra. She's laid three summer dresses out on the bedspread, wondering which one to choose: blue with white flowers, the short yellow one, or the longer white one that goes down to her ankles.

She chooses the yellow one, pulls it over her head and looks at herself in the hall mirror, and she thinks that anticipation is making her beautiful, or at least more beautiful than she has felt for ages.

The interview with Svea Svensson just an hour before. The words echoing inside her: cold hands on the covers, under the covers, snakes on her body.

She remembers what an old man said to her during a previous case: "Desire is what kills, Miss Fors. Desire is what kills."

They had asked about Louise, if Svea Svensson knew anything about her daughter that she thought they should know, but Svea Svensson had refused to answer the question at all.

"Is Sture Folkman still alive?"

Zeke's question to Svea.

"Sture Folkman is alive."

"Do you know where he lives?"

"I think he lives in Finspång with his wife. He had a family."

"And?"

Malin could sense another story.

"God help those poor people."

And then silence, the lips clamped shut as if they'd let out enough memories for a lifetime.

Maybe the white dress after all?

No.

Malin looks round the flat, it looks tidy enough.

She goes down to the car in the parking lot by the church, starts the engine, sees from the clock that she's early, it's only half past seven, Tove and Janne's plane lands at a quarter to two. It takes at most an hour and a half to get to Skavsta. Even if she sticks to the speed limit. But she wants to be there in good time, and might as well be somewhere else with her longing.

As she drives up Järnvägsgatan toward the Berg roundabout, a face comes to mind, she doesn't know why, but she knows the face is important.

Slavenca Visnic smiles as she opens the door of her flat in Skäggetorp.

And a minute later Malin is sitting with a glass of Fanta in her living room, trying to think of something to ask, and it's as if the caution she felt just now, the watchfulness around a person featuring in a murder investigation, has blown away, leaving just a vague sense of significance.

"What do you want to know?"

Slavenca Visnic doesn't seem surprised by the visit, just curious about what Malin wants.

"I don't really know. I just wanted to ask you to try to think if there's anything important that you might not have told us."

"What could that be? I just try to be a good citizen, mind my own business, that's all."

Malin can see how ridiculous her visit must seem to such a down-to-earth person as the woman before her.

"Oh, well."

"Don't worry. Finish your drink. I've got to go up to Glyttinge to collect the day's takings, and have my evening swim. They start cleaning the water at half past nine, and if you swim at the far end of the pool it actually does feel clean there then."

"An evening swim? Nice. I'm heading to Skavsta to pick up my husband and daughter."

Malin regrets saying this at once, Slavenca Visnic lost her whole family, but her eyes show nothing but calm, warmth.

"I'd like to show you something," Slavenca Visnic says. "Follow me."

The next minute they're sitting at a computer in her bedroom, the light of the screen flickering.

Slavenca Visnic has opened ten documents that look like pages of a child's picture book. On the pages she's loaded the few pictures she has of her family, alongside short texts about her childhood, her children's lives, the short lives they got to live.

Slavenca Visnic looks younger in the pictures, her face full of innocent anticipation and responsibility. The children in her arms, beautiful round faces beneath black hair that's been allowed to grow long, her husband: a friendly, fluid face defined by a strong chin.

"It feels good to keep busy doing this," Slavenca Visnic says. "Writing. Trying to recreate life the way it was when it was at its best, all that simple love."

"It's beautiful," Malin says.

"Do you think so?"

"Yes."

"Do you think they can ever come back?"

"No, I don't think so." Slavenca Visnic's question seems entirely natural to Malin, as if resurrection from the dead were possible sometimes, at least for the love itself.

"But someday you'll get to meet them again," Malin says. "And their love is still here in this room. I can feel it."

Slavenca Visnic shuts down her computer and follows Malin out into the hall.

"Drive carefully, they'd probably prefer you to get there in one piece. Your husband and daughter."

"We're divorced," Malin says. "We've been divorced more than ten years."

46

Shimmering dusk.

The day on its way into inescapable darkness, its death throes in shifting shades of yellow, red, and orange.

Forest, open fields, water, red-painted houses huddling by the tree line, cars parked in driveways, light in windows, sometimes silhouettes behind the glass, people like dark dreams, hungry, still not ready to let go of the day.

But the day itself muttering:

I've had enough.

That'll do.

The car creeps up to seventy-five. Can go much faster than that.

A metal bird high up in the atmosphere, where the summer air is too thin to breathe. Soon on its way down, the metal cocoon protecting your bodies.

Keep your eyes on the road.

Dangerously tired.

And the asphalt is a snake sliding past Norrköping, Kolmården, and on into the night.

Stockholm.

The road ends up there. Sometimes she wishes she was back there, in a larger setting, with more regular cases to fire up a detective's soul.

A case like theirs.

Threads like unexploded shells, howling as they approach the ground, and all the police officers involved wait for the explosion, waiting for the truth to burst out and take shape before their eyes. But instead just an unexploded bomb lying in the meeting room and emitting a foul stench, in the open-plan office of the police station, a whistling sound that mocks them, reminding them of their shortcomings.

The media going crazy.

Karim Akbar getting softer each day, and simultaneously worse as a media performer, but better as a police chief.

Sven Sjöman.

Malin has never seen him so physically tired as he has been over the past few days. The heat is tearing the soul from his heavy body. Just let his heart hold out, Sven's good heart.

Per Sundsten. It's impossible to get a grip on him, who he is, what he wants, what he thinks. A good detective ought to know that sort of thing, Malin thinks, because if you're sure of who you are and what you want, then your intuition can fly free, can't it?

What do I want?

Who cares?

No, actually. I have to know.

Waldemar Ekenberg is more obvious than almost everyone else, his masculinity almost comically exaggerated. God knows what he's got up over the past few days, how much he has allowed the ends to justify the means. At some point time will catch up even with him.

And Zeke. The way they work together is possibly simpler and clearer now than ever, no nonsense about each of them going off and doing their own thing, a wordless trust in each other. It's as if Zeke is holding back his tendency toward violence now that Ekenberg is part of the team, as if there has to be a constant balance between violence and empathy, as if this balance is essential if they are to twist the truth out of the clues.

And me.

I know what I'm doing.

Am I learning anything?

I'm slowly getting closer to the girls, that much is clear. If I can feel and understand their fear, maybe I can understand the person who harmed them.

The immigrant lads.

Karin Johannison not yet done with her examination of the dildo. But there's a high probability that it matches the one used in the crimes, so maybe they'll be able to take the day off tomorrow.

The lesbian line of inquiry.

A wicked man in Finspång. Where does this woman-to-woman love lead?

Slavenca Visnic. The kiosks. And the water.

The water.

Tomorrow will bring with it the hypnosis of Josefin Davidsson. Malin called Viveka Crafoord on her way home from their meeting with Svea Svensson, told her that they'd have to put it off, and Viveka had sounded disappointed, saying: "I think I can get something out of her, get her to talk."

The road signs with numbers saying how great the distance between grief and longing is, how far it is until the distance is wiped out and only time remains.

Nyköping twenty.

Seventeen.

Skavsta.

Should I have brought Markus?

It didn't even occur to me.

And Malin parks, goes into the arrivals hall, white beams seeming to float high up under a curved ceiling, a bare room full of peculiar dreams.

The clock on the wall says quarter past ten.

The plane is due in on time.

In two and a half hours the presence of love will replace grief, longing.

*　　　*　　　*

She'll soon be there, Malin, your Tove.

We were up with her and Janne just now, and they were both asleep, exhausted by the long journey, by everything they have experienced.

They were both smiling.

It was a happy moment, just like you will be experiencing soon.

And us?

Sofia and I. We're drifting somewhere below the ceiling of the arrivals hall, watching you and thinking that maybe it would be better if you were concentrating on us, on what has happened, instead of concentrating on your own nearest and dearest.

At least that's what we'd like.

Worrying about your own concerns doesn't disappear where we are. But it's different, it encompasses more, it's as if it encompasses everything that is or has been or ever will be.

Worrying about your own concerns becomes consideration for everyone.

Sofia and I are one and the same here. We are Josefin, Tove, and you. We are all girls and all who have been girls. But we're boys as well.

Does that sound odd?

I can understand that, Malin. It's all very strange, actually.

Where should you start?

Start with your nearest and dearest.

But who wouldn't choose love, if the choice was between it and violence?

Can you hear me, Malin?

This is Sofia Fredén.

My mum and dad are sad, so sad, their sadness can never even be replaced by longing. Unless it can, if only time is allowed to pass? Now they're sitting on the sofa in their flat in Mjölby. The television is on but they can't see what's on the screen.

Their eyes are full of tears.

And they're crying for me, Malin.

You can do so much, Malin.

You can make their tears stop. Or at least take a different path.
Just take a brief moment to catch your breath before pressing on.

Tove is holding her dad's hand, the pressure in her ears is giving her a headache as, foot by foot, the plane descends toward the runway, the lights of the houses in the forests outside the windows are growing, a strip of brightness is still lingering on the horizon, and Tove wonders if the world is disappearing over there, but knows that it carries on for an eternity, that life on this planet is a vast cyclical motion, no matter what anyone might say.

Mum.

I've missed her.

A vibration in the plane as the wheels touch the runway. Lights from the hangars.

Dad squeezing my hand.

I wonder if she brought Markus?

I haven't really missed him much. What does that mean?

"Back on Swedish soil!" Dad says, and he looks happy. "Now to see if your mum's made it on time, or if she's still at work."

Their bags.

Janne hates this part of traveling.

But there they are. Almost the first ones to appear, nothing got held up in the transfer between Heathrow and Stansted.

Their baggage.

Everything as it should be.

"Come on, Tove."

It's nice to come home.

Malin stares at the automatic doors.

Taps her sandal-clad feet on the white stone floor, around her she can see happy people, expectant, focused.

She runs her hands over her dress, pushes her hair behind her ears, feels like she needs to go to the toilet but doesn't want to go off now; the plane landed a while back and they should be here.

Now.

And the door opens once more.

There.

There they are, and she goes toward them, running, and she can see that they're tired, but when Tove catches sight of her the tiredness disappears and Tove runs toward her, and Malin runs and the air lifts and their bodies meet.

Hands, arms around each other.

Malin picks her daughter up.

How much do you weigh now?

Six pounds nine ounces when you emerged from me.

And now?

Malin looks at Janne.

He's standing behind the luggage trolley, seems unsure of what to do now. Malin puts Tove down, beckons him over and then they stand in the arrivals hall, feeling a warmth warmer and more genuine than any summer could ever conjure up.

PART III

You Need to Come, Before Now Stops

ON THE WAY TOWARD THE FINAL ROOM

I haven't finished yet.

I know what needs to happen now.

Nothing can stop this summer from burning, nothing can stop our love from coming back.

The world, our world, will be pure and free and we shall whisper the mute snakes' words in each other's ears, feel how they make us big, invincible.

He must disappear, be wiped out, and you will dare to come back again.

Everything will be white. Burning white, and innocent.

No one will be allowed to stop me.

Claws scratching storeroom shelves, spiders' legs moving over your face.

My summer angels.

They can rest now, and soon they'll have the company and love of someone who shares their history. And the very same love that I shall also receive.

I shall find another girl. She will be you.

Everything will be put right. It won't hurt. Because soon there will be no pain anymore.

47

Tove safely returned.

She's sleeping under a freshly laundered white sheet in her bedroom and Malin thinks that it's like she's never been away, as if Indonesia and Bali and bombers and undercurrents and the other side of the world have stopped existing, even as a possibility.

A mute drive from Nyköping, Tove sleeping in the backseat, she and Janne united in an eternal wordlessness, a silence that never becomes uncomfortable, but which feels more lonely than real loneliness.

Intermittent words.

"Did you have a good time?"

"Are the forest fires under control?"

"It's starting to resemble a firestorm in places."

Janne came upstairs with them, carrying Tove's large green Samsonite case, Malin offered him tea and to her surprise he accepted, said he could ring for a taxi home whenever he felt like it.

Tove had dropped off before the water had boiled and they drank their tea in the kitchen, as the sound of a man and woman arguing rose from the street, and once they had fallen silent the only sound was the ticking of the IKEA clock.

Just half past three now.

"We were never good at that," Janne says as he puts his empty mug on the draining board.

"Good at what?"

Malin is standing as close as she dares, doesn't want to scare him off.

"At arguing."

Malin can feel anger rising up inside her, but suppresses the pointless emotion and manages to locate her calm, her longing again.

"Sometimes it feels like we never had time to really get started."

"Maybe we didn't."

"It's probably good to do a bit of shouting every now and then."

"You think?"

"What do you think?"

"I don't know what to think."

Then Malin tells him about the case she's working on, that she feels like heaven or earth has opened up and released a desperate evil on the city, and that she doesn't know how to stop it.

"Just like the fires," Janne says. "It seems like they don't know how to come to grips with the flames."

Then they stand silently in the kitchen for a while before Janne moves out into the hall.

"Do you mind if I call for a taxi?"

"Go ahead."

Janne picks up the receiver.

Malin goes toward him in the hall, and as he keys in the number of the taxi company she says:

"You can stay here."

Janne stops.

"I prefer my own bed to your sofa, Malin."

"You know that's not what I meant."

"You know it wouldn't work, Malin."

"Why wouldn't it work? Just go into the bedroom and lie down, it's no harder than that."

"It's stupid, Malin, what good would come of it? We're all done with—"

Malin puts one index finger over his lips and his breath is warm against her skin.

Close to him now.

"Shush, don't say anything else. Can't we just let tonight be tonight?"

Janne looks at her, and she takes his hand and leads him into the bedroom and he follows her without any further hesitation.

Hard or soft.

Punishment or reward.

That's what physical love can be.

Janne's chest against hers, one of her legs wrapped around his body, and it was so long ago now, but she remembers exactly how his cock feels inside her, how it takes her over and how her body's independent recognition makes her calm and feverish, knowing exactly how to move to be filled in a way that no one else fills her.

Drops of liquid merging into one.

Is that you or me breathing?

She shuts her eyes, then opens them and sees that Janne's eyes are shut, as if they're both trying to make their bodies believe that if they don't look at each other, then this isn't happening.

And they're young again, far too young again, and a thin piece of rubber breaks and you are formed, Tove. Malin keeps her eyes on Janne, the lower half of her body is heating up with a pain that's more pleasant than anything else she knows.

Awareness catches up with your body over the years.

The distance between feelings and thoughts of feelings disappears. She lies back.

Soundlessly and heavy he follows her, and her hands search his back, every square inch of skin a memory.

She lets go.

Becomes a woken child sleeping on its back with its arms above its head.

Come back to me now.

This is love.

Promise not to disappear again.

There you lie, dear Malin.

In the dawn light I see your lips twitch, you're dreaming, aren't you?

I've just pulled the sheet up over your body.

We won't speak about this tomorrow, or any other day. We'll pretend it never happened.

Goodbye, Malin.

Janne leaves the flat, but first he takes Malin's car keys from the chest of drawers in the hall. Goes down to the street.

He opens the trunk, takes out his case. Goes back upstairs and puts the keys back where he found them.

The dawn is warm, and the gray stone of the church seems to vibrate in the thin blue light of the rising sun.

A faint smell of smoke, hardly noticeable even to his trained nose.

He heads toward the station. Pulling his case behind him.

At the station he changes into his protective clothing and goes with the first engine up to the forest, to the fires, heading straight into the heat and fighting the inferno.

Daniel Högfeldt happened to see Janne, Malin's ex-husband, come out of the door of the building where she lives.

A particular rhythm in his walk.

Daniel was on his way to the newsroom, early. He'd woken up in the middle of the night and been unable to get back to sleep.

Now he's sitting at his desk and thinking about the rhythm in Janne's movements, the way they exuded a softness and, oddly enough, love.

I can never compete with that, Daniel thinks, opening a new document on his computer and tossing the heap of articles linked by the word *rape* into the wastepaper basket.

Can't be bothered to do anything with them.

Can't be bothered even to sit here.

I have to, Daniel thinks, fumbling his way back to feeling bothered, finding it again.

And being bothered is not going to happen if he concentrates on the history of violent sexual assaults in Linköping. Someone else can do that. Maybe you, Malin?

Last night's dream.

A boy by her bed crying, Mummy, Mummy, Mummy, help me breathe.

She cried back.

Can't you breathe?

The boy replied.

No, help me, Mummy.

I'm not your mummy.

You are my mummy. Aren't you?

No.

Help me breathe.

Why?

Because I'm your brother.

Can't you breathe?

No. You have to show me how.

"It's so hot. Has it been like this all the time?"

Tove is drooping over a bowl of milk and cornflakes at the breakfast table. Malin is over by the sink, drinking her third mug of coffee, getting ready to force herself to eat a sandwich.

"It's been horribly hot, Tove. And they just said on television that it's going to carry on like this."

"Great. Then I can go swimming."

"With Markus?"

"With him, or a friend."

"You have to tell me who you're going swimming with."

"Can't I go swimming with who I want?"

"Read the paper and you'll see why I want to know what you're doing."

Tove leafs through the *Correspondent*. They have several pages on the murders.

"Police Silent," says one headline.

"Nasty," Tove says. She doesn't ask whether her mum is working on the case, knows that she must be. "Do you think it's the guy you've got locked up?"

"This one's really bad, Tove," Malin says. "We've got one man in a cell. But you have to be careful. Don't go out alone. And let me know where you are."

"You mean in the evenings?"

"All the time, Tove. I don't even know if the person we're trying to catch makes any distinction between day and night."

"Isn't that a bit over the top?"

"Don't argue. If there's one thing I know more about than you, it's this."

Malin can hear how disagreeable she sounds, the collected aggression of a debilitatingly hot summer, and she sees the look of surprise, fear, and then sorrow on Tove's face.

"Sorry, Tove, I didn't mean—"

"I don't give a damn what you meant, Mum."

48

They're on their way past Tjällmo, heading toward Finspång, driving past the fringes of the fires.

It is now half past nine. They skipped the morning meeting today. They can all meet up later instead.

She's thinking about Janne.

Knows that he's already in there, in the smoke, working and trying to fight the flames, to stop the fires spreading even further.

"He's there already, isn't he?"

Zeke is holding on to the wheel of the Volvo with one hand, his eyes fixed firmly on the road as they pass a fire engine.

"Couldn't wait another second."

"You're so similar, Malin, you know that?"

"In what way?"

"Loads of ways. But I suppose I mean the way you treat your work. You both love your work beyond reason, it's your way of escaping from reality."

"Zeke. I'm going to pretend I didn't hear that last bit. How's Martin's preseason training going?"

"Great, I expect. He loves circuit training."

"Any more offers from the States yet?"

"Apparently his agent is talking to a number of clubs. I daresay it'll all work out once the baby's here."

Martin was picked for the national team for the first time back in May for the World Championships. Zeke traveled to Prague to see one of the matches, forced to go by his wife. Malin knows he hates flying almost as much as he hates ice hockey.

"He's going to be seriously rich, then," Malin says.

"Yes, for hitting a damn puck and sliding around the ice on a pair of skates."

"For entertaining the rest of us, Zeke," Malin says, and considers her hopes for Tove: becoming a teacher or a lawyer, one of the nice, straightforward professions that all parents dream of for their children. Or an author, seeing as she reads like a maniac and writes essays for school that astonish her teachers.

"Hockey's for morons," Zeke says. "That's all there is to it."

"Don't be so hard on him."

"The lad can do what he likes, but there's no way I'm ever going to love that game."

The road forces its way through the forest.

The world around them is deserted, all the animals have long since fled the flames. Fifty minutes later they reach Finspång.

Home to the De Geer industrial empire.

A town built up around the production of cannons.

Neglected.

But a good place to raise children. And a good place to hide yourself away.

Their satnav leads them to the right place.

The street where Sture Folkman lives is an obscure cul-de-sac just behind a run of shops right in the center of town, and number twelve is a three-story block of flats. The ground-floor shop is occupied by the National Federation of Disabled Persons.

They park.

Take it for granted that the old man is home.

The door to the flats isn't locked, Finspång so small that they don't need coded locks, people free to come and go as they please all day long.

They read his name on the gray-green list of names in movable white lettering; he lives on the third floor.

"That's the bastard," Zeke says.

"Take it easy now," Malin says. "He's an old man."

"Okay, so he's old. But some crimes never go away, and can never be forgiven."

"Get lost," says a hoarse voice through the mail slot, and it contains a meanness, a malice that is evident in a way that Malin has never experienced before, and the pink walls of the stairwell seem to turn bloodred and collapse in on them as they stand there.

"I don't want anything. Get lost."

"We're not selling anything. We're from the Linköping Police, and we'd like to talk to you. Open the door."

"Get lost."

"Open up. Now. Or I'll break the door in." The man inside seems to hear that Zeke is serious, and the door is unlocked and opened.

A tall, thin man with a bent back, his body frozen by what looks like Parkinson's.

You didn't do it, Malin thinks, but then they never really thought he had.

A long nose that distracts attention from a weak chin, and Sture Folkman stares right at them, his eyes gray and cold.

Cold as the tundra.

Cold as the Arctic.

Like a world without light, that's how cold your eyes are.

Black gabardine trousers. A white nylon shirt and a gray cardigan in spite of the heat.

"What the hell do you want?"

Malin looks at his hands.

Long, white, bloodless fingers dangling toward the rag rugs in the hall, tentacles ready to feel their way up, in.

Green plush sofas.

Black-and-white photographs of family farms long since sold off.

Heavy red velvet curtains shutting out all the light. A bookcase with books about chemistry, and a complete set of the *Duden* encyclopedia in German.

"I've got nothing to say to you."

Sture Folkman's response when they explained why they were there.

But Malin and Zeke still went into the living room, sitting down in a couple of armchairs, waiting.

Sture Folkman hesitated in the hall.

They heard him moving around in the kitchen, scrupulously clean, Malin noticed that as they went past, old-fashioned knives with Bakelite handles in a block on the draining board.

Then he came in to them.

"Get lost."

"Not until you answer our questions."

"Get lost, back to Linköping. That's where you said you were from, isn't it? Fucking stuck-up dump. I was at your oh-so-wonderful hospital last month. Fucking shit urologist."

He slumped onto a rib-backed chair beside the bookcase.

"I've never had any dealings with the cops."

"You should have."

"What do you mean?"

"You subjected Louise Svensson to sexual abuse, repeatedly. There's no point trying to deny it, we know all about it."

"I—"

"And doubtless you went on to do the same to your new family. Where are they now?"

"My last wife died four years ago. A brain tumor."

"And your two daughters?"

"What do you want with them?"

"Answer."

"One's dead. The other's a long way away. In Australia."

"Does she live there?"

Sture Folkman doesn't answer.

"Do you know anything about the murders of young girls in Linköping?"

"What would I know about that?"

"Do you think Louise could have had anything to do with them?"

Sture Folkman knits his fingers, sniffs them, then lets his hands rest on his black trousers.

"Have you got any other assaults on your conscience?"

Zeke sounds the way he always does just before he explodes, just before violence.

"Well? Have you?"

"Zeke."

Sture Folkman raises his hands toward them, his white fingers a jagged fence.

"What do you really want? What do you want?"

On the way back to the car Malin can see Zeke trembling with loathing and anger.

He tosses the keys to her.

"You drive."

And Malin sits behind the wheel as they leave Finspång behind them. They're surrounded by dense forest when Zeke finally speaks.

"He had a point, the old bastard. What were we doing there really?"

"Following up on a line of inquiry, Zeke. That's what we do. We look back in case it helps us move forward."

"But still. It feels so remote that it's bordering on desperation."

Malin doesn't reply.

Instead she fixes her eyes on the road, thinking about what must happen to your soul if you get nightly visits from those white fingers throughout the years when your faith in other people assumes its final form.

It makes you watchful.

Scared.

A conviction that everyone probably wants to hurt you.

That everyone hates you.

An inability to fit in, instead an urge to seek out anything broken, to validate what's broken within yourself.

Life as a lonely, aimless wanderer.

Everything that could be defined as self-esteem fingered to destruction.

Cracks in doors concealing a darkness that you could tumble helplessly into.

Inquisitive.

"Off you go, now."

Per Sundsten tries to make his voice sound authoritative.

Sven Sjöman hadn't been convinced about their idea: taking him out to the crime scenes to get him to break down, confess.

"His lawyer will have to go too."

"Fuck the lawyer. We haven't got time for that," Waldemar said. "The girls, Sjöman, think of the girls."

"Okay, but take it easy. Nothing unnecessary."

As he sat at his desk in the open-plan office, Sven hesitated, his face wrinkling with awareness of their excesses.

"Get lost."

And Waldemar fixes a stare on the boys until they lumber off, embarrassed, down the little beach and back into the water.

"So this was where you buried her. And was this where you killed her as well?"

Suliman Hajif shakes his head, whispering:

"My lawyer should be here."

"We tried to get hold of him," Waldemar says. "But he wasn't answering the phone. He doesn't give a damn about you."

"It would make sense to confess," Per says. "You'd feel better. Any time now we're expecting the results from Forensics, and then we'll know it was you, and that it was your dildo that was used on these girls."

Suliman Hajif shakes his head again.

Waldemar takes a step forward, grabs him by the neck, hard, but in a way that could look almost paternal to the other people on the beach.

"So you're playing the silent game, are you?"

A groan.

But no words.

"Let's go to the next one," Waldemar says, dragging Suliman Hajif with him, back the way they came from.

Malin gets the call just as they're passing the turning to Tornby.

Karin Johannison's voice, excited behind the formal tone.

49

The beach outside Sturefors in the dying afternoon light. The heat is making Waldemar Ekenberg's jacket stick to his body as he stands beneath the oak inside the cordon.

The holstered pistol is warm against his chest, not even metal shielded by cloth and shade can resist the heat.

Suliman Hajif is standing beside what was Theresa Eckeved's grave, dressed in jeans and a white T-shirt, allowed to not wear custody clothing for the excursion they're in the middle of. His hands are behind his back, the handcuffs fastened tight to make sure he doesn't try anything.

The bathers have found their way back.

When they arrived they stared in their direction from behind their sunglasses, now they've gone back to swimming. Presumably they think that the reason for their visit is too frightening to be allowed to blemish such a dreamy summer's day as this: *That was where they found her. It's the police. It happened. How old was she? Fourteen. Summertime death. Over there, by that oak tree.*

Only two boys, wearing identical blue swimming trunks, are standing outside the cordon and staring up at them through blue-tinted glass. The ice-cream kiosk is closed, otherwise the boys would probably each be clutching a cone.

"It's the same paint. The paint on Suliman Hajif's dildo matches the paint on the one used in the attacks."

"So it's the same dildo?"

"It isn't possible to say that for sure. But certainly the same sort. As to whether the fragments of paint match the pieces that are missing from Suliman Hajif's dildo . . . Well, I've tried, but there isn't a hope in hell of doing that."

Malin feels her stomach clench.

All due respect to the chances of matching the fragments. But how likely is it that two different dildos of the same model would turn up in the same investigation?

"Any other traces on it?"

"No."

"Any other news?"

"Sorry, Malin. No new evidence."

The same dildo.

Synchronicity.

Freud.

On the way to Viveka Crafoord now for the session of hypnosis. Is that even necessary now?

"Thanks, Karin. Are you going to call Sven Sjöman?"

"Of course."

"So it's the same dildo? Okay, just the same model. But then it's sorted, isn't it?"

Waldemar elated behind the wheel of their blue Saab; Sundsten and Suliman Hajif in the backseat, they've just driven through the idyll of Sturefors. Beside them on the cycle path an elderly couple are wobbling along on a brand-new tandem.

"We've got him here, we're coming in. No, nothing. He hasn't said a word."

Without letting go of the wheel Waldemar turns to look at the backseat, saying:

"Okay, you randy little Paki, we've got you now."

Then he turns in to a side road and drives deep into the forest, and Per knows what's going to happen now, doesn't want it to happen, but lets it happen.

Zeke's reaction to the information about the dildo:

"So we don't have to bother with the hypnosis? It's as good as sorted now. We must be able to get a confession out of him now."

"It's not sorted," Malin says without taking her eyes from the road. "We'll go through with the hypnosis as planned. Josefin Davidsson is probably already at Viveka's office. The best we can hope for is that we get ourselves a witness, and no matter what that witness says, it will give us more information, won't it?"

Zeke nods.

Knows she's right.

"I want this case to be over," Zeke says. "I want the people living in the city to be able to read in tomorrow's *Correspondent* that we've caught the bastard and that they can let their girls play wherever they like again, that they don't have to be worried or frightened."

Tove.

Am I worried?

No.

Actually, yes.

"It's coming, Zeke," Malin says. "In principle, the case is cracked. Now we just have to join all the dots."

Waldemar Ekenberg clenches his fist and punches Suliman Hajif just under his ribs, the place which causes the most pain without leaving any visible physical evidence.

Suliman Hajif collapses.

Per Sundsten is pretending to help, picking Suliman Hajif up, but only so he can be hit again.

The young man is still silent.

No words, just groaning as he lies on the ground, hands over his eyes, and the forest around the gravel road is still, the moss thick and yellow and dry on the ground, the maples have lost their chlorophyll, but life is clinging on in there, begging for rain.

"You raped and murdered Theresa Eckeved and Sofia Fredén. Didn't you? And you raped Josefin Davidsson. Didn't you? You perverse little fucker. I'm going to kill you out here if you don't confess."

He must be able to hear from Ekenberg's voice that he's serious.

Suliman Hajif tries to get up, but his legs don't want to obey, he lurches back and forth and Per can see the fear in his eyes.

Waldemar takes his pistol from its holster.

Crouches down beside Suliman Hajif and puts the barrel to his back.

"It's easy. We say you tried to escape and were forced to shoot to stop you. A double murderer and rapist. No one's going to wonder. People will thank us."

Per unsure.

"Get up!" Waldemar screams, and Suliman Hajif scrambles, tries to get up, screaming:

"I can't confess to something I didn't do!"

The pistol against his temple now.

"Don't try to escape."

Then Per takes a step forward, knocks the pistol from Waldemar's hand.

"What the hell are you doing?"

"That's enough. Get it? That's enough."

A wind blows through the maples' shriveled branches and a thousand yellow leaves decide to let go, falling like a golden rain over the scene in the forest.

"I bought the dildo from Stene at Blue Rose," Suliman Hajif screams. "He said he'd sold dozens of them, so how do you know it was mine?"

"Shit," Waldemar whispers, and Per thinks: You're right there, Waldemar, you're absolutely right.

"Why the hell hasn't anyone checked which dildos are sold in the only porn shop in the city? Fucking Internet. People still buy things in shops, don't they?"

Per grabs Waldemar's arm.

"Calm down. This is a crazy summer. We're under pressure from all sides. Sometimes you don't see what's right in front of your nose."

Quarter of an hour later Waldemar is standing at the counter of Blue Rose on Djurgårdsgatan, the city's long-established porn shop.

Stene, the owner, smiles with his puffy, stubbled face.

"A blue dildo?"

Stene goes over to a shelf at the back of the dimly lit premises. Comes back with a pink and orange package in his hand, the blue object inside the pack half obscured by the loud, shouting lettering: HARD AND HORNY!

"These have been selling like hotcakes. I must have sold forty or so in the last eighteen months. None in the last month or so, mind you."

Waldemar spits out a question:

"Do you keep a list of your customers?"

"No, are you mad? Nothing of the sort. Discretion is my watch-word. And I have a bad memory for faces."

"Credit cards?"

"Those bastards take seven percent. Here it's cash that counts."

Malin pulls up in the parking lot of the Filadelfia Church and doesn't bother to get a ticket from the machine. She and Zeke cross over Drottninggatan, ignoring how hungry they are and fighting the urge to stop in McDonald's on the way.

They press the buzzer of number 12 Drottninggatan and Viveka Crafoord lets them in.

In the treatment room, on the paisley-patterned chaise longue, sits Josefin Davidsson, her mother sitting nervously beside her.

Viveka is sitting in her leather chair behind the desk, her face lit up by the light falling from the window looking onto Drottninggatan. A strange, mystical light, Malin thinks.

"Okay," Josefin says. "I want to know what happened."

You're not the only one, Malin thinks.

50

*T*he memory of violence.

    It's somewhere inside you, Josefin.

    Synapses need to be connected to synapses, and then you'll re-member. But do you really want to remember?

We remember. We can see what happened to us, how we disappeared, we'd rather call it that, a disappearance, then how, after a lot of loneliness, we found each other in our shapeless space.

Sofia and I have each other.

Perhaps we're in the beautiful place that exists before consciousness, unconsciousness? Before everything that human beings mistake for life?

We can just make out the people we once were, our space can assume whatever color we like, and we can be exactly the people we want to be, wherever we like.

We're with you, now, Josefin, in the lady psychologist's room.

We need your memories.

Because somehow we need the closure provided by the truth in order to achieve real peace, to stop being scared of the dark. Because that's what our space is like, it can adopt a color that makes black seem like white.

Don't be scared.

It's just memories.

Of course. They're your life, in one way, and we need them.

But remember one thing, Josefin. The only thing we summer angels really have is each other.

The pendulum in front of my eyes.

The curtains, the leather-bound volumes in the bookcases, the etchings of rural scenes. This room is like England.

The pendulum.

Isn't that just something they do in films?

It smells stale here, couldn't she have aired it first? Or maybe put some perfume on?

This peculiar sofa is comfortable, Josefin thinks, trying to concentrate on the pendulum, but her thoughts keep wandering off, her eyes flickering around the people in the room.

The woman police officer.

Malin.

She's standing behind the psychologist lady.

What's her thing? She seems calm, but anyone can see how twitchy she is under the surface. Well, maybe not twitchy, exactly, but definitely pretty manic or something.

She's staring at me. Stop staring! Maybe she can read my mind, because she's stopped staring now.

The policeman with the shaved head is sitting on the black lacquered chair by the window. Calm, but dangerous. He's the dad of that hockey player. And then Mum, terrified. I'm not scared, is she scared that her little girl is going to get dirty? I'm no angel, Mum, stop thinking that.

And the psychologist lady.

Looking irritated. She's noticed I'm not concentrating.

"Look at the pendulum and listen to my voice."

What, has she said something? Josefin thinks, and says:

"I'll try harder."

The psychologist lady says:

"Take deep breaths,"—I take deep breaths—"follow the swing of the pendulum,"—I follow the swing of the pendulum—"feel yourself drifting off," and I feel myself drifting off.

Eyelids closing.

Dark, but still light.

But hang on.

Where am I now?

At last, Malin thinks as she sees Josefin Davidsson disappear inside herself, responding to Viveka Crafoord's commands.

She's written a list of questions for Viveka, who has made it very clear that she, and she alone, would talk to Josefin during the session. That it could be difficult otherwise, and that this wasn't like an ordinary conversation, you had to follow images and words instead of subjects.

Viveka puts the pendulum on the desk.

The sound of cars out in Drottninggatan seeps into the room.

You can hear the five of us, our breathing, Malin thinks, how they are becoming one. Zeke's face is expressionless, Malin knows how skeptical he is about this, even if he'd never admit it now that it's happening.

Viveka takes down the list of questions from the top shelf of the bookcase.

"Can you hear me, Josefin? I'd like to ask you some questions. Do you think you might be able to answer them?"

A white, echoless room.

A strange voice, my own voice.

"Ask questions if you want."

"I'll ask questions."

"I'm tired, I want to sleep."

"The Horticultural Society Park," the strange voice says, and a pure white light shines in through a hole in the wall, the windows go black and then disappear.

"I woke up there."

"What happened before you woke up?"

"I was asleep. Before I was asleep I was at the cinema."

The light is fading now, the room turns gray, and a dark figure is coming toward me, it might be a wolf or a dog or a hare or a person, but what sort of person walks on all fours?

"Take the dog away."

"Was it a dog that put you to sleep?"

"It's gone now."

"Who put you to sleep?"

"Mummy."

The room is white again and I am alone, and up in the ceiling there are storage shelves, like giant lights. I see myself sleeping there, a pair of floating hands are patting me on the back, it smells like a swimming pool, like a dewless summer's morning.

"A pair of hands."

"Put you to sleep?"

"Yes."

"A man's hands, or a woman's?"

"I don't know."

"Do you remember the start of the evening?"

The walls of the room disappear, I see myself cycling through a small piece of woodland, on an asphalt path, on my way through the forest in Ryd down into the city, I don't know why I've chosen that route, why?

"I went through a forest."

"Which forest?"

"The wrong forest. Why?"

The strange voice, the nuisance voice, a woman's voice, older than most.

"Why was it the wrong forest?"

"Because something was lying in wait for me."

"What was in the forest?"

"Something."

"Which forest?"

A force pushing me down, there's only me now, and I fall asleep, wake up to the rumbling sound of a car.

"Then I went in a car."

"Where?"

"To the storage shelves that were in the ceiling just now."

"You got to a storeroom?"

My body on a bunk. The scrubbing, it stings, and it stinks. And what is this body doing with me, its teeth are shining, it's cutting and my whole body hurts, stop pressing, stop pressing.

"Stop pressing, STOP PRESSING, STOP PRESSING, STOP DOING THAT."

The voice, the stranger:

"It's all right, you're safe here, you can wake up now."

I'm back in the white room, the dark figure disappears, and I creep out, wandering through the wall, waking up in a summerhouse, it's morning, and a nice person wakes me up, even though I'm not asleep. Is the person nice?

"I fled, I was awake, but I didn't see anything."

"Who found you in the park?"

"Maybe a person. WAS IT A PERSON?"

"You can wake up now. Wake up."

Black.

Open eyes.

The police officer, the police officer, Mum with gentle eyes, and the psychologist lady. They all have one thing in common. They all look confused.

Josefin Davidsson and her mother have left the clinic. Zeke has stretched out on the chaise longue and looks ready to begin the first of many therapy sessions.

Viveka is sitting behind her desk, Malin by the window. She's looking down at the cars on Drottninggatan, as they seem almost to dissolve in the dull light.

"Well, that was a great help," Zeke says. "Almost, anyway."

"If I understood that right," Malin says, "she was attacked in a forest, driven to a storeroom somewhere, where she was abused until she managed to escape and find her way to the Horticultural Society Park?"

"She was probably sedated in the forest," Viveka says.

"But she didn't say anything about who did it?" Zeke says.

"Not a damn thing," Malin adds.

"I'm sorry," Viveka says. "But interviews conducted under hypnosis seldom give straight answers. The consciousness never wants to remember the very worst things."

"You tried your best," Malin says.

"Can we try again? In a couple of days?"

Zeke converted, he seems to believe in this now.

"I don't think there'd be much point," Viveka says. "The memory is connected to the instinct for self-preservation. She's shut off again now."

Malin feels tired.

Wants to get home to Tove.

Wishes this investigation would finally get somewhere.

Anywhere, almost.

51

The clock on the wall of the meeting room says 6:15. The second hand is firmly attached, yet still seems somehow lost as it goes around. A summing-up meeting instead of a morning meeting. The investigating team gathered round the table.

All of them tired, the greasy skin of their faces damp with sweat, their clothes crumpled and dirty from fine summer dust.

The run-through has just started.

Malin has told them about Svea Svensson and Sture Folkman, and about the hypnosis of Josefin Davidsson.

Bad news from Karin Johannison. The forensic examination of Suliman Hajif's flat didn't come up with anything. His computer contained a whole load of porn, but nothing to connect him to the murders in any way.

Blue Rose had sold thirty-four dildos, and one of the police constables had identified ten sites on the net that sold the same model. So, without a confession or some new evidence, they were stuck as far as Suliman Hajif was concerned.

"How could we have missed checking out Blue Rose at the start of this?" Zeke says.

"We assumed that everyone bought that sort of toy on the Internet," Malin says. "None of our heat-addled brains even considered that tragic little shop."

"Mistakes happen in every case," Sven Sjöman says. "We could have saved Forensics some work. But there's no way we can get anywhere with Blue Rose's customers. Of course we can ask them to contact us, but that won't get us anywhere. No one's going to come forward and say they bought a dildo. I think we can all agree on that, can't we? Hajif. Are we making any progress there?"

"He has no alibi, but otherwise we haven't got anything."

Malin can hear the exhaustion in Waldemar Ekenberg's voice. He probably wishes he was back in his house in Mjölby, with just his usual hooligans to bully.

Another of their constables, Aronsson, had poked about in Sture Folkman's personal history after Malin asked her to. According to the archive, one of the two daughters from his marriage to Gudrun Strömholm, Elisabeth, had committed suicide when she was seventeen. The officers investigating the case never had any doubt about the cause of death, and Forensics had given an unambiguous verdict. Elisabeth Folkman had hanged herself. Reason: unknown.

No longer so unknown.

Aronsson.

The best constable in her year.

She had also checked with the police in Nässjö about the fishing accident in which Louise Svensson's father drowned.

He had been found floating beside a rowing boat out in the middle of a lake, Ryssbysjön, with a wound on his forehead. Gunnar Svensson was assumed to have tripped in the boat, hit his head on the railing, and fallen overboard, unconscious. Traces of blood had been found on the railing.

Sven tells them that they have finally and rather unexpectedly received a response from Yahoo! about the password to Theresa Eckeved's email account, and that the only correspondence was ten emails to Lovelygirl, who, to judge by the content of the emails, was Louise Svensson. Her farm was mentioned by name. According to what they had got from the emails, no meeting had been arranged that could have coincided with the date of the murder. But there was still no answer from Facebook.

You want to keep your grubby little secrets, Louise, Malin thinks. Presumably you hoped that we wouldn't find out what you've been up to? And once we did find out, you went on trying to protect yourself, your memories, everything that you are.

A lonely person living in the middle of the forest. But still a sex offender.

Then Sven tells them that the specialist unit in Stockholm was working on a psychological profile of the perpetrator, but that it would be delayed because the whole department was on holiday at the same time, and the relief psychologist had a bad cold.

"Psychologists, *pah*! Wimps," Waldemar says.

Malin thinks about what Viveka Crafoord said about the killer's profile, but keeps it to herself, it's just idle speculation by Viveka based on nonexistent evidence.

"You'll have to carry on with all lines of inquiry," Sven says. "Try to find new ones. Use every bit of intelligence you've got. Ekenberg, Sundsten, interview all the sex offenders you can get hold of."

Karim Akbar beside Sven, worried, knows that he's the one who's going to have to face the media again, trying to duck their questions without having anything substantial to give them. The press conference has been arranged for seven o'clock that evening.

As they are all leaving the room Karim asks Malin to stay behind.

He asks her to sit down again.

"Malin," he says. "I just wanted to tell you how much I want to get back to the house down in Västervik and go swimming again."

He wants to talk to me about swimming?

"Did you want anything in particular?"

"Yes, I want you to take part in the press conference."

"The press conference? You know how much I hate things like that."

"That's an order, Malin. If I haven't got any new information for them, then at least I can give them a few minutes with the prettiest face in the Linköping Police."

Anger wells up inside Malin.

At the same time she feels reluctantly flattered by Karim's compliment.

"Malin, joking aside, I don't want to stand there on my own again with nothing to say. It would be nice if you could come along and say nothing as well. And helpful. It might calm them down a bit."

"So you don't mean that stuff about being prettiest, then?"

Karim grins.

"Look in the mirror, Malin."

"Can we let them have the dildo?"

"That it was the same model?"

"Yes."

"No, that could lead to everyone assuming that Suliman Hajif is guilty. He doesn't deserve that yet. You saw the papers yesterday. That was bad enough."

The papers had been full of pictures of Suliman Hajif with his face blacked out. Headlines like: *"Summertime Killer Caught?" "Terror in Linköping."*

The prettiest face?

So that's where this crazy summer has got me?

A role as a shopwindow dummy.

Twenty minutes later Malin and Karim are standing before a group of journalists in the foyer of the police station. Of the television stations only SVT is there, but there are several radio stations and maybe ten newspaper reporters, a couple of photographers, presumably from the *Correspondent* and the TT news agency. Twice as many journalists just a couple of days ago, her summer angels are quickly becoming less interesting, selling fewer papers now that the investigation's got bogged down.

"We have spent the day pursuing a number of lines of inquiry," Karim says.

There's a crackle of flash photography before he goes on: "We're expecting a breakthrough in the case shortly, but for the time being I don't have any further information for you."

"What about you, Malin, can you tell us anything?"

More flashes, and Malin squints.

Daniel.

She didn't see him before, he must have been late arriving.

"No."

"Nothing?"

And Malin sees the gang of reporters, the hunger in their eyes, the curiosity and exhaustion, just like their own, and before she knows it the words are pouring from her mouth:

"Well, we've been in touch with a psychoanalyst who has put together a simple profile of the perpetrator. We're probably dealing with someone who has themselves been the victim of abuse, who has a fragile ego and a distorted self-image. A person who is part of society, yet still somehow separate. I can't say any more than that."

"And the name of the psychoanalyst?"

"I'm afraid we can't reveal that."

Karim fills in this last remark, making the best of the fact that Malin is revealing information that no one else knows about, having evidently decided that there's no harm in it.

"The profile isn't official, and was produced in haste, and they're currently working on a more detailed profile at National Crime."

"What about Suliman Hajif? You're still holding him? Any new evidence against him?"

"We're still holding him in custody."

"But you expect to be able to rule him out of the investigation?"

"No comment," Karim says. "That's all."

Several of the reporters want to interview Malin on her own, but she fends them off, saying:

"My daughter's waiting for me at home."

With a start, she realized the cameras were still rolling.

"That's off the record," she said.

How stupid. The last thing she needed was to share personal details with a television audience.

*   *   *

Tove and Malin are finishing off the pizzas she picked up on the way home, no longer hot, but almost nicer in this heat now that they're cold.

Tove still tired after the flight home.

She's slept most of the day away, never got out for that swim, hasn't even met Markus, but she's spoken to him.

"When are you going to see Markus?" Malin asks as she stuffs the last of the pizza in her mouth.

"Tomorrow," Tove says curtly, and Malin can sense the end of the love story in the dull tone of the word.

A shame, Malin thinks, because I really do like Biggan and Hasse, Markus's parents. I appreciate their dinners and their relaxed, cheerful company.

"Did you miss him while you were in Bali?"

"I don't know, Mum. Can we talk about something else? Do you have to go on about Markus?"

From inside the living room they can hear the start of the nine o'clock news on television.

"I might be on it," Malin says, and Tove lights up.

"This I have to see!"

It's the third item and they make a big deal of the profile in the absence of anything else. A close-up of Malin as she answers questions, and she thinks how old she looks, tired and washed out, wishes she'd put some makeup on or at least brushed her hair, but she did none of that in spite of Karim's encouragement.

"You look lovely, Mum," Tove says with a wry grin.

"Thanks, Tove, that warms the cockles of my heart."

"Are you cold?"

"I wish!"

Then another clip of Malin as they ask for an interview, as she brushes the camera aside with the words:

"I'm heading home to my daughter."

Tove gives her a curious look.

"Why did you say that, Mum?"

"I was careless."

Then the weather.

The heat wave is going to continue. No end in sight.

The policewoman.

Malin Fors.

In front of me on the television screen in my secret room. The storeroom shelves are stuffed and the stench doesn't exist for me, just the heat, a hell that I have sought out and must find my way through.

I've seen her swim.

At Tinnis.

Cooling herself down in this inferno.

Does she think she knows who I am? That she can call some psychoanalyst and find out who I am?

And on television? Where anyone can see?

If anything in life was that fucking easy I'd have completed my one single task long ago.

We'd be together again.

None of us would need to be alone or scared anymore.

I shall be like fire. Destroying, creating the possibility of new life.

This violation stops here, you've violated me, like everyone has always violated me.

You're moving inside me.

And what I just saw must be a sign, mustn't it, the scratching of white spider's legs with rabbit's claws in the dust of the bed. Shall I rattle the rabbit's claws above her neck? Is that what you want?

I'll try with the claws. They'll tear you again. I'll scrub with the milky white, that's what I'll do. Your skin will be a white dress. Impossible to trace, of course. Like the dildo. I bought it with cash down in the city last year. He said he'd sold a lot of them. I knew it would come in handy.

I'll show you. She will become you, you will become her.

You're leading me in the right direction, Malin Fors. Pain breeds pain which breeds love again. You mentioned your daughter on television. Why? She must be your whole world. Isn't she?

I just hope she's the right age.
My summer angel.
The pure love of summertime angels.
I can see it in you.
You're longing for resurrected love, just like me.
I'm going to escape my longing, and yours will begin.
Balance.
Maybe that's what's missing?
What I've been missing?
What we've been missing.

52

S ee how Tove rides her bike down there, taking care not to get into trouble with other traffic, better to get there slowly than not get there at all.

The roof of the Hotel Ekoxen, the Horticultural Society Park like a green mirage, the water of the pool at Tinnis like a shimmering blue promise.

She's going to meet someone, isn't she?

Yes, I think so.

Us?

No.

I don't want that, it would make me miserable.

Now she's cycling across the bridge over Tinnerbäcken, then struggling up the slope toward Ramshäll.

That's where the rich people live.

She isn't rich.

No.

Now I can't see her anymore.

She's beneath the canopy of the trees.

But you can sense that as well, can't you, Sofia?

Yes, I can sense it.

She must be careful.

Careful.

*   *   *

Markus.

It's odd. First she couldn't be without him, then everything became sort of normal: not boring or anything, just normal. He didn't exactly turn into a friend, but it wasn't like it was at the start either.

Tove knew that she wouldn't miss him in Bali, she just knew, and she knew what that meant.

It's hotter at home that it was there.

And the light is ten times sharper.

It's a good thing I've got good sunglasses.

Mum doesn't like wearing sunglasses, she thinks they distort reality. I like it when the world gets a bit more yellow.

Her heart is pounding in her chest as she stands up to pedal up the hill into Ramshäll, past the brick houses and the big wooden ones occupied by the most prominent of the city's inhabitants.

Markus's mum and dad are people like that. Doctors, both of them. She'd liked that as well to start with; their big house, not at all like at home, it was a bit like one of the books she'd read: the girl of the people, the man better off, like a prince or duke.

But the house became normal as well, it wasn't like in any of the books. Bali. That wasn't normal.

On her way to the house and Markus now. He wanted to come up with something to do, and he must have been able to tell from her voice over the phone last night that she wasn't sure. She thought about it last night as she was falling asleep. How she somehow can't imagine seeing Markus the way she used to. Of course they can meet up, but not like that.

How to say that to him?

It's like she means more to him.

A white van drives past her, slowly, presumably looking for an address, probably a gardener.

Finally, their white brick house. The big apple trees look sad, the trunks look like they're about to crack in the heat. The front door opens before she's even had time to park her bike on the path.

Markus.

Thin and pale, and he smiles.

Tove smiles back, thinking:

Hope my smile looks genuine.

It's good that he can't see my eyes.

Then she thinks:

Is it always like this? That when you aren't in love anymore everything is just flat? Isn't there anything else?

Karin Johannison is in her office, feeling restless. She gets up, sits down, puts her feet up on the desk, her pink-painted toenails perfectly matching the narrow pink stripes of her Prada sandals. She bought them in Milan back in the spring, when she and Kalle were there on a shopping trip.

Restless.

Karin doesn't know why, but one of the reasons is probably that she and Kalle had sex like idiots all night, they had the windows open and the night heat, damp but somehow fresh, had made them wilder than usual.

She can feel him inside her still, wants him inside her now, is that why she can't sit still?

They don't really talk to each other much anymore.

Not about anything.

And certainly not about the fact that they have never been able to have children, in spite of a thousand doctors and as many appointments. Instead they fuck. They've been doing that ever since they first met, and now their fucking is confirmation, that they're okay, that they still look at each other, and Karin thinks that that gets them a long way, but only a child can get you all the way.

Wordless love is nothing to be afraid of. Words don't get you far anyway.

But there's something more than her residual lust that's making her restless.

Have I missed something important?

Is that why I feel restless?

Karin sits down, switches on the computer, reads through her report about Josefin Davidsson. Watertight.

She reads through her report about Theresa Eckeved.

Probably murdered out at the beach.

Why?

No marks on the body to suggest it had been moved after death.

The soil under her nails matched the soil found at the scene, in both structure and content.

But.

Did I check all her nails? All the soil?

No.

I should have. There could have been different soil under different nails.

Sloppy.

Heat-fuddled sloppiness.

I was probably rushing, wanted to get a report to Malin and the others as soon as possible, and I took it for granted that the soil was the same under all her nails.

Have to check now. As long as there's still some soil left under the other nails.

She remembers the scrubbed-clean body.

Scrubbed, but there were still traces of soil under the nails, even if they were scarcely visible. Why did the killer miss that? Unless it wasn't there for the killer, in his or her dark tunnel.

She's standing beside what was once me in other people's eyes, scraping the soil from under the nails of my left, middle, and index fingers.

I know who the woman is, Dad.

What does she want now?

I've never got used to the chill of this room. The small windows up by the ceiling, the metal worktops, the stainless steel cabinets containing us, the drawer-like metal bed where I am lying now, and then there's the smell of surgical spirit and a lack of fresh air. It's a clean smell, clean, but heavy with sorrow and a feeling that this was how it all ended up, no more, no less.

What does she want with my fingers?

With the soil?

Must you be so methodical, efficient? That's actually me lying there on the stainless steel, my body completely cold, scrubbed clean, the blood stiff in its veins.

But it's still me.

Tell her, Dad.

I want her to stop treating me like an object. Do you hear, you, the one called Karin?

I want you to stroke me over the forehead, I want you to show that I am still someone as I lie there, but you're working quietly and methodically, and that makes me even more scared.

Please.

Stroke my forehead.

Put my hair in place.

Show me that I'm still a person.

The air-conditioning unit in the lab has given up and the building's own ventilation system can do little more than circulate the hot air from outside. For some tests, those requiring cold, this would be a disaster, and Karin has called the engineers.

But she doesn't need cool for soil analysis, and drops of sweat are beading on her forehead, she's not wearing her white lab coat and her pale-mauve sleeveless Ralph Lauren top is glowing under the neon lights.

The body down there just now.

She doesn't know why, but before she pushed it back into the refrigerated cabinet she stroked the girl over the forehead. Several times. Calmly and carefully. Gently stroking her hand over Theresa's brow. She's never done anything like that before.

The sheet detailing the first soil analysis on the worktop.

The new sample in the microscope.

Her eye focuses.

She can see at once that they aren't the same soil. The soil under these nails is from somewhere else. The soil under the nails of the other hand was sandy, its crystalline structure sharper.

She does other tests. This new soil is typical mineral-rich compost, the sort you buy in sacks from garden centers. This soil comes from a garden, or a park.

So, Karin thinks, she could have been moved after death, and if she was struggling to get away, scratching at the earth to get a grip and flee, she did it somewhere other than the beach. The soil from the beach could have got there as the body was pulled down the slope or put down on the ground.

But where?

Malin will probably think this is interesting, even if it doesn't really mean anything at all.

Karin opens the curtain.

She can just make out the yellow-white façade of the hospital.

One week until her holiday.

I'll end up getting ill if I don't get away from here.

Karin looks round the lab. Test tubes, flasks, fume cupboards, eye baths, all of it very sexy in an inexplicable way. She sees herself up on the worktop, her cotton skirt round her thighs, Kalle thrusting deep inside her.

As deep as he possibly can.

Markus three feet or so from Tove on the sofa in the recreation room.

Cooler down here, the indoor pool behind the glass empty for the summer.

"In the summer you swim outside!" Markus's mum, Biggan, had said when Tove asked about it in June.

He wants her to come closer. He doesn't need to say it, it's obvious from his bearing. But Tove doesn't want to, wants to tell him that she has to go, but she doesn't know where to start.

He's going to be upset.

"Come and sit next to me."

His Iron Maiden T-shirt is just childish. Like all hard rock. As if he doesn't want to grow up, even though their bodies do.

But they haven't had sex.

Markus has wanted to, and so has she, but they still haven't. To start with they used to lie next to each other in the recreation room, under an itchy, brightly patterned, crocheted blanket, and she would hold him in her hand, but no more than that, and he would have his fingers on her pants, but no further.

The heat, different from the sort when she just looked at him, scared her.

She doesn't know why.

53

The conversation had been short. Just after a content-free morning meeting.

Karin Johannison had told Malin that Theresa's body might have been moved, and that there was high-quality compost under her fingers, and Malin had pointed out at once that if she had been moved from somewhere then the likeliest place was her home, the beds in the garden were full of new compost. It might be worth a look.

She and Zeke met up with Karin in the parking lot outside the National Forensics Laboratory, best to arrive together even though Karin was driving her own car, its trunk full of the equipment needed for fieldwork.

They pull up outside Theresa Eckeved's parents' house.

As they drove past Malin's childhood home she looked the other way. It was as if the house was calling inaudibly to her, as if it wanted her to go there, and try to re-create what had existed a long time ago.

Secrets, the voices seemed to cry.

Come, and we'll tell you some secrets.

"Are you coming?" Zeke calls to Karin, frowning, his tone aggressive rather than impatient. Malin imagines that he might just be annoyed that Karin may have missed something that turns out to be important, but how many times have they overlooked things? Like the porn shop?

No one is faultless. Things being overlooked are part of every investigation.

"I'm coming. Could you maybe help me with one of my bags?"

Zeke goes over to Karin, picks up one of her large black bags, and they head up a white paved path, the bushes not watered, forgotten.

They ring the bell and Sigvard Eckeved opens the door half a minute later.

Surprise and suspicion, but also anticipation.

Have you got him?

And Malin sees the hope in his green-blue eyes, a flash of life, and she says that they have reason to believe that their daughter may have been murdered in a different location from the beach and that they would therefore like to conduct a cursory search of the house, just to rule out the possibility that she was attacked at home.

"You can't imagine that I, we . . ."

"Not for a second," Zeke says, and Sigvard Eckeved steps aside and his body is heavy, as if the true note of grief had penetrated his system and taken it over.

"If it would help your inquiries, you're welcome to burn the whole house down."

"I don't think that will be necessary," Zeke says with a smile. "There are probably enough fires round here as it is."

"True enough," Sigvard Eckeved says. "Well, do whatever you need to. The wife's in the city seeing her shrink."

Malin is going through the beds around the terrace and pool, searching for clues, broken twigs, signs of a struggle, but all she can find are withered red roses that long ago gave up in the heat.

She's out in the sun and has to keep wiping the sweat from her eyes and forehead. She can see Zeke on the other side of the lawn, where there's a large vegetable patch between the lawn and the neighbor's fence.

Karin inside the house.

Malin thought just now how well she fits in with this chic pool environment, in her skirt and her silly pale-mauve armless designer top.

Then Zeke calls out:

"Over here!"

And Malin can hear from his voice that he's confident, that he's found something important.

"She must have tried to escape next door."

The vegetable patch is full of drooping potatoes, bolted carrots, rhubarb that no one bothered to pick. The signs of a struggle are obvious, almost solidified in the drought and lack of rain and absence of watering, and they can see footsteps, the way her body must have fallen into the plants, then how someone had tried to pull Theresa backward and she struggled, digging her fingers in the soil, trying to cling to life.

"We need Karin," Zeke says. "Whatever she's up to. I imagine she's inside, in the cool."

Sigvard Eckeved has slumped onto one of the chairs on the terrace, his daughter's death even closer now, physically in their home, and it seems to Malin that he's been struck with the realization that they can't possibly go on living here, now that this is—has become—a place of violence.

Malin crouches down beside him.

"I'm sorry," she says.

"It's okay," Sigvard Eckeved says, and Malin realizes what this loss means for him, that things can't get any worse, that there might even be some small comfort in the fact that his daughter was at home when she was attacked.

"But I don't know," he says. "How am I going to tell my wife? It'll break her."

Once Karin has finished in the vegetable garden she turns to Malin, who has been watching from the shade of a pear tree.

"She most likely would have come from the pool," Karin says. "The perpetrator probably attacked her there and she tried to escape in this direction. I didn't find anything inside, no traces of blood or anything."

"You'll need to check around the pool."

"That's where I'm heading next, Malin."

A minute later Karin is going around the pool, and the water seems to simmer in the heat, inviting and off-putting at the same time in its ostentatious blueness. Karin sprays luminol on the wooden decking and the stone edge of the pool, hoping that the liquid will make any traces of blood glow in the relative darkness as she goes along shading the ground with a blue towel.

"I knew it," Karin says when she reaches the part of the pool closest to the garage. "I knew it," she repeats.

Malin hurries over, and Zeke emerges from inside the house.

Sigvard Eckeved remains seated on his chair, his face expressionless.

"Look here," Karin says, waving them over, and under the towel are some twenty small patches surrounded by splashes. "The perpetrator tried to get rid of it. But I can promise you that this was where Theresa received that blow to the head."

"Can you get a blood type or anything from that?"

Zeke hopeful.

"I'm afraid not. Nothing like that," Karin replies. "What you see here are just little ghosts of reality."

Malin is crouching beside Sigvard Eckeved again.

"Who would have had any reason to be here?"

"Who?"

"Yes."

"I don't know."

"There's no one who comes to mind?"

"No one. Sorry."

"No one?"

"No, it could have been anyone."

"No gardener? No one like that?"

"I usually do all the work myself. Together with my wife."

"And the pool?"

"We have someone who comes in early May each year. When we fill it. But this year I did it myself. Last summer we had workmen here, doing improvements to the terrace."

Malin's mobile rings from her jacket pocket.

"Fors here."

"Malin? This is Aronsson. I've finished the expanded background check of Sture Folkman. Do you want me to go through it over the phone?"

"I'm busy right now. Can we take it in an hour or so? Back at the station?"

"Sure. There are a couple of slightly unclear things I want to sort out."

Malin puts the phone away.

Sigvard Eckeved has started to cry, his whole body shaking, and Malin wants to help him but doesn't know how, and instead she puts her hand silently on his arm and doesn't say that everything will be all right, that it will all sort itself out.

Don't cry, Dad.

I'm scared, but I'm okay.

I was scared when it happened by the pool, out in the garden. It was awful, really awful.

But everything's coming together now.

I can feel it.

Evil.

Even that has a pain threshold where everything cracks.

When it becomes visible and can be driven back.

When people can start to enjoy the summer again in peace and quiet, just like they imagined they would, with no pain.

But first things need to reach a solution. What you call the truth needs to be revealed, however terrible it is.

And you, Malin, you have a visit to make.

You need to pay a visit to yourself. Maybe looking back can lead you forward. What do you think, Dad?

I know you're never going to forget me.

As long as you remember me, I'll be there wherever you are.

And that's a comfort, isn't it?

54

The house is empty of people, but when Malin looks in through the living room window and sees the mess of toys, she can hear the sound of children shouting, happy laughter, yelling and crying resulting from clashes about who gets the toy car, the stuffed animal, the crayon.

A young family lives in the house in which she grew up.

She told Zeke and Karin to go on ahead, said she wanted to walk round the area for a bit and that she'd get a taxi back. But Karin said that Zeke could go with her, and Zeke didn't protest, just said, to Malin's surprise: "That makes sense."

She rang the bell, but guessed no one was home, and now she's walking around to the back of the house. The grass is scorched to ruination, probably not watered all summer, and the fence around the terrace is flaking, the wood dry, no one's found time to oil it for several years.

Dad would be upset if he could see this, Malin thinks. The pedant, Mr. Careful, cheered on by Mum, Mrs. Better Than She Really Is.

Mum.

Why couldn't, why can't you be happy with what you are? Excuses about the flat in Tenerife: "We were going to buy a house, but looking after a garden and pool is so much work."

The hedge between the garden and the neighbor's, younger people living there as well now, and she remembers chasing a football around the lawn on her own on summer evenings, with Dad shouting at her not to hit the apple trees and currant bushes with the ball, and Mum lying in the hammock drinking chilled white wine and staring out into space rather than at her, looking like she'd rather be somewhere else.

Winter.

Snowmen and secret paths through the snow, days and nights of darkness that never ended, her glowing cheeks, and how she used to fight with Ida, the neighbors' daughter, once making her nose bleed, and she felt so bad afterward, the violence made her feel sick.

Mum and Dad's silence. The way they would circle each other like silent snakes, Malin with a big black pit in her stomach, the sense that something had gone wrong and must be kept secret at all costs.

What was it that I couldn't see?

Why was I so abrupt with Dad on the phone last time he rang?

And she misses them at that moment. Sees them before her in the flat in Tenerife that she's never been to, Mum in a flowery dress, Dad in a tennis T-shirt and shorts, eating breakfast on the terrace and talking about their neighbors, the neighborhood, the weather, but never about her or Tove.

Why don't they care more about Tove?

Dutiful love. The love of least resistance. She's you, for God's sake, Malin feels like shouting. You.

She breathes in the warm summer air, feeling the years and all the unreachable memories take hold of the person she has become. She crouches down.

What is it that I'm not seeing?

Snow turning to water.

She goes over to the terrace, looks in through the kitchen window, and in spite of the glass she can hear a tap dripping.

The kitchen is new, white IKEA cabinets, the FAKTUM range, shining in the relative darkness, the dining room off to the left, a table similar to the one they had, white-painted pine with uncomfortable, high-backed chairs.

A dripping tap.

Water.

Always this water.

Chlorinated pools, beaches for summer swimming. The apparently aimless movements of girls working over the summer.

What is it about water? Malin thinks. You want something to do with purity, with water, don't you?

Malin walks quickly away from the house, can't get away fast enough.

"What have you got against me, Zacharias?"

Karin Johannison presses the accelerator and Zeke sees the white, long, lace-edged cotton skirt mold itself to her thigh, sees her fine, long blond hair draped across her sharp cheekbones.

"I haven't got anything against you," Zeke says.

"We work together so much," Karin says, "and it would be easier if we got on."

Zeke looks out through the windshield, sits in silence watching the trees on the far side of the cycle path, and wonders why he instinctively dislikes Karin so much. Is it her money? The self-confidence that comes of being born with a silver spoon in your mouth? Is it her nonchalant manner? Or is the cause of his dislike somewhere inside him? A woman. Does he have a problem with the fact that she's a woman, and so damn attractive, and that she doesn't fit the image of what a forensics expert should be?

But that's just my own prejudice, Zeke thinks. Then he realizes what it is. Realizes that he's known ever since the first time he saw her. Impossible attraction means that you keep your distance. If I can't have you, I can always make you feel bad, feel worthless, even if that's the exact opposite of what I want.

"I don't know," Zeke says.

"Don't know what?"

"Why I've always been so abrupt with you. But that's all over now."

Karin doesn't say anything. But after a few long moments she takes her eyes off the road and looks at him with gratitude and warmth, and perhaps also desire.

Police Constable Aronsson has been blessed with a outsized bust which is scarcely contained within her gray police shirt, and Malin knows that she's already a running joke among her male colleagues: Bustbuster, give us this day our daily breasts, making a clean breast of things . . .

But Aronsson is smart and tenacious and has no delusions or testosterone dreams about what the profession is or should be.

She puts her notes down on Malin's desk and Malin and Zeke lean forward in their chairs, listening carefully to what she has to say.

"I've done the expanded background check on Sture Folkman, like you asked."

Aronsson's face is gentle, but her unfortunately protruding top teeth make her less attractive than she would otherwise be.

"He arrived here as a wartime evacuee from Finland. Evidently saw his whole family burned alive in Karelia. He ended up at a farm in the north of Skåne, outside Ängelholm. That's where he took his school diploma."

Aronsson pauses for breath before going on:

"He divorced his second wife in 1980. They had two daughters. One of them killed herself in 1985. The investigation seems to have been fairly straightforward if you read the report, she was found hanged and had apparently been in and out of psychiatric institutions for years."

Cold white hands under the covers.

Stop, Dad, stop, I'm your daughter.

There there, there there.

Malin forces the image from her mind. Some men should be castrated and strung up in public.

"And the other daughter lives in Australia? That's what Folkman implied."

Aronsson shakes her head.

"She lives here in the city. She's been registered at an address in the Vasastaden district for the past couple of years."

"Anything else on her?"

"Her first name's Vera. Forty-two years old. But I can't find any other details anywhere."

A quick, improvised meeting about the state of the case.

It is almost six o'clock, and they're all tired from the heat, from many days' intense hard work, and Malin wants to get home to Tove.

Sven Sjöman at the end of Malin's desk as quiet activity goes on around them in the office. Karim Akbar has already gone home, said he had a migraine. He's never had one before, Malin thinks.

"So Theresa Eckeved was probably murdered at home?"

Sven's voice slightly less tired than in previous meetings.

"We're not sure. But that's where she was attacked. She may have been moved somewhere else before being buried at the beach," Malin says. "So the killer may have some connection to the house. But nothing has emerged from talking to the family and those close to them. And the parents' alibis are watertight."

"Any other news?"

"Vera Folkman. Her father, Sture, said she lives in Australia, but she's registered here in Linköping. We're thinking of going to see her first thing tomorrow."

"Good," Sven Sjöman says. "That's just the sort of discrepancy that you have to look into to make any progress in cases like this."

"We know that talking to Vera Folkman is clutching at straws," Zeke says.

Sven turns to look at Waldemar Ekenberg and Per Sundsten, who are sitting at the other end of the desk.

"What about you?"

"We're checking the last names on the list of sex offenders," Per says. "And we thought we'd talk to people close to Suliman Hajif. It doesn't look like we're going to get much further with Suliman."

"Can we get the prosecutor to hold him for a bit longer?"

"I doubt it, I spoke to him a short while ago and the evidence is far too weak to hold him on grounds of reasonable probability."

"Better to let him go," Sven says, "and watch what he gets up to. What about Louise Svensson? Anything new there?"

"We've been checking on her regularly. But she's just been working on her farm," Malin says. "And I've got my doubts about Visnic."

"Okay, we'll carry on tomorrow," Sven says, looking at Malin with a frown.

"Something you wanted to tell us, Malin?"

"No. Just a feeling."

"So . . ."

"It can wait," Malin says, and Sven lets it go, saying:

"And we still don't know who called in about Josefin Davidsson. And we still don't have any idea what happened to her bike."

Tove isn't answering the phone. Not her mobile, and not the landline at home.

Where is she?

Malin is sitting at her desk, feeling her anxiety get the better of her. She's just called Markus and he said she left his house two hours ago, that they'd spent the day swimming at Tinnis.

Tove.

I told you to be careful.

Malin gets up, goes out to the car.

Malin opens the door of the flat, runs up the stairs. Calls:

"Tove! Tove, are you home?"

Silence.

Silent rooms.

Kitchen empty.

Living room empty.

Tove's bedroom empty.

Bathroom empty.

"Tove! Tove!"

Malin opens the door to her bedroom. Tove, please be lying on the bed.

55

Karim Akbar takes the hot cup of espresso from the machine and looks around the kitchen. The stainless steel draining board that was specially ordered to cover the whole area under the glassy tiles his wife had picked out from one of the international interior design magazines she usually gets from Press Stop down in Trädgårdstorget. The doors were also ordered specially, painted in a color known as British racing green, and the table and chairs are oak, bought from R.O.O.M. in Stockholm.

No migraine.

Just a feeling that he had to be alone.

He thinks about the book he should be writing, but which he will probably never manage to produce.

He doesn't even believe his thesis about integration himself.

The house in Lambohov is silent.

Is there anything more silent than a home in summer when the people who inhabit it are somewhere else?

He and his wife have been arguing more and more since the spring. About nothing, and he's noticed that their son is getting upset, is wary in their company, reluctant to talk, and Karim feels sorry for him but doesn't know what to do, doesn't have the energy to do anything. All the masks he has to wear, at work, in other official situations, and here at home, have exhausted him beyond mere exhaustion.

Why do we argue?

Karim breathes in the smell of their home, as its nooks and crannies become visible in the dim light.

She isn't happy. That much is clear. She finds fault everywhere and maybe she finds me offensive? No. But I irritate her and that in turn makes me irritated.

Their son.

In his formative years.

I, we, mustn't mess him up.

And Karim thinks of his father, and how he found him hanging in the flat in Nacksta one summer's day, almost as hot as today.

I was twelve years old.

I learned what despair was. But I refused to believe that even love has its limits.

I go too far sometimes, Waldemar Ekenberg thinks as he sprays water over the roses in the back garden of his house in Mjölby.

His wife is in the kitchen. Making a salad to go with that evening's barbecue, the pork has been marinating since the morning, the wine open to breathe, no wine-box crap here.

But do I go too far?

My colleagues have reported me, suspects have reported me, but nothing has ever come of it and I deliver the goods, more than other people, and with a case like this one? With a bastard like that on the loose no one cares if someone suffers a bit as long as no one really gets hurt.

That's what being human is.

Sometimes you get squeezed by circumstances, that's just the way it is. You just have to accept it, just like most suffering.

The woman in the kitchen wanted children.

I didn't care that much, Waldemar thinks. But God knows, they tried. Test tubes all over the place, wanking into little pots in dimly lit bathrooms with a cheap porn magazine in his lap.

Then she hit forty-five and all that stopped.

They share that fate with a lot of other couples.

And here I stand in our garden. The sky getting darker. Stars lighting up in distant galaxies. Earthly life huddling together, and I can honestly say that I still love her.

Per Sundsten is standing at the hot dog kiosk in Borensberg. Built in the fifties, it's the archetypal Swedish kiosk with an adjoining waiting room for bus passengers. He's ordered a pork burger with cheese, and is planning to take it down to the Göta Canal to eat it in peace and quiet as he watches the boats, before heading home to his flat in Motala.

The advantages of the single life.

I do what I want with my time. No one to tell me what to do.

"There you go."

The kiosk owner, an immigrant, hands him the burger, the cheese almost running down the sides of the meat.

He sits down on a bench overlooking the canal.

A man and woman, the same age as him, go past on a blue yacht. They're sitting in the cockpit drinking wine, and they wave to him and he takes a sip of his Pucko chocolate milkshake and waves back.

Ekenberg is crazy.

But at the same time it's reassuring to have him by my side. He knows how to do this. I'm probably better suited to the financial crime unit in Stockholm.

Motala. Not too dissimilar to Kalmar, where he grew up, an old industrial town now full of drugs and problems, but still with the appearance of a small-town idyll. But hardly the best place for a thirty-year-old to live.

The case they're working on. He can't get a grip on any of it. The threads are running together and it feels like he's mostly a passenger, that he doesn't have anything to contribute.

Fors.

She's driven and manic and a bit scary. She almost seems frightened of herself. But if anyone can solve this case it's her.

He takes a bite of the fried meat.

Another boat goes past.

A man is sitting in the cockpit. He looks lonely, Per thinks.

Zeke shovels another mouthful of plaice into his mouth. His wife looks at him, then she looks down at the kitchen table, with a pointed glance at the holiday brochures opened at various destinations: Sunny Beach in Bulgaria, Crete, Costa Dorada. Dreams packaged as dreams.

"I can't begin to think about that at the moment. About going anywhere."

She's sitting opposite him, pointing at Sunny Beach.

"This one's supposed to be cheap. What do you think?"

"Didn't you hear what I said?"

The kitchen suddenly seems extremely small, the brown pine units are crowding in on me, Zeke thinks, and he wants to escape into the garden, but she's not about to let go.

"Lennart and Siv went to Crete last summer. They said it was lovely. And it's easy to get deals now that the weather's so good here."

"This fish is good. Plaice is always good at this time of year."

"Or what do you think about Spain? That's still the classic, after all."

She leafs through one of the brochures.

"How about Rimini?"

He looks at her. Martin's mother, his wife. Who are you? he thinks. The investigation, the heat, the light, the dust, and Karin Johannison's legs under white fabric in the car. Everything creates new distances, making him a stranger in his own life.

Karin Johannison is standing naked by the swimming pool on the terrace behind the house, one of the largest in Ramshäll, the garden not overlooked at all thanks to the mature shrubs. The evening smells of sulphur and pine resin.

Kalle in front of the television in the living room.

He's watching one of those old films on TCM that he's so fond of, a Frank Capra comedy.

They had the pool installed back in the spring, they'd both wanted one for years.

They have help maintaining it, a neighbor put them onto a woman who looks after pools. She comes when they aren't at home, cleans it up, adjusts the chlorine levels, and Karin has never met her, but Kalle says she seems to know what she's doing, although she never says much and always wants to be paid in cash.

Whatever.

She thinks about what Martinsson said in the car.

About him.

Almost ten years older, and she's often wondered what he had against her, but she believed him, that there would be no more bad feeling from now on. And the way he looked at me. I could have stopped the car and done what people do at the side of the road.

A long hot crazy summer.

Heat all around me.

Heat within me.

I know how to escape it, Karin thinks, and pushes off with her feet, sailing through the air before her body cleaves the surface and everything becomes cool and miraculously silent.

Malin has crept in beside Tove.

She was lying in bed, still tired after the flight. Malin woke her, told her off. "The battery in my mobile ran out, I just met up with Julia and we got an ice cream from Bosse's, then did some people-watching in Stora torget. Mum, it's no big deal."

And Tove fell asleep again. Malin was feeling tired too. In the kitchen she drank half a tumbler of tequila, thinking that they were finally getting somewhere now, that soon this would all be over. And she felt how worried she was.

Then she went back in to Tove.

Took off all her clothes but her underwear.

Crept under the sheet and felt her daughter's warm skin and the gentle vibrations from her beating heart, reason enough to carry on fighting, living.

56

What are we going to do with all these people? The ones who can't control their desires, the ones who damage other people because they themselves have been damaged?

A bloody big camp up in Norrland.

A suicidal cliff of desire.

Chemical castration.

Real castration.

Electronic surveillance.

It's early in the morning and Per Sundsten can't work out what he thinks as he and Waldemar Ekenberg follow a still sleepy Arto Sovalaski through the hall of his red wooden cottage on the outskirts of Linghem, a bedroom community just to the east of Linköping. They just passed through a neatly tended garden, parched like everything green, with gooseberry bushes in close formation along the gravel path leading to the house.

"I know why you're here. And on a Saturday and all. Shouldn't you be having a day off?"

"At least we didn't have to have a morning meeting," Per says, watching Arto Sovalaski shuffle in front of them. Possibly the most exhausted man in the world, his face wrecked from drink and smoking, with no trace at all of any dreams for the future.

The stench of sweat in the house.

"We shouldn't be working," Per goes on, "but right now Linköping has been visited by the big bad."

Arto Sovalaski, the last name on the list of known sex offenders in their district.

He wore a stained yellow T-shirt with a picture of a bulldozer on the front.

"Do you work?"

Waldemar's question as they enter the living room and Arto Sovalaski has settled onto the yellow-and-brown-patterned sofa, the only piece of furniture in the room. Bottles and overflowing ashtrays all over the wooden floor.

"No, I got an early pension."

Well, thinks Per, I daresay no one really wants to have you around. Four rapes in four months ten years ago in different places, Växjö, Karlstad, Örebro, and one here in Linköping. Since then, nothing.

"So you know why we're here?"

"Yes, it's happened before when there's been some sex-related crime in the city. Then you come running. But you can clear off again, because I was away when it happened, visiting friends over on Öland. Call them."

Waldemar goes closer.

Not again, Per thinks.

But Waldemar backs down this time.

"Have you got your friends' number?"

"Sure."

Ten minutes later they're sitting in the car on the way back into the city, Arto Sovalaski's alibi confirmed by a drunk Finn on the other side of the Kalmar Sound.

"Well, that's that line of inquiry exhausted," Waldemar Ekenberg says. "Let's get back to the station and put the squeeze on Suliman one last time before he gets out."

"They let him go last night," Per says.

"Did they, now?" Waldemar says. "Did they, now?"

*   *   *

A bit of a lie-in.

They indulged themselves seeing as it's Saturday, and it's nine o'clock when Malin goes downstairs to meet Zeke.

The second Saturday of this case. Just over a week has passed since the eruption. But it feels like several years, as if they're dealing with a drawn-out plague.

The heat hasn't improved. It may even be a bit worse.

The gray stone façade of the church is quivering in the air, fading into a sickly yellow nuance, and the quiver in the air means that Malin can't make out the inscription.

Zeke, where are you?

He called ten minutes ago as he was passing Berga, so he should be here by now.

Tove still asleep up in the flat.

Malin walks down the street, taking a look in the windows of the St. Lars Gallery, at the colorful paintings by artists like Madeleine Pyk and Lasse Åberg. She doesn't know much about art, but what she sees hanging on the walls of the gallery makes her feel ill.

Vera Folkman.

How broken is she?

Damaged, damaged goods. We should put in a claim for the damage.

Like that couple in the US who adopted a little girl from Ukraine who turned out to have learning difficulties. The story goes that they sent her back in a FedEx box and that she froze to death en route, in a plane thirty-five thousand feet above the ground.

A car horn.

Zeke.

The next minute she's sitting in the air-conditioned cool of the car. She breathes out. Doesn't notice the white van parked at the top of Ågatan.

Tove stretches out in bed, her mum's bed, it's still nice to sleep there sometimes.

She's meeting Markus later, and today she's going to tell him it's over, that she still likes him, just not like that, and that they can still be friends.

But he won't want that.

She sits up.

Just from the light creeping through the gaps in the Venetian blinds she can tell this is likely to be the hottest day since she got home from Bali.

They ring the bell of Vera Folkman's flat on Sturegatan. She lives on the first floor, but there's no answer; the whole flat gives a strangely abandoned impression from the outside.

"Gone, baby, gone," Zeke says. "Damn, it's hot already. Hotter by the second."

The longer they stand outside the flat, the more they become aware of a smell coming from inside.

"It smells of animal crap," Zeke says.

"Maybe she keeps cats in there?"

"Well, whatever it is, it stinks."

"Maybe she's in Australia," Malin says, turning on her heel and starting to go back downstairs. "She could have left her pets inside."

"It's probably cooler there than it is here, even in Alice Springs," Zeke says.

"That's supposed to be the hottest place in the world."

"Wrong. Linköping's the hottest place in the world."

Tove sitting firmly on her bicycle.

Her pink top tight against her body.

The world sleepy and yellow through her sunglasses.

She pedals past Tinnis, but instead of heading up Ramshällsbacken she turns off toward the hospital, heading back down toward the Hotel Ekoxen. She has a funny feeling that someone's following her, that someone's watching her, trying to get closer. But she carries on pedaling, getting slightly out of breath, and she thinks it must be her nerves ahead of her conversation with Markus that are making her twitchy.

She'd felt it ever since she got her bike from the stand down by the church.

But where were the eyes?

She looked around, nothing suspicious, nothing different, just fewer people in this hot, summertime empty city.

And now she is coasting down toward the hotel, and turns around, and isn't that the same van that was parked outside the flat? At home? The one that drove past her outside Markus's yesterday?

Scared now.

And she stops at the hotel.

Opens the gate leading to the airy, yellowing Horticultural Society Park.

That was where they found one of the girls.

But at least the van can't follow me in there.

A dark figure behind the wheel. Who?

She's cycling fast, her daughter, and I mustn't give myself away, I shall take her like I took the others, it will be quick.

She mustn't see me and she's stopped at the gate of the park and she looks scared.

But I'm nothing to be scared of.

I'm just going to see to it that you start living again. I'm an angel-maker. That's what I am.

But she disappears.

Cycles into the park. She must have seen me. I drive past, pulling my cap down over my face. Time, my time, our time, will soon be here. Hands firm on the wheel now.

What time?

Tinnis, over there. That'll do.

*   *   *

Shall I call Mum?

No.

The van goes past, it doesn't stop, and the person inside it wearing a cap drives on.

I'm just twitchy.

There must be hundreds of white vans in Linköping.

Hardly anyone in the park. She cycles back to the gate by the hotel. No van in sight.

She cycles straight to Markus's house, determined, focused, just like Mum. Just like Mum, she thinks.

57

Zeke is sitting in the shade of a sickly yellow Festis umbrella in the outdoor café at Tinnis. He's just peeled the plastic from a meatball sandwich. Malin wanted to take a swim at lunchtime, and he protested at first, didn't they have more important things to think about than swimming?

But she insisted.

Said she couldn't deal with the gym in this heat.

Wanted to go swimming, and she insisted in a way that was almost manic, in a way that only Malin can be: controlled, but still intense and relentless. He has learned to listen to her when she's like this, knows she's trying to find meanings and signifiers that can lead them on.

The sun has free rein over the clear sky.

The trees on the far side are shading the outdoor pool, and the indoor pools are shut off, empty while work is being done on them.

He doesn't feel like swimming.

Too many people. And even more at lunchtime.

Pools like this never feel clean, no matter how much chlorine they have in them. They met a woman on the way out when they arrived at the pool. She was dressed in white and carried a black bag in one hand and a test-tube holder in the other. Presumably something to do with pool maintenance.

But it doesn't matter, Zeke thinks, taking a bite of the sandwich. Even if they have the strictest hygiene standards, I still don't want to go swimming here.

Malin doesn't care.

She's standing in her red bathing suit on what looks like a sugar lump, ready to dive in.

The water of the pool rinsing her body.

Cool, take long strokes, feel the chlorine cleaning her skin, lungs, another stroke, it's supposed to hurt or it isn't doing any good. The red balls of the lane marker become a red line as she speeds up.

She breathes and her muscles lurch and she takes another stroke, and little by little she fights her way to the edge, maybe thirty yards away now.

The confusion in her head has disappeared.

Nothing but clarity and the sting of lactic acid.

Made it.

She puts a hand up on the tiles, breathes out, sees Zeke sitting under the umbrella up at the café.

She pulls herself up, sits on the edge with her feet in the water, breathing, feeling strangely clean, as if the sweat and the dust had gone forever, as if she has become something new, better. She feels reborn, and the surface of the water sparkles in a thousand shades of blue, and all of a sudden it hits her with shattering clarity.

The Eckeveds' pool.

The water at the beach.

The Glyttinge pool.

Sofia Fredén's summer job last year here at Tinnis.

Josefin Davidsson's summer job, and the article in the *Correspondent* saying there was a problem with the water around the time when she was working at Glyttinge.

Drops like a thread, purity like a mantra.

Violence as a tragic rosary.

*   *   *

Zeke stands up as she comes over to his table.

"Can I borrow your mobile? I need to make a call, right away."

Zeke takes out his mobile, his movements slow in the heat, and a group of children in rubber rings are shrieking from the edge of the pool, too scared to jump and shouting to their parents for encouragement, for reassurance that jumping in isn't dangerous.

Three rings before the call's answered.

"Sigvard Eckeved."

"Hello, this is Malin Fors. There's something I forgot to ask. Do you have someone who looks after the pool for you? You mentioned that someone came last spring?"

"You mean the one who comes out here?"

"Yes."

Zeke looks at her, his eyes fixed, expectant, as Malin squeezes the water from her hair with her free hand. There's a delay before she gets an answer.

"Well, a woman used to come each spring to check the water purifier. Your phone rang yesterday while I was telling you about it. But I didn't really think it was important. You're looking for a man anyway, aren't you?"

"You said it was a woman?"

"Yes."

"What's her name?"

"Her name's Elisabeth."

"Surname?"

"No idea. To be honest, I'm afraid I always paid her in cash. The first time I gave my number to a neighbor and she called me. The way it works is that she calls to ask when she should come. I never got a number for her. Pretty much the way it works with Polish cleaners. But, like I said, this spring I took care of it myself."

"Okay. Thanks. Can I have your neighbor's name and number?"

Silence.

"I'm afraid not. He died of a heart attack a year ago."

"His wife, would she have the number?"

"He was single. But the new neighbors may have kept her on. Maybe they've got her number?"

Sigvard disappears from the line. A minute later he's back, and rattles off a number. Malin memorizes it.

"Thanks."

"What's this about?"

"I don't know," Malin says. "We'll have to see."

She ends the call and turns toward Zeke.

"Do you remember what Sture Folkman's daughter's name was, the one who committed suicide?"

"Aronsson never said when we talked to her," Zeke says. "But I remember from the report. Elisabeth. The only reason I remember is that that was the name of my first girlfriend."

Malin turns and heads quickly for the changing room, making sure that the phone number is still in her head.

It's there.

Like an image, the number in glowing pink neon on a worn house-front in Los Angeles.

Zeke doesn't move, looking out over the Tinnerbäck pool, looking at the people trying to make something good of the heat wave, with these temperatures. The children with their rubber rings the very definition of innocence.

Markus was sad at first.

Not that he cried, but Tove could see him withdraw into himself, his shoulders slumping, his eyes restless. They were sitting at the kitchen table and the sunlight was reflecting off the stainless steel refrigerator, making her squint. They'd had sandwiches and milk, talked about how they were going to spend the rest of the holidays. Markus had been taking it for granted that they'd spend all their time together, maybe going out to his parents' summer cottage, and eventually Tove managed to say it, and when she did her voice didn't sound the way she'd wanted it to.

"I want us to break up."

Like the crack of a whip. Far too abrupt, not remotely gentle.

The words felt brutal in their unambiguous simplicity, and Markus was shocked.

"What did you say?"

"I want—"

"I thought—"

"It just feels like I want to be free this year, and it doesn't, I don't know, it doesn't feel like it did at the start . . . it would be better if we could be friends."

The words out of her mouth fast, as if they were burning her.

"I want to be able to concentrate on my schoolwork."

Markus said nothing.

Like he was letting the words sink in, as if their meaning was gradually taking hold within him. But what could he say?

"I missed you when you were in Bali," he said.

"But I didn't miss you."

And with those words his sadness changed into anger, and he stood up and shouted at her:

"Couldn't you have said this before you went? That you wanted to break up? Now I've spent all summer waiting, not even looking at anyone else at parties!"

"Stop shouting!"

"This is my house, I'll shout as much as I like," and Tove had had enough, she got up from the bench and ran out into the hall, slipping on her flip-flops and opening the door.

He called after her:

"Come back, I didn't mean to get mad," and Tove felt twenty years older, grown-up, when she heard how upset he sounded.

But she still shut the door behind her.

Heard the little sucking sound as it closed.

And then the sound of her own breathing, adrenaline coursing through her body, making her feel giddy.

*   *   *

Let her cycle off. Let her go.

I met your mother just now in Tinnis.

You're a constant source of worry to her.

So just come to me.

Become an angel.

A cleansing angel of resurrection.

Innocence reborn.

She's angry as she rushes out of the house.

Slamming the door.

Doesn't look in my direction, doesn't see the van parked a little way up the hill.

Peace, come and find peace.

Soon you'll never have to be angry again.

Death is over there.

Watch out, Tove, watch out, you don't want to be one of us.

We drift and we roar in unison in your ear, but our angel voices don't reach your eardrums.

Stop, stop!

But you're not listening.

You're fleeing discomfort, toward a warmth that you think exists some-where.

Hear what we're saying.

Stop.

But you're deaf to our voices, they're no more than vibrations in the noise of your inner ear.

Instead you keep pedaling, cycling angrily straight into the catastrophe.

Right into the fire, down, down, into the lowest of all circles.

Who can save you there?

Not us.

Your mum?

Maybe in the end the whole thing will come down to whose love is the greatest?

58

"Water, Zeke, that's the connection in this case."

Malin was talking fast as they headed back to the car parked outside the pool, and she explained what she meant, how all the girls were somehow connected to pools, and had been scrubbed clean with manic frenzy, and how even the smells corresponded, the bleach on all three girls, and the smell of chlorine from the swimming pools.

Malin felt almost feverish in the parking lot, as reality, air, buildings, cars, heat, sky all seemed to be tumbling around her, but she pulled herself together.

"So you mean we should be looking for someone who does swimming pool maintenance?"

Zeke more open-minded than skeptical.

"Yes, one in particular."

"One in particular?"

"Soon, Zeke. Soon."

Zeke breathed out deeply.

"Where do we start? Here?"

"Why not?"

As they went back in again, Malin called the number she'd been given by Sigvard Eckeved, but the neighbor wasn't aware of any pool maintenance woman, saying: "I take care of all that myself," and now they're sitting in a cramped, hot room with yellow tiled walls next to the café, talking to the manager of the Tinnerbäck pool, a Sten Karlsson, a bundle of muscle in lifeguard's trunks and a red vest with the pool's logo, a sea lion with a ball.

The desk in front of them is littered with papers.

"Paperwork isn't my strong point," Sten Karlsson says apologetically. "What can I do for you?"

"We'd like to know who looks after pool maintenance."

"Our lifeguards and our technician. The lifeguards keep things clean with nets and pool bottom cleaners, and the technician makes sure that all the technical stuff works."

"Are all your lifeguards employed on contracts?" Malin asks, feeling herself getting impatient as she doesn't get the answer she wants.

"Yes."

"Is any of them in charge of the chemical side of things?"

"No, we've contracted that out."

"So that was the woman I saw," Zeke says. "She was here about an hour ago, wasn't she?"

"That's right. We have a woman who looks after the chemical makeup of the water."

"Who is she?"

The question bursts out of Malin.

"Her name's Elisabeth. I don't know her surname. Her company is called, hang on . . ."

Elisabeth.

The same woman?

Is Elisabeth Vera Folkman? Acting under her dead sister's name? And, if so, what does that actually mean? If she is Vera Folkman, what have her experiences done to her, what have they made her do?

Sten Karlsson is searching through the sheets of paper on his desk.

"Hang on. Here it is!"

He holds up an invoice. Linköping Water Technicians Ltd.

"Sexy name, eh?"

Malin snatches the invoice from Sten Karlsson's hand.

Reads the address, phone number.

"Do you know where she was going after here?" Malin asks.

"No idea. She's pretty mysterious."

Sten Karlsson points at the invoice.

"She leaves those without a word, except for saying that she wants to be paid in cash. But I can tell you one thing. She knows her job. We've had her for two years, and the water in the pools has been top quality since then."

Malin and Zeke are standing together outside Sten Karlsson's office. Malin is holding a note containing the details of the company: name, address, and company number.

"Number 17, Johanneslundstigen," Zeke says. "I've never heard of a Johanneslundstigen."

Malin reads the phone number: 013 133 02 66.

Calls the number.

An automated reply.

"The number 013 133 02 66 is not in use—"

"Fuck," Malin says.

"Call information," Zeke says. "Ask them."

"Information. May I help you?"

The perky operator's voice annoys Malin.

"That's right, that number isn't in use."

"No, there's no Johanneslundstigen in Linköping."

"Of course, I'll put you through to the tax office."

After a long pause someone else answers. The tax office is pretty much closed on a Saturday in July. Then another long wait to be transferred. Then a new woman's voice, formal and bureaucratic, as she might have expected. Zeke is pacing up and down beside her now, sweat on his forehead.

"Did you say Linköping Water Technicians Ltd., registration number 5-987689?"

"That's right," Malin says.

"There's no company registered under that number, or that name. Sorry."

Malin ends the call once she's made a note of the woman's direct number.

She feels the heat constricting her chest, her heart beating hard under her ribs. How long can you keep a false company running? One year? Two? Three? Maybe longer, if you do it properly. But who knows how long she's been in the city. Unless she really has been in Australia, like Sture Folkman said? And came home two years ago with the very worst baggage imaginable?

"Someone has a hell of a lot to hide," she says, and Zeke smiles, his whole face radiating confidence.

They drive out to the pool at Glyttinge in silence.

Slavenca's kiosk appears to be empty, and from the front it looks like it's closed for good. In the parking lot the smell of smoke is very noticeable; the wind is coming from the northwest, blowing the charred smell toward them, particle by particle.

The owner of the Glyttinge pool.

Hakan Droumani.

A man in his fifties, of Mediterranean appearance, his accent hard to pin down. He's very cheerful, business booming in a summer like this, offering Malin and Zeke coffee in the pool's little café, in the same building as the changing rooms with a view of the main pool.

Quick questions, answers.

"Yes, her name's Elisabeth. Surname? No idea. If I know anything about her? No. Her company is Water Technology, Linköping, Ltd. . . . cash, always cash, that's fine by me, of course, no account number on the invoices, but business accounts cost money so I suppose she's trying to cut costs . . ."

By the pool stands a woman in a burka, ready to jump in.

Hakan Droumani laughs.

"That's the only full clothing I allow."

"You've never had any reason to call her? Like back in June, for instance, when there was a problem with the water?"

"She called me. Health and Safety leaked it to the *Correspondent* before they said anything to me. But otherwise I've never had any reason to call her."

Malin makes another call to information, to the woman in the tax office: "doesn't exist . . . sorry . . ."

"Where do we go from here?"

Malin puts her mobile in her pocket and looks questioningly at Zeke. All around them in the parking lot outside the Glyttinge pool people are walking slowly past, on their way to or from cool relief.

"We can try Vera Folkman's flat again."

Zeke's voice full of certainty. He's turned Malin's theory about how things are connected into a truth, even though they don't know that yet.

"Okay," Malin says. "If Vera Folkman is this Elisabeth."

"It could be urgent," Zeke says.

And they look at each other, two detectives made scruffy by the summer, feeling how violence is approaching, how they're being drawn toward its core, the eye of the hurricane, the ultimate eruption of the volcano.

She feels her stomach tighten.

That isn't fear.

But she doesn't manage to convince herself.

Zeke puts a hand on her shoulder.

"Relax, Malin," he says. But not even Zeke's voice can reach deep enough inside her to suppress her anxiety.

Now you're going into the library.

Thousands of books in there, sentences, words, characters, each one more meaningless than the last, each story more mendacious than the last.

But you love books, don't you?

Their spines, the escape they offer.

You can't escape.
I'll be waiting here for you.
Are you going to go through the park?
Or along the road?
My cleansing angel.
My summertime angel.
I shall bring life to you, that's what I'll do.

59

Tove loves the library.

The nice new one that was built after the old one burned down one cold January night.

She loves all the space above the books, and how the greenery outside takes over the room through the huge windows facing Slottsparken, and the smell of old books, a bit musty but still full of excitement and dreams, suggesting that the planet and all the life on it can be made clear; the smell of mystery, enticing but also, in some indefinable sense, dangerous.

She's sitting in one of the black Egg chairs that are lined up facing the park, immersed in *The Great Gatsby* again, in the parties and Jay and Daisy's passion, so different from her and Markus's infatuation that never turned into love. Unless it's going to?

Am I going to regret it?

And try to re-create a feeling that might never really have existed?

She must have read the book five times now. Precocious was how her Swedish teacher described her essay in school.

Sure.

She can sit here for hours, vanishing among the words, watching the day turn to afternoon, then early evening. Nice weather outside, but then it always is.

Outside in the park some colored men in green overalls are raking up leaves, they've given up early this year, the leaves.

Turning the pages.

Do a bit of reading before I go home and get something to eat.

Zeke's finger on the bell of Vera Folkman's flat on Sturegatan. The heat in the stairwell is oppressive, the glass in the windows seems to bow, and it feels as if hungry flames are rising from the floor and trying to burn the skin of Malin's legs.

No answer, and they stand silently in front of the door for a while. A smell of decay.

"Shall we break in?"

Malin says the words more as a challenge than a question, doesn't want to leave any room for doubt.

"We can't, Malin. You know that."

"So what are we going to do, then? How the hell are we going to find her? She's like mist, smoke, a shadow. Whatever you like."

"Calm down, Malin. Just calm down."

"Sorry. It's this heat, it's driving me mad."

"Let's go back to the station. See what we can come up with. We need a meeting."

"Okay. Let's do that."

Before she gets in the Volvo Malin calls Tove, wants to find out what she's doing, check that she's okay.

A birch tree provides a bit of shade, and in the car Zeke reaches for the cold-air vent by the rearview mirror.

Tove answers after just one ring.

"Mum, I'm in the library reading. You're lucky I forgot to switch my phone off. You're not supposed to have them on in here, but I don't think I've disturbed anyone."

"Aren't you with Markus?"

"I broke up with Markus today."

You didn't tell me, Malin thinks, even if I saw it coming, why didn't you tell me, Tove? And she wants to reprimand her daughter, ask: Why didn't you tell me you were going to break up? But when could she have told me?

There's never any time.

Hence Tove's silence, her secrecy.

And because of something else. Another explanation that makes Malin's gut ache, an explanation that she shies away from.

Malin had been expecting them to break up, but so suddenly?

But perhaps things like that always happen suddenly? Like a revelation?

"Mum, are you there? I said I broke up with Markus today."

"Was he upset?"

"Yes."

"Was it rough?"

"I don't know, Mum, I felt relieved afterward."

"Tove, let's talk more this evening. I'll see you at home."

There are so many books, Tove thinks as she walks through the bookcases in her hunt for something to take out. And so little time to read them.

She pulls out a book from the shelf, it's called *Prep*, American, about a school for rich kids.

Tove has read about it in a magazine.

It's supposed to be good, and five minutes later she leaves the library with the book in her hand.

Food?

I'm not hungry, and Mum won't be home and it's no fun eating alone.

The men in overalls with rakes have left the park, and the shadows under the trees over by the parking lot toward the castle look inviting.

I'll lie there and do some reading, Tove thinks. What else am I going to do?

*   *   *

You're coming closer to me now.

Am I really going to be so fortunate that you're going to lie down in the grass under the oak tree, in the shade, so close to me?

You're steering your bicycle toward me.

I can go up to you if you're lying there, just five yards away, and I can take you with me. No one need notice anything.

Tove leans her bike against the tree, looks over at the parking lot but doesn't notice the van, half hidden as it is behind some low bushes. She's longing to get into the book among the words and letters, into the fiction.

She takes her towel out of her bag, lays it out on the grass, and lies down on her side, opens the book, and starts reading.

The sounds of the city in the background. The siren of an ambulance, cars, and the hum of a choir of hundreds of ventilation units. The indistinct sound of voices.

A sliding door opening.

Soon the sounds of the city are stifled by the rhythm of the words in her head.

I'm heading toward you now.

No one can see anything, it's early afternoon but we're alone here, and I'm going to take you.

No one by the castle, or the county administration office, or in the park.

Or on the path to the library, or inside the big glass windows, and I am approaching your rebirth. I shall take you with me to him for the final act.

They'll say that I'm mad.

And maybe I am beside myself.

But I shall do this now.

Fill you with nothing.

The asphalt of the parking lot becomes grass under my feet, I'm close to you now, we're sharing the shade. The ether in my hand, a soaked rag, and my white clothes are spotless and you don't hear me and I'm kneeling on your orange towel, putting the rag over your nose.

What's this?

A sharp, bitter smell and something damp burning against her nose and Tove twists round, but her body doesn't want to, why doesn't her body want to, and in the corner of her eye she can see a white figure, feeling the weight of someone's arm and the edges of the world start to dissolve and I'm sleepy, so sleepy, but I can't fall asleep here, not here, not now, and I can feel something dragging me over the grass, then something harder, asphalt? And then my sight disappears and the world becomes a dream before everything goes black and cold, dreamless and empty.

Before the world becomes mute, wordless, and therefore ceases to exist.

The heavens quake.

And like in an enchanting dream, full of whiteness, she reaches out one hand against a transparent white film, and feels the film tremble before she pulls her hand back, resting, dreaming herself still in the world, nightmaring herself alive again.

60

Fire is everywhere.

It's jumping from treetop to treetop, thundering as it tears everything in its path into burning fragments.

This summer is hot.

But the hell in the forest is even hotter. Slowly the fires have spread down toward Lake Hultsjön, and Janne and his colleagues have their backs to the lake, their hoses snaking through the vegetation, zigzagging through the still-living soil down to the warm water of the lake, where generators are driving great pumps.

He slept on the floor of the fire engine last night, in the empty space where the hoses are usually kept, the night singing all around him, crackling and rumbling and stinking of smoke, of cremated animals and insects, of soil turned to ash.

The flames an unquiet wall some hundred yards away from them. Approaching faster and faster. Human beings against fire, fire against human beings.

He's wet with sweat, feels like tearing off his clothes and fleeing the heat in the water of the lake.

The fire is the beast.

They stand firm, sticking their gushing knives right into its throat.

*   *   *

Afternoon meeting.

Karim Akbar clears his throat and looks round the meeting room with empty eyes, perhaps trying to find a dancing mote of dust in the air to focus on.

Malin has just outlined her suspicions about Vera Folkman, about the pools, about the false information about her company, a company that may not even exist. She's explained that they haven't been able to find her, that she's "like the smoke from the forest fires, you can't see it, but you know it's there."

"We've got her flat under surveillance," Sven Sjöman says from his chair beside Zeke. The blinds are open, the playground behind them deserted, the nursery still closed for the summer. "Does anyone have any other ideas of how to get hold of her?"

"We don't even know if this Elisabeth is actually Vera Folkman," Karim says.

"We'll have to assume that she is," Malin says.

"We're keeping an eye out for white vans," Zeke says. "That's what she drives. But there are loads of them in the city."

"And we're checking to see if there are any registered companies with similar names," Malin says.

"Any other ideas?" Sven says once more. "We haven't got enough to go into her flat, you know that, Malin. Even if the smell might suggest that she's maltreating animals in there."

Malin thinks: It's starting to fit, Sven, the voices of this case are telling us that, aren't they? And then the other maxim: *It's desire that kills.*

Waldemar Ekenberg and Per Sundsten are silent.

Silent as only police officers who've caught a scent of the truth in a meeting room can be.

"We spoke to the last sex offender on the list this morning. Nothing," Per says.

"As much of a dead end as Suliman Hajif and Louise Svensson. And Slavenca Visnic, she's been busy with her kiosks, although apparently they lost her this morning."

"And she drives a white van," Per says. "So in theory Slavenca Visnic could be this Elisabeth."

"We saw the interior of her van in the forest," Malin says. "She didn't have anything in there that could be connected to pool maintenance. No chemicals, nothing. And the manager at Glyttinge would have recognized her from the kiosk outside."

"Check again, just to make sure," Sven says. "You take that, Sundsten."

Then Waldemar's voice, full of skepticism:

"Could a woman really have done this? Dildo or not? Doesn't this go against a woman's nature?"

"Prejudice," Malin says. "There's no shortage of female thugs and sex offenders in the past, and most of them were the victims of abuse themselves, just like Vera Folkman."

"And Slavenca Visnic," Per says.

"I think we should put the squeeze on Suliman Hajif again," Waldemar says, but no one has the energy even to comment on his suggestion, and Malin shuts out the others' voices, thinking about what it must be like to be Vera Folkman, thinking about synchronicity, how the pools and all the other connections in the case could be coincidence. And maybe Vera Folkman isn't even this Elisabeth?

People who are people who are people who are one and the same person.

A desire to dissolve, to be reborn as someone else.

A person as drifting smoke, above a charred landscape. As one single feeling, one single characteristic.

Love and evil.

False company names.

The desire to be invisible.

Cold white hands.

But how?

"Come on," Karim pleads. "No ideas about Vera Folkman?"

And where are you now? Malin thinks.

*　　　*　　　*

Where am I?

Why is it dark, and what's this over my eyes? My head aches and I feel sick, but that isn't the biggest problem, there's something worse, but what? I'm breathing, Tove thinks, and this is a dream, and she remembers the shade under the tree, the paper of the book under her fingers, but what sort of dream is this, what does it want with me? Markus, is that you, and she can feel how she's breathing, recognizes the smell of detergent and she tries to get up, but her legs are stuck.

She tries to push herself up with her arms, but they're stuck, and Mum, Mum, Mum, where are you, I can't be dead already, is this my grave, Mum, and Tove tries to scream but no sound comes out of her mouth.

Cloth in her mouth.

Why would I have cloth in my mouth if I were dead?

Or if I were dreaming?

Malin looks out across the office.

Six o'clock.

Where has the afternoon gone?

Writing reports.

Looking through the register of companies to try to find any with names resembling Linköping Water Technicians.

Nothing.

You are out.

Waiting for one of the patrols to call in with something positive.

But that never happened.

The search for Vera Folkman and the surveillance on her flat has led nowhere, the shadow remains a shadow. And Slavenca Visnic seems to have gone up in smoke, she isn't at any of her kiosks, and the patrol that went up to the fires couldn't find her either.

One piece of news, though. Andersson in Forensics rang. Facebook had finally got back to him. Confirming that Lovelygirl was Louise Svensson, they'd managed to trace her IP number.

She spoke to Janne over the phone.

He called her. Said that they'd had to run from the fire down by
Hultsjön, that one of their generators had been lost to the flames, that
a hunting cottage had burned down, and that a few idiots came close
to being cut off by the fire in their attempts to save the cottage.

The Murvall brothers' cottage, the brothers in the fire. The Bengt
Andersson case.

"I'm so damn tired, Malin."

"Go home and sleep."

"I can't."

"Why not?"

"They need me here. And I've got this weird anxiety in my body."

"Me too."

Janne's restlessness.

Hultsjön. That was where everything came to a head last winter
in connection with another case. That was where evil caught up with
Maria Murvall.

The same evil?

No.

But who knows?

When we get hold of Vera Folkman she'll have to provide DNA
samples that can be compared with those of Maria Murvall's attacker.
Slavenca Visnic? I've already asked Karin to take care of that.

The clock on the computer says 6:52.

She calls home, hoping Tove will answer.

But no.

Her mobile.

Five rings, then the voicemail.

Anxiety. Hardly unexpected, Malin thinks as she quickly shuts
down her computer and leaves the station.

61

When the room gets too cold and I hear the floorboards creaking out on the landing I try to think of summer instead of the monster.

The summer, like when Elisabeth and I are cycling along the canal, and the warm wind catches our thin fair hair and I see your white cotton dress pressed tight to your body, stroking your skin more and more and more with each pedal, and you're my big sister, I try to keep up with you but for you there's no contest. You stop and wait for me. The light falls through the oak leaves of the ancient trees along the canal and you're standing beside your red bicycle, smiling at me.

Was I cycling too fast? I didn't mean to. You go first, I'll be right behind you, you don't have to keep looking back, I'll be there, making sure nothing bad happens.

I'm twelve, you fourteen.

You are the whole of my summertime world and we go skinny-dipping together, there's no embarrassment between us, and if we cycle far enough along the path that runs along the shore of Lake Vättern we can get to places where we can be on our own. Where the summer can drive the pain from our bodies.

Where he can't reach us.

We share the secrets of the darkness, you and I, sister.

He comes just as often to each of us, and I want to scream and you want to scream, but he puts his long white fingers on our lips, then fingers his way down and we let it happen, because what else can we do?

It is his house and we are stuck in his life.

And it hurts so much and I want to scream, but instead I cry and I hear you cry in the hours when light is about to return, when the pink-painted paneling in our room takes shape again and our whole bodies ache.

A spider is weaving its web across the window in the moonlight, the spider's legs are white and outside in the garden his rabbits are scratching in their cages.

We can never wash ourselves thoroughly enough.

Soap isn't enough. We find dishwashing liquid under the sink in the kitchen and in the garage we find blue bottles containing a milky liquid that smells like his breath, and the liquid stings inside us, gives us more sores, but somehow it feels good to spoil what he wants to take from us. As if there can never be enough pain, and he is so strong, so hard, and his fingers so cold, his whole being is determination.

You choose not to see, Mum, why won't you see anything? Because surely you must see?

He's our dad.

We're his children.

And he comes in the night and there is no way out except deeper in.

How wonderful the summer is.

The wind as we speed along the bank of the canal. The way we pretend it isn't painful to sit on the saddle. The way we still have each other and how our love might yet conquer his fingers, all of him.

And then you see, Mum.

You choose to see, and you take us to Grandma, to her two-room flat in Borensberg, and you argue and fight and I'm scared that he's going to come after us, but he doesn't come and it takes a long time before I realize that he will always be with us anyway.

We huddle in the two-room flat we move into in Klockrike.

I'm thirteen when we go to the doctor, speechless meetings where no one asks for an explanation, cold steel implements inside me, and

I see the distance and the sympathy, but also the fear and derision in their eyes.

It's me they're looking at.

The reincarnation of the monster must be driven out.

And I am living proof of how painful it is to live, a pain that few want or dare to look in the eye.

You fall silent, sister.

Turn fifteen and sixteen on cakeless birthdays and we kept to the trees on the edge of school, kept to ourselves as if everyone knew, as if there were no solace in being with the others, and the summers are colorless, windless, and we lie beside each other on the floor on the hottest days and you say nothing, don't answer when I ask if we can go for a bike ride.

The hospital. You're sitting on a bed in the corner. You're there several times.

I call your name.

You've gone home from school before me and I call your name when I get home.

Elisabeth, I call in the hall, but you don't answer.

The living room is empty and I want to go out again, run away from there, cycle with the wind to another world, away from this rotten little flat where we try to cling to our lives.

But not you.

The bathroom smells of damp, the white tiles are loose, but the hooks in the ceiling for the drying frame above the bath are strong enough to hold your weight.

The white rope is wrapped twice around your neck, your face winter-blue, panic-stricken, and your eyes, my blue eyes trying to burst from their sockets. Your thin blond hair hanging down over your naked and unnaturally clean body, your feet in the air, still.

Small cuts on your lower arms and shins. As if you changed your mind and tried to get free.

Yellow piss on the bottom of the bathtub.

No water from the shower. I missed the water then. Wanted it to be gushing, full of life.

I went over and held you, my dear sister, dreaming that you and I would wait for each other again, sharing the secrets of the darkness once more. But you were mute and cold and I could hear my own wailing, the way it sounded like a concentrate of loneliness.

I held you up, hugged you hard, and felt our lost love flow between us.

You aren't scared anymore, sister, I asked, are you?

But you didn't answer.

There was no innocence left in that moment.

And I promised you, myself, us, that one day I would put all this right.

That the world, our love, would be reborn one day.

62

You were the one who let him in, Dad.

If you hadn't left me and Mum, he'd never have crossed our threshold, come into my life, in under my sheets, into me, in, in, in.

He wanted me to call him Daddy, Daddy, that fucking bastard Folkman.

He came at night.

The floorboards creaked when he came.

And he said: Louise, I'm just going to touch you a bit down there, feel me, the way I feel, and then he would come, his hands were cold, all of him was cold and hard and stank of vodka.

Sometimes, on the nights when the floorboards never creaked, I used to think about you, Dad, and how you vanished, replaced us with other girls, the woman that Mum said you'd met who had two children that you adopted.

Forget him, Mum said.

We don't exist for him.

And I hated you on the nights when he came.

And all the other nights. And I hate you now.

But still, the only thing I ever wanted to happen was for a shiny silver car to pull up outside the house and you would get out of the car and embrace me, saying: I've come to take you away with me, from now on everything's going to be all right, you're my daughter and I'm going to love you the way a father should.

You never came.

When I got older I used to take the car and go down to Nässjö, where you lived then, and I would sit in the car outside your house and watch you coming and going, sometimes I would see your new wife's daughters, grown up now, just like me, and when I saw you together I could see that you loved them, a misplaced love, what should have been my love.

My love.

You never noticed my car.

The way I used to follow you.

But you must have guessed it was me who made the anonymous phone calls, that I was the one who never dared to speak on the other end of the line.

What could I say, Dad?

Because even if I had seen you, you were only a smell, a touch, an image, a voice from when I was little, and I longed for you here at Skogalund, I longed to see your silver Vauxhall coming up the drive, to see you instead of him come into my room in the cellar, among my toys.

You were going fishing that day, like so many times before.

You were starting to get old.

I parked some distance from the isolated jetty and walked over to you.

I was child, girl, and woman, all at the same time.

It was an early-autumn day, chilly but sunny, and you caught sight of me in the forest and you knew who I was, you knew straightaway, and when I came out onto the jetty you shouted at me:

"Get lost, I don't want anything to do with you, get lost, I'm going fishing."

One of the oars was still on the jetty, long and hard, with a metal-edged blade.

Did you know who you were letting in? I wanted to ask. I came here to get your love, I wanted to say.

"Get lost," you yelled.

The oar.

At the reading of your will it emerged that you'd left everything you owned to your new wife and her children.

I got five thousand three hundred and twenty kronor in the end.

63

"Tove? Tove? TOVE! TOVE! Tove? Tove."

Malin is going through the flat, running, walking, searching room after room, but Tove isn't there, not under the sheets of her own bed, nor in Malin's bed, nor in the wardrobe or kitchen cupboards, how the hell would she ever fit in a kitchen cupboard?

Fuck, it's hot.

"Tove!"

Don't panic now, Fors, don't panic, and she sits down on one of the chairs in the kitchen, feeling the sweat on her scalp, and the mantra inside her:

Think, think, think.

Not at Markus's.

Call them anyway.

She takes out her mobile, calls the number. Hasse answers.

Evidently unaware that they've broken up.

"No, Malin, she's not here. You don't know where she is?"

No time for small talk.

"Hasse, my other phone's ringing. I've got to go."

Friends?

Which ones are still in the city? Who did she have ice cream with? Julia? Call Julia.

Malin runs into the bedroom, turns on the computer, looks up
Julia Markander in the online directory.

"Hi, Julia. This is Malin, Tove's mum, is Tove with you? She's not?
Do you have any idea where she could be?"

Filippa and Elise.

Staying in the country.

The clock on the computer says 7:37.

She should have been here by now, or let me know.

Shit.

Don't panic now, Fors, and suddenly she is struck for the first time
by how shabby her bedroom is, how yellow the wallpaper has got over
the past six months, and the curtains look scruffy and old-fashioned
with their mauve-and-yellow pattern, and the lack of plants and pictures on the walls makes the room look sterile.

There are hospital rooms with more charm.

Focus.

Janne. Could she have gone to see Janne? But he's in the forest.

Maybe she'll be home soon. Maybe she's been to the cinema.

But she would have let me know, Tove does things properly and
knows that her mother would be worried to death considering what's
been happening in the city.

Anxiety.

The very worst could have happened.

You should never appear at press conferences.

Who knows what it might trigger off in the heads of the nut-
ters?

She calls Janne.

Three rings before he answers.

"Janne here. Malin?"

"Tove. I think she's missing."

He can hear that she's serious from her voice.

"I'm on my way," Janne says. "The fire will have to manage without
me for a while."

Malin sinks onto the sofa in the living room, rubbing her eyes,
thinking: How the hell could this have happened?

*   *   *

How much do you weigh, little summer angel?

A hundred pounds?

Not more.

I rolled you up in a rug in the van, and carried it over my shoulder into the room that we're in now.

I'm in no hurry.

You're sleeping on a wooden bunk, carry on sleeping, it's always hard to know how much ether to use. On the one called Josefin I used a different substance, one that vanishes without a trace from the body, and I brought her here to this room, my room, and when she was lying on the bunk I scrubbed her clean. I used bleach, and I rubbed so hard, but not too hard, I took care not to damage her skin, because of course you'd need that.

I took her in the forest at Ryd.

As she was cycling home.

They still haven't found the bike.

I waved at her to stop, and she did, then she got scared when she saw my masked face and put up a struggle, but she soon fell asleep.

The cuts and marks on her lower arms. I made them with the scissors I got for my tenth birthday, as I scrubbed and cleaned and purified her, she smelled of bleach and of course I could have got her even cleaner with the swimming pool chemicals, but those can be traced. Then I took all my clothes off and strapped on the blue, letting the rabbit claws scratch freely, I turned my fingers into white spiders' legs, and she woke up and stared at my mask and she screamed, but she was tied down.

Tied down.

Just like you, my little summer angel.

And then I used the blue nothing.

In and out and she seemed to fade away, and I screamed at her to stay, that if you were to have a chance of coming back, my dear sister, she had to be here, and I soon realized that it was pointless.

She wasn't, and never would be you.

That simple bitch could never accommodate you, and maybe this was the wrong room?

I gave her some of the mixture.

Carried her out.

She was bleeding after the nothing.

I let her go down by Tinnerbäcken. She must have walked to the park. She hadn't seen me and she was allowed to live, seeing as she could never be you.

But the one lying on the bunk now, with the caged rabbits and boxes of white spiders' legs, she can be you, she can be the possibility of resurrected love.

I know how it all has to happen now.

What about us?

Why did you kill us?

Don't kill her, let her live. She's not supposed to drift like us, not yet, show mercy, do you hear? Let the hot lava of violence withdraw into the underworld, it's flowed far enough now, give yourself up, show your face, who you really are, people will understand what unlove has done to you, that it's impossible to make an empathetic person out of someone who has confronted the monster where there should have been love.

Janne in the hall of the flat, sweaty, face streaked with soot, wearing white cotton trousers and a yellow T-shirt with the words KUTA BEACH.

They hugged, but failed to press away each other's anxiety.

His question just now:

"Have you called the police?"

And they laughed and then fell silent, fear and anxiety like molten tin solidified in the air, suffocating, destructive.

"Call now, get the search going."

And Malin calls the station, is put through to the duty desk, Löving, and she explains what's happened and he says: "We'll put out an alert at once, don't worry, we'll have everyone on this right away."

Zeke.

Malin thinks. I ought to call Zeke, and he answers and breathes heavily down the phone, and she knows that he knows, that he feels it with his whole body, just don't let it be too late, and Janne is standing beside her looking worried, as if he's wondering what's going on.

"I'm heading out, Malin. And I'll call the others."

"What others?"

"Sundsten and Ekenberg. Sjöman. Karim."

"But where are you going to look?"

"Everywhere, Malin. Everywhere. I'll take Folkman's flat."

"She's got her."

"Yes. Probably. I'll make sure everyone takes their service weapons with them."

"I'll take mine."

They hang up.

"Come on," Malin says to Janne once she's got her pistol from the gun cabinet in the bedroom, the holster hidden under a thin white cotton jacket.

"We'll go back to yours, see if she's there."

"What time is it?"

"Quarter past nine."

"She'd be back by now if she went to the seven o'clock showing at the cinema."

"Shouldn't one of us stay here in case she comes?"

Right thinking, Janne, but wrong.

"We're doing this together," Malin says. "She's our daughter."

Then Malin writes a note and leaves it on the hall floor.

TOVE, CALL US!
Mum and Dad.

64

Something's approaching.

I'm awake, my head is thumping, enough for me to know that I'm awake. Where am I?

I'm lying on something hard and I can't move, what's that scratching behind me, and the smell, it stinks here and I'm not at home, where's my book, did I fall asleep under the tree?

My whole body aches.

Tove tries to pull her arms up, but they're tied down.

Something's approaching.

A faceless face, a nothing face, and now I'm screaming, but there's cloth in my mouth, I can feel it.

Close.

I strain and pull.

Mum.

Dad.

Then cold against my nose, and sleep, miraculous sleep. I want to get away from here.

Because I am just falling asleep, aren't I?

Nothing else?

*   *   *

The house, in a remote patch of woodland just outside Malmslätt, is smothered with scaffolding. The yellow wooden façade is being replaced, the rot has finally won, and Malin looks at the cars, one, two, three, four wrecks, God only knows what make.

Janne's hobby.

Doing them up and selling them.

Making a bit of extra money.

The only problem is that he never sells any of the cars. There are four American cars in perfect condition sitting in the workshop and garage. He never drives them, never puts them on show, he just has them.

She never understood the cars.

Thought they were about as unsophisticated as anything could possibly be.

White trash. And it was only years later that she realized that it was her mother's distaste for anything that could be regarded as unrefined haunting her, that she had unconsciously adopted her mother's attitudes and that this had influenced her relationship with the only man on the planet she can categorically state that she has loved.

They lived here together.

Before the catastrophe.

Before the divorce. Before Bosnia and all the other godforsaken places Janne has been.

You keep the house, Janne.

We won't be there when you get home.

Gathering this "we" together now. This is what we do. Janne opens the front door and they call into the darkness of the house: Tove, Tove, but their shouts don't sound very persuasive.

Janne turns on the lights.

We are here, this is where we ought to live together.

They go from room to room in this house, looking for their daughter, but she isn't there, she isn't anywhere.

"What do we do now?"

Janne's question directed at the kitchen sink, a glass of water in his hand.

"We drive around."

"Shouldn't we just wait at home to be there when she gets home?"

"Do you really believe that's going to work, Janne? Waiting drives me mad. We'll drive around. Looking for her. In parks, anywhere."

"You don't think she could have gone somewhere else?"

"Not Tove, you know that as well as me, Janne."

The kitchen lamp flickers, hesitates before there's a small pop and it goes out.

They stand opposite each other in the darkness.

"Fucking hell," Janne says, then clutches her tightly to him.

Zeke is sitting in his car on Sturegatan, outside Vera Folkman's flat.

Dark as a bat cave up there.

He's been up and rung the bell.

Like the grave.

And the smell.

Cadaverous, more noticeable now.

No sign of her, no sign of Tove.

My problems with Martin and his ice hockey.

Luxury problems.

What the hell am I sitting here for? There could be something up there that could help us. Tove might even be up there.

Malin. I'm doing this for you.

And Zeke gets out of the car, crosses Sturegatan, and goes into the building.

The stench from the flat is overwhelming now.

Something's died in there.

An image in Zeke's mind: a gutted stomach, steaming entrails pouring out.

I can blame concern about sanitation.

Then the lights go on in the stairwell, heavy breathing, someone carrying something heavy up the stairs.

Is that you coming now? Zeke wonders and creeps halfway up the next flight of steps, pressing against a bare stone wall, listening to his own breathing, his heart beating faster and faster.

*   *   *

Janne and Malin drive past the library. The building a dark shape in Slottsparken.

This was where she was the last time I spoke to her, Malin thinks, and says:

"She goes there a lot."

Janne doesn't answer, looking instead up at the park, but he doesn't see Tove's bicycle in the shadows against one of the trees.

"Let's head out to Skäggetorp," Malin says.

Slavenca Visnic's flat is deserted.

Janne asks: "Who lives here?"

"A woman connected to the case."

She told him about Vera Folkman on the way back from his place, that she's got a terrible feeling that the very worst has happened, or is in the process of happening.

The look of panic in Janne's eyes.

This time he needs to save himself. No one else, and he looks tired standing there in the heat, in the light of a streetlamp in Skäggetorp, his cheeks still smeared with soot, his frame somehow diminished by lack of sleep.

"You need to sleep," Malin says.

"How could I possibly sleep now?"

"I can drive you home."

"Malin, leave it. Let's carry on."

Waldemar Ekenberg pushes open the door of Behzad Karami's allotment cottage and Karami leaps up from the bed when he sees who his visitor is.

Waldemar raises a hand.

"Calm down. I just wanted to see if you were alone."

Karami sits down again.

"Do you want some?"

He points at the bottle of vodka on the floor.

"Thanks," Waldemar says.

Karami pours out two glasses of vodka.

"Well, cheers."

"I didn't think your sort drank."

"I drink."

"The fucker's taken the daughter of one of our colleagues now. Can you imagine?"

"Did you come to apologize?"

Waldemar downs the vodka before putting the glass back on the floor.

"There's no room for apologies in this world, lad. Never forget that."

The person carrying something heavy has stopped outside Vera Folkman's door. Panting, trying to revert to more regular breathing.

Zeke has his pistol in his hand, the safety catch is off, he moves down, the sound of the other person's breathing loud enough to hide his footsteps.

Wait?

Or go now?

The stairwell is dark.

Why don't they turn the lamp on again?

The jangle of keys?

And Zeke leaps down two steps, presses the illuminated red button, and the landing outside Vera Folkman's flat is bathed in light.

Zeke holds his gun in front of him.

"Police! Don't move! Okay, down on your knees!"

The man on the landing looks scared and surprised, and next to him is a box with the Sony logo and a picture of a flat-screen television.

Shit, Zeke thinks as he lowers his weapon.

The Horticultural Society Park is completely deserted, and Janne and Malin meet a patrol car on its way into the park as they are coming out.

They called home to the flat a moment ago.

No answer.

They drive out onto Hamngatan, past McDonald's, and Malin asks Janne if he's hungry.

"I couldn't get anything down."

His eyelids are practically hanging on his cheeks, how much sleep has he been getting? Two hours per night? Three?

"You said she worked on pool maintenance?"

"Yes, at least that's what we think," Malin replies.

"Well, you'd have to buy chemicals somewhere. Wouldn't you?"

"And?"

"You get them from DIY stores. In large quantities. Maybe some DIY store has delivered stuff to her? To an address you don't know about? To that company of hers?"

They glide past St. Lars Church.

Malin looks up at the flat. The windows are still black.

Zeke helped the man to carry the television. He lived on the fourth floor, and now the sweat is literally pouring from Zeke's brow.

The man, a pensioner named Lennart Thörnkvist, had never even seen his neighbor, but commented on the smell:

"That's what dead bodies smell like in hot weather."

And now Zeke is standing in front of Vera Folkman's door again.

He looks at his watch.

Just a few minutes before midnight.

He gets set.

Kicks the door as hard as he can, but it doesn't give way, nothing happens.

He takes out his pistol again.

Aims at the lock and fires.

A deafening echo. Zeke's ears are ringing as he pushes the door open and the stench that hits him is unbearable.

A switch. Light.

An empty hall and scratching noises from inside the kitchen and what must be the only room of the one-room flat.

He heads toward the room with his weapon drawn, glancing into the kitchen, where he sees three rabbit cages stacked on top of each other, living creatures behind the bars.

Inside the room.

On the walls.

A sight that Zacharias Martinsson will never forget.

65

I 'm busy with my bag.

I'm going to kill you. You can be resurrected. I am packing up, unpacking, the blue nothing, worms, rabbits' claws, my white spiders' legs, and all the things that are me.

Incense and painted flowers.

Sacrificial offerings in my temple.

How it started? It's always gone on. It's been the meaning and purpose of my life. To the far side of the planet, to the parched interior of Australia, the beaches of Bali. Looking after pools for people with money.

But there is no escape from unlove.

Then one day I was driving my van through the city, along Hamngatan, and I saw a taxi. It was only a few weeks ago, actually. And there you were, sitting in the front seat, Dad. Old, but your eyes, and the fingers against the windshield, were the same, you were probably on your way to the hospital for some sort of tests.

And when I saw you, I knew.

Wisdom and innocence swept through my body and I was forced to begin, just so that what must be conquered could be conquered.

I've been feeling my way.

Fumbling in the darkness for the light.

You're sleeping again, my summer angel.

You're a long way down now, deep down in the darkness of dreams.

You're hanging in the bathroom, sister.

I'm the one to find you, shake you, cry over you.

I'm the one who's going to put everything right.

And then we can ride our bikes together, we can go skinny-dipping together in water that no one else knows about.

Rabbits, splayed open, nailed to the walls, their claws pulled out, red trickles of blood dripping from the paws, some of the animals still alive, their little lungs rising and falling frenetically, whimpering, then others that have been hanging for a long time, the shreds of their rotting bodies slipping down toward the polished pine floor.

A bed in one corner, discarded white surgical gloves, a bunk in the middle of the floor, and then rows of bottles of chemicals along the walls, pots of paint that must have been used to paint the flowers on the walls. Splashes of blood on the floor, bloody scalpels, and a stench that is making Zeke giddy. He lowers his gun and goes over to the window, undoes the catch, and opens it wide onto the leafy inner courtyard, and breathes, breathes, breathes.

He turns back to the room.

Bloody hell.

Like a picture by what's-his-name, Francis Bacon.

But no Vera Folkman.

No Tove.

Janne fell fast asleep just after Zeke called them. Malin could see how he was trying to stay awake on the short drive from the Abisko roundabout to Sturegatan, but his body's need of sleep got the better of him.

He's asleep down in the car now.

His head leaning against the window.

What are you dreaming about now, Janne?

About when we were young?

When Tove came to us?

We're a family. Why have we never been able to see it?

Instead we've rushed off in different directions. Yet still not far from each other.

They're standing in the stairwell outside the flat, drinking coffee Per Sundsten picked up at the Statoil petrol station in Stångebro. Karin Johannison inside, searching for evidence, securing material.

Sven Sjöman's breathing is heavy, his face furrowed with tiredness, Per and Waldemar Ekenberg are quiet, watchful, sleepy too. Karim Akbar is in the background, scratching his cheek.

It's already three o'clock.

Soon dawn will be stroking Linköping's rooftops, whispering: A new day is here, wake up, people, come out into the heat.

Zeke tired, but still alert and keen. He is explaining for the third time:

"I broke in. The smell was so awful that I suspected some sort of criminal activity had taken place in the flat."

"Don't worry, Zeke," Sven repeats once more. "It's fine. Those pool chemicals in there. We're dealing with one and the same person."

"Now we just have to find Vera Folkman," Per says, and no one in the group of detectives wants to give voice to the obvious subtext: We have to find Vera Folkman, because then we'll find Tove, Tove, our colleague Malin's only daughter.

"Any ideas?"

Malin shakes her head, not a no, but to shake off her drowsiness, and she looks at the others, sees in their eyes how they're screaming for rest, that none of them can think clearly, that they might miss the most obvious things, that they can't let it all become too late just because of tiredness.

"Anyone who wants to can get some sleep," Sven says. "We're not being terribly constructive here."

No one replies.

They slowly drink their coffee. Feeling valuable time slip by.

"Fuck!" Malin says, and Sven puts his arm round her shoulder.

"We'll sort this, Malin. It's going to be okay," and at that moment Karin appears from inside the flat, holding up one of the chemical containers in one hand, and pointing at a label with the other.

"This can, and several of the others, were delivered by Torsson's DIY down on Tanneforsvägen. Maybe you should have a word with them? They might know something?"

I'm dreaming now.

Processions of people dressed in colorful clothes, gifts in their hands, they're on the way to the temple to honor the dead. The incense is thick and they're singing, and their song is full of sun and light.

I dream about you, Mum.

That you'll be there when I wake up.

That you and Dad will be there.

Now I'm running across an open field, then through a forest and I can sense that there's something you haven't told me, Mum, and it's something you should say now.

The room around me from when I was last awake is in the dream. It isn't a nice room.

Shutters, concrete walls, cages, walls painted with flowers and fear, and I want to run through a forest now, a burning forest, and the vegetation is chasing me, wants to tear me to pieces, Mum, and I want to wake up, but something's keeping me in the dream, a tickly smell is pushing me down into dreamlessness, Mum.

The home number of the owner of the DIY store is listed in information.

Sometimes you get lucky, Malin thinks.

Her colleagues are staring at her, the stairwell fading around them, and everything is focused on Malin and her conversation.

A sleepy, thick voice on the other end.

"Yes, Palle Torsson?"

"This is Malin Fors from Linköping Police."

"Say again?"

Malin repeats her name.

"Has the shop been broken into?"

"No, we need some information about a customer. Linköping Water Technicians. You've delivered supplies to them on Sturegatan."

The sleepiness is gone from the voice now.

"The pool girl," Palle Torsson says. "You don't get many words out of her. But she always pays cash."

"Do you know anything about her? Have you ever delivered supplies anywhere apart from Sturegatan?"

"Not that I know of. I can check the computer in the store tomorrow."

"Now," Malin says. "I'll meet you at the shop and check. If you're not there in ten minutes I'll personally shove a paintbrush up your ass."

Janne wakes up as they pull up outside the store.

The clock on the dashboard says 3:20, and daylight is starting to flicker, the hint of relief from the heat offered by night has gone and it must already be eighty degrees outside the car.

"Where are we?" Janne asks.

"Wait here," Malin says.

"I'm not waiting anywhere."

The DIY store is a single-story purpose-built construction, with a loading bay beside the entrance. Malin imagines that most of its customers must be other businesses.

No owner in sight, no Palle Torsson.

"We're doing this together," Janne says, and Malin looks at him, then tells him what's happened, what they found in Vera Folkman's flat.

"Here he comes," Janne says once Malin has finished, and she sees a black Toyota SUV stop in front of them and a small, thickset man in shorts and a light-blue T-shirt jumps out.

Malin and Zeke get out of the Volvo and walk up to the man who must be Palle Torsson.

Zeke joins them from his own car.

They've split up once more. Sundsten and Ekenberg are carrying on the search, driving around to see what they can find, Sven and Karim on their way back to the station "to do some thinking."

Malin holds out her hand to Palle Torsson. He takes it, but looks cross.

"Can I ask what the hell this is about?"

His round cheeks are bouncing with irritation.

"You can," Zeke says. "We're hunting the murderer you must have read about in the paper. And now the trail has led us here."

"How?"

"The computer," Malin says. "We need to look at it now."

I put you on the bunk, you've been lying there for a long time now, my white van is outside, and we're going to go to heaven on earth.

Do you believe in the Father?

Or is there only one father for each person?

Faith.

Is that with the Father?

Can you suck the faith out of someone?

You're clean now. I've scrubbed you and you're clean, so clean.

The blue nothing.

Are you heavier now? I'll soon find out. I'm going to carry you again.

The computer screen flickers before Malin's eyes.

She and Zeke and Janne are leaning over Palle Torsson's shoulders. Accommodating now, as he clicks his way through a sales database.

The little office is behind the counter and the walls are covered with bookcases full of files. The yellow linoleum is peeling away from the floor by the walls.

"Let's see," Palle Torsson says. "Vera Folkman, Linköping Water Technicians. 17 Sturegatan. As far as I can see, there's no other delivery address."

"Any phone number?" Zeke asks.

"No, sorry."

"Try under Elisabeth Folkman," Malin says.

Palle Torsson taps at the keyboard.

"Sorry."

"Just Elisabeth."

More tapping.

"Bingo," Palle Torsson says quietly. "An Elisabeth Folkedotter has ordered supplies for Linköping Pool Maintenance. The address is out in Tornby, number 11 Fabriksvägen. There are loads of industrial units out there."

Linköping Pool Maintenance.

No company registered under that name.

Seconds.

Minutes.

Hours.

How much time do we have?

Is it already too late?

Tove.

I don't want to become one of the living dead, Malin thinks, and runs for the car.

66

There you lie.

We're getting closer. I can hear you rocking to and fro, don't be worried, it's not far now.

Theresa.

I saw her by the pool in the garden, she was like you, sister, and I felt it might work.

I followed her.

Rang on the door, said I was there to check the water in the pool. Then it went the way it went, she struggled and I chased her and she screamed but no one heard her, and I hit her over the head with a metal case and she calmed down.

Then I took her to the warehouse. Made some careful cuts with a scalpel, trimmed her wounds, so carefully and neatly, wanted to do a good job, and I washed her with bleach and she woke up, Theresa, and I didn't have my mask on and she stared straight at me and she shouldn't have seen me, because if she was going to be transformed then she would have to start from a state of facelessness, wouldn't she?

But I still pushed the blue nothing into her and I had my cold white spiders' legs to help me, thin as they are, and I thought: I'm hugging you to me, and I wrapped my hands round her neck, but she didn't become you.

I wrapped her in plastic.

Buried her by a fairly isolated patch of water. Maybe her clean, unblemished body could turn into you down there in the ground, sister?

But that animal, the dog, found her before that happened.

God, how I miss you.

My beloved.

I'm coming to you now.

You're coming to me now.

You shall die.

You shall be reborn.

All available cars are on their way to Tornby.

Janne beside Malin, this is a police operation but she can't push him away again. None of her colleagues has probably given it a moment's thought.

Janne.

All the things we haven't done together, and now we're sharing this.

The Berg roundabout.

The sun painting the roofs of Skäggetorp with newly woken rays, the white blocks of flats almost beautiful in their hot, abandoned stillness.

They drive down the hill.

Eighty, ninety miles an hour.

Zeke behind them, but Malin can't see any other cars.

We're first. Janne is breathing hard but says nothing, the adrenaline must be pumping through him just like it is in me, but he's used to it, who knows how many times he's been in the vicinity of death while he was serving abroad? Maybe even in the forest up by Hultsjön as well? At the fires?

They turn in to the Tornby industrial park. Drive past the bloated retail boxes: IKEA, the Ikano Group, ASKO, Willy's budget superstore, the Plantagen garden center, and on into the park, past the Vansito wholesale warehouse.

They turn off, and number 11 Fabriksvägen is a single-story redbrick warehouse, maybe thirty yards long, with four separate entrances along a worn concrete loading bay.

They stop, jump out of the car, run.

Which door?

They run from door to door, listening, looking for signs, but all the doors are unmarked.

The heat and the sharp light no longer exist, only sweat and the exhaustion that is slowly forcing its way through the adrenaline.

Sounds from inside one of the storerooms.

A scratching sound, dripping.

The sound of sirens approaching.

A closed metal shutter, locked. The sun has pressed its way upward and the loading bay is bathed in light. Malin kneels beside the lock, tries to twist it open, but her hands are shaking.

"Hang on," Zeke shouts, rushing up to Malin with his pistol drawn. "Stand back," and Zeke aims the gun at the lock and fires.

A bang, I can hear a bang, Tove thinks, and a dull rumbling sound. Where am I? And her head is throbbing, and she can't move her body, but it's there.

Am I paralyzed?

I can't move.

Mum, is that you coming? Dad? To rescue me from this nightmare?

Something's approaching again.

A sliver of light, is that a door opening? Am I being rescued?

Malin and Janne and Zeke have taken ahold of the bottom of the shutter and are forcing it up, there's no second door behind it, and the sirens are close now, they shut off and Malin can hear police officers shouting to each other, calling out orders, Ekenberg and Sven Sjöman's voices? Karim's?

And the shutter is up.

Janne holds it up and Malin goes into the room with her weapon drawn, sees the empty bunk, the containers, Tove's red top on the floor, sliced open, a book, her sunglasses, and then the rabbit cages along the walls, the pots of paint, a box of white surgical gloves, boxes of chemicals everywhere, empty bleach bottles, scalpels, a dripping tap. The floor is stained with blood, the blood long since dried up, and thin strips of rotting, stinking flesh, the whole room smells of torture decay death.

Fuck, Malin thinks. Fuck.

You were here.

And she sees Janne slump to his knees, holding up the tattered remains of Tove's top, holding it up to her, saying:

"I bought her this."

"Fuck!" Malin screams, before she sinks to the floor and starts to cry, with exhaustion, and despair as well, and Janne crawls toward her, wraps his arms round her, and they breathe together, preparing themselves for whatever will come.

All around them uniformed officers, Sven and Karim talking to Zeke, who sees Waldemar's car just arriving. Only Per Sundsten is missing, but perhaps he's having a nap somewhere, gone home to Motala?

Malin gets up.

Janne behind her.

The other warehouse doors are open, evidently nothing inside that need concern them.

"We got here too late," Sven says. "What the fuck do we do now?"

The bang.

It must be a rifle shot from the forest, some poacher out early.

But it could also be from you, my summer angel.

And you'd woken up.

We've left the fires behind us, and I've sedated you again.

Now you can sleep peacefully in the van until we get there, until we reach the final room.

It's not far now, I promise.

And there's no need for you to be frightened.

You're going to die, but only for a little while, and then you'll be the most beautiful person ever.

Malin, Malin!

We're shouting in chorus now, Sofia and me.

Think!

Think!

Sitting there, dejected and despairing on the asphalt outside the warehouse in Tornby.

Don't listen to the others.

There's still time to rescue her.

There's still time to stop her becoming one of us.

Just think, and make us less scared, rescue Tove and grant us peace.

Let us rest soon, Malin.

You know where Tove is going, where Vera Folkman is going.

They're on their way to the final room, they're very nearly there, the white van is close now.

67

You need to be awake now.

I'm going to tie you up and you will see what I'm doing, if you can see it happen then you'll dare to come back, because there'll be no more fear, will there?

Beloved sister.

I'm parking the car outside the monster now.

He must be asleep.

It smells of summer out here, a summer's morning, and on this day a summertime dream can start, my little summer angel.

I open the back doors.

You're groaning, don't wake up too soon now. You might as well see my face, what difference does it make, soon you will cease to exist, and I don't think faces matter anymore.

Tove squints.

The light is back again. Am I alive? Do I still exist, Mum? I think I'm alive, because my whole body aches. And someone's pulling me, but it doesn't hurt, it just gets hot hot hot when my body comes out in the sun.

Buildings all round.

Gray, concrete buildings, yellowing plants, 1950s buildings that I don't recognize as I look at them upside down.

I have to run.

Get away from here.

But no matter how I try, my body doesn't obey.

Mum.

Now it's there again, the face, but it has features now, a woman's rounded features.

Then she changes her mind.

Lifts me back into the darkness again.

I ring the doorbell.

And ring.

And ring.

Wait, wait, and you open, see me, try to close the door, but I'm stronger now, stronger, and I put my foot in the gap and you yell as I shove you into the flat, press you down on the sofa, tie you up and your cold white spiders' fingers. I throw a blanket over you and you're old now, but the meanness, the transparency in your gray eyes can never, ever disappear, Dad.

Wait.

I'll go and get her.

From the van.

She needs to be watching when you die.

Your eyes are glaring wide open in terror from your skull, it's like your eyelids have lost the ability to blink and the whole of your lair stinks of drink and piss and unwashed old man, but I know all about cleaning, Dad.

Wait here.

She's heavy as I carry her over my shoulder, and I had to put a rag in her mouth to stop her screaming and waking the whole block.

No one can see me now.

Finspång's morning eyes are dead.

I close the door.

*   *   *

How long have I been sitting here now? Malin thinks. Far too long.

Her body is a single emotion molded of many: anxiety, anger, exhaustion, despair, resignation, fury, and heat. An overheated brain is worthless as an instrument of thought, as a rescuer in this hour of need.

The asphalt warm beneath her buttocks.

Malin hasn't bothered to move into the shade, the sun is merciless even just before half past four in the morning.

Janne and Zeke are sitting in the shade, leaning against the wall of the warehouse next to each other, and Malin can see that they're gathering their strength, recharging before the next act.

The final act?

Sven Sjöman crouching beside her.

"Malin, have you got any ideas?"

His breath smells of coffee.

The voices, listen to the voices.

It's desire that kills.

And Malin straightens up, certainty like a sudden strong jolt through her body and she flies up, shouting over to Janne and Zeke:

"Come on, I know where she is!"

Sven steps back, letting Malin past as she races to the car.

"Come on, for fuck's sake!"

All around them officers have stopped what they were doing, as if the desperation in her voice has frozen time at that second and given them all a glimpse of eternity.

Sven called after them:

"Where are you going, Malin?"

But she didn't answer, didn't want a whole fucking army to show up and set off something stupid if it wasn't already too late. She didn't want Sven to call the cretins in the Finspång station, who knew what sort of mess they could make of things.

No.

Now it's me against you.

I know where you are now, Vera Folkman, and I know why you're doing what you're doing.

It's a tragic madness, your madness. Two sisters alone in the world. Don't they love each other endlessly? Do you think you can recreate your sister? Your love for one another? It's a beautiful madness, your madness. But it's my task to destroy it, obliterate it.

It's Janne's task.

Zeke's.

But most of all ours, Janne. We have a child, and we owe her a life.

Malin is sitting in the backseat of the car, Janne leaning on her shoulder. They're forcing themselves to stay awake, saying things about the landscape as they pass through it to make sure that Zeke doesn't fall asleep at the wheel.

"The Roxen looks so inviting in the morning light."

"Vreta Kloster really is beautiful."

"We're going to stop that bitch."

At the start of the drive Malin explained that Vera Folkman must have taken Tove with her back to see her father, Sture Folkman, to conclude a dance of death that had been going on for far too long, that had created a summer that no one in the area would ever forget.

Ninety miles an hour as they pass the golf course in Vreta Kloster, after driving through a deserted early-morning Ljungsbro.

They pass the fires, the lines of cars, and they meet fire engines on their way back from there, their cabs full of exhausted men with soot-smeared faces, resignation in their eyes as if the fire and the heat were too strong for them, as if they had no choice but to capitulate to the flames and let the fire transform all the forests of Östergötland into a no-man's-land.

"Do you wish you were still there?" Malin asks Janne, but he doesn't answer.

*   *   *

Dark, burgundy-colored wallpaper. A creaking wooden floor.
   Him rendered immobile. You soon here on the floor.
   I have everything in place now, sister.
   So that you can be resurrected.
   So that our innocence can be reborn in a radiant whiteness.
   I am in the final room.

68

IN THE FINAL ROOM

I, Sture Folkman, was seventeen years old the first time I gave in
to my lust.

Down by the factory in Ängelholm there was a kiosk where
she, she was eleven or twelve, used to buy cigarettes for her mother.

Her white dress.

It covered no more than her thighs and it was a hot day, almost as
hot as some days have been this summer.

She was walking along the path behind the factory and there were
azaleas, the most beautiful I had ever seen, in bloom there.

I caught up with her.

Brought her down.

And she was hairless and I knew this was the first step of many
for me, it couldn't be stopped, I could see in her frightened eyes that
deep down she loved it, loved me, just like all my girls came to, even if
some of them got ideas in their heads later on. I kept rabbits in cages
to make them happy. Girls love rabbits.

That white dress ended up spotted with blood.

I whispered in her ear as I held her by the throat.

Keep quiet about this, girl, or the devil will get you.

Shame comes before love.

Over the years other people's shame has been my best ally. It was easiest and nicest when I had the girls in the house, God knows how excited I got, hearing my creaking footsteps at night when I was on the way to their room.

They were always full of anticipation.

Lying awake, waiting for me, for my lovely, long, dextrous fingers, for my wonderful presence.

I was always careful.

Pulling the covers from their bodies.

Caressing their young white glassy skin.

My own flesh and blood or someone else's, it never mattered. I gave my love to all the girls who came my way.

You're awake now, little girl, my beautiful summer angel.

We're here now, in the final room, and she shall see me do this first.

I've hammered four big nails into the floor and tied you to them. And you can see in my direction now.

I'm sitting beside my dad on his sofa.

I've got my mask on, so my face lacks definition, I'm wearing my white spiders' legs, holding the necklace of rabbit claws to his cheeks, and I'm scratching and he's screaming, the old man, but there isn't really much life in him.

You're looking away.

LOOK FOR FUCK'S SAKE.

And you look.

She's naked and the mask is on again.

Her head is aching, but Tove can see the scene clearly, understands that she's in a grotty flat, God knows where, and that a woman, naked, is sitting next to her dad and hurting him.

Why?

And she screams at me to look, but I don't want to see this and she scratches his face again and he screams.

She gets up.

Her thin white surgical gloves are glowing in the weak light.

I can't get up.

There's a smell of bleach, the sort Mum uses to get rid of stains.

Mum, Dad. You have to hurry.

I can hear her in another room, drawers being opened, she's looking for something, and the man tries to scream, but she's put a rag in his mouth, just like mine.

Neither of us can move.

Neither of us can escape.

The knife.

The old kitchen knife that Elisabeth and I fantasized about stabbing him with, he's still got it, the rough knife with the Bakelite handle.

I pull it from the block on the worktop.

Hold it. Think what a shame it was about Sofia Fredén. I saw her when she was working in the café at Tinnis last summer, and she used to move the same way you used to, Elisabeth, and with her I thought that if I do everything quickly and in one place then maybe I can achieve what I want through speed and shock tactics, like an explosion or a powerful chemical reaction. I scratched and cut her with the claws, the first one I did that to, but it didn't mean anything. Rabbits are only animals, their love is meaningless.

I scrubbed her in the park. Worked fast.

But she just went limp in my arms when I pressed my hands around her neck.

She died without you coming back.

But, dear sister, you should know that I have never doubted. I know what I have to do now.

Just watch while you're waiting.

Then come to me with love. You should know that I miss you.

*   *   *

She has a knife in her hand.

Tove sees the blade glint, and she screams NOW LOOK as she sits down next to the man on the sofa that Tove thinks must be her father.

She holds the knife in the air.

Screams.

THIS IS NOTHING.

Then she stabs the knife into the man's chest and stomach over and over again and his irises disappear into his head, his eyes go white and his whole body shakes and she stabs the knife into him over and over again and the blood sort of seeps out from the gap between his brown top and gray trousers.

He's still now.

And I'm terrified, but I couldn't be more present.

She takes one of his hands, Mum.

And then the knife again, she saws and cuts and the fingers fall off onto the floor, one by one by one, the blood, Mum, the blood.

Fingerless hands on the fabric of the sofa.

She's done now.

Turns toward me, Mum.

I yank strain scream cry.

But nothing happens.

If you're on your way, you need to hurry now.

69

Finspång.

The time is now quarter past six, and the streets of the industrial community are still empty, Zeke takes a shortcut the wrong way through a roundabout and comes close to running over a bleary-eyed paperboy.

The center.

Gray buildings, a hot dog kiosk, trees shrinking away from the sun, the flower beds not as well tended here as in Linköping, but there's still a feeling of summer idyll, as if the industrial town had come to terms with its transformation into a sleepwalker's hideaway.

But something is happening.

"Turn here," Malin shouts, and her mobile rings, she knows it's Sven Sjöman again, he's called her mobile ten times, and tried them over the radio, but we're doing this on our own.

"Stop."

And Zeke brakes hard and they throw the doors open and pour out of the car. Malin runs toward the building where Sture Folkman lives, pulling her pistol from the holster under her jacket, Zeke hot on her heels with his gun in his hand, Janne shadowing them, crouching, as if he were expecting enemy fire from the windows of the white block of flats.

They creep up the stairs.

Press close to the wall.

Malin puts her ear to the door, making a hushing sign, finger to her mouth, listening for any sounds from inside the flat.

Groaning noises.

A woman's voice saying, there, there.

How to play this?

She's put a blue thing round her waist, she's cut open my trousers and pants with a knife, and I'm naked now.

This isn't happening.

Tell me this isn't happening.

The fingers all round me, in a circle, like worms, like eyeless baby snakes.

I try to close my eyes and cry, but she holds my eyelids open the whole time, it's like I have to see everything and my skin stings as if she's rubbed it with something that burns.

Standing up, she rattles a necklace made of animal claws over me.

"Do you see the fingers?"

Her face is covered by a mask, her hands wearing white rubber gloves, and the blood of the man on the sofa is oozing toward me now, it will soon reach me and it stinks of guts and iron and I don't want it to touch me, away, away with the blood.

And what's she doing now?

Talking, wondering.

"What would be best?"

A curious, expectant voice.

"The nothing, or spider fingers around your neck?"

She looks up at the ceiling, as if she were seeking an answer.

It's happening now.

I'm going to kill you, and you will be resurrected.

The fingers are gone now.

Then we shall cycle with the wind in our hair to a water where love is eternal, where we can lie next to each other and believe that this world, this life wishes us well.

I shall put everything right.

There now, don't be frightened.

I shall start by squeezing the life out of you, then I shall fill something with nothing one last time, and then you will look at him, at yourself, at the world, lying safe and open ahead of us.

You'll see that I've put everything right.

Together we shall fly through the countryside like loving summer angels.

Malin!

Don't wait any longer.

Go in!

It isn't too late for Tove yet, the way it is for us. The truth, you've reached its front yard, and it's behind that door.

The sight behind it is terrible to behold.

But you can do it, both of you, because your lives can be saved behind there, in the darkness.

See to it that this comes to an end.

Wipe out our fear and help us enjoy our insight, our freedom. Give our mums and dads the solace to be gained from putting a name, a face, to evil.

Open the door, Malin.

Do it now.

It's high time.

My hands round your neck.

Stop wriggling.

It won't take long and I understand that you're scared, that it hurts, but you can come back as pure love, as the most beautiful person in the world.

Your skin is warm, so warm, and I press harder now.
Give up, give up, that's right.

They hesitate.
Whisper soundlessly:
"How are we going to play this?"
"Burst in."
"But—"
No buts, no alternatives, and Malin takes a step back, kicks in the door with all her strength, and ten feet inside the flat she can see a bloody human beast standing crouched over a clean-scrubbed body on the floor, human fingers all around, the human beast's hands round the neck of the body, the human beast like black organic magma, its veins filled with glowing worms, and Tove on the floor, and Malin screams:
"LET GO! STOP!"
And holds the gun in front of her, takes aim, and the human beast moves, looks at Malin, stares into her eyes, then turns toward Tove again.
Because that is you, isn't it, Tove?

She looks into my eyes, and I vanish, everything goes white and I seem to be drifting, Mum, is that you shouting, Dad, is that you I can hear?

Your eyes, you're disappearing into them and something new arises.
They're your eyes, sister, and you're back, I look into your pupils and feel an endless love.
So the nothing wasn't needed.
I squeeze and then I explode into sound.

*   *   *

Malin squeezes the trigger.

No time to fight, to lose, just reply to the volcano in kind, become part of the volcano.

Pulling the trigger again and again.

Zeke pulls his trigger.

Over and over again and the smell of blood merges with the smell of gunpowder and Janne screams: "Tove, Tove! Stop firing!" as he rushes into the living room, almost slipping on the blood on the floor, kicks, pushing aside the lifeless body that has collapsed on top of Tove before feeling her neck with two fingers, screaming "Fuck!" And then he presses his mouth to Tove's, forcing air into her lungs.

Malin and Zeke beside him.

The mutilated corpse on the sofa, its hands bloody stumps, face white, bloodless, the naked body next to Tove perforated by dozens of bullets, blood pumping out in gushes over the amputated fingers arranged in a circle, then Janne's order: "Don't just stand there, cut her loose!"

And without thinking Malin grabs a large knife with a black handle and cuts Tove free from the floor, rope by rope, Zeke swearing in the background.

"This is the worst, the fucking worst thing I've ever seen," and Janne pumps in air, counts, pauses, pumps, and Malin sits down beside him, stroking Tove's forehead, pleading out loud:

"Please, please, please, this can't be happening," but nothing helps.

Janne breathing into her.

Lifeless.

Tove.

Where are you?

"Come back, Tove," Malin whispers into her ear.

I'm here, Mum, I can see you, but I don't know how to wake up.

I can see two girls drifting around your body and their mouths are forming words that I can't hear, but I understand that they don't want me with them, that they want me to go back.

Go back where?

Follow the voice, they say.

And I listen to you, Mum, come back, come back, come back, and I feel the air fill my lungs, images return to my eyes, and I see you now, you and Dad, how the fear and grief in your eyes turn to joy and love, to life.

Malin and Janne sitting on either side of Tove.

She's breathing, looking at them with conscious eyes.

They're holding each other, holding Tove, in a soft embrace that all three of them promise themselves will never end, the blood moving beneath them, holding them together, forcing violence back, deep into the holes it emerged from.

Zeke has opened the blinds.

The final room is bathed in light.

Someone listening carefully can hear the song of the summer angels: a wordless song, an ancient murmur about unity and love and belonging, a song people have long forgotten, and therefore never expect to hear again.

But the song exists within the three people on the floor of the room.

The three people hugging each other.

Epilogue

*W*e are together up here, down here, everywhere, in all the spaces that are ours.

It's good enough.

We are the eternally young girls, Linköping's summer angels, and have forgotten the terror.

Our mums and dads are still sad, and not even time can offer any balm for their grief.

But they know what happened.

You know what happened now, Dad. And there is no blame.

And that will have to do.

We, we have each other.

We share everything.

Just the way it was planned.

We can be together now, Elisabeth.

And we can see him, how he suffers, suffers, and suffers, where he is now.

Can we help him?

No.

Instead we drift along the banks of the canal, pretending to feel the wind in our hair, pretending to bathe, pretending and playing, and we are sisters, you and I.

And we always shall be.

Malin is lying in a hammock at the back of Janne's house, watching him and Tove rake leaves that have fallen far too early. The scaffolding around the house is gone.

It's a nice day, perhaps seventy degrees in the shade, the light mild, and up in the forests the fires are finally under control.

Karin Johannison has compared DNA samples from everyone involved in the case to those of Maria Murvall's attacker, but there were no matches.

The same evil, but a different incarnation.

Why did it happen now? *Why did Vera Folkman cross the line this hot summer?*

Malin hasn't found an answer to those questions. Lying awake at night she has thought: history contracted, volcanic ground fractured, and out flooded a concentrate of evil, tired of being held fettered and silent in a hidden darkness.

She called Josefin Davidsson. Josefin said she felt calmer after the hypnosis. They still don't know who called in about her, no one ever came forward.

Malin bumped into Slavenca Visnic in the city. She said that she'd sold the kiosks and was going to move back to Sarajevo.

"The time has come," she said.

Malin's flat by St. Lars Church has been rented out to a student for the autumn and winter. Tove's and Malin's things are still in boxes in the living room of Janne's house.

Tove and Janne are moving through the garden, across grass that heavy rain has made green with life.

Flowers in a myriad of colors have ventured forth, trusting that the heat has gone. Their petals are blowing in a gentle wind, confirming that this present is all that really exists.

Tove and Janne.
You're my people, Malin thinks.
We're each other's people.
We belong together.
And that's a gift that we'll have to learn to live with.

Acknowledgments

Many thanks to Neil Smith, the excellent translator, and to Emily Bestler for publishing my books in the United States.